THE KATE HAMILTON MYSTERIES BOXED SET

INIQUUS SECURITY ACTION ADVENTURE
BOXED SET

BOOK 7

FIONA QUINN

THE WORLD OF INIQUUS

Ubicumque, Quoties. Quidquid

Iniquus - /i'ni/kwus/ our strength is unequalled, our tactics unfair – we stretch the law to its breaking point. We do whatever is necessary to bring the enemy down.

THE LYNX SERIES

Weakest Lynx

Missing Lynx

Chain Lynx

Cuff Lynx

Gulf Lynx

Hyper Lynx

Marriage Lynx

STRIKE FORCE
In Too DEEP

JACK Be Quick

InstiGATOR

Fear The REAPER

Striker

UNCOMMON ENEMIES
Wasp

Relic

Deadlock

Thorn

FBI JOINT TASK FORCE
Open Secret

Cold Red

Even Odds

KATE HAMILTON MYSTERIES
Mine

Yours

Ours

CERBERUS TACTICAL K9 TEAM ALPHA
Survival Instinct

Protective Instinct

Defender's Instinct

Delta Force Echo

Danger Signs

Danger Zone

Danger Close

Cerberus Tactical K9 Team Bravo

Warrior's Instinct

Rescue Instinct

Hero's Instinct

Cerberus Tactical K9 Team Charlie

Guardian's Instinct

Sheltering Instinct

Certified Cerberus Tactical K9

Beowolf

CIA Color Code

Red Line

This list was created in 2025. For an up-to-date list, please visit www.FionaQuinnBooks.com

If you prefer to read the Iniquus World in chronological order you will find a full list at the end of this book.

MINE

A KATE HAMILTON MYSTERY

Mine is a work of fiction. Names, characters, places, and incidents either are the product of the author's imagination or are used fictitiously, and any resemblance to actual persons, living or dead, business establishments, events, or locales is entirely coincidental.

1

Kate Hamilton stared at her Uncle Owen's face. She was barely able to recognize him, resting there against the slick satin of his coffin pillow.

Somehow, the funeral director had molded and painted her uncle's features into a pleasant, peaceful expression. There had never been anything pleasant or peaceful about this man in life.

Everyone in Scarborough would agree that Owen Jenkins was one of the most cantankerous and disagreeable people that God had ever created.

But her aunt, Emma Jenkins, told stories about how Uncle Owen hadn't always been that way. She said that before he left for Vietnam, Owen was charming and gentle-hearted. No one but Aunt Emma could remember that far back in his history. Over the last fifty years, all his meanness had robbed the town of the happier memories of him. Uncle Owen had been the official town curmudgeon.

And now, no one cared that he was dead.

"I'm not expecting anyone to stop by tonight." Aunt Emma turned a page of her library book.

"What about from the church?" Kate asked.

Aunt Emma didn't look up from her book. "Not for paying their last respects. I imagine they'll come to the funeral tomorrow. The paper said I hired Maggie May's for the catering. People will want to get out of the house, get something free to eat, and to gossip. I don't expect a crowd, but it won't be empty neither."

"Surely, your friends will be there to support you."

"Perhaps a few. I pushed the funeral up a day, or I'd have no hope of anyone coming at all."

Kate shifted uncomfortably around in her chair. "Why's that?"

Aunt Emma put her finger where she left off reading. "There's a pig-picking Saturday afternoon with music and politicians, and what-all. The whole town will turn out. Perhaps I'll go, too. Rose said they'll have a soft-serve ice cream truck."

Kate moved to the chair next to her aunt and sat down, yanking the short skirt of her black dress to its full length, as she aimed for modesty. The call telling Kate that Uncle Owen had died had come just as she loaded her last suitcase into the back of her Ford Explorer. She had dashed back into the house and grabbed something black to wear, only to realize later that her dresses ran more along the lines of cocktail party garb than proper mourning attire. She saved the plainer of the two dresses she'd brought for the funeral. Aunt Emma lent her a cardigan to help hide this one's low neckline.

True to her aunt's word, no one showed up for the viewing. An hour had passed, and they had another one yet to go. Kate wished her aunt had warned her earlier, or she had the foresight to bring a book, too.

Kate stared into the forest scene of one of the oil paintings decorating the small room, rubbing her thumb over the Celtic design on the ring adorning her index finger. Her mind wandered back to what had happened on Tuesday and the awkwardness of her goodbye as she left her husband. His decision, not hers.

"I need you to leave, for your own damned good," Ryan had argued.

It had killed Kate to drive away. It was her place—no, her *right* to be by his side, supporting him. But he had said to go, and she was afraid of what he might do if she didn't comply. Thank goodness the school year at John Adams High had wrapped up, and she'd already handed in her students' final science grades. Thank goodness, Aunt Emma had welcomed her with open arms. And, of course, she owed a big thanks to Tim.

Just as his image bubbled up in her mind, Kate turned her head to see Detective Tim Gibbons walking toward her and Aunt Emma.

Aunt Emma was on her feet, opening her hands to welcome him. "How kind of you to stop by tonight," she said.

"How are you holding up, Mrs. Jenkins?"

"Kate's here," Aunt Emma gestured in her direction as Kate came to her feet. "She's such a blessing. I was so glad when she decided to visit for the summer. And then this happened." Aunt Emma fingered her cross pendant. "I can't say this will make her stay any worse, though. I expect it might improve it considerable with Owen gone."

Tim nodded, "He was a hard man to like, but you stayed with him—it speaks of the depth of your love."

Aunt Emma reached out and grasped Tim's forearm, her serenity crumbling. "Some men, they lost their legs or their sight in the war. Owen lost his goodness. He came out of the war crippled and broken. His ugliness was *not* his fault."

Shame and resentment washed over Kate. As horrible as Uncle Owen had been, he never threw her aunt out. Kate rubbed her hand over her aunt's back, her gaze fastened on Tim.

Tim was taller than he had been in high school. The laugh lines that crinkled the corners of his eyes when they were younger now permanently etched his tanned skin. The fifteen years that she'd lived in Boston hadn't changed him much. He looked good. And that was trouble. Kate knew it as sure as she knew that the next thing he'd say would be…

"Look at you, Katydid."

"Not much to see." She dragged a smile into place and pulled the cardigan tighter around her body.

"Boston agrees with you."

"It does indeed." Kate nodded.

"Well, welcome home. Glad to have your help at the police station. Though it's not much of a place to do a CSI internship. You're going to end up bored." He stuck his hands in his pockets. "We still roll up the sidewalks come dark."

"Good. I could use a little boredom." As soon as the words popped out of her mouth, Kate regretted them. Her troubles weren't meant for public consumption.

Tim's gaze locked on hers. He seemed to reach right in and pry her secrets loose. As the lead detective on the small-town police force, Kate imagined Detective Tim Gibbons had honed his dowsing skills—sharpened his people-reading acuity. It was a skill Kate loved about him. One of the many things she'd loved about him. But it felt invasive in this moment, and Kate took a step back.

"Where's Pam?" Aunt Emma asked.

Tim pulled his wallet from his back pocket. "She's home with the boys tonight. Billy has a fever from his new tooth." He grinned at the picture of his family he held out for them to see.

"Oh, they're beautiful, Tim," Aunt Emma gushed. "Your eldest is getting so big. He looks the spitting image of his daddy."

A movement from the doorway caught Kate's attention. "Good evening," she said to the man standing there.

Aunt Emma glanced around. "Doctor Javarti, thank you for coming. Let me introduce you to my niece."

Tim gave Aunt Emma a light kiss on her cheek. "I'm on duty.

I need to head on now. Kate." He nodded in acknowledgment, shook hands with the new man, and left.

"Kate, I'd like you to meet the physician who tried to save your Uncle Owen, Dr. Omid Javarti."

"My condolences," he said to Kate, then focused his attention on Aunt Emma. "I'm very sorry for your loss, Mrs. Jenkins. But your husband has found peace. After so many years of torment, he's at rest."

Kate detected the smallest accent in Omid's English. The way he stood and the European cut of his suit—which she was much more likely to see in her adopted home of Boston than in southwest Virginia—made Kate wonder how this cosmopolitan man had found his way to Scarborough.

"That's very kind," Aunt Emma said. "Owen just wouldn't listen to good reason. Never would follow his doctor's orders. We both knew he was risking a heart attack."

To Kate's surprise, her aunt pulled a handkerchief from her sleeve and dabbed her eyes. Had Kate been married to someone like Owen, she would be celebrating. Upon hearing the news, Kate's first thought was that Uncle Owen dying of a heart attack was irony at its best. Most folks swore the man was heartless.

"Even so, a sudden loss can shock the system," Dr. Javarti said. "Please tell me if you need anything in the next days or weeks—something to help you sleep or to deal with any anxiety or depression." He and Aunt Emma walked to the casket. Aunt Emma touched the handkerchief to her eyes, and Kate realized her aunt was crying. Kate was ashamed of her flippancy. She knew better.

2

———

Even with the funeral planned for early morning, the bright rays of sunshine hammered the top of Kate's head.

Kate glanced around at the guests. They were dressed for a garden party in bright floral sundresses. Though Kate noticed, a few people wore shorts as if Uncle Owen's funeral was their first stop on errands' day, and they'd be heading over to the Quick-Pick Groceries after the service. The guests smiled and gossiped. There wasn't a sad face amongst them.

Aunt Emma and Kate were the only ones in black. Kate's silk dress clung to her thighs as the humidity rose. Kate had tugged off the cardigan her aunt had lent her when they left the air-conditioned comfort of the sanctuary. There she stood, dressed as if for a Friday night martini with the girls, listening to the preacher chanting from the Book of Common Prayer, "Ashes to ashes, dust to dust…"

Kate looked over her shoulder in time to receive Doris Arthur's wilting stare.

"Stay away from Doris if you can help it," her aunt whispered in her ear. "If those looks were daggers, you'd keel over dead and share the grave with your uncle."

"Why? What did I ever do to her?"

"Let's talk about it when we get home. We don't need the gossips revved up, and Sally Jo can read lips." Aunt Emma grasped at Kate's hand.

The preacher ended his words of compassion and nodded toward Aunt Emma.

An acolyte stood with a spade in hand. He stretched it out to them.

Aunt Emma leaned heavily on Kate as they stepped forward.

It wasn't until after Aunt Emma placed the first shovelful of dirt over the coffin that the finality of Owen's death hit Kate. Not that she'd miss him, but what about her aunt? Would she be okay?

Stepping to the side, Kate led her aunt back to the assembly room. Opening the door, a blast of air-conditioned air brought them immediate relief from the heat and humidity.

The buzz from Kate's phone in her pocket stopped her progress. After a quick peek at the screen, she halted. "Aunt Emma, I'll be there in a minute. I'm going to the garden to take this call."

KATE EMERGED from under the tree, her cell phone still in her hand. She bent and used the hem of her dress to wipe away the last of her tears. When she stood up, she found Tim standing in front of her, his hands resting lightly on his hips. He took in her appearance but refrained from comment until they reached the church.

"Why don't you slide in here?" he asked. "It goes to Reverend Pine's office, and he has a bathroom. You might want a minute to yourself to freshen up." He pushed the door open but didn't follow her.

One glance in the mirror told Kate why Tim had shepherded

her away. Red splotches ringed her eyes, her mascara ran to her chin, her hair was a mess of humid curls, and sticktights covered her fanny. She was a wreck—inside and out. She pulled herself together as best she could.

When Kate emerged from the bathroom, she held her head high as she headed back out the side door to find Tim, leaning against the brick divider with his hands shoved in his pockets.

He swept his gaze over her. "You'll be okay. People will chalk it up to grief, though they'll wonder why." He pushed off the wall. "I came by to get you because I'm heading over to a crime scene. I'd appreciate your help. Officer Mandrel, who has the most experience with CSI, is on his honeymoon."

Kate turned her head toward the church doors.

He followed her line of sight. "You're not supposed to start 'til Monday. Your aunt may need you. You can say no."

"Let me check on my aunt and make sure she's okay. Then, should I follow you?"

He looked out toward the parking lot. "Let's leave your Explorer with Mrs. Jenkins. I've got a squad car. They're bringing in the forensics van now, so you'll have supplies." Tim moved toward his car as Kate climbed the granite stairs.

Back in the assembly hall, Kate grabbed a plastic cup of ice-cold lemonade and chugged it down in one gulp. Most everyone had left. There were a few ladies, dawdling over the ham biscuit tray. Doris was one of them. She glared at Kate, her toe was tapping and her hands resting on her hips. She was clearly vexed about something,

Kate sent the woman a bewildered glance, then found her aunt and explained Tim's request. "Would you be okay if I left?"

"It's fine, dear. Rose is going home with me, so I'll have company."

The heat of the day wrapped itself around Kate as she pushed through the heavy wooden doors. She had forgotten the extremes of southern temperatures. Outside, it was a screen door away from hell. Inside, it was iceberg-cold with multiple air units cranked to their highest settings—b*utter in a skillet.* Kate mused as she tiptoed across the graveled parking lot to keep her high heels from sinking into the stones. Thankfully, Tim had the engine running in the car, and the interior was plenty cool as she slid into the passenger's seat. Hot then cold, hot then cold—as a child, it hadn't fazed her, but she'd lost her acclimatizing skills, and the sudden shifts left Kate nauseated.

"You okay?" Tim asked.

"Is there time for us to run by my house so I can get changed?"

Tim glanced at her shoes. "We'll have to. You can't go into a crime scene in heels. You're bound to fall over and destroy evidence." He sent her a smile, but the corners of his mouth remained grim.

Kate's scalp itched with apprehension.

"You've got to make it quick. As soon as hazmat gives us the all-clear, we need to be ready to go."

"Hazmat?" Kate's voice squeaked.

"Just a precaution."

They drove through town toward the river. As he pulled onto the highway, Tim said, "I'm assuming those tears weren't for your uncle."

"No." She brushed at imaginary lint on her skirt. "I can't say I'm sorry that Uncle Owen's gone."

Tim reached over the seat, produced a bottle of water from a cooler on the back floorboard, and handed it to Kate. "How's everything in Boston?"

Kate rolled the bottle across her forehead and the back of her neck before taking a swig. "I'll tell you what, how about you brief me on the crime scene instead?"

3

Kate stood at the rear of the CSI van, gathering camera equipment. Dressed in a Tyvek suit, she carried a pair of booties with her as she walked to the front door. On the way, Kate passed a woman sitting under an oak tree with her legs spread out in front of her. Her face drooped, and her eyes looked vacant. An EMT hovered nearby.

"This is Kate Hamilton. She'll be assisting today," Tim announced, as he pulled his shoe coverings over his boots and signed himself in with the officer guarding the crime scene taped entry.

Kate followed suit.

Standing in the foyer, Kate's breath clouded in front of her.

"We have to get the temperature down on days like this, so we have time to work," Tim said as he organized the equipment.

"No medical examiner?" Kate asked.

"We're too far away. We do their tests and send the information on with the bodies. They have a contract with the funeral home to provide transport. I'll give them a call when we wrap up."

Kate's teeth chattered, and she hugged her arms around

herself. She was glad she had an excuse for her reaction and that Tim would assume she was cold and not lily-livered. This was her first real-world crime scene. And Tim said there were bodies, plural. She didn't want a bad reputation for being an emotional wreck before she even started her internship.

She stood next to Tim in the archway separating the hall from the family room, observing the scene. Two teens lay dead, crumpled like discarded papers on the floor.

One boy lay near the sofa. He wore a pair of basketball shorts and a T-shirt. His legs were thin, and he was barefooted. The beginnings of an adolescent mustache trimmed an otherwise baby face surrounded by a cloud of blond curls. His complexion was gray, and Kate wanted nothing more than to rush in and wrap him in a warm blanket, to rub circulation back into his skin, and for him to wake up and say…anything at all.

The second boy lay near the TV. Like his friend, he was dressed for a hot summer day. He lay on his back, with his arms and legs sticking up at odd, implausible angles. Kate realized this teen had been moved since rigor had set in. *The EMTs must have turned his body over to check for vital signs.* His position made it look like he was flailing, trying to get up off his back. He had the same waxy look as the mannequins Kate's forensics class had practiced on.

There weren't as many flies as she had anticipated, probably one of the reasons they cranked the air conditioning up. The TV was off. There were no obvious signs of trauma. The room was neat as a pin.

Kate opened her mouth to speak; she had to stop and clear her throat before trying again. "This place was checked out for carbon monoxide?"

"Hazmat green-lighted our being in here. That's the mom outside," Tim said. "She came home and found this." He pointed toward the dark-haired boy near the TV. "She turned her son over and tried to revive him while the paramedics were on their way, but the kids had been dead for hours. The EMTs realized the bodies were in rigor. They moved her outside, cranked the air conditioning, and handed the scene over to us. We'll start by taking pictures." Tim gestured toward the black cases.

Kate stared at the boys' bodies. "These are children." Her words were barely audible.

"Kate, get the camera." Tim gripped her arms and spun her toward the equipment. "Your first scene is the hardest. You told me you had done an autopsy."

"I have." Kate's teeth chattered. "But it was a very old man." She leaned down to unzip the case. "I imagined he had lived a full and happy life." She looked back over her shoulder at the family room. "These are high schoolers. They should be…"

"Alive. I know. But we have a job to do." Tim's tone was steady and calm. "The family will need to understand what happened here. It's the only thing we can do for them that'll make any difference. Focus on doing the very best job you can. You're a scientist. You're a professional."

Those were the words Kate needed to hear to spur her into action. She followed Tim's directives as she desperately swiped at her imagination while it overlay a macabre slide show of her own students' faces onto the corpses'. Short, shallow gasps of air kept her stomach from emptying.

Following the protocol taught to her in school. Kate took pictures from various angles. Each set of pictures moved her closer and closer to the bodies until she was focusing her lens on white powdered nostrils.

ODs from cocaine didn't make much sense. Kate turned and stared at the mirror and razor blade that had been toppled from the coffee table. "Tim, we need to be looking for something besides coke that these kids stuck up their noses."

Tim stood beside the couch, dictating notes into his digital recorder. "Why do you say that?" he asked.

"These kids collapsed in the same room. If they had become excitable or agitated, they'd be all over the house. There's no vomit anywhere. At least I can't smell any. What's the drug of choice here in Scarborough?"

"Weed and alcohol, not much else around here. There's no extra money floating in people's bank accounts, especially since the furniture factory closed. Most of our families are living on unemployment."

"This family has money," she observed.

"Yeah, this is Pemberly Bowling's house—well, Pemberly Wilks now."

"That's Pemberly? I didn't recognize her at all. She's Virginia blue blood, trust fund money. What did she say happened? Does she have any clues?"

"She said Chad wasn't feeling well," He flicked a finger toward the dark-haired boy. "He called to tell her he had a bad headache. She told him to send his friends home, go up to the medicine cabinet, and get himself a couple of pain relievers."

"Has anyone checked the medicine cabinet?" Kate asked.

"You are. Pemberly said she keeps all the medicines in her bathroom."

With the camera dangling around her neck by the strap, Kate followed the curved mahogany stairwell up to the second floor. The oriental carpeting underfoot was slippery in her booties. She peaked around the doors until she reached the master suite and walked into the white marble bathroom. It was pristine—not a towel on the floor or a stray hair in the sink.

In the bathroom cabinet, Kate found the usual array of over-the-counter bottles and boxes, nothing that someone could cut into a white powder. When she moved the Pepto to the side, she found three prescription bottles. She picked up the one for Nardil and took a picture of the label. Thinking she'd look up the drug later when she got home, Kate carefully opened the bottle and tapped a pill into the lid.

Orange, not white. This probably won't matter. Kate snapped a photo. The next was for Cephalexin. The pharmacy date made it only a week old. Kate took a picture of the capsule and wondered why anyone would snort antibiotics. The third bottle was labeled OxyContin. The same doctor who wrote the prescription for the Cephalexin was listed on the label. He had given Pemberly fourteen pills. "Take twice a day as needed for pain."

If Pemberly took them on schedule, there should be one left. Kate unscrewed the cap and stared at nine pills. A suspicion niggled in her brain, but she couldn't quite figure out why or what it was exactly. She took several pictures of the tablets and then shouted, "Tim, I have something to show you."

Tim had nodded at the bottles when she held them out, then headed down the stairs to ask Pemberly about them. As soon as he held up the bottle. Pemberly became agitated, her breath caught and released, caught, held, released. Kate stared at the EMT to get his attention. She thought Pemberly might blackout at any minute.

"Pemberly, no one is blaming you for anything. We're just trying to account for the medications in the house," Tim said. "Seven days ago, you were given prescriptions for antibiotics and pain killers."

"Yes, I was up at the Country Club, and Bitsy Blanton backed into me with her golf cart. Ran right over my leg. The ambulance took me to the hospital. Nothing was broken, just a bad bruise. I was in terrible pain. And I needed five stitches."

"Did you follow the prescription on your antibiotics?"

"Yes, tonight's my last dose." Pemberly's limbs sagged from her body as if she was disintegrating in the sun, her words flat and lifeless.

"What about the pain medication?" Tim asked.

Kate hovered in the background, listening.

"Oh, I only took one of them. I got by on Tylenol. I felt so strange when I took the one from Doctor Michaels. I could hardly breathe. I almost called 9-1-1."

"You decided not to call?" Tim asked.

"I fell asleep. I slept for the longest time. When I woke up, I was better."

Tim glanced at the EMT. "Does she have someone on the way?"

"Her sister should be here soon. Her husband is trying to get a flight. He lives in Charlotte."

Tim focused back on Pemberly. "You said you took one of the pills. There are nine left in the bottle. Have you any idea what happened to the four we haven't accounted for?"

Pemberly shook her head.

Two cars barreled down the road. Tim turned to Kate. "Seems the other family has been notified. We need to go back into the house and see if we can find those four pills."

4

Aunt Emma sat in her sunny kitchen, muttering over the jumble from the morning paper, when Kate walked in and headed straight for the coffee pot.

"You look like you're dressed to go to the station," Aunt Emma said without looking up.

Kate glanced down at the navy polo shirt and khaki tactical pants she'd picked up at the military surplus shop. Not her usual style, but she thought she should be in something that resembled a uniform if she was shadowing Tim.

"Tim's working on the case from yesterday, and I had some thoughts I wanted to share."

"It's front-page news. You don't have to be so circumspect. Two little babies not even out of high school. They're saying drug overdose."

"I'm not allowed to comment. I'm sorry, Aunt Emma."

"No need. A tragedy is a tragedy. But it won't stop folks from heading up to Scarborough Knoll for the pig-picking. It'll be good for people to share their grief. It's not going to be the fun-filled hoo-ha that the Scarboroughs planned to help sway people to their side of the fence, though."

"Are you going?" Kate asked.

"I am, maybe a little later. I'm not so interested in politics and propaganda. I wanted the picketers and news crews to get hot and sweaty so as they'd leave before I go."

"That's about mining? I saw a bunch of signs on my drive into town."

"It's a shame the Scarboroughs found the uranium vein on their land. We all got along so much better before this. Now, it's a house divided. You're either pro-mining or against it. In this economy with folks so desperate, it's not a pretty fight."

"Which side are you on?"

"I'm on Owen's side. And Owen didn't want uranium to poison his great granddaddy's land."

"This land? Why would Uncle Owen be worried about that? This is uphill from the Knoll; any runoff would affect the valley between the two properties, and the Scarboroughs own that."

"I can't say that I have a proper answer for you. I didn't pay much attention. There was something about needing a holding pond in this direction, away from the riverfront, to meet some standards. It doesn't matter none. Owen said no. And if they ask me, I'll say no, as well. And right now, mining isn't legal anyway."

"Well, I'm heading into town." Kate rinsed her mug and set it on the drying rack. "You enjoy your soft-serve ice cream." She turned and kissed her aunt's forehead. "Thank you for the coffee."

Aunt Emma reached for Kate's hand. "You talked to him this morning?"

Kate shook her head. "I talked to his buddy Zack. Ryan put his fist through a wall. They took him to the emergency room. Nothing's broken, except the wall, that is."

Aunt Emma nodded. "This is a small town, and you like your privacy. People are going to see those red rings around your eyes and wonder what's wrong. Wonder turns to speculation, and speculation becomes fact quicker than a flash of lightning."

"I know, and I'm sure this won't be the last time I look this bad. I already decided to blame it on my allergies to your cat."

"But I don't have a cat, dear."

"You will tonight. I'm stopping by the shelter on the way home if that's okay with you. Do you have a color preference?"

———

"Good, you're here. Come on. I want to introduce you to everyone." Tim strode down the corridor on long legs. He had been the high school quarterback when Kate was in school. He'd probably put his running skills to good use on the streets, keeping the townspeople safe. But now that he was a detective, he wore a jacket and tie, and he probably left the full body contact to the uniforms.

Kate followed him into the conference room.

Officers filled the chairs in neat rows, all of them dressed with military precision.

Kate glanced around but found no other women. She focused on her boots, trying to still the butterflies in her stomach. Being the focus of attention was a work-a-day reality in the classroom, but the vibe Kate picked up here was that these guys didn't want her invading their man cave.

"Gentlemen." As Tim spoke, the room settled down to respectful silence. "I would like to introduce you to Kate Hamilton. Mrs. Hamilton is a science teacher in Boston. As part of her continuing education requirements, she's taken classes to accomplish a second diploma—this one in Crime Scene Sciences. She's here fulfilling the internship requirements. When she returns home, Mrs. Hamilton plans to use her knowledge to encourage her students' love of science, and maybe a few of them will aspire to join us good guys in our fight against crime. Mrs. Hamilton will be helping me for the next few months. She comes to us with the latest techniques, and I plan to take full advantage of her skills while she's here."

A cough from the back of the room sounded like a veiled, "I bet."

Tim either didn't hear or pointedly ignored the interruption. "Let's give her a warm welcome."

The men clapped, but it didn't feel very warm to Kate.

"Are there any questions before Sergeant takes over with today's briefing?" Tim asked.

One of the officers laced his hands behind his head and leaned back in his chair, stretching out his legs. "Why did you come *here,* to our little hick town? Seems like if you wanted to see crime close up, you could've stayed in Boston." The menace in his voice was unmistakable.

Kate recognized him as Ken Arthur, Doris' brother. She'd dealt with the bullies in her classroom, so she knew she'd need to take the upper hand immediately, or she'd be fighting him from here on.

"Well, Officer Arthur," she smiled sweetly as if unperturbed, "I'm killing two birds with one stone."

Ken Arthur sat straight up, his hands making fists on his knees. "Now, what's that supposed to mean?"

The door opened slightly, and a woman stuck her head into the room. "Detective?"

Tim gave her a nod. "Gentlemen," he said to the room, then turned on his heel and walked out, with Kate trailing behind him.

"What've you got, Helen?"

"There's a woman on the phone, says she's a nurse up at the hospital. Jennifer Baker. She came home from the night shift and found her kids' beds still made. She says that means no one slept in them last night."

"How many kids? How old?"

"Her two sons. They're sixteen—twins."

"Have you sent a patrol to talk with her?"

"No, I thought you might want to go yourself. Mrs. Baker says she read in the paper about the teens dying at the Wilks' house. She said her boys were good friends with Chad Wilks."

"Helen, get me the…"

Helen held out a note with an address written on it in capital letters.

KATE BUCKLED her seatbelt and swiveled to see Tim's face.

He turned the key in the ignition then slid the air conditioning lever to high.

"Did you notice anything unusual about the OxyContin pills yesterday?"

"No, why?" He put his arm across the seat and twisted to back out of the parking space.

"I was looking at the pictures I took at the crime scene last night. Did you send the last of the pills on to the medical examiner's office?"

"I did." They stopped at the road, waiting for a break in traffic. Tim watched Kate rub the heel of her palm into her forehead. "Uh-oh. I know that gesture. Everything out of your mouth now is going to be bad news."

"There were four pills missing. If we assumed the boys used one pill each, that leaves two unaccounted for."

"And two boys missing. You're jumping to conclusions. That's not what a scientist does, and it's certainly not what a detective does. We collect evidence and then try to see the pattern, not create a pattern and try to fill it in with evidence."

"I'm not officially a CSI until Monday. I'm telling you what my teacher's gut is saying. I bet you anything that when we have access to those kids' phones, we'll find two things. One, that someone Googled how to get high on OxyContin. And two, that one of the dead kids either called or texted the two boys that are missing. Remember that Pemberly said she told Chad to send his friends home. Friends, plural. We only found one friend."

Tim flipped his lights on to go around a tractor-trailer. "There's more," he said. "Stop drip-feeding me."

"OxyContin is the prescription name for Oxycodone. Do you know much about that drug?"

"They use it for long term pain management for cancer patients and the like. It's from the opiate family. Abuse was a real problem for counties further west of us out toward Bristol, though, you hear about it less and less. We haven't had trouble with it here."

"Okay, well, Pemberly's prescription threw up all kinds of flags you should consider."

"Go on."

"The strength stamped on the pills was 80mg. The usual dosage is 40mg or less. Anything over 40mg is for opioid-tolerant patients only. As a matter of fact, a dose of 80mg in a day can be lethal to someone who hasn't built up resistance."

"There's an interesting piece of information. So Pemberly's prescription was a potentially lethal dose?"

"Yes, unless she was used to using opioids. Maybe you should get a look at her medical records. Here's another flag, the pills were stamped OC. They should have been stamped OP."

He swung his head to look at Kate before focusing back down the road. "You think her meds got mixed up?"

"Something very bizarre is going on. You see, the formulation of the pills allows the ingredients to be time-released over twelve hours. The druggies couldn't get a good high because of the time-release component. They found if they crushed the pills, they could snort them or shoot them and take the full hit of the narcotic all at once. That was with the first formulation, the OC pills."

"But you said they're supposed to be stamped OP." The muscles in Tim's face became taut with concentration.

"People OD'ed in large enough numbers that the FDA considered pulling Oxycodone. The pharmaceutical company reformulated it, so when a druggy tried to powder the pill to get around the time-release component, all they got was goo. That goo can't be snorted or shot-up. The new formulation is stamped OP. With the OC off the market, druggies turned to easier highs."

"But these were OC pills. And because the pill was a potentially lethal quantity when time-released, we can assume a full dose, shot directly into a teenager's system, would be sure death," Tim said.

Kate rubbed the back of her hand. "That's the conclusion I came to last night."

"Could the pharmacy be dispensing the old pills until they're gone, and then replace them with the new ones?"

"I sincerely doubt it. The formulation change took place a long time ago."

"What's a long time look like?" Tim asked.

"Eighteen months or so. The street price for an 80mg OC pill would be astronomical. You simply can't find them anymore. I would assume the pharmaccutical reps came through, picked up the OC, and swapped them with OP. Even if that weren't true, most meds have a shelf life of about a year. The pill's sell-by date should have expired, and they'd be destroyed."

"These pills should have lost their potency by now?"

"Some of their potency, but obviously not enough."

"And you know this how?" Tim asked.

"I took my final exam in Narcotics and Substance Abuse in May. I checked my notes on my computer when I got home last night."

Tim's grip tightened on the steering wheel. "We need to find out if the pharmacy has distributed these pills to anyone else."

"I would. Where are the teens' autopsies being done?"

"Roanoke."

"Oh." Kate turned her gaze toward the ramshackle houses strung along the railroad tracks as they passed by. The whole town had disintegrated since she'd last been here. Poverty was evidenced in peeling paint and sagging rooflines. The yards were overgrown with weeds; no money for lawn mower gas. "When will you have the official cause of death?"

Tim signaled a right turn. "Toxicology reports usually take two to four weeks, so it'll be a while before we have anything definitive."

Kate gripped her knees. "Do you think the two missing boys are dead?" She sucked her lips in as soon as the words passed her teeth.

"Just between you and me, Katie, I've got a bad feeling we're too late. I sure hope I'm wrong about this. Four high schoolers dead in a week is a hell of a loss for a small town like Scarborough."

"And Uncle Owen. That sure is a lot of dying in a short span."

Tim eased the squad car off the side of the road.

The children's mother stood in the driveway, wringing her hands.

As they popped the doors open, the woman, dressed in blue scrubs, squatted next to her car, one hand stretched to the ground for stability, the other fisted at her chest, sobbing.

Tim put in a call for a paramedic. "Here we go," he said, climbing from the car.

5

"Mrs. Baker." Tim crouched beside her. "Ma'am, I know you're scared. But if your boys are in trouble, they need you right now. I have to have some answers, so I can find them."

Kate pushed some Kleenexes into the woman's hand.

Mrs. Baker pulled them across her face, smearing snot onto her cheek.

"They're big boys. They're good boys." Tim's voice had a solid quality to it that said Mrs. Baker could lean on him, and he would support her. "They're probably having an adventure, and we need to get them home. Do they have phones? Did you try calling them?"

Mrs. Baker nodded and pointed toward the house. She opened her mouth, but a belch and sob came out with no information.

"Kate, why don't you walk Mrs. Baker to the patrol car? See if you can get her comfortable in the air conditioning. It's climbing toward a hundred today."

Tim handed her the keys, then tugged on a pair of gloves as he trekked to the house.

Kate pulled Mrs. Baker's arm around her shoulder and power-lifted the woman to a standing position. She led her to the car and seated her in the back. Reaching into the Igloo, Kate pulled out one of Tim's water bottles and opened the top.

"Here, Mrs. Baker, take a sip. You'll feel better." Kate guided the woman's hands to hold the bottle. "You told the operator that Chad and your sons were good friends?"

She nodded.

"Then you knew Chad very well. This must be terrifying for you." Kate struggled to find the right words. "And as hard as it is to work around those feelings, you understand, the more information we have, the faster we can bring your boys home. When did you see them last?"

Jennifer Baker tipped the whole bottle down. When she came up for air, she seemed to have wrestled her emotions into control. She rubbed the back of her wrist across her chin to catch the water drops. "I saw them yesterday morning. But I talked to them around three in the afternoon, and they were fine. I went to the gym, and then I met a friend for pizza and a movie before I went to work. I was on seven to seven last night. I'm late getting home because of all the paperwork they have us fill out at the end of each shift."

"Are you a single mom? Or was there another adult in the house?"

"Their daddy drives a truck. He's somewhere near Ohio right about now."

Kate nodded. "When you talked to your sons at three, did you talk to one of them or both?"

"Each of them. I told them they had to get their chores done before they went out, and they had to be home before dark. They needed to put the trash can down by the mailbox and unload the dishwasher." Mrs. Baker squeezed her eyelids tightly shut.

Kate looked up to see a bin set out at the end of the driveway.

"You said they had to be home by dark." Kate touched Mrs.

Baker's hand, so she would open her eyes. "Where were they going?"

"Out. They'd meet friends by the river and go floating on inner tubes, sometimes catch some fish and fry them up on a fire. Nothing much."

"Do they have their own car?" Kate asked, watching as Tim strode toward them.

"No, they probably walked unless one of their friends picked them up."

Tim opened the car door and stuck his head in. "Do your boys usually go far without their phones?"

"They don't take them down to the river. I told them if these phones got damaged, they wouldn't get new ones."

"Is there any place else they wouldn't take them?"

"No, sir. Usually, those phones are like another appendage."

"Ma'am, you can go in your house now and get comfortable. Search and Rescue is on the way. They're bringing the bloodhounds, so we should be able to track them right quick. Is there someone we can call to sit with you?"

"I can call someone," she said.

AFTER MRS. BAKER settled herself on the couch, clinging to her neighbor's hand, Kate and Tim headed outside.

"You've slapped that impassive mask right across your face, Tim. I always hated it when you did that."

Tim pursed his lips. "As soon as the sergeant gets here, we're moving on."

"You don't do detective work on missing kids?"

"I talked to my supervisor about what you told me. He did some quick research while I was on the phone, and you were right about all of it. The formulation change would never have come up in an autopsy report. We would have chalked this up to kids making a bad mistake. Cause of death would be accidental."

"But now?"

"Now someone's liable. What the charges will be depends on what our investigation turns up."

"Do you think someone wanted to kill Pemberly on purpose, or do you think this was some kind of horrible mistake?"

Tim moved to his side of the car. "You're doing it again."

"What?" She burned her fingertips on the hot door handle.

Tim reached in and cranked the air conditioning to blow the heat out of the car. Neither of them attempted to get in. "Don't hypothesize. Get a panoramic view, and then start to narrow your scope down until you've caught the bad guy in your crosshairs."

Standing beside the car, Kate was damp with perspiration. She pulled her long brown hair into a ponytail and twisted it around until it made a bun. She used her pen to hold the mess in place and then tried to catch her reflection in the back window to see if she had any semblance of a professional appearance.

"Cute as a bug, Katydid," Tim said.

Kate froze for a millisecond. Her heart pounded against her rib cage, then slowed as she realized it was an old habit. He hadn't meant anything personal by it.

An unmarked car pulled up behind them. Tim sauntered back to talk to the sergeant, and Kate slid into their car. The interior was like a furnace. She turned the vent's blast directly onto her overheated face as she waited for him to return.

"You need some oil for those cogs whirring in your brain. They're squeaking," Kate said, staring down the road. "Where are we headed?"

"Dogwood Pharmacy. That's where Pemberly had her prescription filled."

"Do you have a search warrant?"

"Not yet. They're in the works. I want to do a quick check-see on their OxyContin supply and make sure no one else has the old formula. We should have the judge's signature soon."

The rest of their ride was in silence. Kate chewed on the inside of her cheek and watched the cows lolling in their pastures. Just on the outskirts of town, Tim pulled up in front of Country Kitchen. Kate turned a questioning gaze on him.

"It's a might early for lunch, but why don't you take the opportunity? And if you wouldn't mind, order something for me."

"You're not coming in?"

Tim blushed ever so slightly. "I'll do the pharmacy run by myself. Doris Arthur is the owner now, and I might have better luck if you weren't with me."

"I noticed her giving me the evil eye at the funeral. I haven't seen her since high school graduation. What could I possibly have done to rile her up? And her brother, too, for that matter."

The blush grew brighter, and Tim flicked his eyes away. "I couldn't say for sure."

Kate opened the door and stuck her foot out. "You always were a terrible liar. What do you want me to order for you?"

"What I always get." His smile was sheepish and a little bit relieved.

KATE GAZED at the menu board. It was too early in the day for her to feel hungry.

"The chicken salad is good."

Kate turned to find Dr. Omid Javarti standing behind her.

"They make it with dried cherries and walnuts," he continued. "It's quite refreshing with a glass of lemonade."

Kate gave him a polite smile. "Thank you, that does sound good. How are you? You're not on duty at the hospital today?"

"I work seven days on, seven days off. Today starts my week of rest."

"Wow, I'd like that schedule." Kate stepped up to the cashier and ordered her lunch. "And may I have a double cheeseburger—no condiments, large fries, and a milkshake half vanilla, half chocolate to go?"

"Yes, ma'am. Do you want me to hold off putting that together until you're almost done eating, so it's fresh?" The cashier was an apple-cheeked woman with an ample bosom resting on her over-broad stomach.

"I'd appreciate that." Kate paid and moved to a seat near the window to watch for Tim's return.

"Mind if I join you?" Dr. Javarti asked, his hand resting on the back of the wooden chair.

"Please."

"How is your aunt doing?" He unrolled his cutlery from the paper napkin.

"Outwardly, she's fine, thank you."

"And inwardly?"

"I would never know. Aunt Emma and stoicism are synonymous."

He nodded. "I was serious about her health. If you see her needing a medicinal crutch for the time being, please call me. I want her to be as comfortable as possible under these circumstances. I don't mind writing her a prescription."

"Thank you kindly. I'll remember that." Kate took in Dr. Javarti's appearance. Even on this smoldering day, he had on dark pants with sharp pleats. He wore his hair cut short with a long bang that he swept back, and he sported the stylized five o'clock shadow popular with the fashionable crowds in Boston. This man belonged in New York City, not Podunk, Virginia.

"What?" He laughed.

"Sorry, I just… I can't figure out how in the world you found yourself here. Where are you from originally?"

"Originally? Ahh. So, you want me to tell you a story?"

"Yes, please," Kate said as the cashier brought them their drinks.

"I was born in Karaj, Iran. When I was thirteen, my parents sent me to America to spend the summer with my aunt and uncle to improve my English. My parents disappeared soon after. So my aunt's family adopted me, and I became an American citizen. I went to college, followed by medical school and residency, and then returned home, where I became a professor at the University. And that, as they say here in Scarborough, is it in a nutshell."

"Karaj to Scarborough? That's quite a leap."

"Not as far as you would think. Besides the obvious incentives of my hospital paycheck, which greatly supersedes the paltry amount of money I garnered as a professor, I did my undergraduate work at Virginia Tech. I love the rolling hills and shades of green found here in Virginia. And I became quite a fishing addict."

"Fish?"

"Catfish."

Kate laughed. "I guess there aren't many catfish in Karaj." The waitress set thick white pottery plates in front of them. Kate spread her napkin across her lap. "You said your parents disappeared. Were they ever found again?" Kate's hand shot out, and she touched Dr. Javarti's forearm. "I'm sorry, that was rude. It popped out of my mouth before I could stop it."

"It's natural to be curious." Dr. Javarti took a bite of his sandwich; after swallowing, he said, "I actually returned home to find them. I hoped they were dead."

Kate's eyes flashed wide.

"It sounds callous. I can see you're horrified. Let me explain. My parents were very forward-thinking. They were both part of the intelligentsia. My father was a professor of nuclear sciences, and my mother held a Ph.D. in philosophy—both were educated in America. At Harvard, as a matter of fact." Dr. Javarti took a long drink from his glass. "I love lemonade," he said, pausing. "After they finished their degrees, they returned home. They wanted to be part of the new Iran and hoped the policies coming out of Tehran would vault our country into the modern age, where women would have significance in society. Both of my parents wanted to help move Iran toward equal rights for women."

"And they had you. Do you have any siblings?"

"No. I was a much doted-upon only child, which is how I came to be in America. My parents had been told that the authorities had marked them for reprisal, and they brought me here to keep me safe."

"But they returned home?"

"Yes, equality was their cause to fight, and they needed to be fully engaged. Soon after their return, the SAVAK picked them up and leveled our house to the ground."

"The SAVAK?"

"That was the Shah's secret police force."

"Oh, my." Kate laid her hand over her heart. "Dr. Javarti, I'm so sorry."

"Omid, please. And yes, it was a great loss for my country and for me personally."

"Now you're back in rural Virginia, fishing for catfish and enduring the humidity."

"The humidity is very hard, indeed. I am used to desert heat. This…" He held his hands up as if supporting something physically heavy. "…robs me of my energy."

"Did you retire from teaching?" Kate asked, taking a bite of her sandwich. "Are you back here permanently?"

"A three-year sabbatical. I'm a hospitalist and have a contract with the management company, which found me exactly the kind of assignment I was looking for: a sleepy little town in need of a doctor, with plenty of time to enjoy catfishing." He smiled.

"The Middle East is in a tumult right now."

"Yet another reason to find myself comfortably hidden away in Southwest Virginia."

"Oh?" Kate put her sandwich back on the plate.

"Holding an American passport, and coming from my family's activist history, my presence at the university was receiving a great deal of scrutiny. After a private word with some people in-the-know, I decided that a sabbatical was in my best interest." Omid cleared his throat. "Having told you my life story, I'm entitled to one or two questions of my own, don't you think?"

"All right," Kate said, reaching for her glass.

"Your aunt told me that you came to visit for the summer."

"I have. I'm finishing up some schoolwork. I'm a teacher normally, but I've been studying crime scene investigation. It's very popular with the teens. I wanted to find a less daunting way to get my female students engaged in sciences, so they will consider science as a viable career path."

Omid nodded. "My mother also pushed for girls to go into the sciences. It was a great passion of hers."

Kate read something odd about his body language. Was it shame? Anger? She could understand anger. She wasn't sure why she was reading shame.

"So, are you doing an internship with the police department?" he asked. "Is that why you're here?"

"I am. I'm also here to spend time with my aunt."

"A terrible tragedy, the children's deaths. It's all anyone could talk about this morning at the party on the Knoll. Are you working on that case? I understand they died when they snorted lines of adulterated coke."

"I'm sorry, Omid. I'm not at liberty to discuss the particulars of the case." Kate felt someone staring at her and turned suddenly to discover whom. Behind her stood Custis Scarborough. He stalked over.

"Hello, Doc."

Custis' eyes glimmered maliciously; a sneer masqueraded as a smile. When Kate's spine juddered, Omid reached out to cover her hand protectively.

"What do you want, Custis?" she asked.

"Just being polite. Came over to say hey. I heard you were back in town. Plan to be here long?"

"My plans haven't been set in stone."

The bell jingled, and Tim stepped in. Kate yanked her hand away from Omid and hid it in her lap.

Custis nodded at Tim. "Nice to see you, Detective. Looks like you've got yourself a little competition." He tipped his head toward Omid then glanced down at Kate. "I'll catch up with you. We've got unfinished business."

"No, we don't," Kate said, finally getting herself back under control. "Everything that needed to be said was said. I'd prefer you keep your distance."

Custis ran his tongue across his teeth. "I bet you would."

Tim stood behind her chair. "Custis," he said with a nod. "Surprised to see you in town today. Thought you'd be busy up at your pig-picking."

"Just running a quick errand for Mama. We're having a blast. Hope to see you up there with your family when your shift's over. We plan to have music into the night. Got a big ol' bonfire ready and marshmallows for the kids to roast. Your boys would have a great time—and Pam." With that, Custis dipped his head to give Kate a wink.

The two men had squared off, the pleasantries barely masking their disdain. The cashier waddled over and looked from face to face before she set a brown paper bag and a Styrofoam cup beside Kate's plate and left without a word.

"Thank you for the company, Omid." Kate pushed up from the table. "Enjoy the rest of your lunch."

Tim held the door wide for Kate. His lower jaw thrust out, making him look pugnacious. As soon as they were in the privacy of the car, Kate expected the inquisition to begin. She was wrong.

A call went out over the radio for any units in the vicinity of High Street to respond to a medical emergency; the paramedics' ETA was fifteen minutes.

"Buckle up. That's us. We're only a mile away." Tim responded to the dispatcher, tapped his lights and siren on, and jetted down the road.

6

———

Tᴵᴹ ʀᴀᴄᴇᴅ ꜰʀᴏᴍ ᴛʜᴇ ᴄᴀʀ, ᴜᴘ ᴛʜᴇ ꜰʟᴏᴡᴇʀ-ʟɪɴᴇᴅ ꜱᴛᴀɪʀꜱ, ᴀɴᴅ through the wide-open door. Kate ran right behind him, grabbing at the handrail to keep from stumbling. Tim looked left, then right into the dining room and living room. "Police," he shouted. He pointed Kate toward the back of the house as he took the stairs two at a time to check the bedrooms.

"Here," Kate hollered as she came upon the elderly woman hunkered over her husband, trying to blow life back into his lungs.

Kate rounded the couple and pressed two fingers against the man's carotid artery. She couldn't find a pulse.

Tim pounded down the staircase.

"Kitchen," she yelled, positioning herself for CPR. Her hands shook as she stacked them and interlaced her fingers. She locked her elbows and thrust down with her strength and weight. Tim pulled the woman from her spot and took over the breaths.

Four cycles in, and sweat coursed down Kate's back. Her strength waned along with her original burst of adrenaline.

"On three, we switch," Tim said, then lowered with another breath.

Kate plunged down, counting aloud. "One, two, three."

She rolled to the right, and Tim took over. Kate tilted the elderly man's head back. "Could he be choking?" Kate asked the woman as she squeezed his nostrils, then covered his lips with her own.

"Asthma attack." The woman clutched the front of her dress.

Kate counted the CPR thrusts to time her breaths. She watched Tim's powerful arms compress the man's chest the requisite two inches; they never waned, never sputtered.

As the EMTs jogged into the room, pushed the table and chairs out of the way, and used their equipment to register any sign of life.

Tim and Kate continued their efforts.

One of the responders pulled back the man's eyelid and touched his eyeball. There was no reflex.

The paramedic put his hand on Kate's shoulder. "Ma'am, it's okay to stop now. I'm calling it. Time of death, twelve twenty-six."

A wail rose up in the woman's throat and coursed through Kate's veins like an electrical current, lighting her nerves on fire. Two women, hovering at the door opening, rushed forward to gather up the new widow into their arms.

Tim pulled his phone from his pocket as Kate moved to the sink to wash her hands and catch her breath.

The EMTs packed up to leave.

The women followed after them.

Kate was drying her hands on a dishtowel when the elderly woman, Rebecca Brody, came back in alone.

"Mrs. Brody, I'm sorry for your loss," Tim began.

"I want to thank you both. You did what you could. I guess the Good Lord needed Wayne at his side. He's gone home."

"Yes, ma'am. Mrs. Brody, this is Kate Hamilton, she's working with me for the summer."

"I barely got off the phone when you were at my door. When I found him, Wayne was still breathing." Mrs. Brody spread her arms wide and let them flop to her side. "Then, all of a sudden, nothing. I only got one breath in him. I could never have done what you did. Oh, you must be exhausted. Please come and sit down."

"We're okay, ma'am, thank you. I've called the funeral home, and they're on the way. Because this was an unexpected death, it will be up to the coroner whether they do an autopsy or not."

"Can I cover him?" she asked, pulling a tablecloth from the drawer.

"Yes, ma'am." Tim grabbed hold of the bottom and helped Mrs. Brody. "You said asthma. Did your husband have a recent history of asthma attacks?"

"I'm *assuming* that's what it was. Wayne has…had…Wayne had rather severe bronchial asthma. But I don't know for sure. I wasn't here, you see. I was at the grocery store. I brought in the first bag." She pointed to the floor by the table where a brown paper bag laid on its side. "Wayne was gasping for air. I grabbed up his rescue inhaler and helped him spray it into his mouth, but he wasn't taking deep enough breaths for it to be of any use. I called 9-1-1 and tried to calm him down. Then he was on the floor and not breathing anymore." Mrs. Brody stared at the mound where her husband lay.

Kate realized the woman was still in shock. Not a tear was on her face.

Tim stood back and scanned the room. Kate followed suit. Lunch was on the table—a peanut butter and jelly sandwich with chips and a glass of orange juice. A laptop was set up next to the half-eaten sandwich, but the screen was dark. Tim walked over, wrapped his finger with a napkin, and tapped the space bar. A word document came up.

Tim scanned the page. "Mrs. Brody, the whole town is up at

Scarborough Knoll today. Were you and Mr. Brody going there later?"

"Oh, no. We would never do that. Wayne is an environmental engineer, and he stands…" her breath caught, and she steadied herself on the wall before she continued, "he *stood* in staunch opposition to uranium mining. That's probably what got him riled up into such a state - all that propaganda going on over at Scarborough Knoll."

Mrs. Brody sat down in the kitchen chair. Her hand reached out as she spoke, and she touched and moved things around. Kate wondered if she was aware of what she was doing. Mrs. Brody's voice was compressed like she was forcing words from a tight space. "The Scarborough family is right excited. They think in the next round of votes, the legislature will lift the moratorium on uranium mining. That's what Wayne was working on there. He was writing his opposition paper to give to Senator Orly." Mrs. Brody reached out a hand to point to the computer, but her finger hit the glass and sent orange juice dripping from the table.

Kate rushed forward with the kitchen towel to wipe up the mess, and then she crouched to blot the spill. She tugged a latex glove from her side pocket and wriggled it on. She stood up, holding an inhaler and a prescription bottle. OxyContin 80mg. She held it out for Tim to see.

Tim pulled on a pair of gloves and opened the childproof top. There were five OC- 80mg tablets inside the bottle. He looked at the label, and his face went impassive. "Ma'am, has your husband sought help for pain recently?" he asked.

"The fool put his back out two weeks ago, trying to move the blasted piano all by himself. I had to get the ambulance up here to take him to the hospital. He couldn't walk."

"And they issued a prescription for the pain?"

"Yes, some pain pills. But my daughter-in-law is a chiropractor. She came in and worked on him, and he said he was mostly better and didn't need the medication."

"There's only one missing. Do you think he took it today?"

"I told him he should."

"And why was that, ma'am?" Tim put the lid back in place.

"He'd been hunkered over that computer for hours yesterday and was up moaning most of the night. When I went to the grocery store, I handed him the bottle and said if he started hurting, he should consider taking one."

"Do you mind if I hold on to this bottle?"

"Of course not, but why would you want it?"

"Routine procedure, ma'am."

KATE BROUGHT Mrs. Brody's groceries in. The frozen foods had melted, and the milk had already turned sour. Kate put what foods were salvageable in the fridge while Tim was in the cruiser conferencing with his boss.

Mr. Brody's body was on the way to the morgue.

When Mrs. Brody's friends filed in, Kate felt better about leaving. She offered her sympathy, said her goodbyes, and then went to join Tim.

"Got her settled?"

"The cavalry's arrived."

"Yup, probably only took this long because the word had to get to the Knoll."

Kate looked out at the empty sidewalks as they drove past. "It's crazy how dead the whole town is today."

A smile spread over Tim's face. "Katydid, was that gallows humor?"

"More like a poor choice of words. Are you going to tell me what you found out at the pharmacy?"

"I didn't get much because of HIPPA. I need to get those warrants in hand before we see anything. I'm heading back there now with Wayne Brody's prescription."

"Not much, but something?" Kate stretched around. "I'm grabbing one of your water bottles. Do you want one?"

"Don't you have my lunch somewhere?"

Kate reached down and pulled out the bag. "It's bound to be gross. Your shake is melted."

"Hand me that. Half and half?"

"Of course."

He sent her a wink. "I knew you'd remember."

The heat of her blush spread across Kate's face. She turned quickly, so Tim wouldn't see. She took in the tree-lined street with the picture-perfect white picket fences. Deep porches flew American flags and held bench swings with colorful pillows. This wasn't a place where bad things should happen.

She sent a quick glance Tim's way. "You were telling me about the pharmacy?"

"They keep special paperwork on the distribution of all narcotics. There are laws that apply specifically to that class of drugs. I asked Doris to take a look and tell me when she last filled a prescription for OxyContin. She said it was February."

"Both Pemberly's and Wayne's prescriptions were filled this month."

"Thank you, Doctor Watson."

"Did you check their OxyContin supply?" Kate asked.

"Doris showed me. The highest dosage she carries right now is 20mg. She can order a higher dose if someone needs it. And it's all OP."

"Did you ask…"

"When it was switched out? Yes, ma'am, I did. She said it happened about Halloween time, a year and a half ago."

"How weird is that?"

"Pretty darned weird."

Kate noticed Tim's knuckles whiten as he gripped the steering wheel.

"Are you ready for some bad news?" he asked.

"Oh, no." Kate covered her face with her hands.

"Yeah, Search and Rescue found the boys' bodies down at the river. They had a mirror and razor blade." Tim paused and worked his jaw. "They'd been dead for quite a while. In this heat with all them bugs down there, things progressed pretty far." He glanced over at her. "I'm glad you didn't find them."

Tears dripped down Kate's cheeks, but she reigned in the sob that swelled in her throat. Their poor mother. Even though it was Kate's job to help with such a scene, Kate agreed with Tim: she was glad she hadn't found the boys. These teens reminded her of her students at home and filled Kate's heart with pain.

Tim shoved the gear into park. He patted her knee. "Katie, you stay here. Drink some water. I'm going in to talk to Doris."

7

____

"**A**UNT **E**MMA, I'M HOME."

"Oh, honey, come here. You've had a terrible day. I heard about your trying to save Wayne Brody."

Kate drifted into the kitchen.

"Why, what have you got there?" Aunt Emma asked, tying her apron around her waist.

"This is your new kitty. You didn't tell me what color, so I picked a gray. Do you like him?"

"Oh, so tiny. This is just a baby." Aunt Emma gathered the kitten against her chest and tickled her fingers through its silky fur. "Owen just hated cats. Hated them. I never even asked if I could bring one home."

"Is this okay?"

"Yes, dear. Lovely. I'll call him Bingley." She dropped a kiss on the top of the kitten's head.

"Ha! I never took you for a romantic." Kate went to sit at the table. "You're a Jane Austen fan?"

Aunt Emma gave her a confused glance. "Is there a woman alive who isn't? Thank you, honey. I love him already. Here, let me fetch you a glass of sweet tea."

"Thank you." Kate sat down while her aunt poured. "I talked to Ryan today."

"Is he feeling better? How's his hand?" Aunt Emma handed Kate the glass then adjusted Bingley up onto her shoulder. He rumbled with satisfaction as Aunt Emma's fingers massaged over him.

"You got a kitty, and he got his dog today. It's a German shepherd. A female." Kate took a gulp from the glass and shuddered as her system took a full hit of the syrupy sweetness. "He named her Houston."

"Houston? That's a strange name for a girl dog, isn't it?"

"His sense of humor, 'Houston, we have a problem.'"

"Do you think the dog will help?"

"Lord, I hope so. But no, it's just a piece of the puzzle—meds, therapy, his SEAL buddies, puppy, and time."

"Katherine, look at me."

Kate moved her gaze from her lap to her aunt's face.

"Things have progressed a far piece since the Vietnam War. People are different, care is different, and Owen sure never had a dog to help him. There's hope."

Kate sucked in a deep breath. "That's what I keep telling myself. I love him. I really do. Truly. Deeply. But I'm not you, Aunt Emma. You have that corundum core."

"It's an inherited quality. I see it in you. You'll surprise yourself."

Kate pulled her lips in and shook her head. "I'm not sure we can survive this. He doesn't even want me in the same house with him right now."

Aunt Emma reached out and stroked her hair. "He's protecting you the best he can. He was right to ask you to go. It's too dangerous for you to be there. He needs to deal with this on his own."

BEING a former Prom Queen isn't a bulletproof vest. Watch your back.

Kate blinked at the text message that popped up. Ryan was thinking about her. He was concerned. It was oddly worded, but what did she care? She dialed her home phone and got a busy signal. *Darn it.* Kate needed to hear her husband's voice. Needed some connection with him. She tried again.

"Do you need a minute?" Tim asked.

Kate hadn't seen him come up. "I was trying to reach Ryan. I'll catch him later." She slid her cell phone into the thigh pocket on her khaki pants. "What are we doing today?"

"We're heading over to the hospital. I have warrants to get copies of Pemberly Wilks and Wayne Brody's medical histories. I'm going to send a copy to the medical examiner's office. And I want to make an appointment for us to talk with Dr. Michaels about his role in all this."

"Because his name is on both of the OxyContin prescriptions?"

"Yes, and because he attended both of them in the emergency room. Then, I'm going to drop you off at home. I want you to relax for the rest of the day. Tomorrow morning, we need to go to the first of the teens' funerals and see what we can see."

"What are you doing after you drop me off?"

Tim rubbed a finger over his lower lip. "I need to go to Dogwood Pharmacy. Now that I have a warrant, Doris can answer my questions."

"You won't bring her into the station for that?"

"I need her to access her computers. Besides the records for Brody and Wilks, I need a list of employees. I also want the names of the people on duty when Wilks and Brody had their prescriptions filled."

"Okay, but I was doing a little research last night about Oxycodone and interactions," Kate said.

"And what did you find?"

"In my class, we learned that people die from Oxycodone because it represses the respiratory cycle. I wondered why any doctor who knew Wayne Brody had asthma would write a script for the drug. And if they wrote the script, why would a pharmacist fill it? Pharmacy computers have pop-up warnings to prevent drug interactions. Wayne Brody filled his inhaler and his OxyContin at Dogwood Pharmacy."

"Interesting point," Tim said.

"I have another one."

Tim chuckled. "Somehow I thought you would."

"Pemberly was taking Nardil. It's an anti-depressant and one of the drugs listed as a definite no-no for mixing with Oxycodone. Pemberly had her Nardil filled at Dogwood, also. That shouldn't be possible. The origin of the problem could have been the doctor making bad decisions. But because Dogwood's computer should have prevented the prescription from being filled, the proper paperwork for the authorities was not filled out, and they don't even seem to legitimately carry the drug, this all points to nefarious actions taking place at Dogwood."

"Nefarious actions? Kate, you're reading too many novels. But I will say those are reasonable conclusions to draw. I'll check into it."

8

———

"I'M IN HERE," AUNT EMMA CALLED AS KATE PUSHED OPEN THE front door.

Kate followed the voice back to the kitchen, where she found her aunt putting together a blueberry cobbler. "Oh, yay. Do we have ice cream, too?" Kate asked, sticking her head in the freezer.

"It's there on the right. How was your day?" Aunt Emma spooned the berries into the casserole dish.

"Difficult. We went to the funeral for one of the teens this morning."

"Yes, I was there, too."

Kate took down two glasses. "Can I pour you some sweet tea?"

"That'd be fine."

"I didn't see you there," Kate said.

"No, but I saw you, and more importantly, I saw Pam Gibbons. Go ahead and sit yourself down. I want to have a talk with you."

Kate moved to the table and sat in one of the hard-backed chairs. Kate got the same queasy stomach she used to get when she went to the principal's office in grammar school.

Aunt Emma perched on the chair across from her, their knees bumping. "Seems to me, young lady, you're sitting in a frying pan ready to jump into a fire. I just want to know if you're aware of what's going on around you."

"This has something to do with Pam?"

Bingley jumped up to join them. Aunt Emma reached over and plucked the kitten off the table. "She's scared to death."

"About all the people who are dying?" Kate reached for Bingley and nestled him into her lap.

"Lord, no, why would she be scared about that? No, she's worried you've come back for Tim."

"Ow!" Kate yelled as the kitten's claws pricked through her khakis. She moved him to the floor, where he became entranced with her bootlaces. Kate sat up to see the stern set of her aunt's eyebrow. "Oh, that's just silly. Tim and I were children when we dated."

"He asked you to marry him, Kate. You turned him down and left for college."

"Of course, I did. I didn't want to be a cop's wife, and I sure didn't want to live in a small town for the rest of my life. He always knew I planned to leave town and live in the city."

"Everyone thought you loved him enough that you'd change your mind. He surely did."

"Now, how would you know that?"

Aunt Emma shrugged. "I got eyes in my head, and I'm an old woman. There are no new stories out there, only new names for the characters. The two of you had a special kind of chemistry."

"I'd agree with you there, but I'll tell you just how much I loved him. I loved him enough to go away. If I had asked him to follow me, he would have hated living in the city. Eventually, he would have resented me, and we'd have both been miserable. If I had stayed, it would have been me who martyred myself for his dreams. I did the very best for both of us."

"He was heartbroken when you left. Visibly and tragically heartbroken. Some of us feared he'd do something stupid. Turn to drink, or worse."

"I know." Kate raked her fingers over her scalp. "I'm sorry about that. He's a wonderful person. He deserves to be happy, and now he has Pam and the kids. It's the life he always wanted."

"The life he wanted with *you*. Why'd you really come back, dear? Certainly not to visit an old lady like me."

The question shocked Kate. Why *had* she come back? "Convenience." She shrugged. It was a lame reason. Kate tried to dress it up with more words. "I wanted to visit with you, and Joanna told me Tim was a detective. I knew he'd help me with my internship if I asked."

"Oh now, poo." Aunt Emma smacked her knee. "You were willing to come here and stay with me and your Uncle Owen. No one would willingly spend a summer with that old grump unless they had no other choices. Are you telling me your university couldn't find you an internship with a department that actually had CSI work for you to do?" Aunt Emma crossed her arms over her chest; obviously, she wasn't going to let this drop.

Kate held her tongue.

"Now, granted, things have been popping since you've come back to town, but as far as I can remember, there has never been a controversial death here. The most the cops get to do is catch a child stealing candy from the grocery, or write a speeding ticket for the out-of-towners, maybe deliver someone home who's had too much to drink. Be truthful. There's more to you being here than convenience sake. And his name is Tim Gibbons — and what's more, I'm not the only one who worked that out. Pam has. I'm sure most of the people in town see it."

"Tim and I were over fifteen years ago. Surely that's long enough that people wouldn't think I have ulterior motives."

"You love him. Tell me you don't, Kate. I have eyes, mind you," Aunt Emma said.

"Yes, I love him. I've always loved him, but it's a sentimental love. A 'wishing him well and happy' kind of love. A friendship. Not a steal-you-away-from-your-family kind of love. And besides…" Kate stopped and focused on her glass of tea.

"Besides what?"

She shrugged. "I wanted a place to be safe and quiet for a little while. I guess that's why I came here. But after all you just said, I'm feeling pretty small and selfish."

"Everyone is selfish once in a while, especially when they're hurting. Doesn't seem like you found what you were looking for here, though."

"How could I? What I want is Ryan back in my life. I want him better. So I came to hide out here for a while to give his doctors a chance to get him stabilized. I thought Scarborough would be a safe distraction."

Aunt Emma patted her hand. "Are you in for the night? I was going to have cobbler and ice cream for dinner."

The discussion behind them, Kate smiled. "That sounds great. I'm going to run up to the gym after we eat, though." Kate checked her watch. "I told Omid I'd meet up with him at 7:30."

"That would be the fire."

"I'm sorry?" Kate looked at her, confused.

"Tim was the fry pan in my metaphor."

"And you think I'm after Omid? Seriously? Aunt Emma, I'm married and madly in love with my husband. Omid and I just met. I ran into him at the gas station and mentioned the gym. He happened to be going there tonight, too. I would never ever cheat on Ryan… that's just wrong. No." Kate stood up, thoroughly vexed. "And if you catch anyone gossiping about me, you set everyone straight on all counts, please."

"Easier said than done. You're stirring up more trouble than we've had in a long while. People are looking forward to the fire-works they're anticipating."

"They're going to be disappointed." Kate was emphatic.

"You see that they are."

KATE HIT her stride on the treadmill by the time Omid threw his towel over the machine beside her.

"Hey there, I got a head start on you." Kate smiled.

"I see that. I'll have to work to catch up."

"What are you planning for your week off?"

"I got called back on. I need to head to work day after tomorrow."

"Oh?" Kate asked.

"A doctor's wife had their baby earlier than expected." Omid selected his workout on the computer panel.

"Everyone's all right, though?"

"Yes. The baby's family is doing great." He started with a fast walk. "And a few more catfish get a reprieve."

Kate laughed. "I'm glad you're here tonight. I wanted to ask some questions if you don't mind." Kate lowered her pace, so she would have enough breath to talk.

"Are these medical questions or personal?"

"Medical—hospital policy, to be exact."

"Ah. Okay." He pressed a button and began to jog.

"When someone goes into the ER, do they go home with prescriptions filled through the hospital pharmacy?"

"We don't handle that. The doctors write the prescription, and the patient gets it filled."

"Could someone steal a prescription pad and use it without a doctor knowing it?"

"Not at our hospital. We don't use prescription pads. We send scripts electronically straight to the pharmacy. That prevents the mistakes made with poor handwriting."

"And you do this on a computer?"

"Handheld devices we carry with us when we're working with the patients. That way, we can send it immediately during their consult."

"Could someone get hold of one and send a prescription, as if they were a doctor?"

"I suppose so. Whoever it is would have to be an expert hacker. We have tight security on the devices to prevent such a thing. You're asking these questions because of the children who died?"

"Not specifically. I'm trying to understand if there was a broken link in the chain, allowing bad things to happen that should never have been possible."

"Okay, hypothetically then, the answer is no one could send a fake prescription to the pharmacy by mistake or by premeditation."

"I have another question."

Omid smiled broadly. "It's my turn to ask you a question. Do you have plans tomorrow night? I'm driving to Danville for some Mexican food. I've been craving tacos."

Kate laughed. "Tacos, huh?"

"And I planned to catch a late film."

"What's playing?"

"*Salmon Fishing in Yemen.*" His smile crinkled the corners of his eyes. "Please, won't you join me?"

"Thanks, but I'm going hiking tomorrow - get out in nature. My brain feels clogged," Kate said.

"Why's that?"

"Casework. There's been a lot of death this week."

"Yes," Omid agreed, "more than one would expect." A

shadow crossed over his face, and he offered a tight-lipped smile. "So, you had another question?"

Kate looked up to find Custis glaring at her from across the fitness room. He pointed a threatening finger.

Omid followed her gaze. "Something about that man isn't right," he said.

"Yeah, well, you won't get any argument from me." Kate tapped the red button, and the treadmill came to a stop. She gathered her things to leave.

"Did you walk here tonight?" Omid asked.

"Yes, it's a beautiful night for a walk. I was enjoying the break from the heat. I understand it'll be short-lived."

Omid's gaze searched the room until it landed on Custis, who was lifting weights in the mirror, but his attention was focused on them.

Omid stopped his machine. "It's dark outside. I'd feel better if you'd let me drive you home."

Kate glanced at Custis. "Thanks."

KATE'S FRIEND Joanna was sitting on the porch swing with a glass of sweet tea in her hand when Kate climbed out of Omid's Jaguar.

"Night, thanks for the ride."

Omid beeped twice and drove off.

"Hey there." Kate went to give Joanna a hug. "I didn't know you'd be in town."

"I came in for Chad's funeral. Stupid idiot boy. God, he's caused a world of hurt. Pemberly's out of her mind. The whole town's in shock. How could this happen, Kate?" Joanna shook her head. "I've never seen anything like it. It's as if everyone turned into a zombie, walking around in a daze. My sister is clinging to her kids like they're drowning. She won't let them get more than three feet from her, or she freaks out. I hope Reverend Pines gives a good sermon, so people can snap out of this. It's spooky."

"It's hitting close to home for me, too. My students…I don't know how parents can deal with the death of their own child." Kate blew out a breath and looked up at the sky, focusing on the first stars coming out. "My brain is filled with images of my kids. I wonder if they're making good choices and staying safe. Every time my mind turns to home, I panic."

"That's not a good look for an officer of the law."

"CSI intern. But you're right, I have to be professional. I've decided to be a human magnifying glass and focus on the details in front of me."

"Speaking of details in front of you, was that Dr. J. who brought you home?"

"You know him?"

"He treated my mom's goiter. Do you think it's a good idea to be seen tooling around with him?"

"At the moment, I thought it was the best choice I had."

"Why's that?"

"No reason," Kate mumbled and reached over to take a sip of her friend's tea.

"I didn't mean to pry." Joanna pushed off with her foot, making the swing creek as it swayed back and forth.

Kate plopped down on the stair beside her. "Omid has been nothing but a gentleman. He's just being a friend."

"Omid?"

"He's not my doctor. He's just a guy to me."

"A very handsome, well-educated guy. He's also making up for lost time."

Kate swatted away a fly. "I don't understand."

"The Iranian culture prohibits sexual relations outside of marriage. Dr. Javarti never married, and…" Joanna offered up a salacious grin. "Well, let's just say he's ruffled the skirts of almost every woman in town under forty, married or unmarried." Joanna winked. "He has an excellent reputation for his fine bedside manner."

Kate wrinkled her nose. "I get your warning, thanks, but it's not an issue." Her phone vibrated on her hip. She pulled her cell from her pocket and read the text message: **Karma bites.**

Joanna craned her neck to read. "Karma? You posted on Facebook that Ryan's dog's name is Houston."

"I need to call him."

"Yeah, well, it's late. I have to get over to my parent's house. I just wanted to give you a quick hug and tell you I'm around for a few days."

Kate watched as Joanna climbed into her yellow Beetle. She waved until the car was out of sight, and then she tried called home.

9

————

KATE SMOOTHED HER HAND OVER THE NEW AND MORE appropriate black dress she'd bought the day before. She stood in the back, left-hand corner of the church. Tim took up his post on the right. Between the two vantage points, they hoped to cover the congregation. Pemberly stumbled in. It looked like she'd been given a fist full of Valium to get through the ordeal.

The phone buzzed in Kate's bra. She hated to keep it there; it was sweaty and poked at her, but her dress didn't have pockets. She had left her purse in the car to free up her hands. She turned her back to the congregation and fished out her smartphone: **You don't want to stir this pot.**

What could Ryan possibly mean? Kate looked at the time stamp. He'd texted twenty minutes ago. She wondered why the message hadn't been delivered immediately. Probably had to do with whatever Internet site he was using. Kate held up her phone and waggled it at Tim. He responded with two fingers in the air as he mouthed two minutes.

Kate rounded the building, pressing her quick dial for home. The call rang until the answering machine engaged. "Hey, Ryan. It's me. I guess I missed you." Kate said as she walked down the sidewalk into the garden. "I'm trying to figure out what I've done wrong. Did I do something - or not do something – that's upset you?" Kate saw the portly form of Senator Tredegar Orly in the distance and heard someone yelling angry words at him. "If I did, I'm sorry. I'd like to talk it through with you." Kate sidled up to a tree and peeked around. She saw Custis Scarborough punctuating his diatribe by jabbing a finger at Senator Orly's chest.

Even from this distance, she could tell Custis had whipped himself into full fury. "I'm at a funeral right now, baby. I'll call you later. I love you - never forget that."

Kate pushed the end button as she crept toward the rhododen-dron bush. She wished she could make out what Custis was saying, but the wind blew the conversation the wrong way. The words that Kate picked out were "uranium," "The hell I will" and "governor." Kate moved closer to see Senator Orly was red-faced and mopping his brow. It seemed to her that the men were about to come to blows.

She pressed number three on her phone's speed dial.

"What have you got?" Tim asked.

"Get to the garden right now. Hurry." Over the phone, she heard the sanctuary door squeak open, then bang. Tim's breath was in the phone.

Seconds later, "I don't see you."

"I'm over by the bushes, but you should…oh, no." Kate leaped forward, sprinting toward the men. Senator Orly had pulled something from his pocket and then dropped to his knees. As Kate ran the last few steps, Tim's hand was on her back.

Senator Orly fumbled with a prescription vial. Kate knelt beside him and took it from his hand. Nitroglycerin.

She popped the top and tipped a pill into the senator's open hand. He slipped the pill under his tongue, then fell onto his hip, before rolling onto his back. Tim was on the phone with dispatch, getting an ambulance en route.

Custis stood with his arms folded across his chest, a smirk on his face.

"Katie, I need you to go up to the parking lot and show the EMTs where we are. Tell them, stat."

"Do you have anything in the squad car that would help?" Kate asked.

"Not for this, I don't."

Kate took off at a run. She could already hear the sirens wailing on the other side of town.

IT TOOK THE WHOLE CREW, Tim, and several men recruited from the sanctuary to get Senator Orly up the garden hill to the ambulance. Senator Orly had a reputation for being a lifelong lover of fried chicken, potato salad, and pork barbeque. He must tip the scale at over four hundred pounds.

Custis was not one of the men helping with the lifting. He had wandered off long before help arrived, Kate had noticed. While the men made the climb, Kate returned to the garden. Scanning the ground, she picked up her discarded phone and Senator Orly's medications. She squatted down and put her ear to the ground. She hoped from the new vantage point she would see something she'd missed. Something to tell her what Custis had been going on about.

Tim came back to find her fanny up.

Kate jumped to her feet, brushing the grass from her knees. "How does he look?"

"We'll have to wait and see. What've you got there?"

She held out the Nitro bottle.

"Spit it out," Tim said.

"Spit what out?"

"You've got a theory."

"I don't. And even if I did, it would be unprofessional to have a theory, so I wouldn't tell you."

They started up the path.

"But you've got one."

"Not so much a theory as a concern."

Tim's fingers rested on Kate's lower back as he guided her up the stairs. "Go on."

"Two heart attacks in two weeks. Both men on Nitro pills."

"Most of the men in town over a certain age have them, I'd imagine," Tim said.

"Nitro is for angina, so I don't think so. I'm wondering if we could send this to the lab and maybe my uncle's pills, too. See if they are what the label says they are. Senator Orly didn't seem to respond to his pill."

Tim stopped and touched Kate's elbow, so she'd turn to face him. "All right. After the funeral, we'll go get your Uncle Owen's pills. Realize, though, neither man was healthy. Senator Orly's been a heart attack waiting to happen for over a decade now. This is probably a wild goose chase, but I'm willing to scratch this idea off your list. I don't want it rumbling in the background. We need to stay focused."

10

———

I, Owen Jenkins, being about as sound in mind and body as I ever have been in my adult life, do declare this my last will and testament. Whatever I've got at the time the Good Lord calls me home is to be split equally between my wife, Emma Jane Jenkins, and my niece, Katherine Elizabeth Hamilton (Kate). My niece, though, is the one who should make all the decisions. My wife has got to be off her rocker, or she wouldn't have put up with the likes of me for the last fifty some-odd years. Kate shows much more sense by keeping her distance. So now, Kate has to step up and watch out for my Em.

One stipulation, though. Kate is not to sell my great-grand-daddy's land. Not split it up. Not rent it, lease it, nothing. Not to anyone, under any circumstances. It stays in the family, period. The next in line are Kate's cousins on Emma's side. Kate can pick one of them to be in her will. Kate, make sure that you stipulate that this land is never ever to be sold no matter how many millions they offer for it. This land is not for sale.

Other than that, I don't care much about what you girls do.
Signed before God and my lawyer,
Owen Jefferson Jenkins IV.

· · ·

"WHAT'S ALL THIS ABOUT?" Kate asked.

Neil Oliver, Uncle Owen's lawyer, took off his glasses and rubbed them with his linen handkerchief. "Your uncle insisted on writing his own will. He thought the language that I might incorporate would give folks an opportunity to trick or cheat you into compromising the family land."

"It sounds like this has something to do with Scarborough Mining. Aunt Emma said they wanted to put a holding pond on Jenkins Hillock."

"Yes, well, you're right." Neil Oliver rested his elbows on the arms of his chair, steepled his fingers, and thrust the points under his chin. Kate watched him gather his thoughts.

"The Village of Scarborough is at odds," Neil began. "There are two camps: one camp says progress and economics, the other says tradition and environment. Your uncle lived in the second camp. And he had more power than most when it came to allowing or disallowing Scarborough Mining to fulfill its dreams of mega-wealth. We're talking billions with a capital 'B,' Kate."

Kate scooted to the edge of her chair.

"You see, the topography of the area puts almost the entire vein of uranium under Scarborough Knoll. A smaller vein does run through Jenkins Hillock, but that vein wouldn't be profitable to mine. There's not enough raw product. But your uncle's property does have an important role to play in the uranium production. It is somewhat of an obstacle, actually. Scarborough Mining would be required to set up a containment pond, placed to protect the contents from any effect of flooding, should a flood of biblical proportions like the one Noah faced ever descend upon us. If the river was to flood as far as Scarborough Knoll, which is impossible to imagine, it could create a radioactive catastrophe in the Roanoke River."

"Why can't they use Pemberly's land for that?" Kate asked.

"Oh, they did studies. The Wilks family was very keen on renting their land to Scarborough Mining. In fact, Mrs. Wilks was one of the first investors in the mining company and sits on their board. But their land is too low. It would have to be Jenkins Hillock, or they can't move forward. Not that they can move forward at this time anyway, though many are hopeful about the upcoming legislative session."

Kate heaved a breath. "Ah. The holding pond must be the unfinished business Custis Scarborough wanted to talk to me about."

Aunt Emma tilted her head to the side. "You looked relieved, dear."

"I was afraid he wanted to rehash the time I testified against him," Kate said. "Mr. Oliver, is there anything you need from either my Aunt Emma or me?"

"Not at the moment. There's a series of steps to navigate through. Do you and Mrs. Jenkins wish to continue with me as lawyer, or do you prefer to seek counsel in Boston?"

"For now, we'll carry on with you, Neil, if that's all right," Aunt Emma said. "You know all of our business, and there's no reason for a change." She gathered her purse and stood to shake hands with him.

"Thank you, Emma. I'll keep you and Kate updated on how things progress with probate."

As they moved from the icebox-cold office out onto the sweltering street, Kate pulled the sweater from around her shoulders.

Aunt Emma seemed not to mind the heat at all.

"Did you hear my stomach growling in there?" Aunt Emma whispered from behind her hand. "I was so embarrassed. I need something to eat. How about you?" She pointed down the street to Country Kitchen.

It looked too far to walk on such a hot day and too close to drive.

Her aunt walked on, and Kate walked dutifully by her side.

The bell jingled brightly as they went in. The apple-cheeked cashier stood behind the register. After ordering sweet tea and egg salad sandwiches, they moved to the two-top tucked in the far corner.

Ever since Kate had seen Custis yelling at Senator Orly, she'd had some questions she wanted to run by her aunt. "Aunt Emma, do you know anything about Pemberly and her husband's breakup?" Kate asked.

"Well, I do, and I don't. I can tell you what the gossips are saying. How true any of it is, I can't say for sure. It's more to do with that blasted Scarborough Mining."

"Was he pro-mining, too?"

"Oh, he was very much pro-mining. The problem was that American Mine Works offered to buy out Pemberly's shares in Scarborough Mining. It was a good offer by all accounts. Many of the other investors have already sold their shares to them. The Wilks family would have made a tidy profit, but not the hundreds of millions that Pemberly is anticipating. She believes those millions are close at hand because of the upcoming vote. Her husband thinks the vote will fail again, especially with Tredegar Orly standing so staunchly against it. Jason Wilks wanted Pemberly to take the deal. The fiasco turned into a drunken fight at the country club. Pemberly threw her mint julep in his face." Aunt Emma leaned out of the way to let the waitress put their plates down. "Thank you, dear. That looks lovely."

When she and Kate were alone again, Aunt Emma continued, "Afterward, he hightailed it back to Charlotte, where he took a job in finance and hasn't been back to Scarborough since."

"But there's more to this than getting the bill through the legislature. I read that the governor swore he'd veto it if it crossed his desk."

"Owen said that's politics. The man needed to watch how he was viewed in Northern Virginia. He couldn't win a gubernatorial election without a good number of those folks. He probably said what needed to be said. Can you imagine the tax dollars he'd be turning down? He'll sign it in the end. At least, that's what Owen believed."

"Aunt Emma, why would Senator Orly's vote be so significant?"

"With age comes privilege. Tredegar Orly has served in the state senate for nigh on forty years. Since this is his hometown, folks would respect his vote and follow along." She took a sip of her sweet tea. "Have you heard anything about how he's doing?"

"Last I heard, he was in critical condition, and the doctors were doing what they could. Tim said Omid is his doctor."

"There's a blessing. Dr. Javarti is a professor, so he'll know the very newest and best things to do."

"Wasn't Omid Uncle Owen's physician, too?"

"Owen saw a man up at the VA in Richmond. We'd drive up there every few months for them to take a look-see at how your uncle was getting along. He drove Owen batty with his lectures on nutrition and exercise, tried to get him to stop smoking if you can imagine such a thing. I tried to switch Owen to turkey bacon once. You never heard such a commotion. Nope, nothing changed Owen. Not a blessed thing."

"Aunt Emma, did American Mine Works ever offer Uncle Owen any money for Jenkins Hillock?"

"Why yes, I believe that's what brought on your uncle's heart attack. The ladies from my Bible study group had come for tea. We heard Owen in his office blustering away, then it sounded like he was in pain, and I rushed in. I found him there on the floor, the receiver still in his hand. I put a Nitro pill under his tongue, and Rose called 9-1-1. The paramedics collected him and took him up to the hospital. Dr. Javarti said while they were racing the gurney to the ICU, Owen slipped away from them."

Kate and Emma quietly ate their sandwiches, each focused inwardly. As she wiped the crumbs from her lips, Kate asked, "You miss Uncle Owen, don't you?"

"I do. He's been part of my life since I was six years old. Feels like I lost an arm and a leg. But there's also a certain amount of peace. He's in a better place now, and all the torment he lived with is over."

Kate fiddled with her straw wrapper. "Did he ever talk about what happened in Vietnam?"

"Never. Kept it all bottled up inside." She tipped her head. "Has Ryan ever talked to you about what happened to him in the Middle East?"

"No, ma'am. But his buddy Zack read the reports, and he told me the gist of it. Knowing what happened, I can understand Ryan's brain's reaction. Nobody should be able to live through a day like that and walk away unchanged. A normal human being shouldn't be able to see what Ryan saw, lose the number of brothers he lost, and go on his merry way. Now that would truly be sick."

"That's exactly how I felt about Owen."

Kate's phone buzzed, and she glanced at the caller ID and saw it was Tim. She excused herself and did a half-turn before answering. "It's my day off."

Tim cleared his throat. "I thought you should know. Tredegar Orly just died."

11

"I'M WALKING THIS UP TO THE POST OFFICE. YOU WANT TO KEEP me company?" Tim asked.

Kate stood on the first stair going up to the station house and wasn't really in the mood to walk in the heat, but she found herself saying yes anyway.

They had gone about a half-block when Kate asked, "Seven deaths in just over two weeks. Okay, is it me, or is this pretty strange?"

Tim grinned. "I'm blaming you."

"How so?" She tilted her head in confusion.

"You came to town, and suddenly we have no room at the funeral home for any more bodies. You might be the Angel of Death."

Kate smacked his arm.

"It's wrong for me to say this," Tim said, "but those floods in the Midwest are well-timed."

"How does the Mississippi River have anything to do with this?"

"Four small-town white kids - and that's not me being racial, it's just me stating the reality - dead within a week from an overdose? It just doesn't happen. If this were a slow news cycle, we wouldn't be able to move for all the reporters that would be swarming us. Right now, everyone is focused on the folks who truly need the exposure and help."

"I've seen a few reporters at the funerals."

"Right," Tim said. "But they're Virginia reporters. It hasn't spread like smallpox to the national news cycle. If we got thronged by them, it would make everything that much more complicated."

"And it's complicated enough. What do Pemberly and Wayne have in common? Wayne isn't Virginia blue blood, so they don't move in the same social circles. He doesn't have anywhere near her money. They're a generation apart. They were on opposite sides of the uranium deal. There must be some other connection, though." Kate had to stretch her legs to keep stride with Tim.

"I'll see if I can dig anything up today when I interview the drug store employees."

"While you're at it, you should drag Custis Scarborough's sorry ass in and ask him a thing or two."

"Katherine Hamilton, did you cuss? What are you learning up there in Boston?"

"Excuse me, his sorry behind. He was furious with Senator Orly, red-faced and spitting when he yelled at the senator. If it weren't for the wind, I'd know what brought on Orly's heart attack."

"They were fighting about what they always fight about. Tredegar wanted to protect the river, and Custis wants to be a billionaire."

"Still, there might be something there that would help. If you asked me to lay money on an outcome, I'd lay it on Custis' head. He's the only psychopath I know."

"Psychopath, huh? How'd you come to that conclusion?"

"He's anti-social. He hates people, unless, of course, they're serving his purposes, and then he'll charm the pants off them. And he's bright but shiftless. What does he do for a living exactly?"

"He's listed as the CEO of Scarborough Mining, which means he gets a paycheck from their investors, but there's probably not a lot for him to do day-in and day-out. He's got time on his hands. But I wouldn't say shiftless. He does have a law degree from the College of William and Mary. They don't exactly hand those out."

"True. But the summer of our sophomore year - the fertilizer factory. Arson is a big flashing neon sign for psychopaths and serial killers, especially an arson that was that spectacular."

"Thanks to your eyewitness testimony, he spent three years in juvie. You'd think their psychiatrists would have flagged his file."

"Have you seen his file?"

"No, and I won't, because it was sealed when he turned eighteen. Go back to 'charms the pants off people.' Custis ever do that to you?"

Kate stilled. "You know the answer to that. You and I were together all through high school. But I will tell you who he was doing it with – Doris Arthur, and she still has the hots for Custis."

"Says who? You weren't around for the last fifteen years."

"Says my Aunt Emma, who saw his hands up her skirt at the country club last month. She keeps me up on all the scuttlebutt."

"Sounds like you have a storyline forming in your head, and that's just bad detective work. I've told you this."

She kicked at the gravel. "I'm not here to play detective. I'm a CSI intern, here to help gather evidence at crime scenes and process it for use in supporting possible trial cases."

"So all of these insights you've been sharing since you've come back into town…"

"That's just me running my mouth—feel free to ignore me."

"As if that were possible."

They walked along without a word. Tim went into the Post

Office, and then they turned back to the station. Kate took in the number of empty storefronts. The shops that were open looked run down in the heel. Clean, but well worn.

"Nothing in on the tox report for the teens?" Kate asked.

"Nothing yet." Tim shoved his hands in his pockets. "The lab understands there's the possibility of an ongoing risk, so our reports got bumped to the top of the list. I'm expecting them sooner rather than later. The preliminary ME report says that all the kids died of respiratory distress."

"As did Wayne."

"I have nothing on him yet." Tim returned a wave from a couple across the street.

"How long for the feedback on the Nitroglycerin?"

"I can't say. It all depends on how we show up in the queue. Tredegar Orly's name on the file pushes it up on the list."

"It isn't supposed to work this way. I mean, in the movies, those reports turn around in a few hours, a day at most."

"Welcome to the head-banging-into-a-wall reality of police work."

"When I'm studying this in the classroom, we learned that it takes x amount of time to process. It feels very different than this. It's so frustrating. Have you thought about getting a judge to order a shutdown of the pharmacy?"

"I don't have any evidence to suggest that to him, but I did talk to Doris. She's gone back, pulled the names of everyone on Nitroglycerin, and is swapping out their meds. That's what she's doing today."

"Is she bringing the old prescriptions back for analysis? Shouldn't an officer be with her, or shouldn't I be with her, for that matter, so the medications can be properly gathered as evidence?"

"Do you think Doris has committed a crime here, Kate?"

Kate stopped and stared at Tim. "If two men died because of

issues surrounding their medications, culpability should be assigned. This has to lead to something more sinister."

"Are you always this paranoid?" He tapped her on the back to get her walking again. "Right now, we have two heart patients who died. I'm betting the medication composition reports come up normal. I'm really only having the analysis done on the off chance you're right."

"You're placating me?" Kate's voice jumped an octave. "So *no* to the officer following Doris around. And no to her collecting the evidence properly. No to a proper chain of custody."

"That's right. The answer is *no*. No proof that there's a problem. No other person who's even questioning events. There's *no* way I can move forward with this until I get lab results. Remember, in order to collect the medication as evidence, I'd need a warrant. And *no,* I have nothing to present to the judge other than, 'Katie has a hunch.'" He said the last words with air quotes.

"You could do the collection if folks were willing."

"No, I couldn't, because of HIPPA. Now drop it." Tim sounded more than a little exasperated. "I have to figure out how the old Oxycodone formula got through the cracks and into the hands of Pemberly and Wayne. Let's not make this bigger than it is. Now, when I interview the drug store employees, you can't be in the room with me, but you can watch the feed with the other officers. Just keep your mouth shut, so the officers can focus on their body language."

"Is Doris Arthur going to be answering more questions?"

"Yes, but not today."

"Can I be there?"

"It's best if you're not, Katie." His tone softened.

"Seriously?" Kate lifted her chin. "Why not?"

"The Arthurs are a tight-knit family. They tend to huddle up when they feel one of their own is under attack."

"I'm not attacking Doris. I just want to hear her answers."

Tim shuffled his feet. "It's not about the pharmacy. She's Pam's cousin."

"Oh…" Kate walked a few paces, processing that information. "Am I creating grief in your family, Tim? I don't mean to."

"I never thought you did," Tim said. "Pam is very insecure, that's all. She'll get over it."

"Once I leave."

"Yup. Pretty much."

"So why'd you say yes to me when I asked for an internship with you if you knew that I'd be making waves?"

They stood outside the front door of the police station. Tim turned to face Kate. "You've always made waves in my marriage. Pam was around when you and I were together, and she compares our marriage to what I had with you. I agreed to your coming down because I thought if Pam saw us interacting professionally, she'd give it a rest. Seems it's got her more riled up than before, though. She says she can tell that..." Tim scrubbed a hand over his head. "I also agreed because you sounded like you were in a bad place. You'd have to be if you were willing to live a whole summer with your Uncle Owen. I told you a long time ago, Katy-did, I'd always be there for you. And I meant it."

Kate pushed a strand of hair behind her ear. "Am I hurting you? Should I leave?"

Tim pushed the door open. "No, to both questions."

12

Standing behind the two-way mirror, Kate observed Tim questioning the woman. "Ma'am, on that date, you are listed as being scheduled to work, but you're saying you weren't there. Who covered your shift that day?"

Jenna Sue Ridgeway caved her shoulders in as if she were trying to fold herself into something smaller. "Carter Simpson took over for me."

"I don't have Carter on my employee roster."

"Carter doesn't work at the pharmacy anymore since he made all that money with the online gambling," Jenna Sue explained. "He quit to stay home with his daughter."

Tim wrote down a few notes. "That's my last question for today. Thank you for your time and cooperation."

Tim walked into the viewing room, where Kate sat next to the other two officers. "Mandrel, do you know anyone named Carter Simpson?"

"Sure," Officer Mandrel said. "The Simpsons go to my church. They've been on the prayer list for months."

"Why? What's going on with their family?" Tim pulled a metal chair over and sat down.

"During the ice storm, their daughter, Betty, was in a car accident. The dad worked at the pharmacy. The mom quit her job cleaning houses to take care of Betty. The girl's a paraplegic now, and they didn't have any medical insurance before she qualified for Medicaid. Their house was approaching foreclosure. It was a big mess. Then about two weeks ago, Carter came to church and thanked everyone for their prayers. He said God had blessed his family with respite from their financial crisis, though they still needed prayers for the recuperation of their daughter, but his financial issues were over. It was a joyful thing for our congregation."

"I'm sure it was," Kate said.

Tim scraped back his chair against the terrazzo flooring as he stood. "I'm heading over to Carter's place to see if he'll come in for a chat." He pointed at Kate. "Do you want to ride with me? Or do you want to take off for the day?"

"No, I'll come with you."

THE WOMAN STOOD at the front door with her eyes opened too wide. She blanched and staggered.

Kate grabbed the woman by the shoulders and helped her to the sofa. Sitting beside Mrs. Simpson, Kate reached for her hand. "Can Detective Gibbons fetch you a glass of water, ma'am?"

Mrs. Simpson raised her head. "Just tell me quick. Is he dead? How'd it happen?"

Tim crouched by the woman's side. "Oh, no, ma'am. I'm so sorry. Probably the last time an officer showed up at your door, they came to tell you about your daughter's accident."

Mrs. Simpson nodded.

"No, ma'am. We came by to ask Carter a few questions about his time working in the pharmacy, that's all."

Mrs. Simpson took a minute to recover. Her face turned bright red, and she fanned herself with her hand.

When she seemed to have regained her equilibrium, Tim asked, "What time are you expecting your husband back, ma'am?"

"He went fishing this morning, said he'd be back by lunch, but here it is dinnertime." A buzzer sounded from upstairs. "That's my daughter. I have to go check on her." She pushed herself up. "I'll be right back."

While she was gone, Tim looked around the room.

"Everything looks new," Kate said. "Smells new, too - carpet and paint."

Tim looked like he was chewing something over, so Kate sat quietly and let him process.

Mrs. Simpson walked back into the room. "She's fine. She wondered what was going on down here."

"Ma'am, what kind of car does your husband drive?"

"He has a Ford 150 pickup, brand new this week." Mrs. Simpson smiled.

Tim walked to the window and pushed the lace curtains aside. "Looks like you have a new van, too."

"Yes, we needed one to accommodate Betty's wheelchair when we take her to her therapy."

"Does the insurance cover that?" Tim asked.

"Oh, no. It would be wonderful if it did. My daughter's accident has been very costly."

"It seems you're coming through okay." Tim moved back into the room. "The pharmacy said that Carter quit."

"Yes, he did, to help with Betty. She's my daughter by my first marriage. I'm considerably older than Carter is. But he's always loved Betty like she was his own flesh and blood. Couldn't ask for a better step-daddy." Mrs. Simpson pointed at the ceiling to indicate her daughter upstairs. "And I'm so grateful he's home. She's a teen and too heavy for me."

"How was he able to afford to do that, ma'am? To quit and stay home?"

A big grin swept across Mrs. Simpson's face. "He won the money off the gambling sites." Sudden concern filled her eyes. "I hope that's okay. Carter told me it was legal."

"He won a lot of money, then?" Tim tilted his head.

"Oh yes, enough to pay off Betty's bills, do some repairs around the house. And we have enough put aside to get us through retirement."

"Is he still gambling?" Tim asked.

Kate wrapped her hands around her knees and held her tongue.

"No, no. I asked him to stop," Mrs. Simpson explained. "Gambling can be addictive, and after what we've been through – it's enough. No, we prayed for a miracle, and God gave us the right playing cards, and then Carter stopped. We have everything we asked for, except, of course, Betty being able to walk. But we're sure with prayer and hard work that will come, too."

"He went fishing today?"

"Yes, up at his favorite spot near Scarborough Knoll. He and Custis fished it since they were boys together in Sunday school."

"Thank you, ma'am. We'll stop in another time to talk to Carter."

Tim worked his jaw as they walked toward the squad car.

"What?" Kate asked.

"It feels like we're about to hit a dead end."

13

KATE WALKED DOWN THE ROAD. THE SEARING HOT PAVEMENT rose up through the soles of her shoes. It was the kind of day where people would say you could fry an egg on the pavement. That was about all the awareness Kate had of her surroundings. Her mind was chewing on the details of the medications.

The beep-beep to her right startled Kate from her thoughts; she turned her head to glance over her shoulder. She smiled and waved as Omid pulled up beside her.

"Can I give you a lift? You look like you're melting in that black shirt."

Kate made her way around to the passenger's side and let herself into the Jag. She was grateful for the air conditioning. "Hey, there," she said.

"I'm on my way to pick up one of Maggie May's boxed meals," Omid said as he drove down Main Street. "I'm heading to the old train trestle to watch the sunset. Want to come? Looks like you have too many emotions brewing to be comfortable inside. Big emotions take space and fresh air."

"I do have a lot on my mind. A picnic sounds nice. I was

hoping to run into you, anyway. I have some questions about who has access to medical records and how they're stored."

Omid pulled over to the curb. "Glad to help. Why don't you stay in the air conditioning while I run in?"

THE SPOT OMID chose was picturesque and serene. The river bubbled twenty feet below their dangling feet. The sun's last rays licked over the surface, making the water glitter. Fireflies flickered from the shoreline.

Dinner had been simple and delicious. No one made homemade bread like Maggie May. She deserved her reputation as the best cook in the county.

"Did you have enough to eat?" Omid asked.

Kate groaned in reply. "Too much. It was too good to stop. 'Fat as a tick.' Do you know that expression?"

Omid chuckled and reached out to tuck a stray curl behind her ear. "You could never be fat or anything but beautiful." He lowered his lips to hers.

"Oh," Kate gasped, leaning away. "Oh, dear. No. Omid, I'm sorry if I gave you the wrong impression." She wiped her mouth with her napkin. "I'm here only as a friend."

Omid rubbed the back of his neck. "It's me who must apologize. I read the signs incorrectly. Forgive me."

"I'm married. I thought you knew."

"I heard this, yes. But you left him. And you're no longer wearing your wedding ring. I obviously made assumptions… I jumped to conclusions…"

"I'm wearing my wedding ring, see?" Kate held up her left index finger with the thick platinum band engraved with Celtic knots. "It's my husband's wedding band, though. And he's wearing mine on his pinky." Kate twisted the ring around and around. "When I left Boston, we both needed a reminder of the other person's commitment. We both understood our own. So we exchanged each other's rings."

"Why didn't you do your internship in Boston and stay with your husband?"

"He's not well." She rounded her shoulders, caving inward. "He's home from the war. PTSD. He has violent episodes with dissociative reactions, and he's hurt me because of it - not bad, just bruises. But it scared him. I was afraid he might become suicidal if he thought it would protect me."

"How's he doing now that you're out of the picture?"

Kate breathed in deeply, letting her gaze follow the graceful descent of a blue heron, landing on the sandy shore below. "He says he's making progress."

"But you don't believe that."

"It's going to take a long time to heal. I want him to learn to feel safe enough that I can come home. I miss him terribly." Kate reached out to gather their wrappings and stuff them back in the cardboard carton. "It's this feeling of missing him that's worse than when he was in Afghanistan. I have him back physically but not mentally. I'm going to have to adjust to being married to a new Ryan."

"I can imagine this is very difficult for you, Kate. And on top of everything, you came to Scarborough even though you hate it here," Omid observed.

"I don't hate it," Kate said. "I just don't fit."

"I know the feeling. When I'm in the U.S., I dream of Karaj. When I'm in Karaj, I dream of…"

"Catfish."

"Exactly." Omid chuckled.

Kate's phone buzzed in her pocket. Tim.

"Kate, you've got to get up to the Knoll. I need your CSI expertise."

Fear gripped her throat as Kate tried to speak. "Is it Carter?" she rasped.

"I found him floating in the water."

14

———

KATE MOVED CAREFULLY DOWN THE EMBANKMENT WELL AWAY from the taped off area. Tim had sent a cruiser to collect her. Kate had asked the officer to take her by her house for her waders, in case she needed to take pictures of the shoreline. The waders were in her backpack, which restricted her arm movements, as Kate held onto the branches and then made a final leap to the water's edge.

Mosquitoes whined through the air.

Kate had doused herself with bug spray, hoping to keep the worst of them at bay. The high humidity made her skin tacky, and gnats swarmed her. Kate gazed up the river, hoping a breeze would accumulate over the water and whisk them all away. It was wishful thinking. Tonight, the air was still as if the Knoll was holding its breath, waiting. The land, though, was a different story. All about her, the woods came alive. As the evening songs of the birds died down, the tree frogs and crickets filled in the empty spaces, growing their discordant notes into a full country-evening symphony. Deepening indigo painted the sky; the first stars offered tentative twinkles.

The police department had set up massive LED lights, making

the taped area as bright as daytime. A command tent was set up. The ambulance slowly pulled its way up the slope toward the dirt road. The flashing lights were off. That was confirmation enough that Carter was dead. A hearse moved into the vacated spot.

Kate's thoughts went back to Carter's wife. Mrs. Simpson had been sure they were there to tell her bad news. Premonition? Conditioning from her daughter's recent accident? Or did she believe Carter was in danger? Maybe his death wasn't an accident.

Kate raised her hand in the air, a childhood trick she remembered. The gnats were supposed to swarm the highest point of your body. It hadn't worked for her then, and it sure wasn't working now - at keeping the pests away, that is. It did catch Tim's attention.

He moved toward her, answering questions and re-directing his men as he wended his way. "Good. You're here."

"Yup, put me to work. What have you found?"

"About a case of empty beer bottles. Looks like Carter got drunk, tripped, and drowned."

"Looks like?" Kate asked, slapping at the mosquito that landed on his cheek. He ducked before her hand landed.

"Henry said you got your waders. Put 'em on and follow me."

Rubber encased up to her chest, Kate grabbed hold of the rope someone had tied to a tree and used it to move hand-over-hand down into the water. Here the current was manageable, but Tim reached for her hand to keep her steady. They moved further out into the water, and then Tim turned and pointed toward the shore. "What do you see?"

Kate took a deep breath and stared at the shore.

"Don't overthink this. Just tell me what you see."

"There's a log where people would lean for comfort under the overhang of the tree that would keep the sun off. There are a lot of beer bottles. They all look to have the same label, and they're stacked in a pile. I'd assume they're recent since the labels aren't sun-faded or peeling off. I can make out the box they came in. There are two footprints in the mud, but it comes from the slope, not from the log. Long steps, like someone was running."

"Those are my footprints," Tim said. "I saw the body face down in the water and ran over, hoping I had caught him in time. But he had been dead for a while. This heat makes quick work of decomposition."

"I'm confused. From where the fishing tackle is laying, surely there should have been some other footprints."

"Should have been."

"And why is it muddy? It hasn't rained since I've been here."

"Good question. If I were a betting man, I'd say someone used that bucket over there and threw some water on the ground to hide evidence."

"Not an accident, then." Kate lost her balance and wriggled to keep upright. Tim reached around, grabbed her waist, and pulled her to him. He was solid.

"I'm a detective. I don't come to any conclusions until all of the pieces are put together. Right now, there are a bunch of missing pieces."

Kate pushed away from Tim but kept a tight grip on his hand.

Tim gestured with his free hand. "We need all this carefully photographed from out here before I put up the number cones. We'll leave footprints when we do."

They moved together toward the shoreline, away from the crime scene tape.

"How'd you get his body out of here?" Kate asked.

"I did the initial photographs, and then we put him on a back-board and floated him down to where you found the ropes tied. I wanted to keep the area as intact as possible."

"Did you already tell his wife?"

"Our chaplain does our notifications. She's already braced for it."

"That was my feeling. You might want to get hold of Carter's computer to see about his poker history."

"The warrants came in while you were taking your dinner break. A unit already went by and picked it up."

"Do you think Betty's accident wasn't an accident?"

"Doubtful. She was driving in an ice storm. The girl in front with her died at the scene. The girl in the back told the cops what happened, and she walked out of there without a scratch. Hard to stage something like that. Are you a conspiracy theorist?"

"No, why?"

"Just seems to be your mindset. You used to be inquisitive, and now you seem…"

"Paranoid? There is something odd happening. And I think when you've got all the data, it's all going to boil down to one psychopath. Custis Scarborough."

Tim chuckled. "That's what he said you'd say."

"You talked to him?"

"Yup. I wondered if he'd had the hair of the dog down here with Carter, or if he had seen Carter at all today. He said no, and his maid said she had brought his lunch to his room and woke him up. His dad said they had an argument about his drinking, and his mom said she didn't want any of the emergency vehicles messing up her lawn."

"So no one without a vested interest in keeping Custis from going back to jail saw him today? Look over here. There's a beer bottle tucked behind this log." Kate snapped pictures from various angles.

"Myopia is a bad trait for a detective," Tim said.

As she used her pen to lift the brown bottle from the dried leaves, some beer spilled out onto her hand. "Here's a bad trait for a beer – it's blue."

Tim stared down at the liquid on her glove.

"I'd have the ME run a tox report on Carter to check for Rohypnol poisoning," Kate said. "I think he was roofied."

"And the beers over there?"

"I'll bet you my next paycheck that not a one of them has a fingerprint. I'd say that site was staged. But you're the detective. I collect and process crime scenes."

"You work for free, so that's not much of a bet." Tim helped her climb the bank, so she could keep the bottle steady on her pen. "You've got the wrong calling. You should reconsider your job title."

"Teaching? I wouldn't give it up, but why do you say that?"

"I had a bunch of reports sitting on my desk when I came in. The teens found at Pemberly's house both had the same results: Oxycodone overdoses. The powdered residue is from the old formulation, and the kids shouldn't have had access to it. Also, Wayne Brody died of respiratory failure attributed to the use of a high dosage of Oxycodone with a pre-existing asthmatic condition. I don't have anything on the twins yet. I'm hoping that'll come in tomorrow."

"Okay. So there's negligence involved."

"I have more," Tim said. "The Nitroglycerin tablets were placebo pills - sugar."

"All of the pills from the pharmacy, or just the pills for Uncle Owen?"

They made their way to the CSI van.

"Your uncle and Senator Orly had placebo pills, and the other pills Doris picked up were legitimate," Tim said.

"Why would anyone do that? Nitroglycerin helps people with angina. Angina isn't a heart attack; it just feels like a heart attack. They take a pill, wait five minutes, and then take another one. If they're still in pain, they know it's a heart attack and to call for help."

"How would thinking you were having a heart attack change things?"

"If someone gave Uncle Owen and Senator Orly placebo pills, all that would do is make my uncle or the senator *think* they were having a heart attack. Whether they were or not, they'd go to the hospital. The hospital would confirm the heart attack or see that it was angina…" Kate's eyes were unfocused as she concentrated on this newest twist. She turned suddenly to catch Tim's eye. "Doesn't that sound weird to you? And everyone else in town got the real deal? Huh?"

"We can't place blame with Doris straight out. Someone could have switched the pills that Orly and Owen had at any point after they left the drug store. Making a connection directly to the drugstore would be difficult." Tim opened the back door of the CSI van and pulled out a collection bag. He bent over to fill in the information.

"For the placebo pills maybe, but not for the Oxycodone. It has the name on the label."

"Yup, looks like we've got us a mess."

15

KATE WENT HOME, BUT SLEEP ELUDED HER. WHAT DID SHE KNOW? Eight people who shouldn't be dead were dead in a matter of weeks.

Five deaths were intended: Pemberly, Orly, Owen, Wayne, and Carter.

The teens were mistakes.

Pemberly was alive.

Somebody had been switching meds.

Somebody had been giving folks meds they shouldn't have, and they seemed to be generated at the pharmacy.

Carter had worked in the pharmacy, and he had suddenly come into a boatload of money. The day they started to question the pharmacy staff, he drowned.

How convenient was that?

Not so much for his family or for the police solving the case, but very convenient for the mastermind behind all the murders.

Was any of this random?

Sure, Uncle Owen was a terrible person, and not a soul liked him, but would someone want him dead?

Tredegar Orly was well-liked. His funeral was huge. Not a dry eye in the place.

Pemberly was a country-club-going, tennis-playing, garden-partier. Her husband had left her. But he had been in North Carolina. Surely someone would recognize him if he had come to town prior to Chad's funeral. But according to the town gossip, he only came back after he'd been contacted to tell him Chad had died.

Around and around, Kate's mind went until she was dizzy.

Kate's phone buzzed on her night table. She reached out and squinted at the text. **Little girls who play with fire get burned. I smell smoke.**

She stared at that message for a long time, then she pressed the number one button on her quick dial.

"Baby, I'm scared," Kate said to Ryan after he answered her call.

Ryan sounded groggy as if he was just waking up. "What's going on?"

"Why did you send me that text?"

"I can't text you, Kate. I refuse to use cell phones. You know that. What text did you get?"

"You haven't sent me texts over the Internet?" Kate's voice warbled.

"I didn't even know that was possible. What did they say?"

"Um. Random things. They didn't make a whole lot of sense. If you're not sending them, then who is?"

"Kate, what did they say?" His voice took on the calm evenness he used when he faced a crisis.

Kate skipped over his question. "If they aren't from you, do you know how I could find out who sent them?"

"Zack's here. He can figure this out. Hang on."

Kate chewed off three fingernails before she heard, "Hey, sweetheart."

"Hey, Zack. I'm a little wigged out."

"That's what Ryan's saying."

"Now that I know these texts aren't from Ryan, I'm scrolling back. They look kind of threatening."

"What did your boss say? Tim, isn't it?"

"Yes, Tim. I didn't show him. I thought Ryan had sent them until just now. When I read them that way, the texts don't sound menacing, just kind of…off."

"Do you have access to your computer?"

"Yes, my laptop." Kate reached over to her bedside table and pushed the on button to boot up.

"Good, I want you to plug your phone in. I'm e-mailing you a web link that will let me go in and take a look around. You'll want to take any nudie pictures you sent to Ryan out of your photo album. I don't need that in my head."

"It's all PG, I promise. Your email just came. I'm all hooked up. Should I press 'accept'? You don't think Ryan did this and forgot or…"

"He couldn't have, sweetheart. He was at the VA during the day, and I'm with him at night. Besides, he threw his laptop out the upstairs window, so it's a fallen soldier."

It was seven in the morning when Tim looked up from his desk. "Why are you here?"

Kate walked into his office and set a Styrofoam cup of black coffee in front of him. "I couldn't sleep."

"Occupational hazard of police work."

"Good thing I'm a schoolteacher. It occurred to me last night that Pemberly might be in danger. And she's also probably the only person who could tell us whether she picked up her prescription from Carter."

"It occurred to me, too. She's safe for now. She's in Roanoke in the mental hospital on suicide watch. Her husband took her down there yesterday and signed her in."

"The whole story, please?" Kate sat down and pried the lid off her coffee so she could blow on the surface, cooling it enough for her to take a sip sooner rather than later.

"We knew she was taking Nardil for depression. But the how and why she ended up on suicide watch? That I don't know."

"Her husband does. And from what Aunt Emma says, he's a pretty big narcissist. I bet he'd answer your questions just for the attention."

"I tried. He said he's not interested. He said he has no information, and it's not in his best interest to talk to us about anything that might further incriminate his wife."

"Well, that's you. What about a reporter? I've been reading along in the Scarborough Sun, and their reporter, Eva Mason, seems sharp."

"She does a good job." Tim reached over to the side table and picked up the morning's paper. "Did you read her article today?" he asked.

Kate scanned through the Scarborough Sun's front page. "'American Mine Works is an offshore company that no one has ever heard of before. They're buying up stock in Scarborough Mining.'" Kate glanced up.

"Keep reading." Tim nodded at the paper.

"'American Mine Works is buried beneath so many layers of shell companies and secrecy that the reporters couldn't figure out who owns it.'" Kate focused on Tim again. "Do you think that someone associated with American Mine might be involved? Someone who's lurking in the shadows?"

"Lurking in shadows, Kate?" Tim's eyebrows came up.

"You know what I mean."

"No, I'm not sure I do." He leaned forward, posting his elbows on his knees.

"Let's go back for a minute to why I brought up Eva Mason. What if we made a list of questions we'd like peppered into her interview, and she went in and talked to him about his family's tragedy? She could play the sympathetic role. It would give him an opportunity to lay out the story he wants to be known, and there might be a thread of truth in it. She could get him on tape. A narcissist would eat that up like pudding." Kate stretched her legs out and crossed them at the ankle.

"No 'g,'" Tim said.

"What?"

"You've been up north too long. You say all the 'ings' now. 'A narcissist would eat this like puddin'.'"

Kate rolled her eyes but noticed he was looking up Eva Mason's phone number as he said it.

"Sweetheart, you need to head out of town," Zack said.

Kate's hand trembled as she held the phone to her ear. "Is Ryan okay?" She looked under the stall doors in the police station ladies' room to make sure she was alone while she talked.

"He's hanging in there," Zack said. "I talked with a SEAL buddy of ours, Striker Rheas, who's working for Iniquus in D.C. like I said I would. I needed access to Striker's hot-shot hacking equipment to figure out your threats. The IP address that sent you those texts belongs to a Custis Scarborough."

"I *knew* it."

"I have a home address if you need it," Zack said.

"No, I'm well acquainted with Custis Scarborough."

"There's more. Striker found two tracking apps. One is run by that Scarborough character. He's tracking you on his phone. Anywhere you take your phone, he can find you. And the other is more concerning because it's a ghost tracking app. It takes specialty equipment to find it embedded in your codes. Striker traced the connection to a burner phone."

"How did the app get on there?"

"Have you ever put your phone down while you were out in public?" Zack asked.

Kate's mind went immediately to the scene of Senator Orly's heart attack. Custis had been there, and she'd thrown the phone on the ground while she was trying to help the senator. She remembered finding her phone later when she was looking for evidence. "I'm sure I have."

"This is why Ryan's so paranoid about cell phones. It's easy enough to do. Striker said the second one's configurations are professional. He also said a true professional would have redundancy. Do you always carry the same purse with you?"

Kate slid her black hobo bag from her shoulder. "Yes, I only brought the one with me."

"Okay, I need you to empty the bag onto a solid surface and look for anything you didn't put in there, a pen, a lighter, anything odd…"

She turned her bag upside down on the counter and spread the contents out with her hand. "How about a lipstick?" Kate pulled off the top of the golden tube and corkscrewed the red lipstick up. Definitely not a color she would wear.

"Bingo. See if you can take it apart. Are there any electrical components?"

Kate fiddled with the case. "Yes, there's a false bottom. Here's a wire. Should I pull it all the way apart?"

"I'd hand it over to Tim and ask him what he wants to do. Striker ran the texts by his colleague, Lynx. Apparently, she's got a nose for finding trouble spots. Her feeling is that these are a juvenile attempt at scaring you or intimidating you, but she doesn't think there's intent to follow through. I'd take that with a grain of salt, though. I've never met the woman, and she's running on very little information."

"Um, okay. I don't know what to do with that."

"Striker says he's only four hours away. He's glad to come out and check on you. Would you like him to do that?"

"No, thanks, Zack. I'll give this to Tim and make a plan."

"Watch your six."

Kate pressed the end conversation button and stared at the phone. Juvenile intimidation, that was Custis. There was also a high-rent person who had the ghost-ware and the lipstick tube. Why would anyone care who she spoke with or where she went?

Kate's heart was thumping in her chest as she made her way back to Tim's office.

"Katydid, I'd say you kicked a fire ant hill," Tim said after she'd passed on her information and handed him the lipstick tube. "I get that Custis was threatening you and keeping an eye on your movements. It seems like something he'd do. But do you really think he'd follow through by hurting you?"

"Eight people are dead, Tim. Do I want to be number nine? Not so much."

"And you think Custis killed everyone? Why? How?"

"I believe he and Doris had a plan. He has the motive – Scarborough Mining - and she had the means and the opportunity, even *if* she's your kin."

"I'm not as worried about the texts, which are pretty childish. I *am* concerned about this unknown person putting trackers on your phone and in your purse. That your data is going to a burner phone tells me that someone with some skills is involved here. If this has something to do with the uranium, and they think you're getting in the way of their success, you could well be in danger. We're talking about billions of dollars in revenue if the bill passes through legislation."

Kate sat at the edge of her seat, her knees pressed tightly together, her coffee cup forgotten in her hand. "And I may very well be in someone's way," Kate said, then explained her Uncle Owen's will.

"If this were clearly an anti-uranium killing spree, Pemberly wouldn't have been caught up in it," Tim said.

"Unless they're trying to muddle the case. Can you think of any other connections between Wayne, Orly, Uncle Owen, and Pemberly? The killer probably drowned Carter, so he couldn't tell us what he knew from working at the pharmacy, and the kids were most likely mistakes." Her heart clenched as she said that. She set her coffee down as her hand started to shake. "Whoever did this was clever, too. We could have labeled every single one of their deaths accidental or inevitable."

"I probably would have, to be honest," Tim said.

"So, what's the plan?"

"That depends largely on you."

Tim's thought was interrupted when a knock sounded at his door.

There stood Carter's wife, shaking from head to foot.

Kate jumped up and grabbed the woman's hands and led her to the seat Kate had just vacated.

"Mrs. Simpson, are you all right?" Tim asked.

Mrs. Simpson dropped her purse at her feet then started wringing her hands.

Kate moved to a seat in the corner of the office, out of Tim's way. Tim would know how to handle this. Whatever *this* was, and Kate didn't want to be a distraction.

The room filled with silence for what Kate thought was an overly long time.

"He was desperate," Mrs. Simpson whispered under her breath.

"I'm going to tape this conversation," Tim said, pulling out a micro recorder and laying on his desk between them. "All right?"

Mrs. Simpson looked at it distractedly. Then nodded. "Yes. Fine. I want to talk to you about the money that Carter won at the computer gaming. You took his computer. You'll figure it out. My husband wasn't a gambler. Carter was approached with an offer of money. A lot of money. We needed it desperately." She pulled her clasped hands to her chest as if she were in prayer. "Carter thought he could suddenly give us what he always wanted to give us." She looked down at her hands. She was gripping them so tightly now that her fingers were bloodless. "We didn't go homeless." Her eyes sought Tim's. "Imagine the pull a man felt with a step-daughter in such desperate straits."

"What did he do for that money, Mrs. Simpson?" Tim's voice was gentle and encouraging.

She reached down and pulled her handbag to her lap. She pulled out an old-fashioned videotape. "When Carter was approached about slipping the wrong meds into a few pharmacy bags, he videotaped the whole thing." She handed the tape to Tim. "I didn't know." She tapped the tape. "I found this when I went to look for Carter's will, so I had his funeral directives. As you see on the label, it says I should watch this straight away if he was dead or imprisoned." She chewed on the inside of her cheek. "In the tape, he said he knew his chances of surviving weren't spectacular. He wanted to make sure that if he got caught, he didn't go down alone. And if he were killed, that we would know the truth. Anyway, it's the whole conversation about the medication switch up at the pharmacy, the way it would be covered up, the exchange of money from when they made their agreement—a down payment in good faith. Then the second meeting where Carter was paid in full, you know, for succeeding in making the switches. It's both of them in the picture." Tears rolled down her face, and she didn't wipe them away.

"Did you watch the whole thing, ma'am?" Tim asked.

She nodded.

He wiggled the tape. "Did you show this to anyone else?"

"No. But I'm going to go have a talk with Custis after I leave here since he's our family lawyer. I just...well, anyway." She stood and walked out.

17

———

Kate stood on the baked clay footpath, still hardened despite the recent rain, looking toward the dense woods. She was wearing her hiking boots. She checked the side pockets of her day pack, reassuring herself that she had two full water bottles.

"Thanks for inviting me to tag along, Omid. I appreciate your letting me pick your brain about the medical questions I have over the recent spate of deaths. I want these cases wrapped up before anyone else gets hurt." Kate spread her arms wide and tilted her head back to take in a lungful of air. "The air feels so perfect after that thundershower. Mmm, it smells like pine and raindrops."

Omid chuckled as he pulled a backpack from his trunk. "Whenever it got too hot in the city, my family would drive to the mountains. I equate walks in the woods with a calm spirit." He handed her a can of tick spray. "It's always nice to have company to share the inevitable discoveries, and I'm happy to help if I can."

After handing the can back to Omid, Kate pulled her phone from her pocket, checked that it was fully charged and on, and that this far away from town, she had enough bars. She stooped and double-tied her bootlaces. The roar of an engine made her pop back up.

Custis Scarborough jumped down from the cab of his Ram pickup, shotgun in hand. Mrs. Simpson climbed out and cowered behind the fender.

"You sonofabitch." Custis' shotgun pointed at Omid, who dropped his sack and reached his hands out to the sides, palms exposed.

Kate put her fists on her hips. "Custis Scarborough, have you been drinking? Give your gun to Mrs. Simpson and let her drive you home." Kate was surprised to hear her schoolteacher's voice. She felt anything but authoritative and in control.

"Heck no, I ain't climbing back in my cab. I've got a varmint to shoot."

Mrs. Simpson put a hand on top of her head. "Custis, please, Carter wouldn't have wanted this."

"Carter," Custis said, looking at Omid. "Did you know he was my friend? Yup. Since we first went to Bible camp together. And now he's dead. Everyone would think he got drunk and passed out too close to the water. Who drowns in the three inches of water at the shoreline?" He was red-faced and sweating. His eyes were hardened with hatred. "The problem with that picture is that Carter is a three-beer guy. In my whole life, even when we were teens, he never had more than three beers. You?" He glanced briefly at Carter's wife. "You ever seen him drink more than that?" Tight-lipped, Brenda Simpson shook her head.

Omid took a step backward.

"Uh, uh-uh. I've been huntin' in these woods since I could walk," Custis said. "There ain't no way I'd miss a shot, no matter what you did. You step right up here. Get on your knees. Spread your legs wide. Now, hands laced on your head."

Omid followed Custis' directives.

"As soon as I heard all them beers got him drunk, I knew someone killed him. Normally, the coroner would say accidental death. I imagine he wouldn't even check blood alcohol levels or see if someone poisoned him with some medications, huh, Doc?" Custis pointed the gun at Kate. "What about you? Did you chalk this up to an accident?"

"I thought someone slipped him a roofie and pushed him in the water to drown."

"You know why someone might want to do that? Huh, Ms. Boston Smarty Pants?" Custis demanded.

Kate could feel her hands and feet vibrate as blood rushed to her limbs, ready to help her vault to safety. Her heart pounded hard as Custis's words echoed in her ear. A shotgun at this distance would devastate both her and Omid. Her brain worked to figure out how to get Custis back in his truck.

Custis focused his aim back on Omid Javarti.

"You knew Kate was going to figure all this out, didn't you? She's smart, she is. The killer had to be someone who could access medical records. It had to be someone who could get hold of the wrong, or I guess in his mind, the right medicines—a string of bad luck. Eight people dead. Four of them kids." Custis spat on the ground. "They all lie on your head and look at you. Cool as a cucumber. Not a remorseful bone in your body."

Kate glanced down at Omid; her mouth had gone dry.

"Kate," Custis shouted. "Use your science. What kind of person does something like that? Kills eight people?"

Kate licked at her lips. "A psychopath, or maybe a sociopath would."

Custis glared at her. "Dr. Javarti is neither. I had to learn a lot about psychos with my shrink in juvie because apparently psychopaths and serial killers like to start fires in their youths."

Custis scowled at Omid. "I bet you my dog Toby, who is the

one I love most in this world, that up until today, Kate had me pegged for the murderer. I'm sure she was trying to put me back behind bars. Right, Kate?" Custis turned angry eyes on her. "Psych 101? Psychopaths start off as arsonists. Only I was less an arson than an idiot who couldn't figure out how a prank could go so damned wrong. I didn't mean to burn down the building and hurt those families. But there's *no way* I could hurt Carter or anyone else for that matter." Custis nodded his head toward Omid. "Except you, of course. I plan to shoot you. So, smarty-pants, who else would do it?"

Kate's mind went blank. *What should I say? What should I do?* They all stood there, waiting for her to come up with some kind of answer. "Um, someone with a vengeance."

"Nope. It's not that, either. He's got no gripe with any of us here."

Kate hated this game. The sun beat on her head. Squinting past the glare, Kate tried again. "People will kill serially for a cause they've taken as an oath, like soldiers."

"Bingo. That's it, isn't it, Doc? You're a college professor in Iran and got a sudden hankerin' to go fishing? So, you packed your bag and came to Scarborough, Virginia, with three stoplights and an ice cream shop." Custis stalled and stared into the woods to their right. "I bet it's killed you, hanging out with all us hicks. I bet you were thrilled to have someone from Boston show up. Only you weren't counting on that someone turning out to be a pain in the neck, know-it-all. She figured out OC tablets are a scarcity. She figured out the Nitro was sugar."

Kate was astonished that Custis knew all this.

Custis moved his attention to the tree line behind her. Goose-bumps prickled Kate's flesh.

"Small towns have trouble keeping their secrets," Custis murmured.

Kate looked over at Brenda Simpson. Brenda had her gaze fastened over Omid's head.

"Smartypants thinks she knows why they died," Custis said. "She thought it was all about the upcoming vote on mining. That's my motive for killing everyone. Let's see how that works out. Let's tick them off. Tredegar Orly was a big one. No one would thwart him in the legislature. Oh, look, he's no longer an issue. And then there was Wayne Brody. He was leading the opposition on the environmental front. He was a real crusader for the river. Wasn't he? And what do we know about groups and their leaders?"

He waited expectantly, but no one answered.

"Nothing to say? Well, America knows what to do. Look at Al Qaeda. Take out the leaders, and the rest run around like headless chickens, not knowing what to do next. That's pretty much true for any group dynamic. Last-minute like this, there's no time to rally the troops. The environmentalists are floundering. So, check them off the list. Now there's Pemberly. Why, oh why, take out Pemberly? She was on uranium's side. Maybe I was trying to throw the cops off the scent? Could be. Damn sure if the legislature got wind that people were getting killed off to make the vote go through, they couldn't very well vote 'yes,' now could they?"

Kate looked at Brenda Simpson. She nodded her head, then climbed in the cab, shut and locked the door.

Custis kept talking. "I'll tell you why. Pemberly was not only expendable; she was strategic. She didn't want to sell her investment in Scarborough Mining to American Mine Works. She wanted to hold on and go for the mountains of cash rather than take the moolah hill and be happy. Her hubby, on the other hand, thought differently, now didn't he? If Pemberly were dead, hubby would sell their Scarborough Mining investment to American Mine Works as quick as he could get his signature on the paperwork. My understanding is that he has power-of-attorney now that she's batshit crazy and locked up in a loony bin. Maybe Pember-ly's husband Jason was the mastermind behind all of these deaths. He wanted the legislation to go through, but if it were looking bad, then he could just sign the American Mine Works' papers. Either way, he never had to lift a finger for the rest of his life. He's cousins with Doris Arthur. He had access to the pharmacy."

Custis took in a deep breath and shook his head on the exhale. "Yeah, but Jason's also an idiot. Which leads us to here and now. Why am I holding a shotgun on Dr. Omid Javarti?"

Kate tasted the tang of blood from where she'd chewed a small hole in her lip.

"Now everyone knows I've got no love for that woman." Custis briefly directed the shotgun at Kate.

Kate's stomach heaved like she was plummeting from a very high roller coaster.

"Quite frankly, I'd like to see her suffer some. But I'll be damned if I'm going to let some outsider come to *my* town and kill *my* people and let *her* get caught in your net."

Kate desperately wanted to sit down. Her knees shook. Fear and heat made her dizzy. She had never had a gun aimed at her before.

Custis refocused on Omid. "That's why you're here with her tonight, ain't it? You planned for her to have a little accident. Can't drown her. You already did that to poor Carter."

Kate could see disdain curling the skin by Custis' nose.

His voice took on an eerie softness. "So here you are with Kate. You can't drown her like Carter. You can't mis-medicate her like the others. She wouldn't dare take a prescription filled in Scarborough." He canted his head. "How did you kill Tredegar and Owen once they were in your care? I'm thinking air in their IV lines. Am I right? Something undetectable so it would never get traced back to you. Your handlers back in Iran put you here, didn't they? The American Mine Works has nothing to do with

America, does it? You all just need you some uranium. How best to git hold of it? Own a damned uranium mine. Don't matter if it's in Scarborough, Virginia, or on Mars, as long as your country gets what it wants. A few people dead along the way? Not a problem. I bet you've even convinced yourself you're a victim here. Bet they got your friends and family in a vice. You do what they want, or your kin will pay the price."

Omid blanched.

"Bet you think it's a fair price to pay, some hicks in back-woods Virginia for your friends."

Fear filled Omid's eyes. His jaw dropped, and he was panting.

Kate thought Custis had probably hit on the truth. Someone was manipulating Omid. And the story he told her about his parents being taken and killed and his home being destroyed would have been a heavy burden. If someone knocked on his door and said, "You know what we did to your parents? Well, here's a list of your cousins, your friends, your colleagues..." Under those circumstances, Kate wasn't sure what she'd do.

She honestly didn't.

"And now you have to kill again," Custis was saying. "This has to be a good one. Kate, go check his bag over there."

Kate did as she was asked. There was silence while she rifled through Omid's things. She sat back on her heels, staring incredulously at two vials of insulin and hypodermic needles.

"What you got there, Kate?" Custis called.

"This would do it." Kate held up the vials. "We studied the Kenneth Barlow case where he injected his wife's buttocks with insulin, and she died. Modern tests would easily show an excess of insulin in the tissue."

Everyone stood silent, watching her studying the vials dangling in her fingers, mind far away.

"It's so hot," Kate said. "What if I went for a hike? Omid gave me the shots and then called the police to say I went missing, and he couldn't find me. If he started the search off in the wrong location…we're expecting hundred-degree temperatures for the next three days. My body would be too decomposed for them to find insulin."

She stood, moving closer to Custis, her eyes fixed on Omid. "If I were in a hypoglycemic coma, you could crack my head down on a rock to make it look like I fell."

Custis took a step forward. The barrel of the gun hung a mere foot from Omid's head. "You sonofabitch, I'm gonna tell you something certain. You know, just like I know, just like everyone in the whole blessed town knows, Tim and Kate were a thing. And they still care for each other. That spark never quite left his eye. And if Tim thought someone had hurt Kate? Shoot, he'd follow that sonofabitch into the bowels of Hell to make things right. Wouldn't you, Tim?"

Kate spun around to see Tim and four other officers step from behind the trees.

Tim came forward and cuffed Omid, then pulled him to his feet.

"You can't arrest me on the ranting of that man. He's insane," Omid scoffed.

"Oh, but I can arrest you on murder charges. I've got a videotape that Carter made of you two. We were just hoping for some of the finer details as Kate talked through possible scenarios with you today."

Tim focused on Kate. "You okay, Katydid?"

"About time you showed up." She reached under her shirt and pulled at the wires taped to her belly. "Guess we don't need this after all."

Tim grinned. "Wasn't sure what to make of things when Custis beat us to the punch."

Kate looked at Tim, then at Custis. "He did that in spades. Thank you, Custis, for trying to save my life."

"Weren't just me." He pointed his finger around the circle. "Small towns stand tight."

Kate moved a step closer to Custis. "They do indeed."

This is not THE END
Follow along on Kate Hamilton's adventures in her next mystery YOURS. Keep turning the pages for more.

YOURS

A KATE HAMILTON MYSTERY NOVELLA TWO

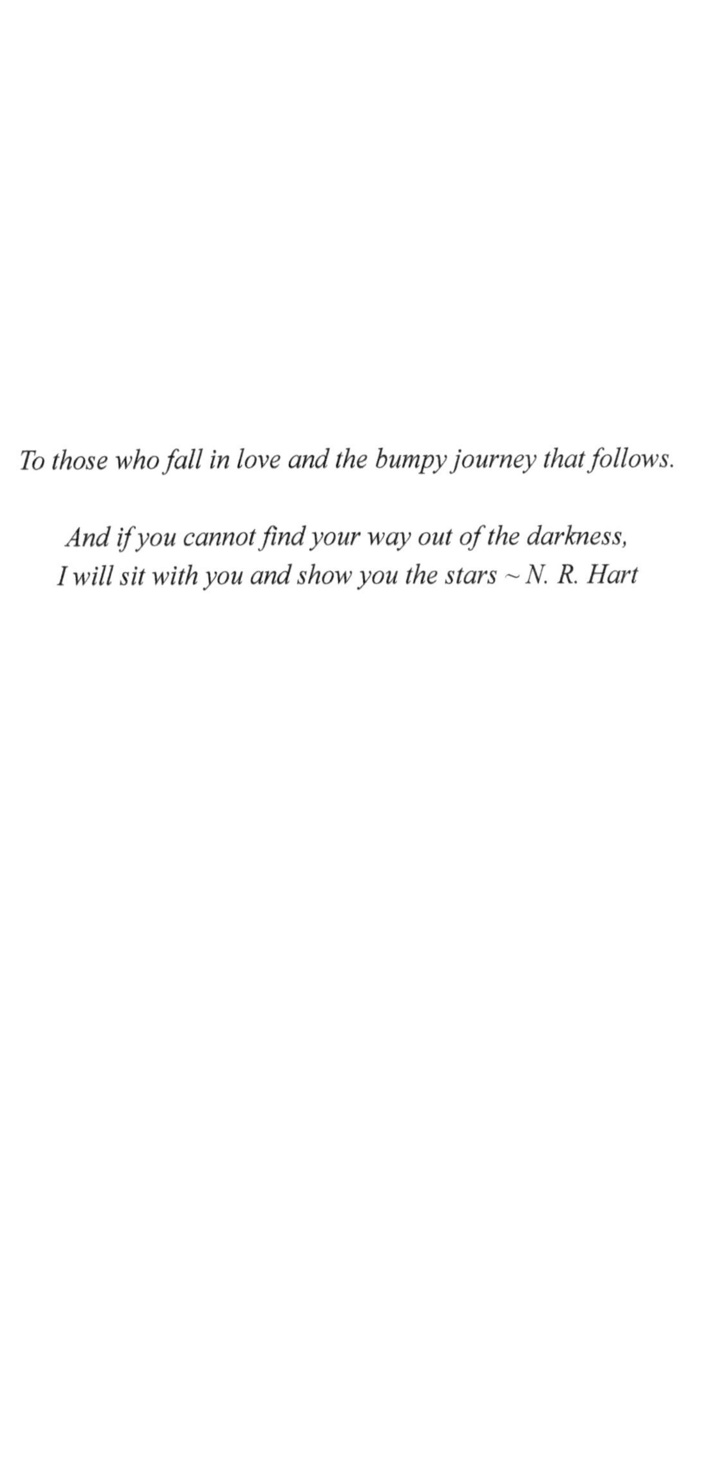

To those who fall in love and the bumpy journey that follows.

And if you cannot find your way out of the darkness,
I will sit with you and show you the stars ~ N. R. Hart

1

———

SUNDAY

KATE HAMILTON's gaze scanned the objects she'd laid on her bed —a pile of spent brass Tim had gathered for her at the police shooting range, a Moon Pie wrapper, an old knitted hat, and a yellow rubber ducky.

Aunt Emma walked into Kate's bedroom with bathroom cleaner in one hand and a box of tissues in the other. "I'm just putting these under your counter," she said, glancing at Kate's collection as she moved through the room.

Kate added an orange magic marker, and a pink candle stick to the objects she'd placed on the towel she was using to protect the quilt underneath.

The quilt had been handcrafted back in the nineteen-forties by Granny Jones. Granny Jones crafted dozens of handstitched quilts. She said she had to have something to keep her mind and fingers busy as she worried about her new husband and her four older brothers who were all over in France, fighting the Nazis.

Aunt Emma hadn't liked to sew as much as her mother had.

When it was Aunt Emma's time to fret about her new husband off at war, she kept herself busy by crocheting shawls for the folks up in the nursing home.

While Granny Jones's family came home just fine, Aunt Emma's husband had been disabled in the war. His challenges were what the doctors at the VA labelled Post-Vietnam Syndrome while the elders in Scarborough called it shell-shock or battle fatigue.

War disabilities of one kind or another ran in Kate's family. That's what happened when you had a family tradition of taking the oath and marching off into the sunset.

Yes, Kate mused, women keeping the hearth fires burning was a tradition for her ancestors in every war since 1812.

Kate was just another generation to weather the storms of military family life and its aftermath.

She drew her finger along the circle of the wedding ring pattern on the quilt done up in bright summer colors against a snow-white background. Then she touched her own wedding ring —well Ryan's wedding ring—that she wore on her index finger. He'd been off on a top-secret mission in the Middle East and had come home with both a brain injury and a desire to keep her safe by kicking her out of their house in Boston.

Ryan's explosive and sometimes violent outbursts needed space. Space that didn't endanger Kate.

He loved her, so she had to go.

Of course, Ryan had packed a bag and wanted to do the leaving, but that was more than Kate could handle. "I'll go," she'd said in a panic. "I'll just head down to Virginia and stay with my aunt for a little while."

That was how Kate ended up here, staying with Aunt Emma in rural Virginia, sleeping under Granny Jones's wedding ring quilt.

Sleep had indeed come a little easier for her since Aunt Emma put the quilt on her bed, now that it was the beginning of September, and nights could feel brisk up here in the mountains.

She hadn't expected to be here this long.

She'd packed up and left Boston after her grades were submitted last June, planning to head back up to her teaching job as soon as her CSI internship under Detective Tim Gibbon's supervision was complete.

In her experience, life didn't follow along planned trajectories.

It would be best if she could just learn to go with the flow, but that wasn't really her nature.

Though she'd grown up here in Scarborough, Kate had left right after high school with the firm intention of never spending a significant chunk of time here again. She was a city girl through and through.

But Ryan had asked her to stay away.

For his health's sake, she'd let her job as a biology teacher in Boston go and had accepted a position made possible with a STEAM (science, technology, engineering, art, and mathematics) grant to teach CSI sciences at the high school in the neighboring town. Boonestown was just a thirty-minute drive over the mountain. It was a one semester gig.

Yup, six months was about as long as Kate thought she could stomach being away. She missed the bustle of Boston, the life she'd made there, her friends, and mostly she missed Ryan.

Her eye caught on her tennis shoes in the corner, and Kate added one of them to the pile on the bed and put a lime green weight next to it.

She glanced up from her project when Aunt Emma emerged from the bathroom, holding Kate's prenatal vitamin bottle.

"I didn't mean to snoop. But this caught my eye." She set the half-full bottle on the nightstand then smoothed the back of her skirt as she sat down on the bed, sending Kate a sympathetic glance.

Kate shifted to sit on the other end of her bed. She'd been avoiding this talk.

"Oh, honey, when did you find out?" Aunt Emma reached for Kate's hand, clasping it tightly. There was a lot of emotion running down her aunt's arm, through her fingers, and into Kate —trepidation, concern. A lot of hope. But no joy.

Kate knew what the trepidation was about. She knew that this was going to be a big problem with her being here and pregnant. Everyone—possibly even Aunt Emma—would be thinking this was Tim's baby. Kate and Tim loved each other, after all. They had been high school sweethearts, and everyone had anticipated their wedding—especially Tim—until Kate hauled herself off to Boston.

That's where she met and married Ryan.

And Tim had married Pam. They had two little boys.

Tim and Kate were friends.

Just friends.

No benefits.

Well, there was a lot of benefit to being friends with Tim. No romantic benefits.

They loved each other in a sentimental kind of way. But Pam, and most everyone else in the town of Scarborough, thought that since Kate's husband's brain got scrambled on a mission, that Kate was back in town for the sole purpose of winning Tim back into her life.

This pregnancy was going to make waves. Waves in a small town quickly took on the height and destructive power of a tsunami. And the grip that Aunt Emma had on her hands proved her aunt anticipated just that.

"It's not Tim's baby."

"I didn't ask that now did I?" Aunt Emma tipped her head. "I asked how long you've known."

"I did the test the morning I left Boston back in June. The doctor says I'm just now fourteen weeks along."

"Ryan knows?"

"I was waiting."

"How long did that wait look to you?" she asked.

"When I came here for the internship, my plan was to give Ryan the space he needed to get himself stabilized, then I'd go home. I thought I'd tell him then." She took in a deep breath and sighed it out. "When he insisted that I not come home, I thought, well, I'll get through my first trimester. If I were to miscarry, I didn't want to…" She let her gaze stray to the wall with its antique wallpaper in pristine condition. It was hard to look at Aunt Emma right now. Kate felt too vulnerable, so she left her gaze resting there on a nosegay of flowers. "It's just been easier not to have anyone judge me."

Aunt Emma patted Kate's hand with understanding. "So now you're on to the beginnings of your second trimester, don't you think you should let Ryan know?"

Kate pursed her lips and nodded. "I'd better also have a chat with Tim. The gossip mills will be working overtime when I really start to show."

"See?" Aunt Emma laughed. "Right now, everyone's saying that you're getting chubby since you've been here because I feed you too much berry cobbler and ice cream for dinner. And I was feeling a might guilty." She turned her head to look at the bed. "What are you getting up to with this stuff?"

"A project for school. These are things I'm going to put along a clue trail to see what my students believe they know about crime scene investigation. They might be more advanced than I think, and I can move them on to harder things, or I may need to go in and un-brainwash them from the television shows they watch. I'm curious to see just what I'm going to find when we go out into the woods."

2

Monday

Kate stood at the front of the classroom listening to her students' chatter. Bookbags were slung between their feet as the kids fished out pens and notebooks.

"All right, so here we go." She shifted her voice to the authority that would quiet the room. She waited for a moment for final adjustments to chairs and focuses. With a nod, she said, "Today, I want us to start by talking about CSI and television. With a show of hands, how many of you watch TV programs that focus on the use of crime scene investigation?"

Every single hand in the room shot up enthusiastically.

"Okay, put your hands back down." She backed up to rest her hips on her desk. "This is both a positive and a negative. Has anyone ever heard of the term CSI effect?" She lifted back to her feet and went to scrawl the phrase on the whiteboard then turned back to see if anyone had their hand up.

The class looked around blankly.

"Okay, great, so now we know that you're going to learn something today. Prosecutors—and who is the prosecutor?"

"He's the dude who is the lawyer for the legal system trying to send the criminal to prison," Dakota said. His blue jean clad legs shot straight out under his desk. There was mud on the cuffs and the bottoms of his boots. Too bad they weren't talking about Locard's Exchange Principal today. He'd be a great example.

Kate made a mental note to mention it at her mock crime scene.

"What do you mean 'he's the dude?'" Lucy asked, jerking her head back, taking offence.

"Generic dude, meant to cover all genders." Dakota sent her a slow smile that he used to smooth over little hurts. Easy. Laid back. Likeable. He also had a little glint in his eye that made Kate want to warn the girls off. That glint meant there was heartbreak hiding behind that smile.

"Prosecutors," Kate plowed ahead, "have noticed that jurors who, like you, watch a lot of CSI shows come into the courtroom with higher expectations for what forensic evidence will be presented by the prosecutors than do jurors who don't watch those kinds of shows. What might the CSI-watching jurors be looking for at a trial?"

A hand shot up and without waiting to be called on Amy said, "DNA."

"Right. Why is DNA not always something presented in court?" She turned to the board and wrote out the list that the students called to her: expense, the crime is too minor to mess with it, it's not applicable to that particular case.

She turned back around. "Give me an example of that please. Who said that? –'not applicable.'"

Melissa raised her hand. "If it was a crime where the victim knew the person who was attacking them and could easily identify them. Or it was like a cybercrime."

"Right." Kate nodded. "Anyone else? Any other instances?"

"They weren't able to collect DNA," Pam shouted from the back of the room.

"Why wouldn't they be able to?" Kate asked, glad that her class was engaged.

"Maybe time?" Lucy threw out. "Maybe the bad guy was careful not to leave any."

Dakota turned in his seat. "Seriously? You get on me for saying the prosecutor is a dude, but you throw out that a guy is bad?"

Lucy wrinkled her nose. "In this case, it's statistically probable that it's a guy who's perpetrating a crime, especially if it's violent."

"Yeah, well same for me," Dakota countered. "It's statistically more probable that it's a dude who's the prosecutor."

"For now," Lucy said, "but not for long. I'm going to get my CSI degree, then my law degree, and bad *guys*," (heavy emphasis on the guys) "watch out."

Kate saw how this could devolve quickly. "All those ideas are right. Good. But if you are used to DNA being presented and there's no DNA…"

"What do the jurors do? Say there isn't enough evidence?" Dakota asked.

"Sometimes, yes." Kate tipped her head. "And if the CSI-watching jurors sound more knowledgeable and more personally convinced in a jury room, what do you think would happen?"

"The jury would think there's reasonable doubt," Heather said.

Kate picked up and uncapped a red pen and scrawled in capital letters REASONABLE DOUBT on the whiteboard, underlined it, then clicked the cap back in place. "All right, now let's think like a criminal. Do you think they could watch shows like that too? Do you think they could make their plans based on what they learned from CSI shows, and then manipulate their crime scenes?"

A chorus of yeses was punctuated with bobbing heads.

"What might they have learned?" Kate asked, turning back to make the lists on the board.

"Wear gloves to avoid fingerprints."

"Use bleach to destroy evidence."

"Leave your phone at home or leave it in a friend's car, so it's pinging somewhere other than in the crime area."

"Yeah! Get a burner phone."

Kate turned back around. "Are these shows messing everything up? Are they training the criminals to be smarter about their crimes?"

"Only an idiot would be a criminal," Pam said.

"Making the jurors more demanding," Kate said. "Increasing the cost of bringing a case to trial…"

"But isn't that what we want?" Lucy asked. "We want to be absolutely sure that the person who is being jailed is the one who committed the crime, right? I mean, if you arrest and jail the wrong person, you're ruining an innocent life, you've got a false sense of security because you think the bad guy's locked up. And the bad *person*," Lucy looked pointedly at Dakota, "is still out there feeling successful, and therefore more likely to commit that crime again, or a worse one."

"Good," Kate said.

"And aren't these shows why you're here teaching us this for our science class?" Laura asked. "People are interested, so they want to go into careers in criminal investigation."

Kate smiled.

"And couldn't the shows be a cautionary tale?" Patricia asked. "In the shows, the crime is always solved, the bad guy always goes to jail—well, for the most part. If I were thinking about doing something criminal, I would be totally freaked out that I left a clue that would put me in jail, and they found that clue and proved their case because of all the things we know about CSI."

"A perfect segue," Kate said. "What do you all actually know about CSI? I want to figure that out. And to that end, I am going to stage a crime scene. Today, I want you to work as a class. Figure out what tasks will need to be done at a crime scene, what order these tasks need to be done, and who will do them. I don't want you to do any research, I'm assessing your starting point to see where I need to design your curriculum, so this class is interesting for you."

Kate picked up her water bottle and took a swig before continuing, "I don't want to be going over the same-old, same-old when you're ready to move on. I don't want to move on when you don't understand the fundamentals. Now." Kate moved around to the front of her desk and sat on the edge. "There's a list of available equipment posted on our class webpage. I need you to tell me what you want me to have on site when we do our exercise on Wednesday. Know that we will be out in the woods, so come prepared. It's still tick season. You all know what to do about that, and if you don't know, then email me."

Excited chatter rode like a wave across the room.

"When you get here Wednesday," Kate had to raise her voice to regain her students' attentions, "don't even put your backpacks down. We're going to head right out the door. You'll need every moment possible to gather the information from the crime scene. The better your planning today, the better your execution Wednesday. Okay." She clapped her hands. "Let's get to it. Show me what you've got!"

3

Tuesday

Kate laid out her clothes for the next day. She was going to wear a pair of khaki tactical pants and a navy-blue collared shirt. They were the same thing she'd planned to wear every day to class to look like she was on an investigation team. She thought it might make her lectures seem more authentic and interesting to her students, especially if she presented cases at the beginning like a police briefing.

That and having a self-prescribed uniform made everything so much easier. No early-morning fashion choices.

She didn't really need to lay anything out, Kate was just procrastinating, and she knew it.

She lay her pants across the top of the chair. She'd bought them online after she'd accepted the job teaching in Boonestown. She'd bought two sizes up and got the kind with the extra stretch elastic for women who needed to get their pants smoothly down over their hips —one would assume so they could efficiently pee in the woods, so maybe police officers and forest rangers. Kate had thought that the elastic would give her a little extra time until she needed to buy pregnancy pants. It turned out, those thoughts had been too optimistic. The pants' elastic only stretched when both the inner and outer buttons were undone, and the zipper was down. So, unless she wanted to go around with an open fly, these wouldn't do for much longer.

Her field boots lay neatly side by side under the slipper chair next to her dresser. Socks, panties, and bra were stacked. There really wasn't anything else left to do but make the phone call.

She sat down on the corner of her bed, dread washing up from her stomach. She'd love to label this morning sickness, but it was neither morning nor had she felt physically unhealthy since her period was late, and she'd taken the over-the-counter pregnancy test.

No. This sensation was dread.

Kate needed to tell Ryan they were going to have a baby, and she couldn't imagine that this was going to go well. If she had any delusions that she might be heading home by Christmas, Kate knew that any danger Ryan thought he was putting her in would be augmented a thousand-fold once he knew she was carrying his son.

Ryan had been on a classified mission. He'd walked away with a chest full of medals on a uniform he wouldn't wear at work anymore. Retired. Medical discharge. He'd been too close to the blast site. He was lucky he'd survived, though Ryan would dispute that.

He didn't get to die a hero, which was the way he'd always meant to go.

At least that's what he'd said when they started dating, and he first joined the Navy.

That had been hard for Kate to hear, knowing he was going to be out there without the normal survival instincts.

That wasn't quite right.

He'd wanted to live. He hadn't been suicidal. It was just that the idea of dying for a higher ideal—a higher purpose— appealed to him.

By the time they married, Ryan had quieted the rhetoric to the idea of fighting to protect his team and get home whole.

What he was most afraid of was coming home as damaged goods. He wanted to be healthy or dead.

As if we got to make choices like that.

He had been especially worried about being "mind-broken" as he called it. He could get by without legs or with half an arm, he'd told her. But the thought of not having control over his brain? Nope. He wasn't going to live that way.

"I jinxed myself. Now, I'm living with the demon." Ryan had said in one of their through-the-night talks when he was still in the hospital. "And I'll be damned if I'm going to let that demon touch you."

Demon was about right.

His brain injury meant that he had violent episodes of dissociative reactions. He'd grabbed Kate one night and thrown her to the floor, thinking he was saving her from an ambush. When he got himself back to the here and now, he saw the cut on her forehead and the bruising on her arms and back, and he kicked her out of the house.

For her own safety.

No, darn it! He wasn't going to listen to her argue.

At least he'd let her stay to finish teaching the school year in Boston before she came to see her Aunt Emma for the summer— now fall.

She'd fought to keep him in that house. Not only for her own mental health's sake, but because Ryan's buddies took turns spending nights there and making sure he got to all his medical appointments. They took good care of him.

There were some good parts to being the wife of someone on the Teams. You knew they always had your back.

"Okay," Kate said aloud. "Churning this over and over and over in your mind isn't going to change circumstances. Suck it up buttercup, make the call."

She pressed the quick dial for her home phone number, it was Zack's voice that answered the phone. "Hi, sweetheart."

Zach and Ryan had joined the Navy together, trained for Hell Week together, made it through SEAL training together, and ended up on the same team in Norfolk. Zack was the big brother she'd never had and never knew she needed until he came into her life.

"Hey Zack. Did I catch you at a bad time?"

"Nope. I'm just about to put some steaks on the grill. Let me call you back from my cell phone."

Ryan wouldn't use a cell phone; that's why Kate had dialed their landline. "Thank you," she said. Relief washed over her, thinking she might postpone this another few moments.

Staring down at the screen, Kate let the phone ring four times before she answered it.

"Kate?"

"Hi."

"Is everything okay?" Zack asked.

Kate huffed out a breath.

"Ryan is out for a run."

"Okay."

Zack laughed. "Wow. I'd say this is one of our weirder conversations, but we have a history of weird conversations. I'm guessing you don't want to say whatever needs to be said or you would have answered on the first ring."

"It's complicated—no, it's not complicated. It's…complicated." Kate put her elbow on her knee and bent in half, feeling the roundness of her belly, and the tenderness of her breasts in the motion. "How is he?"

"Pretty much the same. Tonight's my night with him. He had PT today, and his range of motion and his balance are both improving."

"But his volatility?"

"Is still unpredictable. By *me* anyway. Houston seems to know its coming and does what she can to distract him."

Houston was Ryan's new service dog. They were in training together. Houston was learning Ryan's disabilities and how to best help him.

"She brings him a ball to throw and that oddly seems to work, at least sometimes. I can't say it's a miracle, but at least he has a heads up that he's ramping up. That's why he's out running now. Houston alerted, and he's out burning through his agitation."

"Okay. Thank you. I'll call back another time."

"All right." Zach sounded as if he were confused. "Should I pass him a message? Is there anything I can do to help?"

"I think you're going above and beyond as it is," she choked out.

"He saved my life. If I give him one night a week, it's the least I can do. I still have a night to give. I still get to see my kids growing up and be with my wife. He made that possible."

Kate swallowed. She never knew what to do with statements like that. So many people told her the same thing. Ryan was a hero. Ryan was the reason they were still around.

Kate wanted to be around, too. But Ryan kicked *her* out.

To protect her.

Like a hero would.

And she resented it *mightily.*

"Enjoy the rest of your evening. Thank you, Zack." And before he could press her, she tapped her phone off.

She startled as her ringtone sounded again. Kate rolled her

lips in. She wanted to mope and not talk to Zack, but she couldn't ignore him. Kate turned her phone over to swipe the screen when she saw it was Tim.

Could she ignore Tim?

"No," she said. "He's next on the list of phone calls, anyway." She swiped the screen. *Might as well take the bull by the horns.* "Hey there."

"Hey, yourself," he said. "is everything okay? My Kate meter is pinging at like an eight on the Richter scale."

"I have something I need to tell you."

"Aww crud. Is it your Aunt Emma?"

"My Aunt Emma? No, she's fine. It's about me. I thought I should tell you. You're the first person I'm going to tell. Aunt Emma knows. But I didn't tell her. She found out on her own. So yeah, I'll tell you first."

"Katydid, I am not following you at all."

Kate looked up at the ceiling. "I'm pregnant. I'm going to have a baby boy."

Tim's whoop startled her. She wasn't in a whoop mood. She wasn't even in a smiling mood. She much preferred her Aunt Emma's reaction, a steady "we'll get through this." It seemed a more reasonable way to look at this picture. But here Tim was laughing.

After a moment, he seemed to figure out that his response and her feelings about the situation differed diametrically. He sobered, and after a moment's silence, he asked, "Kate is there something wrong with the baby?"

"No, he's doing just fine."

"You?"

"I'm doing fine, too."

"Then…I sense there's a problem," Tim said, and he seemed to have his detective's hat on, filtering through the data. And then he must have landed on it. "How far are you along?"

"Fourteen weeks."

"For cripes sake Kate! How long have you known?" he growled.

Tim didn't growl, and Kate was startled.

She knew he might be mad. She knew this would start the Scarborough rumor mill running. "The day I left Boston," she said, miserably.

"Then you knew when we were investigating the murders in June?"

"Yes."

"You offered to let me wire you, so you could talk to the killer and gather information. You were going to walk out into the woods with him. Pregnant. You not only were willing to put yourself at risk, but you risked your child?"

Back in June, the pregnancy was just a pink plus sign on a plastic stick. There was nothing else other than a late cycle that had clued Kate in. She was focused on the murder cases to keep from going crazy with grief over her husband's health and her flailing marriage. "You were right there in the tree line." Her voice sounded so patient. It wasn't how she felt at all. She felt attacked. "There were four other officers. If anything were to go awry, you'd be by my side instantly."

"*If* we saw his move. What if we hadn't? What if he had his syringe of insulin out and ready, and he stabbed the needle into you when we didn't see it?"

"I would have yelped, and you would have come."

"But it would have been too late for us to help you, Kate. The insulin overdose would already be in your system. Don't you see what you risked?" Tim wasn't even trying to mask his anger at her decision making. "You have to think of your baby first."

Kate had to admit…he was right. She'd just not been thinking straight. She wasn't sure she was thinking straight now. "Until recently, it was a bizarre concept. I didn't feel pregnant."

Tim's voice was quieter as he asked, "Now you feel differently? Are you not well?"

"I'm fat," Kate whined. "The elastic on my tactical pants isn't stretching as much as I want it to."

He chuckled.

Kate was scrambling to keep up with his emotions. Kate guessed he'd been through pregnancy twice with his wife—he probably knew more about this than she did.

"Promise me you'll put the baby first from now on," Tim said.

"Of course."

"All right. Well, congrats to you and Ryan."

"Tim, I'm not telling anyone yet. Just you. I wanted you to have forewarning. Because…" She didn't know how to spell this part out without it sounding like she was insulting his wife.

"Pam," he filled in. "Yeah," he finally said. "Yeah…" He blew out a long breath.

Kate wanted to tell him how sorry she was. She thought she'd be gone before any of this was a problem. But it didn't really matter. That information didn't help. Their silence hung there.

Both of them feeling the weight.

Kate wondered just how bad things were about to get.

4

—————

Wednesday

Her students were both excited and nervous. They stood on the edge of the parking lot facing into the dense growth. The woods were dark and moist. Gunmetal-gray skies, saturated with humidity, weighed heavily on their skin. Though the air was still, sudden gusts of wind whipped the girls' long hair about.

Kate couldn't have ordered up a better, more spooky day for this project.

CSI meant facing things that were scary and often gruesome. And this day totally had the makings of a horror film.

These were rural kids. They grew up in the woods; but still, Kate could see they were unnerved.

Kate stood beside her green garden wagon filled with equipment. The kids were zipping up their full-body Tyvek suits and hopping from foot to foot, leaning on each other as they pulled on their booties. Kate was taking pictures. The class was almost exclusively girls.

All girls and Dakota.

She wasn't sure how she felt about that yet.

Some research literature said an all-girl class meant that girls naturally took on leadership roles. But Kate knew the world of crime fighting was still significantly male. She thought that females learning to hold their own and push toward leadership in the presence of males was a more practical approach.

She wasn't even sure how this phenomenon had taken place. Were the girls just more interested in CSI so signed up right away and filled all the spots? Or, maybe the guidance office pushed girls toward this as a "softer" science than say physics. Traditional gender roles were still a big thing around this part of Virginia.

Science was science in her book. But who knew…

Dakota, though, seemed happy when he walked in and saw that the girl-boy ratio was 19:1.

As the bustle stopped and the chatter started, Kate called out, "Who can tell me why you're wearing these protective outfits?"

"So we don't get cooties from people's blood and pee," Deborah said and laughed.

"Fair point." Kate lifted her camera and snapped a few pictures of her students.

"Locard's Exchange Principle," Patricia called from the back of the swarm of students.

"Good," Kate said. "Who knows what that is?"

Half the hands went up.

"Yes?" Kate pointed to Elisa who was waving her hand around, making enthusiastic oo-oo—ooo sounds to catch Kate's attention.

"Wherever you go, you pick stuff up and drop stuff off you. As CSI professionals, we don't want to leave strands of our hair, or cut ourselves and leave drops of our blood, because then we're corrupting the crime scene by adding to it."

"Good start," Kate said. "More?"

"The criminal can take stuff from the crime scene, too," Dakota said, not waiting to be called on.

"Examples?" Kate asked.

"Bugs in the car grill."

"Mud on their shoes."

"Cat hair."

Their voices peppered the air with ideas.

"Nice, okay, so now that you're protecting against Locard's Exchange Principle, go to it. Let me see what you've come up with from your planning last class."

Kate had to say she was mighty impressed. This was looking good.

The first thing they did was put up crime scene tape. A student moved just inside the perimeter with a notebook, and she took notes of everyone who was crossing into the space and the time they went in.

Not everyone went behind the tape.

They got points for that, too.

"Three people went into the tree line. The rest of you are out here. Why is that?" she asked.

"The more people, the more chance that they're going to mess up the crime scene, tramping over shoe prints, or tripping over something. We said we'd take turns. They're just in there laying out the crime scene a-frame numbered evidence tents, so others can go in and do other stuff."

Kate said, "Crime scenes take a long time to process. The amount of detail work depends a little bit on what kind of case it is. Obviously, we aren't going to be able to process this area thoroughly in the next hour. Some of this I need you to talk me through. Like, what might change that would force a CSI crew to speed up and maybe miss something?"

"They have to pick up their kids from soccer practice," Amy said.

There was a general laugh.

"Weather?" Joy asked.

"Tell me about that," Kate said.

"If there was a wind storm or a snow storm. If it was a small space you might be able to put up a tent or something, but if it were a big space, you couldn't protect it."

"If the rain is making rivulets and pooling, it could run into a footprint and ruin it," another student called.

"As a CSI professional with an outside crime scene, is checking the hour by hour weather report instructive then? What would you do with that information?"

"Yeah, well you could do your best to collect everything properly and not, you know, take too much time doing it. Stay focused."

Kate pointed at her student and nodded.

"You could prioritize the things that would get hurt first, like you could do footwear impressions first if you thought they might get rained on."

Kate nodded. "Good. Who else has an idea?"

"You could set things up to protect them as much as possible —like the tents that were mentioned."

"Mrs. Hamilton! Mrs. Hamilton!" the call came from her clue trail.

"Coming," she called in return.

Kate walked up to the student who was keeping the log. "Kate Hamilton," she said accepting the booties to go over her shoes that were held out to her. After the student clocked her in, Kate made her way onto the trail. A numbered evidence marker stood next to the stuffed dog, the weight, her shoe, and the candle. So far, they'd found four of the fifteen clues. "Hey, what do you need?" she asked as she approached the three students who were crowded around a boulder just off the trail she'd laid that morning.

"We think it's blood," Barbara said. "It doesn't look like theater blood, so we thought maybe we should ask you if you'd put it here."

"Nope. I didn't lay out any blood." Kate moved closer to the rock. "You're right, the pool here, then the drips there, across the rock…" Kate stood up and looked around. This was definitely off her trail.

Kate wondered what would happen if she had accidentally laid a clue trail on top of a crime scene. And there they were playing at processing stuff and messing up actual clues. She scratched the side of her face, realizing just how much she would have possibly destroyed by her traipsing about.

"Can you all stay still for just a moment?"

Kate moved back out to the parking lot to a semi-circle of expectant faces. "They found a substance that looks like blood. I'm going to take a presumptive field test in and just see if we don't get a positive." She walked to the green cart and started to look through the supplies. "Why do they call it a presumptive field test and not just a blood test?" she asked.

Kate couldn't tell which student said, "Because it can tell you if it's not blood or if it's possible that it's blood, but you need another test to prove that the substance is blood."

"Good." Kate rattled through the bag looking for the HEME-test. "And what is it called when it's a definitive test?" She pulled the tube out and stuck it in her pocket along with a hunter's flashlight. As she stood, her hand came to her lower back as she felt her muscles bunch.

"Confirmatory," someone called.

"Right. Good. Listen," Kate said. "I'm going to do this real quick. When I come back, I want all of you to go into the woods and participate in the crime trail. The way you have this set up is wonderful. But we only have the hour. As I was asking about weather earlier or other things that could create time constraints, one of the ways that you can move things along is to get more hands on deck. And that's what's required here. Take a moment to get a new strategy together. I'll be back in a minute. You all are blowing my mind. Really good stuff."

Kate stepped from the hard surface of the blacktop onto the soft carpeting of pine needles and crunchy deciduous leaves and made her way down the trail to her students. This time she took the video-recorder with her. On another day, she'd show her students what the first three had found, and how to use this presumptive blood test, then they could try it in their classroom.

She'd probably rub something that was about the right color on the classroom walls, ketchup, Catalina dressing, theater makeup, what have you, and let them take turns testing. She tucked those plans into a mental file.

"Hey, y'all. Here we go." She gave the recorder to Elaine. "Can you video tape all this?" Then she pulled out the HEME-STIX. "Now watch. First, I'm going to rub this swab onto the suspected fluid. This works on a stain, as well. But this is still wet enough. Then I pop it back into the tube and secure the top. Now, look. See that? There are two ampules inside. We want to mix the chemicals. I break one." *Snap.* "And the other." *Snap.* "And we mix it up. Ta da! See that deep blue color?"

She held it up to catch a little light from between the leaves.

She waited for her students to nod.

"That tells me that we should treat this *as if* it were blood, but it does not conclusively tell me it's blood." She pulled her hunting light from her thigh pocket. It worked better at night in tracking blood, but she might as well give it a go here.

In the back of her mind, Kate was still cognizant that this might actually be a victim's blood trail. While the chance was pretty minimum, Kate still wanted to tread lightly, so to speak. She chose to walk on rocks and downed limbs to stay off the substrate where a shoe track might be found.

Kate followed the blood spatter as long as it was still visible to the naked eye, then she switched on the light. It wasn't perfectly clear, but Kate felt she was on a good trail. Within fifteen strides, she stopped and called her students to her. "It was a racoon. Then he was somebody's dinner. Part of the food chain. See the flies are already landing? They're laying their eggs. This is part of the decomposition you'll encounter in the field."

Kate made another mental note that she needed to get permission from the principal to set out a dead piglet here in the woods, so the kids could monitor the entomological effects of bugs on a decomposing body. And she should do that before it got too cool.

Standing up, Kate cupped her hands around her mouth and hollered out, "Okay, class, come in and see what you can find on the clue trail!"

It wasn't a crime scene after all.

Kate was relieved.

Wouldn't *that* just have been a horrible turn of events?

5

WEDNESDAY

STANDING in the driveway next to the trashcan with a laundry basket at her feet, Kate was sorting through her student's evidence bags. As she pulled the items out, she carefully preserved the bags for future lessons—they didn't come cheap, and her grant covered little past her salary.

With a squeeze of the rubber ducky, she tossed it in the basket, and reached for the next bag in the pile on her back seat. Kate had used a GPS mapping photo app when she had laid each item out. It made finding and gathering the things that were left unnoticed by the students that much easier, and she'd be able to show the class the pictures to make her point: Even with a keen eye, it was easy to miss things.

And they needed to understand that.

Everyone came to a crime scene with their own past. This meant that each searcher saw things through a different lens. In quick searches for clues, multiple sets of eyes could make a difference, especially in a wide area search.

Searches of rooms had the potential to be easier, and Kate would set up a crime scene in the corner of their classroom to demonstrate just that.

First, she'd have them search for macro items, like this potato chip bag. Next, for smaller items, like strands of hair. Then finally for micro-evidence not seen by the naked eye, like DNA.

She reached for another evidence bag and opened it. Kate hadn't told the students a time frame for the supposed crime. It was one of her tests. Would anyone ask? And no one did. That's why she found this rusty soda can in the evidence bag. She tossed that into the recycling bin.

The next bag she opened, she looked in and pulled out a watch. A nice one, too.

Not something she'd think she'd see in such an economically depressed region.

She hadn't planted this on the trail.

She looked it over. It ran on solar. The time was correct.

Expensive was the thing she couldn't get past.

Here in Boonestown.

It wasn't one of the students' watches, they had on the Tyvek suits and someone would have noticed during the collection.

Besides, Dakota was her only male student, and this definitely looked like a man's watch. A large man—not a Dakota-sized guy—if she considered the circumference of the links on the strap.

The face was simple though. Black, with sweeping glow-in-the-dark hands. She could use it as a class presentation. Talking about how items from a crime could be interspersed with things that were there by happenstance, part of that Lockard's Principal. Someone passing innocently through an area didn't mean they were in any way culpable of or connected to a crime.

And that's how innocent people got locked up for circumstantial evidence.

Maybe she could even get them to do some research on the watch.

Kate considered the design. It reminded her of a dive watch Ryan used with the ports on the side. But this definitely wouldn't function under water.

A specialty watch of some kind.

If it didn't belong to one of her students, maybe that specialty could help them narrow it down to who had lost it. Fun! She pulled at the Velcro closure on her cargo pocket and slipped it in. She'd do some Internet sleuthing on it tonight, so she could help steer her students' searches and get them headed in the right direction with their questions. She didn't need them wandering down some rabbit hole and wasting their precious class time.

"Dinner's on," Aunt Emma called past the screen door.

"I'm starving. What are we eating?"

"We're taking advantage of the last of my blackberry harvest."

"Cobbler and ice cream?" Kate asked.

"Now that I know I'm not making you fat with my poor choices, I thought, why not?"

Kate chuckled, tossing the last of the garbage in the trash and smoothing out the evidence bags. "I can't see how it's a poor choice. All those fresh berries? You top it with oatmeal. Dairy in the ice cream." She tucked the evidence bags into her laundry basket and hefted the whole thing up, realizing she had to switch the basket to her hip since her tummy was bigger than usual. "I think the baby grew today."

"They have a tendency to do that." Aunt Emma pushed the door wide for Kate as she made her way inside.

After setting her things at the bottom of the stairs, Kate washed her hands at the kitchen sink and sat down to tell her aunt about the adventure of the day.

"Turned out to be a racoon that didn't get away." Kate raised a spoonful of warm berries to her mouth and savored them before swallowing. "My students were spooked. These kids were all born and raised here in the mountains. I was surprised by their anxiety. I mean, it was palpable."

"Can't say I blame them after what all went on at that school."

"Something happened at the school?" Kate left her spoon in the bowl and wiped her mouth, waiting to hear the story.

"It hasn't been that long ago. Spring two years ago," Aunt Emma said. "One of their teachers disappeared. Young thing. Beloved. It choked the town. You saw how things got here in June with all them kids dying of overdose, you should have seen what happened over there. The whole town turned out. They searched every square inch for miles around. Never did find out what happened to her. Just poof."

"Wow," Kate said. "Nothing? No clues at all? No leads? No suspects?"

"Now, I didn't say that. They found her car out at the mall. Her purse and phone were gone. They assumed she left with someone she knew."

"It's not on camera?"

"Well, sure. They saw her pull up. They even saw her walking with someone. What the camera couldn't see was who it was. The security cameras took pictures every three seconds. The lucky person was walking by the fence, and they couldn't have timed it better if they tried. Every time the photo was snapped, there was a post in front of their face."

"Did she look like she was under duress?" Kate reached down to untangle her aunt's kitten's paws from her shoe laces. Her boots were one of Bingley's favorite play toys.

"She looked fine. Which told the detectives—Tim included—that she went off with someone she knew."

"Surely they had a suspect list. Old boyfriends, colleagues…"

"They checked them. Her fiancé was in New York City at a

business meeting. Lots of folks could vouch for him. He was some kind of torn up, too. Came down and helped organize the searches and what have you."

"You know, criminals who have committed murder often come and join in on the searches, so they can pick up information. I was out with a group once looking for clues for a missing girl. Someone found the handle of her bike sticking out of a mound of dirt. The guy on my team ended up getting arrested right there in front of me. He didn't do anything that set off my alarms, just happened to be the only guy in the area who had access. Turns out he'd killed her and wanted to make sure the searchers didn't see how he'd covered her over."

"I never said it was a murder," Aunt Emma said. Her lips curled into a sad frown. "I'd hate to think that folks in this area are so vulnerable. Murders just don't happen out here. I would have sworn to that just a couple years ago. But I'd also have sworn that your Uncle Owen would never die from being murdered. I always thought he'd just up and stop breathing one night."

Kate reached out her hand and laid it on her aunt's arm in sympathy. Uncle Owen was buried the day after Kate had arrived in Scarborough. They realized it was a murder a couple of weeks later.

"But yes. Carolyn Lambert. High school science teacher. She disappeared without a trace. And I suppose, it's too suspicious to just call it a missing person. Her family is hoping to find her body and bring her home for burial. Find some closure. The wondering and what-if-ing is like a cancer."

"And you think this teacher's disappearance is why my students were having trouble going into the woods up at the school?"

"Well, see, the teachers and faculty were all considered suspects. Especially the principal. He's still a person of interest."

"Mr. Caldwell? Why especially him?" Kate went back to eating her blackberry cobbler.

"Carolyn was a pretty girl. More than pretty, beautiful. She went through college on beauty queen scholarships. And Caldwell's wife didn't like that Carolyn was working at the school—and working so closely with her husband on different projects."

"Seems there's a lot of jealousy going around," Kate said, thinking about her own predicament with Pam's unfounded concerns about Tim and her.

Aunt Emma shrugged. "Small population. Means there's not much of a choice in the genetic pools. I'm not saying slim-pickings. Well, yes, I guess I am. Small populations and all. You'd have to go out of town to school and what have you to meet up with new folks. And everyone knows everyone, so unless you have a tendency—like you do—to self-preserve by not telling anyone anything about anything, then your life is fodder for discussion. We all played telephone as kids to learn how each time a story is told it changes just a bit. So someone sees the teacher and the principal bent over a project and next thing you know, they were seen kissing. It goes from innocent to sinful in the blink of an eye."

"Did they have an affair?" Kate asked.

"Can't see how that's reasonable. Beautiful, intelligent, young Christian woman like Carolyn, who was dating the kind of young man that one would think she should be dating, and then you stick Caldwell into that picture."

Kate wrinkled her nose. "He's not my type, I'll grant you that."

"Not most people's type. But here's the interesting thing. On the day Carolyn disappeared, Bill Caldwell's wife packed up their car and drove off into the sunset. She insists that Carolyn and Bill Caldwell were having a torrid affair. She insists that her husband was crazy in love and crazy jealous. She thinks that Bill Caldwell went into a rage and killed his mistress because Carolyn had just become engaged to her young man…I can't remember her fiancé's name. He didn't live in these parts."

"And the woods?" Kate asked.

"I can't say for sure. They had searchers all over the place when Carolyn disappeared, which they said on the news was a shame that that happened. Sometimes good intentions lead to bad outcomes."

That Kate knew for sure. Sometimes good intentions did indeed lead to bad outcomes. Ryan and her marriage was a prime example. "These were untrained searchers?"

"The students all got on their phones, and they showed up, stood in a line and walked the county for days on end."

"Killing any scent for the dogs."

"That's what I hear. That and footprints at her house. So *poof* gone just like that. I'm supposing that knowing their teacher just up and vanished, and you heading them out into the woods on a day like today, working on a crime scene, reminding them what all happened back then."

Kate's phone buzzed in her pocket. She pulled it out and looked at the screen. "Aunt Emma, this is Zack. I need to take it."

"You go on now," Aunt Emma said. "There's not much to do in the way of dishes. I'll just tidy the kitchen." She sent Kate a worried look. "You tell Ryan yet?"

Kate swiped her phone. "I will. I'll have to."

6

WEDNESDAY

"**H**EY ZACK," Kate said, walking out of the kitchen and heading for the stairs.

"Hey, yourself. I'm calling to ask a favor." He paused. "I shouldn't have started that way. Are you alone? Can you sit down for me?"

Fear effervesced through her system. Her hair prickled across her head.

Pushing through her bedroom door, Kate turned and closed it behind her and went to lie down on the bed. She was mentally preparing herself for the worst. Did Ryan do something to hurt himself?

She swallowed hard.

"Ready," Kate said, though the truth was she wasn't ready at all.

"Tony Branson died."

Her hand came up and covered her eyes. "How?"

The long pause that followed told Kate everything she needed to know.

"Suicide?" she whispered.

"Yeah," he said quietly.

So many. So many good men and women who had served in the armed forces. People she knew personally or peripherally and not just another number going onto some statistical chart.

Tony, she knew.

He had been in Zack and Ryan's Hell Week. He had gone on to SEAL team 3, stationed in Coronado California. And after retirement, he came back to work at the Pentagon. A SEAL. A man who never gave up no matter what was flung at him.

This hit way too close to home.

Vulnerability washed in waves over her, and she couldn't quite catch her breath. "Marybeth and his kids." Was all Kate could think to say.

"Yeah."

They were both quiet for a long moment. She thought Zach was probably giving her processing time.

Finally, Kate managed, "You opened with you need a favor."

"I do. Ryan has an appointment for an MRI tomorrow. He's waited six months. He needs it. I really don't think it's a good idea that he puts it off and moves his name back to the bottom of the list."

"Agreed. You told him about Tony?"

"He knows."

"Okay so, tell me what you need from me. Just ask, and it's done," Kate said, pulling herself up to sitting, hopeful for a task that would get her moving and busy, keep her from sinking lower into her depression.

"I need to stay up here with Ryan and make sure he gets to this appointment. And frankly, to keep an eye on him after this news. I was hoping you'd go to the funeral and represent Ryan and me. Take some flowers for us. Make sure she knows she wasn't left alone. We've got her and the girls. We'll make sure they're okay, always."

The sobs crawled out of Kate's soul, clawed up her throat and burst out of her. Zack let it happen. Kate was horrified for Marybeth and her kids, and she was equally horrified for herself. Without even thinking about it she blurted out, "Zack, I'm pregnant. It's a boy." And then, just to make sure that Zack didn't question her loyalty, "I'm fourteen weeks along. I knew when I was still in Boston."

"But Ryan doesn't know," Zack said evenly.

Kate could tell Zack had slipped into operator mode. Steady. Focused.

"No. I was waiting to get home to tell him in person."

"Congratulations," he said, but it sounded nothing like Tim's first reaction.

Tim didn't understand her circumstances, Zack did.

"I'll need to tell him soon." She cleared her throat. "In the meantime, I would be honored to go to the funeral. I just need the details."

"Short notice. I'm sorry. Marybeth didn't let us know until a few hours ago."

"Did she say why?" Kate's hand came up to her throat.

"I didn't talk to her. I got the call from Striker. He's the guy who works for Iniquus and helped figure out who was tracking your phone last June."

"Yes," Kate said. Striker Rheas. He'd offered to make the four-hour drive to come check on her. A retired SEAL. One of the people who had her back. She should feel more supported. She *did* feel supported. She felt more lonely than alone. She just wanted to crawl into a corner and lick her wounds.

And she wasn't even the one physically hurt.

She was depressed that she was depressed.

She was disappointed in her emotions.

She'd always thought…yeah, she didn't know what she always thought other than that she'd handle life better than this.

"Striker knows you're coming," Zack said. "He wants to know if you'd like a place to stay. His fiancée has a furnished home, she is opening it up to people who need somewhere to stay. There are three bedrooms."

"To be honest, I think I might like the privacy of a motel. I'll drive there in the morning. I'm too tired and emotional to drive safely right now." She was bone tired. Marrow of the bone tired. Kate could barely move her lips to speak.

"I'm going to text you the details. And I'll also text you Striker's and Lexi's contact information. If you need anything, let them know."

Kate stared at the round circles on the quilt. Round and round they went without beginning or end. Just around. A full circle.

"Kate?"

She stirred. "Yes, thank you. I'll go tomorrow. I'll take the flowers. Can you also text what you'd like the card to say? I'll sign it with your names."

After she tapped her phone off, Kate sat numb for a good long while.

She roused herself to go take a bath. As she let the water run in the tub, she undressed slowly in the mirror. She looked at the swell of her breasts, the roundness of a tummy that had always been flat.

She let her pants slip over her hips. They had dug uncomfortably into her waist all day. Kate's fingers traced over the red marks the band left, and the ripple of skin from where the elastic pinched at her.

Tomorrow was Thursday and the funeral. She'd stay some extra time in Washington. Maybe drive back on Saturday. Friday she could look for maternity wear. Go and look at baby clothes.

Buy a book of baby names and start a list. That was something that she had daydreamed about in her early marriage—the fun of starting a family. Figuring out the perfect name. She'd teased Ryan that she would call their son Alexander Hamilton.

But Ryan had not been amused.

She lifted her clothes to toss them in the hamper.

It was time for her to own up to her new circumstance.

It was time to start acting like a mom.

As her pants hit the bottom of the basket, Kate heard a clunk and remembered the watch. She dug it out of the pocket. Good, she thought. Once I get my pajamas on, I'll call the school to let them know of a death in the family—and the SEAL teams were nothing if not a tightly bonded brotherhood. And then she'd research this watch.

She turned it over again in her hand. She'd never seen a watch like this before. She laid it on the counter. "I'm glad the students found you," she said aloud. "I can use the distraction of a mystery."

7

SITTING DOWN AT HER COMPUTER, Kate lifted the watch for inspection.

Ryan had had a watch with similar ports on the sides that he used for SCUBA, she thought again. He used it to keep a log of his descent, the times he spent at each depth, and other pieces of information that were beyond her interest.

Kate wasn't a fan of SCUBA diving.

She always felt too compressed under the water. She didn't like the feeling of vulnerability. Sure, there were beautiful fish and coral to be seen. But then again, Boston had an amazing aquarium. She could go there and still breathe air. But in this moment, Kate regretted not listening to all of the geekery that Ryan had spouted about his watch. It might have helped her now.

This didn't look like a dive watch, but it must hold some kind of data, she mused. And if she could see that data, she might be able to find the owner.

There was no sticker on the inside, no numbers that she could find. It would be easiest if this watch had a specific set of identifying numbers that were registered to protect a warranty.

But then again, if that were the case, the manufacturer, Sunko, would simply ask her to mail it back to them, and they'd contact the owner. In this day and age, there was no way the private contact information would be handed out to a stranger on the phone.

Which was neither here nor there.

While the mystery was a distraction, Kate's real goal was to get this watch back to its rightful owner.

Now that she was heading to Washington D.C., she'd have to wait until Monday to ask if it belonged to any of her students.

In the meantime…

Kate opened the search engine and typed in the manufacturer. She scrolled through the pictures on the company's website looking for a match. The Sunko watch line was geared toward people who were involved in outdoor sports, GPS watches for hikers, and so forth.

And while the designs seemed close, Kate couldn't quite find the exact match.

Watches were both functional and a fashion accessory, she reasoned. Fashions changed from season to season and year to year. This particular model was probably no longer in distribution.

She took a picture of the watch with her phone and sent it to the search engine's image search.

Helpfully, the search engine told her it was "probably a watch."

She shook her head and reached for her water bottle. "All right, dead end." She had to wait as a shudder of dread worked its way out of her body.

She rubbed her baby bump. "Sorry about that, little guy, Mommy was just having a moment." She shouldn't use phrases like "dead end" on days when she was getting ready to go to a funeral. She took a swig, replaced the cap, and poised her fingers on the keyboard.

Kate typed in: Sunko Watches, catalog, then last year's date.

She scanned.

Nope.

It took her three more tries before she found the right watch.

It was a tiny success; but still, a little bubble of hope might help keep her afloat. She clicked on the image.

Sunko's Alpha Team Hunting Watch, it said. Kate started reading about the watch. She was mainly interested in learning what the download ports were about.

Sunko Alpha Team hunting watch was developed with the serious hunter in mind. This newly developed technology works best when worn on the wrist on the side of the hunter's trigger finger. This state of the art hunting watch registers rifle and shotgun fire. This watch is not intended for handguns or other firearm use.

Our tech team has developed a highly precise algorithm that includes the acceleration of the time piece measured by the accelerometer integrated in the design of the watch along with the pattern of gun recoil.

"Accelerometer." Kate tried on the word. She lifted the watch, bobbling her hand to assess its weight. "Huh," she said, laying it back down.

The shot detection computer will keep track of the number of shots and locations. It is suggested that the wearer download the data onto their computer and clear the history to avoid filling the memory.

Other features of this watch include sunrise and sunset alerts, green background light to protect the hunter's night vision. And a waypoints button to mark important places on your trail.

Kate skimmed down to the fine print: *Results may vary. Use of certain accessories such as suppressors and firearm choice can affect data collection.*

Make sure the watch is tightly secured to the wrist to help eliminate false data collection from movements unrelated to shots fired.

Download it to a computer. Kate would need the proper cord, and she knew she didn't have anything that size.

She examined the clasp and saw that it had been damaged. The clasp didn't snap down any more, which meant it had slipped off the owner's wrist. Other than that, it was in pretty good condition. It didn't look like it had weathered or filled with grit from the soil.

Kate squinted at the ports. They were clear of debris as far as she could tell.

It *might* have been lost very recently.

Kate downloaded the pictures from the digital camera her students had used to document the evidence they'd found on her clue trail. She scrolled through the file to find the picture of the watch, wanting to gather information about what kind of substrate was underneath it when it was found.

Finally, she arrived at plastic numbered marker nineteen, a watch on a rock under the overhanging trunk of a very wide downed tree. Safe from the elements.

How had her students even seen this? Someone must have put their ear to the ground to scan the area. Smart kid. So impressive. They were doing great. Kate was going to have to revamp her plans for this semester to keep her students on their toes.

She drummed her fingers on the laptop, wondering where she'd find the answers she wanted.

A hunting watch.

There was a lot of deer hunting in these parts. People put food on their table for the year by filling their freezers with wild game. It helped stretch food budgets.

Again, Kate was confused by the price tag on this watch. Who around here made the kind of money that would make *this* watch affordable? Whether it helped them hunt or not. Five hundred dollars, that was a *lot* of money when there were no jobs to be had.

But the good news was, since the watch wasn't new, perhaps the memory hadn't been downloaded and cleared.

With data, Kate could figure out where the watch registered a shot. Then it was a matter of public record who owned the property. Kate assumed it had to register date and time, not just GPS data. That information might take her right to the watch owner, or maybe help the property owner figure out who was hunting their land that day.

This might be a really fun project to have her students trace. But of course, she needed to go through the steps first on her own.

She didn't want to get her students involved in anything where she didn't control the outcome.

Or at least had reasonable control of the outcome. Kate had learned that control was an illusion.

She went back to the website to search for information about downloading. She wondered how much a replacement cable cost. If it was a few dollars, she might just send for it.

Okay first, they wanted forty dollars for the cable. That was a nope. Kate was curious, but forty dollars could buy a pair of maternity pants or maybe a cute top or two.

Her eye scanned further. Docking port…two electronic connectors…data flows from the watch and into the computer… the GPS coordinates…check your retailer for assistance.

Okay, Kate thought, that's a pretty good idea. She typed "nearest Sunko distributor" into the search engine. It asked for her zip code. She typed that in and saw that there was a distributor in Richmond, one in Bristol, and four in Washington D.C.

I can kill two birds with one stone, she thought. Then instantly regretted the idiom as once again, dread flashed through her system.

8

THURSDAY

KATE HAD CHANGED out of her yoga pants at the Washington motel. She was wearing one of the black dresses she'd bought last June to go to the funerals for the four dead high schoolers who had OD'd.

She planned to burn this dress after today.

It had been a loose sheathe when she'd bought it. Now, it was more form fitting than was necessarily comfortable. When she went to the maternity stores tomorrow, she'd pick up another black dress.

Seemed like she'd be needing it.

Death and despair.

It was all around her.

She put her hand under her belly. "Sorry little guy. It's the world you're coming into. But I'm going to work on this. I'm going to find a way to feel better myself and protect you as long as you need me to." Kate was talking out loud as she slid her feet into her black flats. "I really do need to work on your name. You know, your daddy has two names. I call him Ryan, but his friends call him Reaper, like in the Narnia book. Well, not really. His friends gave him the name thinking more of the grim reaper. But I prefer the Narnia character Reepicheep. He was a mouse who was friends with Aslan, who was a lion. I'll read that book to you when you're a little older. Reepicheep is a fine role model for you. And it's so much less, well, *grim* than Reaper."

Kate gathered her key card and purse. She paused to check her reflection in the mirror. She looked washed out and sad. Today, that seemed fitting.

She opened the door and headed to the church.

THE SIDE DOOR was heavy as Kate pushed her way into the church.

She was hoping to find a quiet pew off to the side rather than having to prance down the middle aisle. She realized her belly was showing and people would guess that she was pregnant. It was unfair that everyone knew and Ryan didn't.

Later today, she'd try to tell him.

Not try. She'd *do it* today, no more excuses.

Kate would be brave for little guy's sake.

She stepped forward into the dim interior and let her eyes acclimate.

The church was designed like a cross. The main section of the church was full. It looked like Tony's squad was across the aisle on the right-hand side of the altar. Three of them had dogs with them. She knew that two of those dogs had been working dogs and once they were retired, they were adopted by their handlers. The other one was probably a service dog.

As Kate slid onto the smoothly polished pew, she wished she had a dog at her feet, and she could rest her hand on his head.

She looked over and saw a young woman watching her. Athletic, long blond hair, she sent Kate an encouraging smile.

The doors at the back of the church opened and a Naval officer in his white uniform walked in with Marybeth. She was clutching her baby tightly to her chest with one hand and held the hand of her other little girl tightly, stretching the child's arm and making her hop-walk up the aisle. Kate couldn't remember the child's name or age. By looking, Kate would guess she was six or seven years old.

With her child sobbing and stumbling along, Marybeth's eyes were focused forward on the flag draped coffin.

She made her way slowly forward.

Grief sluffed off Marybeth in layers. It covered the aisles and swelled into the air. It made Kate gasp and clutch at her chest.

Marybeth sat down at the end of the aisle. Her whole body spasmed. Her older daughter's cries turned into wails. The baby looked like she was being crushed and was screaming at the top of her lungs, flailing her little fists.

Kate couldn't handle the horror of watching this family's grief.

The young woman with the supportive smile sent Kate a look. And Kate knew immediately what message was being telegraphed. *We have to get the kids out of here.*

The woman walked to the front and slid in next to Marybeth and gently pried her hands away from the baby.

Kate was on her feet and moving to their row. She slid in and reached her hand out toward Marybeth's daughter.

The child grabbed at her like she was a life line.

Kate pulled, to slide the girl toward her, then the two of them pushed out the side door and away from the scene.

Walking down the outer corridor, with the child's howls echoing off the stone, Kate found a little sitting alcove with a couch. Light filtered through the prismed glass. The seating cushions were deep and comfortable.

Kate was at a loss as to how best to help. She wished she could remember the little girl's name. She wished she knew if the child liked to be touched and cuddled. Or hated strangers to be too close.

Any clue, really, to help her help or bring comfort, would be appreciated.

The child was sobbing with abandon. She'd pulled her feet up onto the couch, wrapped her arms around her bent knees, and made animal yowls of pain.

"Let it out. Let it go," Kate crooned. After a moment, the little girl pushed to the side. Now, she was lying curled on the sofa with her head in Kate's lap, hiccoughing.

Kate combed her fingers through the child's damp hair.

Speaking past her jagged breath she said, "Everyone in there knows this is my fault my daddy's dead."

Kate stilled and tried to process that. "Do you feel like your dad's death is your fault?"

"Well, sure," she said, sitting up. She lifted her dress and mopped the drips from her face. It was hard to understand her words spoken through the hitched breaths that came after a hard cry. "If I was a good girl, he'd never have wanted to leave. But I made him mad all the time."

"Baby," Kate said. "Your daddy may have been mad all the time, but it had *nothing* to do with you."

"He *told* me to clean my room. I hadn't done it yet. I planned to do it. I just didn't get to it yet."

Kate's heart squeezed. What a heavy burden for this little wisp of a child. "Your daddy isn't dead because you didn't clean your room. Your daddy isn't dead because of a single thing that you ever did or did not do. Your daddy is dead because he had an illness."

Her eyes opened wide. "He was sick?" she whispered.

"Yes, baby. He was sick. And there is nothing you could have done or not done that would make him better. He was sick. And sometimes, sick people die. And sadly, your daddy was one of the sick people who died. I'm so sorry."

The little girl slid up closer to Kate, and Kate tucked her in tight, wrapping her arms around the child. The little girl rested her hand on Kate's belly.

And there they clung together.

The child opened her mouth and let out a sigh, let go of a burden. Just let it go. And now they sat in peace as the last strains of the hymn was belted out by the choir.

Soon the doors would open. The peace would be broken. And they'd need to go to Arlington.

Kate wasn't sure she could keep her promise to Zack to go and represent Ryan and him. Kate was so sad for Tony's daughter, and so sad for her own son.

All she wanted to do was crawl under the covers and sleep.

9

THE LITTLE GIRL'S gaze popped up when the sound of clicking heels approached. The blonde woman came into view holding Tony's baby. "Hi Lexi." The little girl scrambled to sit up but still leaned against Kate's body. Her fingers curling into the fabric of Kate's mourning dress.

"Hi Riley. I see you have a new friend," Lexi said as she moved over and sat next to them on a wooden chair. She smiled with warmth but not happiness. "This is Charlotte, Riley's baby sister," she said then bent to kiss the head of the sleeping baby.

Riley reached out her free hand and grabbed at her sister's foot. "Charlotte had her first birthday yesterday. She didn't get a cake. We were going to make one. I picked out a unicorn to go on top. Maybe we can use it next year."

"Your mommy is feeling sad right now. She said that you two would probably be more comfortable at my house. What do you think about going to hang out with my dogs? Beetle and Bella could use some petting, and we can bake Charlotte a cake."

Riley nodded but gripped Kate's dress tighter.

"You're Kate. I'm Lexi. I'm Striker's fiancée."

"Oh," Kate said, wondering how Lexi had put together her name with her face. They had never met before.

"If it's all right with you, I told Marybeth that you and I would watch the girls for her until her brother picks them up at my house after dinner. That will give her some time…" It was adult code for Marybeth struggling to keep it together for her kids, and she just needed time to fall apart.

"Of course." Relief warmed Kate's frozen muscles, letting them release. She wouldn't have to go and see them lower Tony's coffin into the ground. "Do you have their car seats?"

"One of the guys moved them to my car already. Shall we go before there's a crowd? Did you drive? You could follow me."

LEXI'S HOUSE WAS LOVELY. It felt like a comfortable old friend. Riley had obviously been here before. She knew just where the crayons and coloring books were stored. She lay on the living room floor flanked by Beetle and Bella, Lexi's Dobermans, and Riley seemed to be distracted from the emotions of today.

Baby Charlotte was in a pack 'n' play in the dining room, where she could nap undisturbed.

"Whatever you said to her back at the church seems to have helped," Lexi said, handing Kate a cup of tea and nodding toward Riley. She sat down with her own mug, curling up on the other end of the couch to face Kate.

Kate stretched her lips upward in a kind of a smile then took a sip of tea.

"Zack and Striker are friends. Zack called us and told us you'd be here by yourself."

"He was playing big brother. He wanted you to look out for me."

"Yeah, he did." Lexi grinned. "He's got a strong mother-duck streak in him. He needs to make sure all the ducklings are safe and accounted for. He was telling me that you're out in the western part of Virginia teaching CSI, for the time being."

"Normally, I'm a biology teacher. I just finished up certification to teach CSI in high schools. This is a one-semester grant that I'm working on now."

"Then you'll head back to Boston?"

"I'd love to. I'm an urban girl. I enjoy being with my aunt, but the country lifestyle just isn't right for me. But Boston… I'm not sure it will work out." Kate didn't like talking about her personal life. She'd learned from her small-town upbringing that holding your private life close to the vest meant staying off the gossip train. Kate was relieved that Lexi seemed to understand and slid the conversation to another topic.

"Beetle and Bella are search and rescue dogs. At Iniquus, where I work, the K-9 trainer works on their scent skills a bit each day. And I work them in the field whenever I can. I really enjoy going out in the woods and watching them in action."

"What kind of scent work do they do?"

"They can trail. Bella's better with air and Beetle's better with ground scent. But they can do both. And they can do HRD."

Kate sent a glance down to Riley. HRD stood for human remains detection, and she wondered what the circumstances were of finding Tony's body. Kate didn't know anything about his death. Didn't *want* to know anything about his death. But from her studies, Kate knew people often want to die looking at something beautiful, so they'll go out in nature. This kept their loved ones from the shock of finding their body, often needing search and rescue volunteers to find them.

Kate didn't know how long Tony had been dead. If he had

gone missing…and to tell truth, she never wanted those details spelled out for her. She wanted to remember Tony as the loving husband and devoted dad he'd always been.

Sometimes, things just don't make sense, like Tony being lowered into the ground.

"I'm actually training out your way next weekend. Just outside of Blacksburg, there's a big tri-state K-9 SARex. You'd be welcome to come if you've never seen one before. It's Sunday, a week from now."

"I wish it was a little later in the month. It would be great if I could organize a field trip for my class to see that. It's not all that far. About an hour."

"Or I could come to them." Lexi shifted to curl her foot under her hip. "I have the next Monday off. I'm staying with a friend and was planning to spend the night anyway. I could bring the girls and do a question and answer for your class. I could even do a demonstration of my girls in action."

"Are you serious?" Kate asked. "I would so love for them to see that. I'm going to say yes quickly before you change you mind. *Absolutely*. That would be awesome." Kate looked at Riley to make sure she was still distracted. "There was a case out my way, Carolyn Lambert. Did you and your team work on that?" The missing teacher had been niggling at the back of Kate's mind ever since Aunt Emma had told her she'd probably frightened her students with their class project in the woods.

"I get called out to Maryland and West Virginia. I've actually never been west of Richmond before."

"I work at her school, the school where Carolyn worked. They have a little memorial set up for her, hoping she'll come home soon."

"I can't even imagine what her family and community are going through. When my late husband, Angel, was a Ranger, he went on a mission in the mountains and was out of communication for months. In the back of my mind there was this clawing desperation, knowing he was in danger and that there was absolutely nothing that I could do. I couldn't even know where he was working."

"I'm sorry for your loss," Kate said.

"Yeah, me too. It's funny how—" She stopped and stared at a picture of a handsome man in his class As sitting on the side table. "Since he had a closed casket, I never saw him," she said softly. "I've never been able to convince myself that he's really gone." She spun the diamond and sapphire ring on her finger. "And there I was, at Angel's funeral, thinking he was still alive somewhere, and the ceremony was all just theater. It just hasn't taken hold. My therapist says it might never feel real to me." She shook her head. "That poor family. I don't know how they can survive one day to the next."

Kate could see the pain stretch under Lexi's skin, watched as grief filled her eyes.

Lexi opened her mouth and exhaled hard.

Kate reached out to squeeze her hand.

"Lexi." Riley rolled and looked over her shoulder them. "I'm hungry and so are Beetle and Bella."

Lexi's smile was forced. "Okay, buttercup, let's get you all snacks."

The dogs licked their chops when they heard the word snack.

Lexi turned toward Kate. "Would you like a snack too? I have both sweet and savory."

"No thank you." Kate stood. "If it's okay with you, I'm going to go outside for a moment and call home. My husband had a medical appointment today, and I want to hear how it went."

Lexi pointed toward the back of her house. "The backyard is comfortable and private."

KATE WAS PERCHED on the edge of the little bentwood rocking chair under an arbor of honeysuckle vines.

After tapping the quick dial for home, the phone rang three times before Kate heard a hello. It was Ryan who answered, and Kate froze up. She had assumed Zack or one of the other guys who took turns staying at the house would grab the phone.

He's on the phone. This is your chance. Tell him about the baby.

This was it.

Now was the time.

"Hi," she managed.

"Good," Ryan said, business-like. "I needed to talk to you."

"I needed to talk to you, too." And then she chickened out. "How did things go today with the MRI?"

"They stuck me in a tube. I listened to some music. They pulled me out of the tube."

"Okay. Did they say when they might get the results?" Kate picked at the hem of her dress.

"That's not what I want to talk to you about."

Kate didn't like the tone in his voice. It sent up warning flares in her survival system. "What do you want to talk to me about, then?" She wrapped a protective hand around her belly.

"I can't keep on like this. I need to cut you free." His voice caught, then he continued gruffly, "You deserve a life that I can't give you."

Ice washed through Kate's system. She bent over, as if she could shield the baby from hearing that his daddy was rejecting her. She whispered, "You want to divorce me?"

"I'm not able to be there for you in any capacity. None."

"No." The word barely made it out. Then the anger started to boil. "I mean *no*. I made vows to be there in sickness and in health."

"But you're waiting for me to get better—I'm not going to get better."

Kate closed her eyes. "I know all about this—I had my Uncle Owen to show me that life isn't rainbows and blue birds."

"You hated him," Ryan said flatly. "I want you to walk away before I smother every little flicker of love you had for me."

"*Have* for you. You don't get to tell me what I feel. Besides, Uncle Owen never did this to my aunt. She stood by her husband —he allowed her to do that. You're not giving me a chance." Kate opened her eyes again and focused on the late season roses along Lexi's garden wall.

"You deserve more. You deserve better." His words were adamant. "I'm going to send you the papers, please sign them."

She should tell him about their baby boy. She should. But it seemed like such a desperate move. Like she was using the baby as a trap. "I'll tell you what," she said, "you bring me those papers. You put the pen in my hand, I'll sign them."

"You know I…that's problematic."

"Yah think? You're asking me to break my vows that I still feel in my heart. You are stopping me from being with you and standing with you. I want to be there. I love you, Ryan."

"I'm not Ryan anymore. I won't be Ryan ever again. Never. I'm a different person. A stranger. You don't even know me anymore, Kate."

"Okay." Tired. She was so darned tired.

"Okay what?"

"Okay, bring me the papers. Put the pen in my hand."

"Darn it, Kate!"

"You want me to make this easy for you, and I won't. Sorry. Not sorry."

"You're sounding like one of your high school students."

"Whatever."

"You're trying to get a rise out of me?"

"No, I want you to tell me I can come home. I don't want to be here. I want to be with you."

"I *don't* want to be with you," he said.

"Okay, that was hurtful. I'm going to hang up now." And without waiting for him to say another word, she swiped the phone to end their conversation.

He'd stabbed her in the heart.

He was trying to kill their marriage.

Well, whether for better or for worse, he was going to have to include his son in this equation. She opened a browser and sent Ryan an email, knowing that he checked his inbox throughout the day, since he didn't trust cell phones. Kate attached a picture of her last ultrasound, choosing the picture with the little digital arrow pointing between the baby's legs, and the word "boy" typed in white font. She put READ IMMEDIATELY! in the subject line. And in the body, she simply typed: **YOURS.**

10

MOST TIMES when Kate met new people, Kate's reticence to talk about herself—rather than say books, or art, or hobbies—made people think she was standoffish. That's not how Kate felt inside, she just really valued her privacy, free of judgement and unsolicited advice.

When Kate went back inside after her death-knell of a conversation with Ryan, Lexi had been ready with a hug.

Honestly, Kate felt like she'd known Lexi for years on end—that they'd always been friends. Kate truly appreciated the rare times when surprise encounters brought comfortable friendships like this.

Lexi felt like a safe place—like a dock rising solidly from a swell of choppy waters. Being in Scarborough, well, it had been a long time since Kate had been around someone she considered a friend.

There was Tim…but that was different.

Even though she'd grown up in Scarborough, all of the

women in her high school circle of friends had moved elsewhere for college and kept on moving after graduating. And since she was about to leave Scarborough at any moment—at the moment when Ryan said, I'm sorry, please come home—she hadn't bothered to try to forge new relationships.

KATE WAS glad to have Lexi's company at the mall the next day, as she set off to buy maternity wear. It was nice to have a girlfriend moment.

Kate had missed this—girl time.

Lexi and Kate were on to their second stop of the day. First, Lexi had taken her to a shop that specialized in women's tactical wear, including maternity sizes. Kate didn't want to invest a bunch of money in her work pants, but after her little guy was born, she could always sell them online.

They had stowed her bags in the cargo area of Kate's SUV and were headed back into the mall now to go to the jewelers.

Kate tapped the watch zipped into her pocket. She hoped for information. Something interesting so she could show her students some detective work, even if CSI wasn't about detective work. Still, since they were involved, it would be a totally cool lesson. And it might inspire some of the kids to consider police investigation as a career path.

The shop had three salespeople. Two of them were occupied with customers. Kate approached the older man who looked like he held the keys and the authority here. "Hi." She smiled. "I'm Kate Hamilton. I teach CSI to high schoolers."

He tipped his head with curiosity.

"We were out doing a class project in the woods, when I found this watch." She pulled the piece from her pocket and stretched it out toward the guy. "I looked it up. It's pretty expensive. I'm hoping to get it back to the owner. I thought you might be able to help me, since you sell this brand in your store."

He took the watch from her hand and rubbed his thumb over the face. "There's no way for me to tell who owns this watch unless it was bought here at the store, and the customer registered their number with us."

"But there are numbers?" she asked.

"In the paperwork we send home with them. Not on the watch."

"It has a computer system to indicate where the hunter used his shotgun, or rifle." She reached forward and tapped the face of the watch. "Is it possible to download that information?"

The jeweler pulled his brow in tight and sent her a look that made Kate feel guilty. What this guy might be thinking, Kate couldn't even guess. "If for example, he shot consistently on a private property, I could take the watch to that place," she said, trying to appease the jeweler's skepticism. "I'm living in Scarborough. It's a small town out in the western part of Virginia. There are lots of farms and lots of hunters out my way." She glanced back at Lexi then focused again on the man. "I'm here in D.C. visiting friends for the weekend and thought I'd take the opportunity to do a good deed."

The guy focused over on the two saleswomen and saw that they were busy showing off merchandise. Without a word he went into the back room.

Kate wasn't a jewelry kind of woman. She didn't like the way it felt on her body and would only wear it when she absolutely had to. Except for her wedding ring. She reached her thumb up and twirled Ryan's wedding ring with its Celtic knots that she wore on her index finger.

When Ryan asked her to leave, she'd asked for his ring and gave him hers. These were symbols of their vows. Kate wanted to remember that Ryan had made vows to her. She needed him to wear her ring to remind him that he'd promised to stick with her in sickness and in health—but those vows didn't stipulate that it would be her sickness. Those words could just as easily be his sickness. He was sick, and he needed to stick with her and keep his promises.

The emotions around her marriage swung back and forth from anger to depression on a fulcrum of love and commitment. Right now, there was no joy. But there had been. There *had been* bliss and laughter and peace.

The guy walked back in with the watch in one hand and a piece of paper in the other.

He handed her both. "There you go."

Kate accepted them and glanced down at the paper. There was a list of numbers. The first row were dates. The second row indicated the time of the shot. The third row was a string of numbers, GPS coordinates. She looked up and focused a smile on the guy. "Thank you for taking the time to help me." She reached out to shake the man's hand, then turned and walked out of the store.

Lexi followed alongside.

As they moved back toward the car, Kate handed the list over to Lexi.

"I know this doesn't look like much," Lexi said. "But it's really very good information. I have an app for search and rescue. Searches on public lands are only some of our missions. If we get a missing person, we often need to go look on private land. The app tells me who owns that land and sometimes even contact information, so we can get permission before we go traipsing around."

"That's pretty cool. I need to tell my students about that. On a CSI job, they'd have warrants in hand. But it's an interesting piece of information. Have you ever had someone say no to you when you wanted to search?" They arrived at her Explorer. Kate slid the key into the lock.

"Kind of." Lexi walked to the passenger's side. "This guy met us on the porch. I had a five-person team, and I was working with Bella that day. This guy waggles his fingers toward my map that I have in a silicone cover, hanging from my backpack strap. I handed it over to him, and he's looking it over. I have our mission area circled in highlighter. He pulls a pen from his pocket, leans over so he can press the map against his thigh." She stopped talking as she climbed in.

Kate pulled her door open and a blast of hot air that had been accumulating in the interior blew past her as she slid under the wheel.

"Now, this is my mission map," Lexi said, "and I don't want him drawing on it. But since my mission was all on his property, I bit my tongue."

"What was he doing?" Kate clicked her safety belt in place then adjusted the strap low on her hips.

"He blacked out two sections and told us we could look where we'd like, but we couldn't go to these two places."

Kate raised her eyebrows. "What do you think was there?" She cranked the engine, smacking the vents downward, so they didn't blow hot air into their faces.

"Well, it wasn't dead bodies. Bella would have followed the scent, black spot or no black spot," Lexi said, as Kate swiveled to see out the window as she backed up. Once they were under way, Lexi said, "I'm guessing meth lab. Maybe moonshine. Who knows? I brought it to managements' attention as soon as we got out into the woods, and let the LEO handle it if they wanted to go to those areas."

"Did the police follow up?"

"When I got back for debrief, they asked if Bella was curious at all about those spots. Since she's live find and HRD, and I said nope, I guess they figured they'd leave it alone. No one was in danger or dead back there."

"Wow," Kate said.

"Yup. We never did find the guy. Our search and rescue team never gives up, though. We'll go back if we're asked to. Sometimes clues show up."

"The teacher I was telling you about, Carolyn Lambert, from the school I'm teaching at has been missing for a couple years. They never found her either."

"Did you know her?" Lexi asked as they pulled to a stop at the light.

"No. She's from the town over from Scarborough, and I haven't lived there in fifteen years. I left right out of high school."

"I can't even imagine what the family goes through."

11

Friday

Kate was in the bathroom of her motel room, changing into yoga pants and a fresh shirt. She'd felt dirty and sticky after being out in the high humidity of the September swelter in D.C.

She'd left the door open, so she and Lexi could talk as Lexi tapped at her tablet, pulling up the information about who owned the properties.

"You're heading back tomorrow?" Lexi called.

"Actually, I thought I might go ahead and get on the road once I have your list. I thought I might go knock on some doors tomorrow. It's Saturday and folks should be at home. Sundays, sometimes they're at church or with family most of the day." She emerged from the bathroom, pulling her hair into a pony tail.

"Are you serious about not staying in Scarborough after this semester is up?" Lexi asked past the pen she held between her teeth, her gaze on a map she had on her screen.

"My contract is only for the fall semester, and it only equals about half the paycheck I used to get back in Boston, since I only teach the one class. Sometimes, you take what you can get. It was an opportunity, and I took it. Once the contract is up, there are no other jobs in the area. If I want to pay the bills, I'll have to find something else."

"So I have a possibility." Lexi moved a file. "I'm going to email all this to you. Maps, names, everything that this app brings up. I have two more locations to go."

The printout had filled the page top to bottom. So the hunter must have been shooting multiple times in one general location.

"Thank you," Kate said, sitting on the corner of one of the queen-sized beds to put on her shoes.

Lexi looked up from her work. "My neighbor across the street from my duplex is an old family friend. His name is Dave Murphy. He's a detective."

"Oh?"

"They're developing a system of community-based policing, and they have a grant to help them achieve some goals in the neighborhoods. One of the things they want to have is an outreach educator who basically teaches the kids K through twelve what police do. And what they can't do. And they think a big piece of that is to make it fun. The curriculum that they're developing is—"

"CSI in the classroom."

Lexi sent her a grin. "Bingo. Washington D.C. inner city. You and an officer. The officer would just smile and look pretty. You would be teaching. Interested at all?"

"Very. But D.C. is almost as expensive as Boston. Is the pay okay? Does it have benefits?" Kate massaged her hand over her stomach. She would swear the baby grew the moment he knew she was getting clothes big enough to accommodate him. Sweet kid.

"It's a full-time job with the police department. It has a pretty good benefits package. And as to the expense, you saw that my house is a duplex. I own the whole thing. Striker and I spend most of our time at Iniquus, but I keep one side of the house, the one where you visited yesterday, for when we're not on call and rent out the other at a bargain-basement rate, because I only want people there who feel like family. And I wouldn't take advantage of family. I'd love for you to be my neighbor."

Lexi smiled at Kate, and Kate choked up.

She was wanted by a stranger.

Was welcomed as family by a stranger.

Rejected by her husband.

Lexi must have seen the emotions fighting her face muscles, because she tucked her chin and went back to work, giving Kate some privacy. Kate hoped Lexi thought she was a hormonal mess because of her pregnancy.

Kate would give her hormones some credit but most of this was just…life.

"There, done." Lexi tapped enter on the computer. "That will be in your email as soon as you get home. I put Dave's contact information in the email. But I'll walk over to his house tonight and talk you up, so you won't be cold calling if you reach out to him." She stood up and started tucking her things away in her backpack. "You'll have to keep me up on what you find out about this watch business. I love puzzles like this."

"Thank you so much."

"Were you serious about leaving right now? I can help you get the things out to your car."

"Yeah, thanks. I think that's what I'm going to do. I think if I stay here, I'll be too antsy to rest. I get that way when I want to know something."

"I completely get that." She walked to the closet and pulled out Kate's new bags. "Why don't I take these?"

Before Kate left the room, she gave it one final look-see to make sure she wasn't leaving anything behind. She pulled her roller bag behind her. It would be months before any of the things in there would be worn. When she wore them again, she'd be a mom.

Wow. Wasn't that mind boggling?

Kate handed in her key card at the desk, and they made their way out the door and over to Kate's SUV.

She'd popped the back hatch when a guy on a motorcycle with a full helmet on his head caught her eye. He was sitting in his riding leathers under a tree on the far side of the parking lot.

Ryan.

She knew it.

Lexi's gaze followed Kate's. "You know him?" she asked.

"I think that's probably my husband."

The guy swung his leg off the motorcycle and pulled off his helmet.

"Yes, that's my husband, Ryan."

Lexi sent her a look of confusion and maybe a little alarm, then looked back as Ryan made his way across the parking lot toward them.

"I…you both seem really stressed," Lexi said. "Is this okay?"

Sure, Kate must have reeked of anxiety, but how Lexi knew Ryan was stressed was beyond her. Ryan looked his normal cool-as-a-cucumber self.

He must have gotten on his bike as soon as he got up that morning and saw her email.

Must have jumped on his bike and headed straight for her.

To hand her the papers.

To put the pen in her hand the way she'd told him to.

His footsteps slowed as he approached, but he wasn't looking at Kate, he was looking at Lexi. He only turned to Kate once they were standing side by side. His gaze moved from her face, down to her belly, then he closed his eyes. Held. Shook himself. And when he opened his eyelids again, he was looking at Lexi.

"Are you Lexi Sobado?" he asked.

Lexi stuck out her hand and sent him a smile. "Yes, I am. I'm sorry, have we met?"

"No, ma'am. I've seen your picture. I've heard stories. My team ran a series of missions with Angel's Ranger unit. He's a brave man."

She touched a hand to her heart. "Oh, you probably haven't heard, my husband died while he was on a mission. It's been almost two years, now." She pursed her lips and tipped to the right. "Whew," she whispered as Kate reached out to steady her. "The pain is as fresh as if it were yesterday. I can't seem to own the fact that he's gone. Every time I tell someone he died, I feel like I'm lying."

Ryan's lips twitched like he was about to say something to Lexi. Kate focused on her husband. She knew him better than she knew herself, and there was something there. Something he knew about Lexi's husband, or that mission, or his death. He got that look when she asked him for information that was mission specific. When the thing she wanted to know was something that he couldn't tell her. Classified and unknowable.

Kate turned to see if Lexi was reading that, too.

Lexi was looking off at the tree line. She turned. "Would you excuse me? I think I'm going to head home and give you two some privacy." Lexi reached out to squeeze Kate's arm, turned, and walked away, digging her keys from her pocket.

Normally, Kate wouldn't let a friend drive away looking emotionally fragile, but Ryan was here, and she had troubles of her own.

"I got your email," he said.

Kate stood absolutely still.

"I don't want a baby."

She snorted as she laughed at that. "Little late. No putting the genie back in the bottle."

"I *don't* want a child. I am not sane. I can't keep a baby safe any more that I can keep you safe."

"Ryan, you have a brain injury. You're not a psychopath."

"I'm not taking chances with you or my...or the boy. You have full custody. *Full.* I will not be part of that child's life. I'll send you money for him, but that's it."

Kate's mouth went dry.

He meant this. He was serious right now.

She couldn't believe it. She never thought Ryan would abandon her.

"If he needs a father, you'll have to find someone else who's willing to take it on. I'm sorry. I'm saying this for your own darned safety, Kate." He reached in his motorcycle jacket and pulled out a packet of papers from the inside pocket. He handed them to her.

Kate looked down at the first page. She couldn't believe this. *Couldn't.*

He pulled out a pen and pressed it into her hand. "You said if I brought you the papers and gave you a pen you'd sign."

She ripped them in half and threw the papers in the air. "I lied." Pushing past Ryan, she got into the front seat of the Explorer, locked the door, and pulled on her seat belt. Her wheels squealed as she stomped the gas pedal to the floor and flew out of the parking lot.

12

———

KATE WALKED out the kitchen door at her aunt's house with a bag of garbage in her hand.

Ryan was dead set on divorcing her. He probably thought he was being a hero. He'd follow through, though. She saw it in his eyes as she ripped those darn divorce papers in half and threw them like chunky confetti into the air. He'd head home, and first thing Monday morning, he'd be on the phone to some lawyer asking to have this go to trial. Trials took a long time to schedule. She had room for a miracle.

Kate looked up. "How about a miracle?" she asked the sky.

She thunked the kitchen trash into the outdoor bin and plopped the lid back in place. Turning to go back in, Kate thought about Lexi and her husband's death. She obviously loved her husband, Angel. Obviously was grieving. And yet, she was engaged to Striker Rheas. One emotion didn't stop her from living her life. She had a comfortable home, job, friends. She gave back to the community with her dogs that she doted on like they were her children. She had children, like Charlotte and Riley who obviously adored her.

Dogs and children were always the very best discerners of character.

While Lexi's life was full, her life wasn't perfect.

Kate reached out and grabbed the handle to the screen door. Before she went in, she looked up to the sky and said out loud, "She's a great role model. I can learn a lot from her, but seriously, would you consider a miracle? Can I have my marriage back?"

"What's that?" Aunt Emma called.

Kate chuckled as she went in. "Sorry, you caught me talking to myself." She stopped when she saw her aunt had lipstick on. "Are you going out?"

"I'm heading over to the church to help them organize for next month's fall festival. I thought I'd get a pizza for lunch, and we'd have the leftovers for dinner. I figured I'd get the loaded veggie kind, so the baby gets his nutrition. Does that appeal?"

"That would be nice. No cooking. No cleaning."

"I'm liking both of those," Aunt Emma said as she tucked a cardigan through the strap of the purse hanging from her shoulder. "I won't be too long. What are you getting yourself up to today?"

"I told you that my class found a watch out in the woods."

Aunt Emma tipped her head.

"I have some printouts about where the watch has been, and I thought I'd work on finding the owner."

"Like a GPS in a watch?"

"As far as I can tell it doesn't have those capabilities. But I really don't know too much about the technology. It's a hunting watch that registers rifle shots. That's about all it says on their website."

"Okay, good. Expensive watch like that, someone's going to want it back. It's nice of you to go to all that trouble."

"It gives me somewhere to focus." She took a deep breath. "I told Ryan about our baby."

Aunt Emma stood still, waiting for the outcome.

"He asked me for a divorce. He drove his motorcycle all the way down to Washington to hand me the papers he'd had drawn up."

"That's about an eight-hour drive."

"Yeah, he shaved off three hours drive time by catching me there at the hotel instead of coming out here."

"Oh, honey. What happened?"

"I tore them up and threw them in his face, jumped in my car, and drove away."

Aunt Emma nodded sympathetically.

"So there's that." Kate wrapped her hand around her belly. She was wearing maternity pants for the first time, and she was so much more comfortable.

"Life rarely goes the way we want it to," Aunt Emma said. Coming from anyone else, that might sound trite. Coming from Aunt Emma, there was a world of experience and heartache behind the words.

"Okay, then you need a plan," Aunt Emma said. "You can always stay here with me, but you're not happy here, and there are no jobs. Once your contract wraps up. I don't know what you'd do with yourself all day." Aunt Emma bent to gather her kitten who was lacing in and out of her legs. She pulled Bingley up for a kiss then tucked him into the crook of her arm.

"There's a possible job that I'm going to apply for in Washington D.C."

"What kind of job is it? Teaching? You could possibly still have your teaching job in Boston to go back to, don't you think?" When Bingley started to squirm, Aunt Emma set him down.

"I can't imagine being in the same city as my husband and not being able to see him. I'd end up like a stalker, he'd have to get restraining orders, I'd have to go to jail. It would be bad."

Aunt Emma laughed. "All right, well I'll be back in a few hours with pizza. Good luck on finding the watch's rightful home."

Kate climbed the stairs to her room and opened her laptop. She scrolled through the three-page list of shots and the corresponding property info that registered on the watch.

Lexi had highlighted four lines in yellow.

Studying the information, Kate realized that those four yellow highlights represented four different locations. Three of which had been visited on multiple dates. At the end of the read-out were the four corresponding location addresses. Three were commercial hunting clubs here in Virginia. One of those three was fairly local. Name, address, website, contact phone number. The fourth was for private property over in Boonestown. It had a name, a P.O. box mailing address, no phone number. The last page was a satellite photo of a turn of the century farm house. The page after that was driving directions from Main Street in Scarborough to that location. Thirty-eight minutes from downtown.

Kate dialed the first number and a man answered, "Lightfoot Lee Hunt Club, Harrison speaking."

"Hi, Harrison. My name is Kate Hamilton. I'm a teacher over in Boonestown." She stumbled along not sure of how much information she needed to mete out. "My class was in the woods on a project, and I found a hunting watch. I took it to the jewelry shop, and the readout said that there are three days that it registered shots fired at your location, three years ago. I have the specific dates and times. I was wondering if you had a data base and could look up who might have been there at those times. I'd love to get this watch back to them. The list price is—" She stopped and rethought giving that information. The guy could just lie and keep the watch for himself. She didn't know him. He could have the ethics of Buddha or he could be a scoundrel—"not cheap."

"You have a list of times and dates that one of our members was here, and you want me to look that up and tell you who they are?" he repeated back.

"Yes, please," Kate said.

"Are you kidding me right now, lady?"

"Well, no. I uh—"

"First of all, that's a heck of a lot of research to look back that many years ago. Second, we have privacy policies. For all I know you haven't got a watch at all and you're up to no good."

"I uhm—"

"Yeah, that just isn't gonna happen."

"Maybe if I could talk to your manager, or the owner…"

"Lady, I am both the manager and owner, Harrison Lee."

"I'm sorry. I didn't mean to offend you in any way. I just thought there might be layers of management that had more authority. Since that's not the case, have you happened to see anyone with a hunting watch or hear someone talking about their hunting watch?"

"From years ago?"

"I don't know. It's kind of novel to me. Maybe it was something interesting that you might remember."

"Nope."

"All right. How about this. What if I sent you an email with the dates and times."

"Hang on a minute." With his hand over the phone Kate heard a muffled, "Peggy, hey, come here and talk to this woman. I've got things to get to, and I don't have time for this."

At which point a new and female voice came over the phone.

Kate tried again.

"That's not too hard to do if you have the date and time. I can pull that up on the computer. I can even put it into a spread sheet and see if I can't narrow it down for you, seeings how you said they had to be the same person here on multiple days. What I can't do is give you any of the information."

"Hmmm. Okay. I—"

"What I can do, is shoot the folks that fit the bill an email and tell them that a watch was found. And if they can describe it to you, they can have it back. That work?"

"Yes, thank you, that works really well. And I'm so appreciative."

"Where should they contact you at?"

Kate was about to give her cell number then thought twice about that. She didn't want her phone number sent out to a bunch of strangers. "I teach up at Boonestown High School. Someone could leave a call-back number there with the secretary."

After Kate read off the number, Peggy said, "This is kind of exciting. Like being part of one of them CSI shows or something. What do you teach up at the school?"

"CSI." Kate laughed.

"Well listen, if someone was to call and claim this watch, I'd love to know about it."

"I'll be happy to call and let you know. I'm writing your name down," Kate said.

After getting Peggy's email address, Kate said good-bye and hung up. It wasn't quite the direction she'd hoped. But to be honest, Kate didn't know what to hope for in that conversation other than maybe, "Oh, Danny asked us to be on the look out for his watch. Black face, black band, silver ports, made by Sunko." That would have been easy.

Maybe too easy.

Kate wanted a distraction.

And this gave her mind something to gnaw on besides her own problems.

She went on to the next hunt club and the next. All three

conversations were the same: They were willing to pull up the data, they were willing to send out an email, but only Lightfoot Lee Hunt Club was willing to go the extra step and narrow down the list to only those who were there at overlapping dates and times.

And for everyone but Peggy, it seemed like this might go on their to-do list and get pushed down until it was forgotten altogether.

But still, even if Peggy was the only one who followed through, at least the watch-wearer would get one email. And if all of them followed through, the watch-wearer should get three emails.

The possibility for success was there.

So now, Kate was down to the residence.

She closed her laptop. Might as well drive out that way.

Tim's anger about her behavior last June when she was going hiking with their suspect came to mind, along with his admonishment to act like a mom.

If she thought things looked concerning, she didn't need to stop. She could always just leave a note on the mailbox if she didn't feel comfortable knocking on the door.

Kate sat on the floor to pull on her tennis shoes, laced them up, and scampered down the stairs with the map in her hand. She'd have to see what there was to see.

13

—————

Saturday

Kate stood next to her car on the otherwise empty gravel driveway.

The house was tucked behind about a hundred yards of tree line. The space opened up enough for the house and a small field with a manmade pond, then more trees. It was in good shape. Nicely kept up. But no one seemed home.

No cars.

No lights.

She listened and didn't hear any dogs barking. The stable doors were closed, but Kate imagined a tractor was in there and garden equipment. She doubted that there were any animals.

Seeings how no one was around, Kate pulled out her phone and tapped on the free GPS app that Lexi had shown her. When it came up, she followed the instructions to recalibrate her phone's location by drawing figure eights in the air. When prompted she chose high accuracy, though it warned her that this would suck battery.

After typing in the exact GPS point that the watch had registered for two shots, one right after the other, Kate wandered up to the front door and knocked.

Waited.

Knocked again.

She held open her phone and followed around to the GPS coordinate associated with the property.

Two shots from the same spot.

She found herself on the back porch right in front of the kitchen door.

She knocked.

Waited.

And knocked again.

No answer.

She cupped her hand and looked in.

It was neat as a pin. No mail on the kitchen table, but there was a salt and pepper shaker sitting in the middle of it, so there was that.

Kate pulled the stapled printouts from the thigh pocket of her new pregnancy tactical pants. Now that she had stretchy yoga-pants at the top, instead of a solid waist strap, zipper, and button, Kate was going to have to forgo putting heavy things into her pockets, lest the weight pull her pants down.

She flipped to the page that gave the date and time, and she focused on the time. It would have been dusk. The shooter could have looked out the window, seen a herd of deer come to drink at the pond, and taken a shot.

She looked at her page again. If that were the case, it would have been illegal. April wasn't hunting season, for deer anyway. Could have been anything. Maybe it was dove season or something.

But still you can't hunt after sunset.

That was presupposing that the person who shot the gun was hunting. They might have been cleaning their gun and it went off by accident.

That didn't quite work out either. There were two shots less than a minute apart, she reminded herself.

Kate heard the crunch of gravel and the growl of a motor coming up the drive. She folded the paper and put it back in her pocket as she rounded the back of the house. Her finger was on a panic app that a friend had asked her to have and use. This app would call everyone on her emergency contact list if she lifted her finger.

An old blue F150 pulled up beside her Explorer.

The man pulled his way out of the cab. She'd guess he was early seventies, snow white hair, thinning, and a little greasy. As he stepped toward her, Kate saw he wore jeans and well-worn boots.

Kate smiled. "Hi, I'm Kate Hamilton. Are you Thomas Parscale?" It was the name Lexi had listed on her printout.

He nodded his head, then looked toward the house.

"I knocked on your front door, Mr. Parscale, then decided to take a peak out back to see if you were working out there." She walked forward.

"Yeah, well I have a driveway alarm. I was a cross the way helping my sister when I heard it go off. What can I help you with?"

"I was wondering if you were missing a watch," she said, coming to a stop by her fender.

He stretched his left wrist. The sleeve of his cotton plaid shirt slid up a bit, so he could show off the silver toned watch on his wrist. "Nope," he said then bent his head to spit tobacco juice into the Coke can in his other hand.

"Have you ever heard of a hunting watch?"

"Nope."

"I found one. A hunting watch that is. And I took it to a jeweler." Kate felt like an idiot. No, she felt like a high schooler who was talking her way out of some trouble. And the adult who could give her a reprieve was having none of it. "They gave me a list of all the times the watch detected a hunter taking a shot. And it said that the last two shots came from your back porch."

"It's that precise is it?"

"To be honest, I have no idea. It says it can be a few yards off. But that's their advertising. For all I know it could be miles off." Which was where Kate wanted to be right then. Miles and miles away.

"No one's up here but me and my kin. When was this the shots was taken?"

Kate thought of Tim, again, and how angry he'd be if he knew she'd come out here on her own, help-me app or no help-me app. He would just reiterate that it didn't matter if help was hidden behind the tree, three feet away, if the bad guy was planning to stab her with a needle.

Bad things can happen in the blink of an eye.

It was almost as if Tim was right there. She could almost feel him worrying about her.

Kate started toward the driver's side of her SUV. "April, two years ago. Well, sorry to bother you. I'm just trying to get the watch back to its owner." She pulled on the door handle.

"Nah, your information couldn't be right. Me and the misses were supposed to go on a cruise down to the Bahamas beginning of April that year. A big storm blew through the gulf and we got cancelled. We stayed in Florida with her sister that month, instead."

"Okay, well. Nice to meet you. Sorry to disturb you with the alarm and all. I'm sorry the watch isn't yours." Kate slid into her SUV, started the engine, and locked her doors. She didn't pull her safety belt on or let the app know she was safe until she'd pulled out of the drive and was well on her way down the road.

She could still feel Tim worrying about her. "Well, I'm never going to tell you about this little adventure," she said, out loud. "I don't need any more trouble."

14

It didn't surprise Kate at all that Tim's car was sitting in her drive when she pulled up at her aunt's house.

She'd felt him brooding ever since she left the Parscale's place.

They'd been connected like that back in high school.

It had taken a move to Boston and concerted effort to get him out of her emotional space.

He was a habit that she could easily slide back into if she wasn't careful.

When she went in, there were the two untouched pizza boxes on the kitchen counter and murmuring voices coming from the living room, a room Aunt Emma only used for special occasions.

Kate walked in to find a sad-faced Aunt Emma, Tim, and his friend Toby sitting there looking uncomfortable.

Tim and Toby stood as she moved into the room.

Kate scowled. "What's going on?"

Tim gestured toward the sofa where Aunt Emma was sitting.

"Kate, I'm not dressed in my uniform, but I've come to talk to you both as a friend and an officer."

That didn't bode well.

Kate perched on the edge of the couch.

"Ryan was in a motorcycle accident in Washington D.C. He was taken to Suburban Hospital."

Kate shook her head.

"He's alive," Toby said quickly.

Kate blinked at him, then turned her attention back to Tim. "I just saw him last night. He was fine. He was heading home to Boston." She had assumed he was…

"The officers got your Boston address from his wallet. The Boston officers went to the residence to inform the family. Zack Tullis gave them your contact information. Boston PD called our station. And the station called me to come talk to you."

"He's alive," she whispered, her lids held rigid and unblinking.

"Last we heard. Yes."

"I…" Kate looked around the living room, not actually seeing anything. "I have to go."

She stood up, at a complete loss as to what to do next.

"I packed you up a suitcase already," Aunt Emma said. "Tim's going to drive you in your car to Washington."

Kate focused on her, trying to comprehend her words.

"Toby's going to follow you all, so he can drive Tim back. They're taking you to your new friend Lexi's house. Zack called her. She's going to be with you when you go to the hospital. You're not alone. You have help. You just need to breathe. Take this one step at a time."

"One step," Kate said. Her body vibrated.

She watched Aunt Emma nod at Toby. Toby went over and picked up the suitcase and headed out the door.

Tim reached over and caught her arm. "Come on. Let's get

you in the car." He turned. "Mrs. Jenkins, would you mind if I took the pillow and throw from your sofa? I want to get Kate comfortable on the drive."

Kate's lips were so heavy that they pulled down her chin until it rested on her chest, and she couldn't lift her head back up.

She saw with her peripheral vision an exchange of color from Aunt Emma's hand to Tim's.

Then Tim pulled her to get her body in motion.

Ryan was in an accident.

As far as they knew, he was alive.

15

———

SATURDAY

TIM DROVE her straight to the hospital.

By the time they'd got on the highway, Kate's brain was functioning again.

She'd been through this before when she got the call about Ryan being injured in Afghanistan on his mission. They'd sent him to Germany, then sent him home, and time moved forward.

Now, time seemed to bend in two. She had been at her aunt's and, just like that, here they were pulling up at Suburban Hospital.

Tim and Toby walked her in and handed her over to Lexi. After giving her hugs, they'd turned and left, heading back over the mountains, and back to the banality of their lives.

Kate had led a banal life.

She'd been inconvenienced with shoveling snow, not wanting to cook dinner, and wishing that her student's tests would grade themselves.

That life seemed so lovely.

She couldn't believe she was nostalgic for cleaning up Ryan's muddy boot prints on the stoop and listening to his snoring. The rhythmic saw that either lulled her to sleep or woke her up when he wasn't deployed.

Lexi checked on Kate's well-being and brought her to the nurses' station to introduce her around. When the doctor came over, Lexi excused herself to go get them something to drink.

She wasn't back yet, and Kate used the opportunity to call Zack.

"Hey, sweetheart."

She could hear it in his voice, guilt. Kate led off with, "You did nothing wrong. You did everything right. I so appreciate you. Let it go." She actually didn't know what she was exonerating him from, but it didn't really matter.

"You're at the hospital? What did you find out?"

"The police said it wasn't his fault. There was a drunk driver. The driver was arrested at the scene."

"You sound like you thought he did that on purpose."

"I came to Washington Thursday for Tony's funeral. I'm back again Saturday night with my husband unconscious. I have my brain primed to consider suicide."

"Ryan's not suicidal," Zack said.

"I didn't think Tony was suicidal. His wife didn't think Tony was suicidal. We don't actually know if Ryan is suicidal or I am or you are or anyone for that matter." Her voice was ramping up. A nurse sent her a look—not exactly punitive, more assessing.

"I hear you." Zack's warm, even tone was a balm to Kate's over-exposed nerves.

She felt fragile, like a paper-thin china tea cup. One poor placement on a hard surface, and she would shatter.

"Can you tell me what the doctors are saying?" Zack asked.

"I have notes, just a second." Kate fished in her pocket for the little notebook and pen that she'd learned, after Ryan was injured on that last mission, were important tools to carry in these circumstances. "Okay." She looked at her tick marks and started to read them off. "His helmet split in two at the time of the accident. He has no alcohol or drugs in his system. This is a second traumatic brain injury, that's a problem. They're classifying this one as moderate, since he only lost consciousness for four hours. He was sleepy, but arousable after that."

"Okay…"

"Right now, he's in a medically induced coma. They said that his body was having an inflammatory response to the injury and that was causing extra fluid and nutrients to accumulate. The doctor said this was helpful in other parts of the body but not so much for the brain, since the skull is rigid. If Ryan's brain fills his cranium, then the pressure will—can—cause further brain injury, and that can even cause death."

She exhaled hard to push those words away from her.

Kate saw Lexi coming up the corridor with a drink tray and a white paper bag.

Lexi slowed her steps when she saw Kate on the phone, probably to give Kate privacy. Kate didn't feel the need for that around Lexi, so she lifted her hand and waved her toward the chairs.

"Did the doctors say how long that might go on, the swelling and the coma?" Zack asked.

"Five days." She flipped the page in her notebook. "The first goal of his treatment was resuscitation. They did that at the accident site. And now they're focused on minimizing complications. There's a doctor here called a neurointensivist who is in charge of coordinating his care. She's the woman I spoke with. Dr. Michele Carlon. I filled out paperwork, so you can speak directly to her and to the hospital and get the new information. I'm just catching you up with what I know."

Lexi slid into the seat one down from Kate and used the chair between them as a table. She wrestled one of the cups from the carrier and handed Kate a cup of hot tea.

"I appreciate that, Kate," Zack said. "If he's in a coma, how do they tell how he's doing?"

Kate took a sip of the tea, heavy on milk and sugar, tasting warm and sweet, and smiled a thank you toward Lexi before she continued. "They have a monitor inserted into his brain tissue. It tells them about his brain oxygen and cerebral blood flow. They have it bolted to his skull. I'll text you a picture."

"That's okay," Zack said, and he sounded a little green around the gills. Zack wasn't great around blood, which made his old job as a SEAL a bit of a head scratcher.

"They also stuck a catheter in the ventricle of Ryan's brain to drain off excess fluids."

There was a pause then Zack said, "I had no idea he was taking off until I found the letter on his bed."

"Yeah, he hunted me down at my hotel to hand me the divorce papers, because one death in a day wasn't enough, apparently, and he wanted to kill our marriage, too."

"I'm sorry."

"I didn't sign them. He's going to have to get better, and then fight me tooth and nail before I'll allow him to divorce me."

"He was trying to protect you and give the baby a chance at a normal life. Ryan and I are both friends with Striker. You haven't met him yet, but you know his fiancée, Lexi."

Kate glanced at Lexi, smiled, and got up to walk through the stairwell doors, so she wouldn't overhear her name.

"You know that Lexi is in mourning. Ryan saw Lexi, and even though she's torn up by her husband's death, she's found love again with Striker. Ryan thinks that could be the same for you. The sooner he cuts you loose, the better your chances."

"I'm an adult. I can make up my own mind about what I feel is right for me. And Lexi's being a widow is not the same as me being rejected by my husband and him divorcing me. That's a false equivalent, and quite frankly, patriarchal and insulting."

"Kate, I don't have an opinion. I'm merely telling you what Ryan's thoughts were. Let's change the subject. I know you just got there, but have you made plans? Where are you staying? At the risk of sounding patriarchal and insulting, I hope you'll stay with Lexi. She's good people, and I'd hate to think of you alone in a hotel room."

"I don't think I can stay here at all. First, Ryan doesn't want me in his life, so if he knows I'm in his room, it could impede his getting better. And second, I made a commitment to a class full of students. If I was helpful and a positive here, you couldn't drag me away. But being here just to stake my ground, seems selfish."

"I'm not disagreeing, though I'd choose other words. You can check in throughout the day and come back when he's awake. Scarborough is only a four-hour drive."

"I hate trying to act like an adult right now." Kate scraped her hair back from her face. "I'd much rather throw a temper tantrum in the middle of this stairwell and scream about how unfair it all is."

"Yeah."

The silence that followed felt comfortable. Just knowing how much Ryan was loved and respected was helpful. After a moment though, Kate told Zack that she'd send him a text of names and contact numbers he would need. And then said good-bye.

Kate slid back into the seat near Lexi.

"I brought you a snack. Some protein and some salt. I find that helps." She held out the bag.

Kate looked in at the wrapped sandwich. Nutritionally, these were the right things for her to eat. Emotionally, Kate would have preferred a scotch.

"I know Dr. Carlon personally," Lexi said. "She was my neurointensivist. Twice."

Kate wasn't sure if she should ask questions about that or not.

"I was attacked once, and about a year later I was in a near-death accident. My story is similar in some ways to Ryan's. I'm telling you this because I feel that Ryan is in very good hands. Dr. Carlon and her team do cutting-edge research and are out of the box thinkers."

"But you're fine," Kate said, then stumbled around to back away from those words. "Seem fine. So did Ryan on the surface. I'm sorry, I shouldn't have assumed. I know better. Wow, was that disrespectful."

"I'm not fine," she said kindly. "But I am okay. I have some complications that I live with. Nightmares, anxiety, sometimes… well, it's an invisible disability. I'm always concerned about exacerbating my injuries, hurting my head again." She reached in the bag, pulled out the sandwich, and unwrapped it. "Once, I hit my head by accident and went in for a check-up. My doctor suggested I just wear a motorcycle helmet whenever I was awake." She chuckled as she pressed the sandwich into Kate's hand. "I'm glad Ryan was wearing a helmet. He has a chance. And I'm glad you have him on your insurance. He can be here."

Kate brought the food to her mouth mechanically, took a bite, and knew that she needed to eat it. It felt good to have something in her stomach. And it gave her some quiet time in which to think.

After Kate had balled up the wrapper and placed it back in the bag, Lexi said, "I have my guest room set up, should you like to stay. And, if you'd like company, Beetle and Bella are good feet warmers at night. Both can lie very still. And I find, when things crawl out of my emotional basement at night, they're good to pet. They seem okay sponging up the uncomfortable emotions. I'd be happy to share one of my pups with you. Though, I always need at least one of them in bed with me."

"You're really kind. I was just talking to Zack and telling him that I'm kind of useless here right now. I only have so many sick days and personal days to expend. I already used one for Tony's funeral. I need to keep my insurance. I can't lose this job."

She nodded.

"If I'm at school Monday, then maybe I can come up Friday after my last class and spend the weekend with you? No wait, you'll be gone to the field training exercise with your dogs."

"No worries. I can give you a key and the alarm code. You've been to my house. Your bedroom will be the yellow one in the front of the house. Though I can show you all that when we leave. I planned to have you stay the night at my place."

"Yes, thank you. I'd appreciate that."

"Good." She smiled. "Oh, wait. I have an idea. With Striker and the team down range, I'm doing computer work this week. I can do that from anywhere. What if I followed you home tomorrow, well as far as Blacksburg, then I come to your school Monday morning with the dogs? I can do that lecture we talked about, and you don't need to be in front of the class all day, trying to hide your emotions. It'll give you a little time to adjust."

Kate paused, but only for a moment. The respite would be really helpful.

"You know what? I'm going to take you up on that. Thank you." She looked up the hallway toward the telemetry wing.

Lexi squeezed her hand. "We're only projecting good things. We won't focus on any negative what-ifs. Facts. Science. Data. And hope."

Kate nodded. "Hope."

16

───────

SUNDAY NIGHT

KATE WAS JUST CLIMBING into her bed at Aunt Emma's Sunday evening with her Kindle in hand when her email dinged.

It sent a spark of adrenaline through her system.

She was so afraid that more bad news was going to come in about Ryan.

But, of course, that was kind of silly. They'd call. They wouldn't email the news.

Nevertheless, Kate pushed the wedding ring quilt to the side with trepidation as she went to check.

It was from her principal, Mr. Caldwell: **Call me.** Followed by his phone number.

Kate's hand shook as she picked up her phone to dial. Was she in trouble? Maybe someone's parents had complained that she'd taken the kids into the woods.

"Mr. Caldwell? It's Kate Hamilton."

"I understand you found a watch on the school grounds," he said without a hello.

"I did. I found it on the east side of the school in the woods. But how would you know that?" she asked.

"I've had two emails today come in saying that I was at the range on the day that the watch registered shots fired from their location. They gave your name and our school phone number to make contact."

"Oh, is it yours?" That was perfect! She could definitely use this for her class, then her class could make a show of giving it back to Mr. Caldwell. This was *excellent*.

"No, it's not mine," he said, dashing Kate's hopes. "There are processes for dealing with things of value that are found at the school."

"Yes, sir, I'm aware. However, I was trying to find the owner. Since the students found the watch on a clue trail, I wanted to see if I could find the owner and then talk about investigators and the role they play vs the role of a CSI."

"Regardless," his voice was tight and angry, "that should have been a discussion we had."

Kate couldn't understand why he sounded so riled. It was a watch that was found in the woods. She hadn't even been back to the school since she'd discovered it to follow the protocol or discuss it with him.

"Rules are rules. Bring it in on Monday."

"Yes, sir. Oh, in the vein of exposing my students to professionals they might encounter as a CSI, I have landed on a unique opportunity for them. On Monday a friend of mine who is on a K-9 search and rescue team is visiting in our area. She will be bringing her dogs in to tell the students what they do and answer questions. I think—"

"I can't have those dogs in the school. Students have allergies."

"All right." Kate worked to modulate her tone. She really wasn't in the mood to deal with any of this right now. "How about if I had the handler and her dogs in the parking lot and any of my students with allergies could either stand well back or could stay in the library during our class time? This really is a unique opportunity, and I will be logging this with the STEAMing Ahead Program in the hopes that they'll afford more grant money to our school district when they see the students engaging in meaningful experiences like this."

"Parking lot? All right. Your friend is credentialled?"

"With her dogs? Yes. And her job is in intelligence work. She works with the FBI and the CIA, so I'm sure she's been through all kinds of background checks." Kate was stretching. She knew that Iniquus was a for hire bridge between different intelligence agencies, and Iniquus was hired in to do things like rescue folks from pirates in Djibouti. But she didn't know what Lexi did. And she didn't know what kind of checks on Lexi's background had been performed. But Kate had to assume that if she were in that building with all those secrets, that she had been significantly vetted.

"Fine. All right. But you need to bring the watch in and log it into lost and found. Once you've done that, because of its value, we'll call the police and hand it over to them."

"Yes, sir." Yeah, that sounded like the thing Kate should have done from the start. But she'd been curious and excited.

From the time she was little, her mother had cautioned her, "Katie, you be careful now, you know how curiosity killed the cat."

Kate had never really learned her lesson.

17

KATE STOOD in the hallway with her classroom door locked behind her.

Her students swarmed around her as the rest of the students moved toward their classes, trying to beat the bell and a tardy slip.

When the last door was shut, Kate grinned at her class, a shhh finger to her lips and her other hand over her head, calling for silence.

"I have a surprise for you," Kate said.

Everyone stilled.

"Remember the evidence trail I laid for class last Wednesday?"

The students shifted on their feet. Kate felt that same wash of anxiety run through their ranks. She hadn't forgotten, but Kate had thought at the time it was the odd weather and dark woods that had set them off. Today was absolutely gorgeous.

Kate hesitated, wondering briefly if this was a good idea or not. In the end, this was too good of an opportunity to pass up.

And the dogs were both here, that should help calm her students' nerves.

"I have a guest here today. She has two scent trained search dogs with her. First, I'm going to introduce you, then she'll do a demonstration, then we can do a question and answer. Because of regulations, Mr. Caldwell has asked that we be outside while the dogs visit us. Does anyone have a dog allergy?" She looked around.

No hands were raised.

Now there was a wave of excitement. Smiles lit her students' faces. They moved en masse toward the side doors and out into the parking lot.

I walked them over to Lexi's SUV, she had the back up and Beetle and Bella were lounging with their front paws draped over the lip of the cargo area, sniffing at the air.

Lexi did a hand signal; the dogs looked the students' way but didn't move.

"Class, this is Mrs. Sobado. She lives and works in Washington DC. Her dogs are Beetle and Bella. They're Dobermans. And these dogs have a very special function. Lexi?"

"Hey everyone. How about a show of hands how many of you have owned dogs?"

The hands shot up.

"How many of you who have owned dogs who worked for you, used them for herding, hunting…?"

Most of the hands stayed up.

"Beetle and Bella are hunting dogs. They hunt a scent, so for example, if a bad guy jumped out of his car and ran into the woods—" she pointed behind her at the tree line, "then my dogs could sniff the seat where he'd been sitting, pick up the scent, and track that scent to find the suspect."

The class grinned.

"The other thing they've been trained to do is find human remains. They're certified in HRD, human remains detection."

Dakota stuck his hand up but didn't wait to be called on. "There's lots of dead stuff in the woods. Wednesday on the clue trail there was a dead racoon."

"HRD dogs are trained to only find and indicate on remains associated with humans."

Another hand shot up. "Can the dogs tell the difference between blood from a live person and blood left by a dead body?"

"Great question," Lexi said. "They smell the same to the dogs. Once the blood leaves the body, whether that body was alive or deceased when the blood left the body, that blood is no longer being oxygenated and receiving nutrients, so it starts to decompose. So no, there is no scent difference between a live subject's blood and a deceased subject's blood."

"How old could the scent be? Like, do the dogs have to find it in a certain amount of time?"

"Another good question." Lexi reached out to scratch first one dog, then the other. "The answer is they can detect extremely old cases. My dogs, while they were training, were part of a search effort to find an old pre-Civil War family burial plot. And they were successful. The remains in that area were almost two hundred years old."

The students nodded.

"Can we pet them?"

"Let's hold off until the end. They tend to get riled up when they get loved on, and we want them to be focused as I show you how they work. This morning I placed a tooth out in the woods. The dogs will work off lead. If they were tracking and found someone they would come back and sit at my feet and raise a paw. Since we're looking for human remains, once they make their find, they'll lie down and will send up a howl. Not all search dogs do that, most don't. That's just what my girls do. Each team is different and unique. Are you ready?"

She snapped her fingers and pointed to her feet. "Time to work."

Beetle and Bella's composure changed immediately as they jumped out of the vehicle. Their bodies were primed. Their coats quivered with anticipation and excitement. Lexi chuckled, then said something in a foreign language.

The dogs' noses went up in the air and both trotted straight into the woods, taking separate entrance points.

"What language was that?" Kristen asked.

"Secret language," Lexi said with a grin. "I don't announce it to anyone. I want my dogs following my signals alone. If a bad guy were to figure out how I direct my dogs, they might try to use my signals against me."

"It was Klingon," Miriam said.

"Bad *guys*, hear that Dakota?" Lucy asked.

"Bad guys is a figure of speech," Lexi said, "but in my experience it's more likely. Now I wanted to show you that the dogs got started on a foreign language signal, once they make a find, I switch to English. So from here on you'll understand."

Almost immediately a howl went up. "That's Bella," Lexi said.

Everyone walked in the direction of the alert.

About thirty strides into the woods, Bella lay with her pink tongue hanging out, looking thoroughly proud of herself.

There was no indication of anything on the path near her.

Lexi approached, waited for the class to make a horseshoe around her then asked, "What is it, Bella? Show."

Bella stood and patted her paw on the ground.

"Away, sit," Lexi said.

Bella stood, moved off the path, and sat down.

"Doesn't she get a reward?" Maryann and Beth asked simultaneously, both sounding indignant that a treat wasn't meted out immediately.

"We have to prove she deserves it, first." Lexi bent where Bella's paw tapped. She brushed at the dirt, uncovering a plastic top with holes dilled into it. She pulled out a shallow container and held it up so everyone could see the tooth. "*Now* she gets her treat."

Lexi pulled a bag from her pocket.

Kate wondered where Beetle had gotten off to and turned to scan. There, right behind her, stood a thoroughly ticked off Mr. Caldwell.

18

KATE PUT a hand to her throat as she took a step back, so Mr. Caldwell wasn't right up on her. "Hey there, I don't know how much you saw, but Bella just found the buried tooth." She tried to smile. "I'll introduce you to Mrs. Sobado in just a moment. She needs to reward her K-9."

"I thought I told you to bring the watch to the front office this morning."

"You told me to follow the protocol, yes. You didn't mention first thing this morning. As we have a guest speaker, I wanted to help her get set up before the bells rang.

"Where's Beetle?" a student called out.

Lexi let her gaze search amongst the trees. "I don't know. She's off searching. I'll call her in in a moment. Eventually, she'll make her way back here to the tooth."

"You brought the watch?" Mr. Caldwell asked.

And his persistence made Kate feel protective of it. "It's in my car. I'll get it after I'm done teaching. I'll bring it right to you if it makes you feel better. You got the emails about the watch because I was trying to find the owner. It's not like I'm trying to steal the thing." Okay, that sounded a little more self-defensive than Kate felt about the watch. But she had some red flags going up for her. One was, Kate realized in a flash of awareness, that the last time there was a record of a shot fired on the watch was April two years ago.

And the teacher, Carolyn Lambert, had disappeared in that time frame.

A chill washed over her.

Maybe she'd found a clue to Carolyn's disappearance. And maybe what she found was a watch that had its memory filled two years ago, and those two time periods overlapped. The watch could have been lost yesterday, she scolded herself.

It was bad science to jump to conclusions.

It was bad science to have an emotional reaction.

But Kate decided that before she did anything with the watch, she'd call Tim and ask him what he thought, since Aunt Emma said he'd helped with the case.

Just then, the school bells rang.

Time had flown out here in the woods.

"Class," she called out, "I'm going to walk you to the edge of the woods and watch you get back to the school building. I want to stay here and help Mrs. Sobado with her dogs and set up for the next class who is coming out after first lunch. Let's keep this a secret, so they can be surprised, too."

Mr. Caldwell stared hard at the tooth in Lexi's container. Then turned. "I'll see them in. Let's go," he growled, then strode off.

"Wow," Lexi said, once they were alone in the woods. "He's kind of intense, isn't he?"

"Yeah, it makes me wonder."

"About?"

"I told you there was a missing teacher, Carolyn Lambert. Our principal, Mr. Caldwell," she pointed toward where the class had walked down the path, "is still a person of interest."

And that's when the howl went up that lifted the fine hairs on Kate's body.

"That's an alert. Beetle made a find," Lexi said, putting her hand on Bella's collar and her other hand on Kate's arm. "I only planted the one clue."

Kate was doing some deep breathing as she followed behind Lexi. Her limbic system was bright with awareness. She could feel her senses stretching out to keep her safe. She thought about that walk in the woods she was about to take with the killer last June, not yet aware that she was on his kill list.

Tim might not like her out in the woods right now, but Kate wasn't about to abandon Lexi.

Bella was snapped onto her lead and was walking at Lexi's side. Flanking might be a better word. Bella looked like she was on a mission, focus level at code red.

The woods had an eerie feel.

"Whatever you're imagining right now, clear your mind," Lexi said. "Beetle could have found an old gravesite, or she could have found a place where someone walking through cut themselves and left some blood."

"Definitely human, though, right?"

"Right," she called over her shoulder.

Beetle sent up her signal again.

Lexi looked toward the parking lot, then toward the place where Beetle had signaled.

Kate followed Lexi's gaze. She imagined in her mind how far they were from Beetle and how far Beetle was from the parking lot. "Less than a hundred yards to the cars," Kate whispered.

"That's what I calculated, too."

And in that calculation the stakes for what they'd find were raised.

In novels and on TV shows, bodies were hefted over someone's shoulder or dragged in a tarp deep into the woods, the criminal would dig a grave, a nice deep grave where the creative who came up with the plot line would show them standing shoulder deep, throwing soil over the top.

That just wasn't the reality of things.

Dead weight was heavier than live weight.

It was difficult to maneuver.

Holes were horrible to dig. Especially in the woods where rocks and roots would stop the progress.

What criminals would do is drive up to an overpass with water underneath and throw the body in. The other thing they would do is follow the fictional plot line. They'd go to a woods and try to get the body way, way, way back. But even the biggest and strongest of men couldn't get a body but so far before they were exhausted.

A hundred yards was about it.

Lexi, as a searcher, would know that.

Kate stopped and looked around.

They were now standing on the path where she had laid out the clue trail. She held perfectly still, in a squat, fingers pressed into the dirt.

Lexi signaled her dog and came to an immediate stop. "Are you okay?"

"The watch," Kate said.

"You found it near here?"

"The students did. Somewhere on this path. I have pictures of it."

"A big guy wore that watch," Lexi said.

Kate tried to remember Mr. Caldwell's wrist. He wasn't big in an athletic sense. He was a big guy though.

"Okay," Lexi said calmly. "We might have a situation on our hands. Just from where Beetle is, and the watch mystery, my antennae are up. I don't want to mess up any forensics if forensics are needed. But I need to get Beetle. And we need to have something verifiable before we call in to the police. Here's what we're going to do. We're going to walk on hard surfaces as much as possible. We're going to walk single file, where I step, you step."

Kate nodded.

"When I get to Beetle, I'll put Bella in a down stay next to you. I'll walk in, take a look, and make a decision."

"Okay."

And that's how they proceeded, but it wasn't very much farther.

There lay Beetle, her coat shimmering in a little stream of sunlight.

The sun had creeped through a hole in the tree canopy where an ancient oak had toppled, exposing its roots, and leaving a concave depression in the soil.

"Not good," Kate said.

"How about you wait there?" Lexi said, then signaled Bella, who pranced over and lay at Kate's feet.

This was what criminals looked for in the woods.

A large hole from where the roots of the tree were pulled from the ground.

After dragging the body as far as their strength and energy would let them, they'd contemplate digging a deep enough grave, and they'd just have no more energy to give. And truth be told, if they took the clothes, a root burial was an effective way to dispose of a body that would allow for quick decomposition from exposure to moisture, bugs, and scavenging animals.

When they found a tree that had fallen with the carved depression where its roots were pulled from the soil, it was a simple matter of pulling out the accumulated debris, dropping the body in, and pushing the debris back in place. The longer the body went undiscovered, the more camouflaged it became as the bones mineralized to the colors around them and more debris landed and decomposed along with the body.

Lexi picked up a stick and lifted a mat of leaves. Holding that in place, she pulled her phone from her pocket, snapped several pictures, then gently lay the stick straight down, and snapped pictures of her disturbance. She took pictures of Beetle laying in place, nose pointing exactly where Lexi had lifted the debris.

Now the two were tracing their steps back to Kate.

"Have you seen pictures of the teacher? Did she have long blond hair?"

Kate knew that bones, teeth, and hair were the last to decompose. "Carolyn Lambert? Yes, she was a blonde."

Lexi nodded and tapped zero on her phone. "Operator, could you connect me to the non-emergency number for Boonestown, Virginia Police? It's urgent but not an emergency."

19

———

MONDAY

KATE LAY in a deep tub of hot water still trying to comprehend today.

While Lexi was on the phone with the police department, Kate had called Tim. She was little afraid of what he'd say about the sequence of events that landed her at a crime scene, but if Tim was upset with her, he modulated his tone so she wouldn't know.

Which was a good thing.

Pregnancy hormones, coupled with fear and grief hormones, coupled with the horror of the discovery—even if she didn't see anything herself—was about all the bad feelings Kate thought she could heft that day.

She'd handed over the watch to the detective, outlining what she'd learned about it, and what steps she'd taken since she'd found it. She ended with her description of the talk with Mr. Parscale at his house.

Tim was supposed to come over tonight after he'd helped Pam

put the kids to bed, so he could pick up her print out from the jeweler.

The more she thought about the watch, the more questions she had about the technology.

The advertisement had said that a hunter could press one of the buttons and store waypoints. That was a function of a GPS.

Kate hauled herself, pink fleshed and warm from the bath, toweled off, and pulled on a pair of sweats and a shirt.

She put the papers in front of her and looked up Sunko on the web. They were a California based company. She looked at the clock and subtracted the three hours, yup, someone should still be around. Kate tapped at the bottom of the webpage where it said technical support and dialed the phone number that popped up on the screen.

Her wait time wasn't but a few minutes.

"Hi there," she said and was at a loss how to proceed.

The man introduced himself as Daryl. "Are you calling about a watch that you've purchased?"

"No actually, I'm calling about a watch that is a bit of a mystery." As soon as that popped out of Kate's mouth, she wanted to backtrack. That wasn't a good way to do this. "Actually, I found a watch, and I was trying to get it back to the rightful owner."

"Hmmm," he said.

"I took it to a jeweler who gave me a download of the shots that were registered on the watch. But the last shot was more than two years ago, and that doesn't seem very helpful."

"If you don't have the registration number…"

"No, I don't. But I did have a question. The ad said that the watch can register waypoints. That requires GPS tracking. Like a phone that pings off cell towers, isn't that right?"

"That's right."

"But the jeweler said that this watch doesn't record that, it only registered waypoints and shots fired."

"That's to preserve as much memory on the watch as possible. The GPS is continually following the watch."

"That's what I thought you'd say. But that's not stored, and I'm not sure how that works with the memory. That information has to be somewhere doesn't it?"

He waited a beat. "Why do you ask?"

"I thought I could follow the GPS to the owners house and hand him back his watch." Actually, she wanted to know if the watch moved from the Parscale house to the woods at the school.

"Yes, well, that data is stored in the owner's cloud account. The owner could access it, but no one else can. And an owner wouldn't know to ask for the information. We don't advertise the cloud memory on the hunting watches."

"Why not?" Kate asked. "I would think that would be a selling point. They could track their hikes and game trails, what have you."

"That's our cross-country hiking watch. Same design, same technology, different client. A hiker wants to track where they've been. Our hunters tend to not be as trusting. They're a little suspicious of Big Brother and government intrusion."

"I get that," Kate said. "But if there were a warrant, that information could be accessed?"

"Sure, I suppose. Why did you say you were asking questions?"

"Oh, now I'm just being curious." Kate smiled as she said it to lighten her voice and make her sound conversational and not like she was interrogating the guy. "Thank you so much for your help. At least I know this isn't a path I can take to get the watch back to its owner. Have a nice night."

Kate hung up.

She turned the first page of the watch printout over. She noted the website, Daryl's name, the phone number, date, and time. Then she noted what he said about the continuous GPS tracking that was held in a cloud account. That right there could exonerate the owner from any wrong doing. And conversely, it could track a killer in real time right up until he'd carried the body into the woods.

Kate contemplated how that might have happened. Hyped on adrenaline and fear, the murderer was taking the body back into the woods for burial.

Why the woods at the school?

Personal connection? A personal story? Part of the how and why of the murder? Someone with a connection to the school. Or someone who wanted to be close to the body…

Mr. Caldwell's name popped into her mind. She let that thought slip right on out, again. She knew better than to try to frame the narrative without evidence. And no one had verified that the body Beetle had discovered belonged to Carolyn Lambert.

But someone had buried the woman's body.

Someone could have tripped and fallen, broken the catch, and been unaware as they hefted the body back up, that the watch was dragged from their wrist and left behind.

They might have even discovered it later and gone back to look for it. But unless they did what Kate's student did, and lay with an ear to the ground, the person wouldn't have seen it there under the log.

That reminded Kate, she pulled up the photos of the evidence trail and downloaded them onto a flash drive. She'd hand that over to Tim, as well.

Kate turned the jewelers print outs over and looked at the highlighted places.

Caldwell had received two of the possible three emails. It could be he was only in the right place at the right time twice, or it could be that only two places had sent them. Or maybe, they didn't want to mess with it and just sent an email to all their members, no matter the date and time they'd gone or not gone.

Kate turned the paper over and noted that information for Tim.

She looked at the map of Parscale's home, letting her thoughts bubble up.

There was almost a year's lag between the date the shots were fired at the last range on her list, and the shots fired from the Parscale property.

She pulled up a search for the date when Carolyn went missing.

No, there wasn't an apparent connection.

The last shots fired at the Parscale property happened a full two weeks after Carolyn's disappearance.

It didn't have to be Carolyn out there in the woods, Kate reminded herself. But Kate knew in her gut that it was. She'd lay a good wager on it.

Bets and speculation were poor science. "Good thing I'm not a detective," she said out loud as she picked up her glass of water and drained it down.

Now here was a story line that could work with this time frame, Kate thought. Carolyn went missing. Searchers, both townsfolk and professional, came in and did their best to track Carolyn down and didn't find her. The searchers in Boonestown would have come and gone. If Carolyn was still alive and held prisoner somewhere, no one would have found her—the dogs wouldn't have found her.

What if the watch did tie in? If these shots recorded on this page were the shots that had killed Carolyn… Maybe she had gotten away and was running out the door, and then someone had shot her.

Mr. Parscale would never have been able to get the body out to the woods by the school by himself.

And why would he need to? He lived in a house surrounded by woods. Heck, he could have had a bonfire out by the pond and burned the body, mixed the cremains with some cement and tossed them in the middle of the water. "That's what I would have done." She told the screen, as she typed "Lambert disappearance, Parscale."

As her eye scanned down the articles, Kate thought, Mr. Parscale was in Florida with family for April. Someone could have known that and was using his house.

She reached out and tapped open an article. This article listed the persons of interest in the Carolyn Lambert case, and then indicated why each couldn't have done it except Mr. Caldwell.

Mr. Caldwell might have fit the watch; he was acting off.

And maybe he had deteriorated over the last two years after his wife left him and as he carried the burden of being a person of interest in a murder. But Kate simply couldn't see him having the physical stamina it would have taken to get a hundred and fifty pounds of dead weight out of his car and back that far in the woods.

A weight lifter, someone who worked manual labor—construction, maybe.

There had been a mention of a Benji Parscale, but the article had said he had been out in the Gulf of Mexico on an oil rig. You can't get much better an alibi than that.

Kate went back to read more carefully. Why had anyone even thought Benji was a possibility? It seemed there was a restraining order. Carolyn had taken an interest in him and had tried to help him get his grades up so he could graduate, but he had read that as more than it was. He'd professed his love to her, and when she told him to leave her alone, he started stalking her.

Yup, he would definitely be at the top of Kate's person of interest list.

Kate looked at his picture. And she didn't get any vibes from him one way or the other.

"But in April, Carolyn disappeared, and the shots were fired and recorded with the watch—whether those things intersect or not—you were on the rig." She told his photo.

In the Gulf. Huh.

Didn't Mr. Parscale say that there was a weather system that cancelled their cruise?

Kate went back to that date and checked for which storms were causing problems in the Gulf. April wasn't a month when she'd expect to see weather events like hurricanes.

But yes, there it was: heavy rains, high seas, coastal flash-floods, and tornadoes.

She looked up oil rig shutdowns for that month. Nothing there, but there was a link that said, "What's the difference between a shutdown and a turnaround?" And that's how Kate learned that refineries had specific times when they closed for maintenance.

She wrote on her list for Tim. "Did anyone ask the company where Benji Parscale was working if Benji was there that April, or if they were even running? Possible turnaround time."

Kate's phone rang. The readout said Suburban Hospital.

And her heart stopped.

20

Monday

"Hello?" Kate whispered into the phone.

"Kate Hamilton, please. This is Dr. Carlon."

"This is she." Kate glanced around the room like she was looking for an escape hatch. Were they calling to let her know Ryan hadn't made it? Was she wrong to have left him there without her?

"Your husband is being monitored and his state has not improved, and it has not deteriorated, Mrs. Hamilton. I want you to know that right away."

"Please call me Kate. Yes, he's the same. Okay, thank you." Not dead.

"I've been in contact with Ryan's doctors in Boston. They've sent his records down, and I have a copy of his latest MRI, which is excellent to have on hand. We will be able to compare what his brain looked like on Thursday before the accident to what his brain looks like after this accident. Of course, that picture will be clearer as the inflammation and fluids go down. It's rare that we have that data for comparison. I'm very excited about that. I'll be able to tell what and even if any further damages developed."

Kate gripped her throat. "Yes," she said. She didn't know what else to say.

"One thing I noticed—no, I think I'm going to back up a little here. My notes say that you're a biology teacher?"

"Yes," Kate said.

"I like to note things like that down, it helps me to know how best to offer information. In your case, I feel I can get a little more technical, but if it's *too* technical I need you to stop me. I know this is a recent event, and you're probably still adjusting."

"Thank you."

"Okay, well, diving in... Studies have been performed on soldiers who have returned from Iraq and Afghanistan who were diagnosed with blast concussions the way Ryan was. It was discovered that a significant portion of them develop a hormone deficiency."

"They did blood work? I don't remember his doctors ever mentioning this to me."

"While about twenty percent of the soldiers coming home are diagnosed with blast concussions, very few, in fact, have their hormones checked, which is a shame, because of those veterans with blast concussions who are tested, around forty-two percent seem to have developed hormone levels that are associated with hypopituitarism."

"Who would check for that? An endocrinologist, right?" Kate asked. "That seems a really large patient pool. Almost half of the twenty percent. That's something like eight out of a hundred soldiers coming home have developed these issues."

"That's roughly correct, a little over eight percent of those who served in the Middle East have this medical condition. And yes, they should be checked by an endocrinologist. But they usually aren't."

"You're telling me this for a reason." Kate slid her feet into a pair of flats and jogged down the stairs.

"Yes, I've looked at Ryan's charts, and I wanted you to know I'm pursuing this aggressively."

"What would it look like, his experiencing a hormone issue versus TBI, or I don't know... PTSD?" She walked out the kitchen door. Standing in the driveway, looking up at the black velvet sky, she watched the galaxy of stars winking at her and felt supported by the heavens. Her emotions had grown too big to be indoors. "They said at the hospital people who have TBIs often exhibit symptoms of PTSD, and you're saying that it's not PTSD, it's a hormonal dysfunction. Well, roughly half the time it is."

"This might account for Ryan's anxiety, depression, feelings of isolation. Anxiety can effect cortisol levels, his fight or flight responses."

"He sometime has dissociative moments."

"Those too might be something that Ryan would find relief from if his hormones were balanced."

Kate felt hope sprouting, and that scared her. "But this isn't for sure, you haven't done any tests."

"I *have* done the tests. I'm sorry I wasn't clear about that. I have done the tests, and I see that this is an issue for him. We've started hormone therapy."

Kate squatted in the driveway. Squeaking, choking noises scratched their way out of her throat.

"I know this is very emotional information. It's a lot to take in."

"He...he might get better? He might be better? Ryan might be all right?"

"He was in a very bad accident. He has a long way to go. But from all the data I have in front of me, I am cautiously optimistic."

Cautiously optimistic, Kate gripped at the phrase. She'd take it and cling to it as hard as she could. She hadn't had anything even close to optimism for a very long time now. "Thank you," Kate whispered.

"I have some other calls I need to make, but let's talk again tomorrow after you have some time to absorb this, and I'm sure, given your background, do a little research."

"Thank you," Kate said. There was absolutely nothing, *nothing*, that she could say that could convey the enormity of her gratitude.

As soon as the doctor hung up, Kate let herself sob. Big ugly sobs that came up from her gut and spilled out into the night.

"Hey," a stranger's voice slurred drunkenly. "What you doing laying in the driveway crying like that?"

21

———————

Monday

Kᴀᴛᴇ's ᴛᴇᴀʀs ᴅʀɪᴇᴅ ɪɴꜱᴛᴀɴᴛʟʏ.

Under the side door light stood Benji Parscale. She recognized him from his picture in the newspaper article.

His eyes were bloodshot and glassy. Was he high? Drunk?

What kind of drunk? Kate had grown up with drunk. Her dad had died from his drinking.

Was Benji a mean drunk?

A stupid drunk?

A violent drunk?

From the set of his jaw, Kate would guess violent. She didn't want to move and antagonize him, but here on the ground was a vulnerable place to be. Without looking around and giving herself away, she tried to find an escape plan. Her car was locked, the house was a trap. Her aunt was gone to the movies with her friends.

There were no neighbors near enough to hear her cry out.

She was alone.

"You're a teacher, aren't you?" Benji asked. "Your name is Kate Hamilton."

"I am. But I don't know who you are. How did you know who I was and where you could find me?"

"It's a small enough town." He shrugged. "Science teacher, huh? I'm particularly fond of teachers." He sent her a wink. "I used to like my science teacher, back in the day. Her name was Miss Lambert."

"You look off balance, why don't you sit down?" If Kate couldn't get up, maybe he'd get down. She gestured with an open hand, as if inviting someone to sit on the gravel drive with you was something that was done.

He nodded and sat.

"Why are you here? Can I help you with something?" Kate asked.

"Oh, yeah. I came for my watch. I got three emails saying you had it. And I got a call from my uncle. He was right mad. He'd told me not to go by his house anymore a couple years back. But he said he know'd I'd been there. He said you'd shown up, slinking around the back of his house, bringing trouble."

"I'm sorry he thought that. I was simply knocking on his back door, so I could return the watch."

"Yeah, I'll take that now."

"I don't have it," Kate whispered.

"What was that?" Benji cupped his hand around his ear. "Did you say you don't have it?" Kate knew from her dad's volatility, that things were ramping up in Benji's system. Funny, Kate thought in a flash of insight, even when Ryan was having a dissociative episode, she'd never been afraid of him. *This* she was afraid of.

"I'm so sorry. I don't have your watch anymore. When I couldn't find the rightful owner, I told the principal, and he asked me to give it to the police for their lost and found. Which I did. I'm sure you can get it there."

"You gave my watch to the police." He looked like he was chewing that over. "How did you know how to look for me in the first place?"

His voice filled Kate with cold dread.

"I looked it up on the Internet." *Tim is coming. He's putting the kids to bed and coming right over.* "I saw it was a hunting watch. I had to go to Washington for a funeral and took the watch with me." What if Pam found out that Tim was going to see her tonight? Word of Kate's pregnancy had spread like wild fire. Aunt Emma had said it was laced heavily with speculation about the baby's daddy. If Pam got angry or ordered Tim not to come…

Tim might not come.

"Why are you telling me about Washington?" Benji asked.

"Because they could tell me…" Kate didn't know how to tiptoe around this. This seemed a thin tightrope over a deep chasm. "I thought they could tell me who had registered the watch, so I could mail it to the owner. It's a lovely watch. I thought you'd like it back."

"I liked that watch, but I lost it."

Kate sat silent.

"You're good at finding stuff."

Kate didn't like where this was heading. She didn't know how to steer the conversation in a safe direction.

"You found two of my treasures. I'd say that was pretty good." His eyes were unfocused and travelling about. He worked his jaw and nodded his head.

Kate needed a plan. She needed it now. Her phone was in her lap, but she couldn't imagine that Benji would let her swipe her emergency app and signal she needed help. And honestly, Tim was right. She couldn't imagine anyone was close enough to get here in time to help her.

And her baby.

"I guess I found your watch," Kate said. "I'm really glad for you that you'll get that back."

"And you found Miss Lambert where I planted her under the tree."

"What?" Kate asked. Now any guess work and speculation was gone.

Confessions meant danger.

Confessions meant the murderer wasn't afraid for you to know their secrets.

Benji had killed Carolyn and brought her to the woods at the school. Kate glanced at his arms, his wrists. His muscles were like steel from his job on the rigs. He would have needed the wide circumference of that band.

Kate's lips were sticking to her teeth.

"You know, I thought I'd be sad when Miss Lambert had to die. But I wasn't." He shook his head. "It was actually kind of fun killing her. I liked it."

He paused as if he were remembering. The right side of his face pulled up in a smile. He nodded. "Yeah, that felt real good. I liked it."

In the distance an engine powered up the hill.

Benji turned his head to look, and Kate's hand shot out, without any thought or plan and grabbed the metal lid on the trash bin. She wound up and cracked it against Benji's head with the full might and wrath of a mama bear.

She felt it—the biology of survival. It boiled in her blood. She swung again as she leapt to her feet and then swung out a third time.

Benji was on his feet, yelling at her. Tall. Huge.

Kate kicked at his knees.

She screamed as loud and long as she could to warn her aunt

not to come if it was Aunt Emma, who'd parked in the drive and to maybe get some help if it was someone who could help.

"That's right fight me. I like that!" Benji grabbed her wrist and was pulling her in as he bent down, his lips extended for a kiss. Kate grabbed at his belt to use as leverage, and she slammed her knee up into his crotch again and again and again.

"Kate!" A man's voice yelled.

Kate was driving her knee into Benji fast and hard.

"Kate, back away, now!"

That was Tim's voice.

She focused on what Benji was doing. He gripped at his crotch with one hand and held his other up in surrender. His face was slashed and bloody. His eyes disoriented.

Kate turned to see that Tim had his gun trained on Benji.

She backed up. One step then another and another until she was at the kitchen door.

She walked in and turned the lock behind her.

She was okay.

Her baby was okay.

Tim was outside, arresting the bad guy.

Carolyn's family could mourn.

And Ryan—she thought as she slipped into one of Aunt Emma's kitchen chairs—Ryan had a chance.

All this might take a minute for her to absorb.

This was a lot.

"But we're okay, little guy." She rubbed her belly. "We're okay. I'll do everything I can to protect you. I love you. I'm really glad I get to be your mommy."

This is not the end, keep turning the pages to follow along with novella three, OURS.

OURS

A KATE HAMILTON MYSTERY NOVELLA
THREE

Ours is a work of fiction. Names, characters, places, and incidents either are the product of the author's imagination or are used fictitiously, and any resemblance to actual persons, living or dead, business establishments, events, or locales is entirely coincidental.

PROLOGUE

Sunday

The January air nipped at Kate's nose as she stood on the gravel drive beside her great aunt's house. Kate was wrapped in her husband Ryan's black winter jacket, which hung almost to her knees. She liked to wear it because it smelled like him. Somehow, that was comforting, like he'd wrapped Kate up and was keeping her safe—even if that was all just wishful thinking.

Last June, Kate left their house in Boston to stay with her great aunt, giving Ryan some space and some time to get himself to a safer place following a traumatic brain injury he sustained in theater.

Ryan was okay with his SEAL brothers stepping up and helping him.

But he was hellbent on keeping Kate away from the fray.

Fine, she'd give him some space. While he was up in Boston, Kate was down here in her childhood home town, wishing she weren't. She spent last summer working on a CSI internship here, then she got a grant to teach CSI sciences at the high school one town over for the fall semester.

September arrived, though, when Kate was sixteen weeks into her pregnancy, and she couldn't keep it secret any longer.

She knew…

She knew all along that if Ryan found out she was pregnant; he would do everything he could to keep his son safe. And her.

In Ryan's great wisdom, he rode his motorcycle down from Boston to get her to sign divorce papers while she was representing him at a fallen SEAL's funeral in Washington D.C.

Ryan thought he was being a hero, letting her off the hook, giving her a clear runway to take off on a new life with a new man.

That thought made Kate nauseous.

Kate tried very hard not to blame herself for the accident that happened just minutes after she tore up those divorce papers and flung them back in Ryan's face.

She'd left to head back to her Aunt Emma's house where she'd been laying low.

Ryan left, presumably to go back to Boston, but a drunk plowed into his Harley, sending Ryan flying through the air.

Into a coma.

A second traumatic brain injury.

And while things had been bad before, at least Ryan hadn't been in physical pain. He was able to play with his service dog, to exercise, to be with his military brothers. He had some semblance of a life.

Now…?

He lay there in his bed at the long-term care facility, refusing pain meds because "the hell he'd become an addict." He lay there with terrible pain that radiated across his head and down his neck.

The experts were trying to figure out the cause; but so far, there were no answers. That wasn't unusual though. It was almost expected, she'd been told.

When she visited Ryan on the weekends, Ryan would only say, "Please. Please. Please sign the papers."

And she would play deaf and dumb.

So today, this coat, wrapping her and her pregnant belly, was a source of comfort at a bleak time.

Kate enfolded her Aunt Emma in her arms. "I'm feeling guilty about leaving you." She ended the hug by rubbing her hands up and down her aunt's arms as if to warm her. "There's room in the house I'm renting. Why don't you come down and stay with me, at least until after the baby comes?"

"You're going to miss my blackberry cobbler, are you?"

"I don't like the thought of you rattling around in this house all by yourself." Kate gestured back at the Georgian home that had been in Uncle Owen's family for generations. When Ryan kicked her out, for her own safety, Kate was on her way here to stay for the summer, and just happened to arrive the same day her uncle died. Her great aunt seemed to have shrunk over these last months. Aged. Grown more diaphanous. Kate was worried about her being here alone.

"I couldn't leave the mountains around Scarborough and be happy. You can understand that. Same with you, hungry to get back to city life and the bustle. You just don't fit here, never did."

"I have to go…with the baby, and Ryan, I have to—"

"Be in a job that has insurance. You tell me this *every* day. You can let that guilt go. Your priorities are lined up right. Your family needs you."

"You're family," Kate whispered.

Aunt Emma patted Kate's arm as Kate's friend Tim rounded from behind the Ford Explorer where he'd tucked her suitcases in the back. "Ready?"

"She's already on a guilt trip. I'd say, the sooner Kate gets herself down the road, the better she'll feel."

Tim caught Kate's eye. "I'll keep an eye out for your aunt. We already have a plan, right Mrs. Jenkins? As soon as Little Guy comes into the world, I'll be driving her to Washington so she can give you a hand."

"And he's going to come pick me up again when I can't stand the city for another second." Aunt Emma poked a finger into Kate's arm.

Aunt Emma was *fine*.

This was going to be *fine*.

"As a member of the police force here in Scarborough, I can't get rid of you fast enough." Tim rocked back comfortably onto his heels and sent her a wink. Tim was the town's detective. The town hadn't really needed a detective—until Kate arrived last June. Then, murders seemed to come out of the woodwork. "I'd agree to almost anything to get you out of town so our crime rate can drop back to zero," he punctuated that with a grin.

Tim and Kate had known each other all their lives, dated in high school, and were back to being—well, more than friends, more like family.

"I'm *trusting* you to watch out for Aunt Emma." Kate sniffed back her tears. She turned to plant a kiss on her aunt's papery cheek.

"Will do," Tim said, as Kate turned her belly out of the way to give him a hug good-bye. "You're going to be fine, Katydid. I have every faith in you." He dropped a brotherly kiss onto her head.

Kate tucked her chin and made her way to the driver's side door, forestalling the sob that crawled up her throat. *Stupid pregnancy hormones*.

Tim held up a hand to wave as Kate slid her ungainly belly behind the wheel.

Thirty-one weeks along, now, Little Guy was due at the end of February.

Too soon.

She needed more time. "It's okay, sweet boy. We'll figure it out," she said softly, shutting her door, and fastening her safety belt low across her hips.

"Call when you're there and safe." Aunt Emma took a step to stand closer to Tim, and he wrapped her in a protective arm.

Kate gave two toots to the horn as she backed out of the gravel drive. Tomorrow would be her first day at her new job, she hoped things would start turning around for her in Washington.

But wherever Kate went, bad things seemed to trail along behind her.

1

———

Monday

Monday afternoon, Kate waddled across the parking lot at William Howard Taft High. Dressed in her CSI-styled maternity khakis, a navy-blue collared shirt, and wrapped in Ryan's winter coat, she paused to wait when she saw Dave pull into a parking spot.

Detective Dave Murphy was going to be co-teaching this class with her. While this special-invitation class met every afternoon, last class of the day, Dave would only be joining her two or three times a week to add his expertise.

"Hey there." She raised her free hand. "Good timing."

Dave held up a finger while he stalled beside his car to answer a call.

Setting her bag by her feet, Kate tucked her hands into her pockets to wait. Kate was pretty sure that Dave was the reason she had her position with the Washington D.C. Police. She didn't know what favors he pulled. It wasn't easy to get a new job when you would be needing maternity leave a couple months into the contract period.

In her new position, during the weekdays, Kate would rotate between various public middle schools doing special presentations for classes. Mostly, this meant that science teachers could get her to step in and teach a class, hand them ready-to-go teacher plans, and follow up assignments. Kate had developed most of her curriculum during her last semester teaching CSI in Boonestown, Virginia. There, she'd gotten a feel for what worked and what fell flat, at least for rural students.

Whether teaching in the lower grades or coming here to the high school for the intensive CSI course, through all her student interactions, Kate was an ambassador for the Washington D.C. Police Department. She was supposed to make them look cool. That was a stretch, making the police look cool while she looked and felt like a sack of potatoes.

She'd give it her best shot, though.

The most important aspect of her job, as she was told by her employer, was to develop a high school curriculum as a recruiting tool.

Okay, that's not quite how they put it.

There was an initiative, that was funding her employment, with several worthy goals. The DCPD wanted to address the need for a diverse police force. They wanted to bring students through the pipeline who had lived in the areas where there was statistically more crime. The thinking was that those who knew the area culture, and had relationships with the citizens, would know best what worked and what didn't work in bringing safety to the streets.

The police also wanted to focus positively on at-risk youth who hadn't yet given in to the streets, helping them with skills, mentorship, and with the successful completion of this class, the opportunity for scholarship money to study in the criminal justice field.

Dave slid his phone in his pocket and made his way over to her.

"I got my roster of students this morning." Kate pulled her hand across her long brown hair as the wind swept it across her face. "All males. Not a *single* female was identified as a possible future police officer?" She stooped to grab the handles of her bag.

"All guys?" Dave asked.

"I thought the goal was diversity. Were they only talking about skin color?"

"Languages, religions, LGBTQA…there was a spectrum. Gender was one of the demographics on the list." He reached for Kate's bookbag to carry for her. "What the heck you got in here, bricks?"

"Presents."

"Gonna bribe them from the beginning, so you're their favorite? Didn't even give me a heads up so I could bring them some doughnuts or something?"

"Doughnuts!" She swung her hand out to catch his arm. "Dave, that would have been a genius first day surprise."

"Too bad it's too late." He slowed his pace, so she didn't have to struggle to keep up. "Only guys. That's a problem. It was the school resource officer and the guidance counselor that sent the invitations last semester. I wasn't involved in all that. It could be that the invitations went out and only the males took us up on this honor." Dave stood about five foot ten, balding, a little paunchy, a little unkept, also incredibly smart and invested in his job from everything Kate had gathered.

"If that were the case, the females should have been brought in and the chance at scholarship monies and your other perks should have been made clearer. Now, if it's the case that no females were invited, and neither the SRO nor the guidance counselor noticed, that's a problem that might have ramifications for the girls across their school experience."

"Egg shells, Kate. We're here as an experiment and a resource."

"Still!"

"I hear you. You sure you want to get bent out of shape before we go in there?" At least he didn't say it in a placating/mansplaining voice. This was more about pragmatism.

"No. I'm not." She took a few paces, trying to stuff her outrage. "*All males*, Dave," she grumbled under her breath. This was the exact opposite issue than what she'd had last semester when they filled her classroom with girls thinking that CSI studies was science-light.

"I'll follow up." He pushed the bar on the door and went in to hold it wide for her. "Remember, we're guests in this school. Our goal, our whole reason for being here, is to make sure we set the stage for future crime solvers."

2

Monday

Kate and Dave made it all the way down the hall before the school bell sounded.

Soon after, the students worked their way into the classroom, sent an assessing glance toward Kate and Dave to size them up, and took their seats.

Kate noticed the way they caught each other's eyes as they sat down and lifted their chins in greeting. They all knew each other already and were friends or were friendly.

Dave took center stage. "Welcome." He turned to Kate and she moved up beside him. "I'm Detective Dave Murphy. I work mostly homicide with the DCPD. I'll be co-teaching this class on criminal justice. I made the decision to go into criminal justice when I was 'round about your age. I got my degree in criminal science, and then started off as a beat cop, learning the ropes. Over time, I worked my way up to my position. I've been a detective for just around ten years now." He looked over at Kate.

"And I'm Mrs. Kate Hamilton." She turned and pointed to the board. "That's my email and my phone number. Please don't hand it out, but it's available if you need my help. I'd appreciate it if you would all text me with your names and emails sometime today, so I can add you to my contacts, and I know who's texting." She paused and smiled. "I've been a teacher for about a decade, as well. I taught biology in Boston up until this year. While I was teaching, I went back to school and got my certification in crime scene investigation with the idea that it would make a wonderful high school science class. Last semester, I taught CSI in South West Virginia. I moved to your city just yesterday." Another pause to smile and assess. The class wasn't warming up to her. "I'm now working with the DCPD in this partnership with the Washington Public Schools. I hope that you really enjoy and will gain from being in this class with us."

They looked back at her expressionless. *Well, that fell flat.*

A student in the front seat stretched his leg out and slid down in his chair, focused on her. "But you never worked on crime just studied it in a book?"

"I'm trained in crime scene investigation. I've also been involved in helping to solve crimes."

"What kind of crimes?" He tipped his head and squinted his eyes. He didn't believe her.

Mmm. Not something she meant to tell them, but if they did an Internet search, they'd know. "Murder." She limited it to one.

"How many?" He sat up and leaned forward, craning his face toward her. "You said crimes."

Observant. And combative. Okay, she and this student might be butting heads this semester.

Lots, Kate wanted to say. But she didn't want to talk about the four teens who died last June. Those boys were younger than these seniors. It still twisted her gut. Still filled her visual field. She was glad that there were people who could do that job day in and day out… Kate certainly couldn't. "Two murderers went to prison," she said as a compromise.

Kate made a quick pivot to gain back control. "My point is that I am trained as a crime scene investigator and not as a detective, like Detective Murphy is. Many of you read crime novels or watch TV and movies about what happens at a crime scene. For the most part, that's purposefully constructed for its entertainment value not scientific correctness. I wanted to take a moment and talk about the differences between detective work and crime scene investigatory work."

Dave caught her eye, interjecting, "Detectives on TV walk up next to the CSIs and look at the body, poke around at any evidence that they might see, pick it up give it a once over, set it down. Some detectives might actually do that. It's not the best practices and can even be held against them in court if they're testifying. I *will* go onto a scene if the victim is alive. If there's plainly a body involved, I wait to be cleared for access."

"Why?" Kate asked as she looked over her class.

"You might be destroying evidence," came from the back.

"Exactly," Dave said.

"But the CSI people are with the police department, right?" a student asked.

"Yes." Kate reached for her book to take roll and start putting names with faces. "Though, they're not necessarily police officers. Some jurisdictions, like here in D.C., have large enough departments to hire CSI techs with that being their sole focus. Where I came from in the mountains of Virginia, there were only a handful of officers, and a single detective. When I did my CSI internship there, I was taking over for one of their officers who had had specific training for that. In small precincts, police have to wear more hats."

"What if they're so small they don't even have that? My mama comes from a little town with a sheriff and that's it."

"Typically, they'll call in someone from the state police to help out," Dave said as Kate picked up her pen.

"Quick roll call. Make sure I'm pronouncing your names the way you want me to, and if you have a preference other than he/him if you would let me know, I'd appreciate it."

She moved quickly through the roster of sixteen names. They had purposefully decided to keep the class size small this first time around. Both from the practical side of doing the experiments to the amount of money they had to hand out for scholarships. If this proved successful, the next class would be bigger.

That success rested squarely on her shoulders.

Kate went to the white board and picked up a marker. "Back to our discussion." *Why two professions: CSI and detectives?* She wrote in even script across the top of the board and underlined it. She turned and the students were all tilting their heads and knitting their brows. She looked back at her neat writing and turned once again to the students, confused.

"They don't teach script here anymore," Dave said.

She picked up an eraser and rubbed out the words. "Sorry about that, they still teach it in the school I came from." She quickly put up the topic again in printed letters.

"Checks and balances," Antonio said.

"Good. Like what?" She jotted down Antonio's words.

"He's a bad detective on the take. He want to plant some evidence, or he want to hide some evidence. No one's there to call him out."

"Okay. That could happen," Kate said with a glance at Dave.

He seemed unperturbed.

"It's a lot to do, right?" Jamal offered. "I mean, one detective has to process the crime scene quick so nothing messes it up. And he's got to talk to folks who saw something quick before they take off and no one can find them, or they forget, or they talk to someone else and change their story."

"Good." She noted that down.

"Yeah." A student leaned out into the aisle. "I'm thinking it might not be corruption. Someone might threaten him. But threats gets smaller if a bunch of people were involved."

"More?"

"They have a bunch of people who documented the same thing and put it in their reports and all. It would be harder to make all of that just disappear."

"I'm sorry, I'm still learning names."

"Oliver," the student said with his hand to his chest.

"Thanks, Oliver. And good. There are threats, there are enticements, these careers have to do with criminal elements. Possibly, people who have killed. It's certainly a factor to take into consideration when making a career choice. In this career, you will have to walk in with a solid code. When my husband was a SEAL, they deployed to parts of the world where no one would know if they did something wrong." Kate was fully aware that she was using her husband's past service as the "it" factor to gain some respect. Wrong of her, maybe. But there it was. "They could cover up just about anything. They walked in, though, with a code. That code kept them focused on right actions even in the face of temptation."

"Yeah," Oliver clicked his tongue, "except that SEAL that was shooting up them women and kids for the fun of it. And he got let off by the president. He didn't work no code."

"It doesn't seem so," Kate said. "The SEALs in his unit did, though. When they were in theater, the team did what they could to stop him, and he was reported and brought before a judge."

"To basically be set free." Royce, he was the one that had started off challenging her, and he still had that defiance in his eyes. "That's what they call entitlement on full display."

"His sentencing isn't up to the CSI or the detective or even the prosecutor." Dave had his arms crossed over his chest, shoulder against the filing cabinet. Not even a tweak of frustration to his emotional volume. "The judge has his job to do, too."

"Pshh," Royce said.

Yup, they'd be butting heads.

"You can disagree about the rightness of that outcome. It's like the SEALs Mrs. Hamilton mentioned," Dave said. "You do your job and pass it on to the next person to do theirs. If you do a *good* job with your evidence gathering and your detective work, it should make the job of those further along the trajectory easier and more fair."

"This CSI stuff isn't just for the police though is it?" Oliver asked. "I mean there are other professions that use it. CIA…"

"The CIA is an intelligence gathering agency." Kate came around and rested her hip on the edge of her desk. "So perhaps some techniques, like fingerprinting, might be used. But yes, not just police, the FBI, the ATF, and other national law enforcement groups need professionals to stop crimes."

"That's what I'm gonna do. I'm gonna join the FBI." Oliver painted a hand down his chest. "I'll be *Special* Agent Winder."

Kate smiled. "Luckily, Oliver, one of our guest teachers this semester will be Special Agent Steve Finley, domestic terror. So future Special Agent Winder, make sure you've done your homework, come in with pointed questions for him, impress him, and see what comes of that." She reached back and tapped her marker on the board to get the young men back into focus. "To sum up. A CSI's job is to scientifically and thoroughly collect evidence and present it without bias to the detective." She held out a hand to Dave.

"The detective's job is to use that information to drive the scope of the investigation, to point to new channels to try to identify the criminal and bring them to justice. Now, there are lots of people that line up and work together. Crime solving is a team sport. You guys play sports?"

"Not on a school team," Antonio said. "But we play basketball in the neighborhood, sometimes challenge other teams to a game."

Interesting that they already hung around together, Kate thought. Maybe that was how they had stayed out of trouble and got invited to this initiative. "In this class we'll be going over a lot of different positions on the team, jobs that maybe you've never heard of before. Maybe one of them will spark your curiosity. Maybe your curiosity will lead you toward your career. As many of you observant young men might have noticed, I am very pregnant. I expect my baby to arrive at the end of February and will be taking six weeks away from the classroom. Detective Murphy will continue to come in, unless an investigation is pulling him away. Though, we don't anticipate that being the case. During that time, I have seven different professionals from fields as diverse as search and rescue team, to criminal and trauma psychologist, to the special agent from the FBI." She stopped to blow out when Little Guy jammed his foot up into her diaphragm. "I hope you're looking forward to learning a lot in our time together. While this class will talk about public safety and crime," she pulled her bag across the table, "another thing we're going to work on this semester is to build your brain skills. Whatever job you have, your number one tool will be your ability to think, to process, and to come up with solutions to problems that present themselves." She pulled a travelling chess board from the bag. It was about the size of a tablet and had magnetized pieces. Kate had found them seventy percent off at an after Christmas sale at the local drug store. She had been mighty pleased with their quality. She waggled the board in her hand. "My greeting gift for you is a chess board. Has anyone played chess?"

The students faces displayed a spectrum from dubious to disappointed. No one was an admitted chess player.

Dave picked up the bag and made the rounds handing the sets out.

"Of course," Kate walked to the board, "you can play chess on the computer. But why might you be better served by playing with an opponent?" She started a list: *You can start to observe body language,* was her first point.

The students started throwing out ideas right away.

"You can work on your own body language so they can't observe you. Like poker, right? A detective's gotta have a good poker face."

"You can learn to be quiet while facing someone," she heard as she jotted the last answer. "What a wonderful observation— why would that be important?" She turned to face the class. "Learning to be quiet while facing someone?"

"We don't do a lot of quiet, music and podcasts in our ears and what all. Someone always pinging our phones. Sitting in quiet means you're building concentration."

"Good. More?" Kate scanned the room.

"People don't like quiet in a conversation when they're uncomfortable. My mama—" Romeo started.

The students snickered.

His mama had a reputation, apparently. Kate nodded to encourage him to finish.

"My mama," Romeo tried again, "she just puts her hand on her hip and tips her head." He acted it out comically. "When she do that. I get so nervous. I start saying anything I can to get out of trouble. She doesn't say anything. She know I handed her a line. She tip her head the other way and raises her brows up." He shifted around to make a face; the class cracked up. "And I try something else. When she presses her lips out into a flat line, I know she's had enough, and I tell her what really happened. She never says a word. It's being nervous around her and wanting to fill in the silence that has me spilling my guts."

"Exactly," Dave said. "Silence is one of my best tools. Build rapport, and then allow someone to vent, tell their story. Ask short questions and sit in silence. Not only might someone explain the truth, sometimes the truth isn't that they did the criminal action, but they did something that would endanger them that they didn't want out there. The guy cheating on his wife might not want to hand you his alibi. It saves a lot of time and effort if you can get to that place and not spend investigatory time on the wrong suspect. Chess, then, builds your capacity to think, to strategize, to try to figure out your opponents' game plan so you can try to outmaneuver them, and you can win the game. This is an important tool. But tools sitting in your tool box won't fix a problem. You have to take them out and use them."

"And get the bad guy in jail."

"That's not the goal," Dave said. "The goal is to get the *right* criminal in jail. Our job is as much about proving the innocent person is innocent as the person who committed the crime committed a crime."

"I want us to be very careful in this class about calling people the 'good guys' and the 'bad guys'," Kate said. "It's a bit on the politically correct spectrum to some people, but there's a reason for us to be careful about this. We aren't looking for a bad guy. That closes the brain down. It makes a specific box. What if it's a good guy who committed a criminal act? Can anyone give me an example of that?"

"Yeah, I can," Antonio said. "There was a guy who was a youth minister and a Boy Scout leader. He was out running a race. Those are all good things. But he run up behind this reporter lady who was live on air, and he slapped her on the a—he uhm…"

"That's okay," Kate let him off the hook. "I think we all saw this on social media."

"So he goes on the morning show and tries to convince people that he got carried away and he sorry."

"Still criminal?" Kate asked.

"Sexual assault is what he got charged with. You don't put your hands on someone's body unless they beg you to." Romeo smoothed a hand over his hair. "Like the ladies do for me."

"Sexual assault," Dave said after the laughter fell off. "On paper, that guy is a stand-up citizen. Someone might put blinders on and say he's a good man who does good things. He's fit and healthy, he has a spiritual life that's also his job, and he gives back to the community. But does the community want this good man to be out and around if he has an impulse control problem with sexual assault?"

Kate was glad Dave was the one to ask that man to man.

Things were defrosting. Interests were starting to spark. Kate felt some of the tension ease from her shoulders as a general "no" rose from the class in response to Dave's question.

"So good man, criminal act. How about a bad man who might be innocent of the crime? Could that happen as well?" Kate put the top back on her marker. "He's got an arrest record as long as his arm. He was in the vicinity. He had a motive. Must be him."

"Then he might get thrown back in the prison for a crime he didn't commit while the person who did the crime gets away," Royce said.

"Exactly." Kate nodded. "In this class we'll refrain from 'good guy' 'bad guy'. We're looking for the *criminal* who committed a *crime*. We're going to find someone or several some-ones we think did it. We don't get to decide that. Only a judge and jury can. So we think this is the person who did the crime, we call them the 'suspect' or even the 'subject of investigation'. Later, that could change to the 'accused' or the 'plaintiff'. And until they are found guilty, a subject cannot be called 'the criminal' in a case." Kate stopped to check the clock and clapped her hands then rubbed them together. "We have just enough time to get you going with your chess sets. I want you to divide up into partners.

We're going to learn how to set up the chess board and what the basic moves are for each of the pieces. Your homework tonight will be to get some exercise after school, and then play a game of chess."

Dave gave them a nod. "This is your first step on your journey to solving crimes."

3

MONDAY

HER BACK WAS KILLING HER. Kate wriggled around to get out of her car. When she got home, she'd put up her feet, put on some mindless television, and fall asleep on the couch after she polished off a peanut butter and jelly sandwich dinner with a glass of milk. She didn't have the energy to cook and clean up tonight. Maybe over the weekend she could batch cook and put a bunch of things in the fridge for next week.

Shopping. She needed to add that to her list at some point. She'd ask Dave where his family did their groceries. Maybe even splurge for one of those services that culled and bagged everything for you, so you just drove up, paid, and took your stuff home.

The thought of carrying grocery bags into the house felt exhausting.

Kate stopped with her hand on the car door to squeeze her knees together while Little Guy punched her in the bladder. "Stop!" she called down to her stomach.

He didn't listen. He never did.

Stubborn, just like his daddy.

She petted a hand over her belly with a smile, and when she thought that Little Guy had gone on to elbow safer parts of her anatomy, Kate shut the car door and pressed the fob to lock it.

Before she could settle in and review the school day—what worked, what didn't, how she should handle tomorrow—she needed to tell Ryan she was safely moved into the left side of Lexi Sobado's duplex conveniently situated across the street from her colleague, Dave Murphy.

Lexi was family, by way of the SEAL code. She was engaged to Striker Rheas, who had retired from DEVGRU—SEAL Team Six. Now, Striker worked at a company called Iniquus. Iniquus did government contract security work. And they were the best allies anyone could have. They had been golden to Ryan—well, "Reaper" as they called him.

One of the Iniquus folks from Strike Force stopped by the long-term care facility every morning on their way to work to feed Ryan's service dog, Houston, then take her out for a run and to potty. Around lunch, someone from their Cerberus Tactical K-9 team picked up Houston and took her for training at the Iniquus K-9 facility until dinner. It kept Houston, who was only two years old, in good working condition. Fed. Exercised… It gave Ryan at least four points of contact throughout the day when fellow retired soldiers were in his room, giving him the kind of stability that Kate wasn't allowed to give him.

Above and beyond.

Thank goodness for Striker and Iniquus.

Other than for them, Kate couldn't figure out a way that Ryan could keep Houston as a service dog. Ryan needed her—Houston, that was.

Displaced by a dog, Kate thought, pulling open the heavy front door to the facility. *Ain't that a bitch.*

That was bitter. Honestly, Kate was grateful for anything that gave Ryan any kind of relief. And she was tired. She wouldn't beat herself up too much about her sour attitude.

Kate signed in at the desk, gave the reception lady a finger wave, then headed down the hall toward Ryan's room.

When she pushed through the door, he wasn't there.

The bed was made.

It always made her panic.

"Mrs. Hamilton," a voice called, and Kate spun with her hand to her throat. "Your husband's in physical therapy. The therapist was running late today."

Kate nodded her head and leaned over to rest her hands on her knees.

"Are you okay?"

Blame it on the baby. "Ha! This kid just took exquisite aim and kicked me in the diaphragm."

"Do you need a chair? Or…"

"I'll just go wait for Ryan in his room." Kate closed her eyes and let out a long hot breath, then rounded into Ryan's room and perched on the corner of his bed, smoothing her hand over the quilt she'd brought down from her Aunt Emma's house. Something that wasn't so clinical and cold as the white cotton blankets that they provided here. The bedspread had been quilted by her Aunt Emma's mother in the wedding ring pattern, but she hadn't told Ryan that.

"You can't fool me."

Kate looked up when Dr. Carlon walked in the door.

"I watched your face when you saw the room was empty." She took a seat opposite Kate.

Kate swallowed. "I keep thinking that… We don't know why he's in so much pain. It could be anything and that anything might just take him away from me."

"About that," she said.

Kate pulled her eyes up. She put her hands on her wide spread knees and locked her elbows out.

"No new news on Ryan's condition." Six feet tall with honey blond hair cut in a short flattering style, bright eyes, and a bit of a pixie smile, Kate had come to lean on Dr. Michele Carlon. She was kind and honest. She was dedicated and tenacious. Yeah, they'd lucked out when Dr. Carlon took on Ryan's case. "I found a study that's underway, and I contacted them about Ryan."

"Okay."

"It's not going to make him better. Our problem right now is that we can't see what's wrong. Our imaging is amazing—"

"But not good enough."

"Exactly. Not good enough." She pulled her phone from her pocket and swiped, looked, and placed it on her knee. "With that in mind, I started looking for a different kind of imaging."

"Okay." Kate kicked off her shoes and laid down on the bed, pulling the pillow around to support her stomach and propping her head up on her hand.

"The Army Research Laboratory and Northwestern U. are working on high energy x-rays that they beam onto human skulls."

"This is on live humans?"

"No, they're using Advanced Photon Source, APS. It's a deeply penetrating x-ray that can view the structure of matter. You can imagine it like a giant microscope that uses high-energy x-rays that are a billion times brighter, but useful on a scale that is impossible for a microscope."

"Are we talking molecular level?"

"And even atomic level."

Kate let out a low whistle. "Why are they using APS on skulls? You said it was the Army Research Lab involved? Is this about soldiers and TBIs?"

"Better than fixing a TBI is preventing one."

"Absolutely."

"They want to understand the mechanics of the skull bones so that a better more protective military helmet can be developed."

"And motorcycle."

"One would hope. So their findings are new. They're still being analyzed."

"You're bringing them up for a reason," Kate pointed out.

"Some of the new data shows that skull bones don't actually move in the same direction, which is what I learned in med school. They've been looking at how energy is dispersed inside a skull when it takes a blow. My thinking was that Ryan's bones moved in a way that was not anticipated, that might be a reason why he has the radiating pains. I called and talked to them about what they could anecdotally tell me, to see if it were something that I could follow up with. They put me in touch with a researcher who's been working on just that problem."

Kate swung her legs around to sit up, hugging the pillow to her. "Yes?"

"He's still in the research phase."

Kate frowned. Dead end.

"He does have a study going. And if Ryan would like to participate, he could add to the body of work. If he participates, the researcher would be willing to share the raw data with me and discuss what that raw data might mean."

"Lots of conditionals."

"We're not going to find the answers in a conventional way."

Kate sucked in a lungful of air, held it, and let it go in a rush, hoping to blow some stress out of her body. "Where is this?"

The door popped open and Houston rocketed onto the bed, bowling Kate over with doggie kisses.

"Sorry, Kate," Tripwire said. "Love is more powerful than commands when you're a two-year-old." Tripwire tugged Houston off Kate, petting the German shepherd until she calmed down, giving Kate a chance to get herself upright. "Where's Reaper?" he asked.

"Physical therapy." The Iniquus guys weren't supposed to leave until they handed Houston to Ryan. "I'm glad to take control of Houston until he gets back. I'm not leaving."

Tripwire didn't look comfortable with that.

"It could be a while. It's fine. I promise. Did she have a good workout today? What was she training in?"

"She's learning to relax draped over my shoulder, in case she ever needs to be hiked out of a situation. It gets her ready for fast ropes and sky diving, things like that."

Kate put her hand under Houston's chin. "You're a brave girl." And she got a full-face lick for the compliment. "I'll tell Ryan. Thanks so much, Trip." She touched her hand to her heart. "I appreciate everything you do."

"No problem." Tripwire gathered the lead and handed it to Kate. "Lay down. Stay," he commanded.

Houston lay down with her head draping off the side of the bed and her tongue hanging out.

"Just call if you need anything. Ridge is picking her up tomorrow." With a nod to Dr. Carlon, he gave Houston a final scrub to the ears and a finger wag. "Be a good girl." And left.

Dr. Carlon looked at Kate and fanned her face. "Wow," she mouthed.

"I can't disagree." Kate chuckled as Dr. Carlon launched herself at Houston to give her a belly rub.

4

Tuesday

"YES but," Royce said, followed by a *tsss* and a shake of his head.

Kate was determined that by the end of the semester she'd win him over. "Great! Thank you, Royce, for cueing me up—'Yes but' is the perfect way segue to this last part of today's lesson."

Eye roll.

No back talk this time, she'd take it. Day two. Baby steps.

"Why does 'yes *but*' stop us in our tracks?" She looked around and got blank stares. "'Yes but' is agreeing and then not agreeing. And when you do it, it closes down creativity and critical thinking. We're training our brains in this class. Why would 'Yes *and*' be different? Give me a problem and let's try this out. Problem?"

A couple of students offered up some problems.

"My kid sister keep telling my girlfriend all my business."

"The hot water shut off in my apartment, and I gotta go to my friend's house to take a shower."

"Yesterday, my mama," Romeo started, and the snickers swept the room. "She tell me I gotta babysit my one-year-old sister. I said, 'Yes, but I gotta lot a homework to do like eat a snack and play basketball for my science class. I don't really have no time for the baby.'"

Kate wrote the sentence out on the board and turned back to catch Romeo's eye. "And how did that conversation go?"

"She whoop my a— butt for that." Romeo made a face that had the class cracking up.

Now to use Romeo's class clowning skills for unity instead of student-teacher division this semester.

"Let's help Romeo out with his mama."

They turned to look at her.

"The 'but' in this sentence"—she underlined it— "is the thing that created the tension. It says that there are no alternatives. What if instead, Romeo said, 'Yes, ma'am. I'm glad to help out babysitting *and* I also have school obligations. Here's my list of things I need to do. This is the time I think it will take me to do them. Can we figure out the schedule so everything can get done by my bedtime?"

"Romeo's mama kick him right out the door," Antonio said. "She'd think he was an imposter being that respectful and responsible. She'd think he high."

"Maybe at first Romeo's mother would be astonished," Kate agreed. "But soon, she'd get used to his maturity." She paused. "Your assignment for this entire semester is to catch yourself before you say, 'yes but' and amend it to 'yes and'. Help each other, call each other out on the 'yes buts' because we're building good brains this semester. Reflexive thoughts like 'yes and' can pave the way to success. They allow you to be creative in reaching your goals."

"CSI is supposed to be science stuff. How does creativity step in? This ain't no music class." Royce asked.

"You don't think Edison was creative when he came up with his idea for the lightbulb?"

"Psh. Edison's a genius." Royce pulled himself up and leaned forward to challenge her. "Ain't no geniuses in this classroom."

"Maybe. I think that depends on your definition. Let's talk about that. Someone name a creative. A musician—"

Oliver leaned into the aisle to catch her attention. "Sir Mix-a-lot."

Kate nodded. "Old School. I like it. Sir Mix-a-lot of 'Baby Got Back' fame."

The class laughed.

"Sir Mix-a-lot is a really great choice for this discussion, thank you, Oliver. Did you all know that Sir Mix-a-Lot rapped Baby Got Back with the Seattle Symphony?"

"What?" Oliver squeaked.

"Seriously. I'd play it for you, but I think I'd get in trouble for the lyrics. It's on YouTube, though, and you can search it when you get home if you're interested in seeing him. It was a pretty amazing performance. Everyone seemed to have a great time." She picked up her phone and started scrolling. "Now, one that I can play for you is a woman by the name of Kelis—does everyone know her?" She looked up briefly then went back to typing into her search engine. "Another classic, 'My Milkshake Brings All The Boys to the Yard.' Here it is." She dropped her phone to her side. "When Kelis was still in elementary school she sang in church choirs and played violin, piano, and saxophone. Her parents kicked her out of the house when she was sixteen because of her behavior. But despite this set back—"

"*And,*" Romeo corrected.

Kate pointed at him and nodded. "*And* despite this set back, Kelis kept up with her education at a music and performing arts high school. Eventually, she got a deal with Virgin Records. Here is one of her songs where she, like Sir Mix-a-Lot, used classical music to add to her contemporary music. Listen to this." Kate pressed the play button and sat on her desk while they listened to Kelis singing "Like You."

Kate hoped she'd scored some street cred points for being able to talk music, albeit older music. "Do you hear that high note? Isn't it amazing?" She stuck her finger in the air to follow the note.

At the end of the song, Kate put her phone back on her desk. "That stratospheric high note was a high F and it comes from the Queen of Nights aria in the Magic Flute by Wolfgang Amadeus Mozart in 1791 at the age of thirty-five. Kelis's song is an example of how music is not created in a void. Music is accumulative. That means that musicians practice, practice, practice songs that have already been composed. From this practice, musicians build their own creativity. Kelis is a creative—she was inspired by Mozart. She used that inspiration to create something new and interesting. Maybe more overtly than most but all musicians are like this. Science, too, is accumulated. Scientists study what is known. They practice the art of being a scientist, they know enough to start posing their own questions. They also know how to search for an answer. Scientists must apply a marriage of creativity and expertise to answer their questions. I'm going to circle around to that in a minute. First, though, I want to address the idea that the students in this classroom are not geniuses."

Nope, they were tuning out. But she'd already started down this path. Maybe she could bring it back around.

"Kelis used Mozart in her music. Let's talk about Mozart and some ways that he and Kelis are alike. Mozart—you all hear about him?" She takes out her phone and plays a couple of minutes from the Magic Flute. "He's known as a genius, Right?"

"Don't mean we want to listen to him, though," Royce said.

She ignored him. "Many people think that Mozart was a born genius. So none of you are destined to be as amazing as Amadeus Mozart, right? You weren't born with that genius in you? What if I told you that probably isn't the case at all. Mozart most likely was born with a musical gift, but not a genius." She walked to the board. And started listing:

Amadeus Mozart

Composing at age 5

Public performance violin and piano 8

Salzburg Court musician as a teen

600 compositions but died in his mid-thirties

SHE READ over each one and punctuated it with a tap of her pen. "Amazing right?"

Nothing by way of response.

"What if I told you that Amadeus's dad, Leopold Mozart, wrote a book on how to teach violin that came out the same year his son was born? Daddy Leopold started Amadeus's intensive violin training at age three, using his child to test the theories that he had written into his book. Amadeus was a science experiment." She tapped the board on 'composing at age 5'. "Of the compositions that little Amadeus created, Daddy Leopold edited two hundred and seventy-one of them." She tapped the six hundred number. "Almost half of them. What did Amadeus have that made him into a genius?" She wrote on the board as she enumerated. "Study. Practice. Mentorship. Intrinsic motivation."

The classroom door cracked open, and Dave stuck his head in. He nodded at her then came in and sat in one of the chairs by the door. This was Tuesday, he wasn't supposed to be here today.

Kate turned back to the class. "When I said that Mozart was

probably born with a gift, I'm talking about 'intrinsic motiva-tion.'" She stopped to take a swig from her water bottle. "Intrinsic motivation is doing tasks out of the love of doing them rather than the obligation."

"What if you do them, and you don't love them like, say, homework?"

She wrote 'external motivation' on the board. "You might have the external motivation to do your assignment because you were told to and if you don't, you will be punished with a bad grade, and a bad grade will affect your GPA, and your GPA will possibly affect your future. Some of you will do your homework for an external motivation. Some of you, though, will do the assignments I give you because it sparks your curiosity and your desire to know more and have command of the subject matter. Some might find criminal justice a topic that makes you feel hungry and focused and inspired." She rounded back to the front of her desk and cast her gaze over her students. "Have you ever done something where you were just lost to the experience, then you look up and hours have passed by?"

"Yeah, playing basketball," Jamal said.

"Good! Yes, athletes talk about that a lot. Artists do too—being lost in the zone. When you're in the zone, things just seem to work. It's golden. Magical." She stopped to smile. "I hope you find your thing that gives you intrinsic motivation. For each of you it's different."

"What you do that's intrinsic?" Jamal asked.

"For me it's teaching. I love it. I love thinking about it. I love doing it. It's what I wake up every morning and want to do. Even at night, even on the weekends, over breaks—I'm always on the lookout for interesting things to share and ways that I can be better. I'm new to teaching CSI. Like I told you, I've taught science for over a decade, but CSI is a new degree and a new subject. I only have one semester of teaching under my belt when it comes to CSI. So I hope you'll be giving me constructive feedback from a student's point of view to help me improve my skills, just as Detective Murphy has promised to help me hone my knowledge base of the subject matter from the depth of his experience in the field. Criticism, even when it hurts, if offered by people you trust to want the best for you, so they help you reach your goals, is a precious gift. Now, today's homework—"

There was a groan.

"Pay attention to every time you hear a 'yes but' or you catch yourself saying 'yes but'. If it's someone else, correct them. Repeat back, 'Yes, *and*.' If it's you who made the mistake, stop and say, 'Excuse me, I meant yes, and.'"

Xavier spun around in his seat. "Yeah, you go home and try that on your mama, Romeo, and report back."

The class guffawed.

"Practice once for me, Romeo," Kate said.

"Mom, can I go play basketball?" Antonio waggled a mother like finger at Romeo. "Yes, *but* you have to do your homework first, and watch the baby, and clean yo room."

"Yes and." Romeo put his hand under his chin and batted his eyelashes. With a smart-alecky voice, he said, "Mama, while I know my homework be important, and I will get it done, my science teacher says it's better for my brain success to take this time to exercise for half hour. I should have a healthy snack before I hit my books—she say that science proves it'll turn me into a genius!" Jazz hands.

"Yeah, good luck with that, man." Oliver reached forward and patted him on the shoulder.

"And there's the bell!" Kate raised her voice over the din as her students grabbed up their books and made for the door. "I need those CSI articles tomorrow, play chess, and remember a half hour of exercise before you study."

"And a good snack," Jamal added.

"I want a report back on how 'Yes and' does for you all. See you Wednesday!"

Whew! Done. Thank goodness. She moved to a chair near Dave and put her feet up.

"Long day?"

"Just a lot going on right now." She sent questioning eyes toward Dave. "I'm surprised to see you here, what's up?"

"A meeting with the SRO and guidance counselor to see how the dynamic happened in this classroom. It's a political problem, and I need to talk to you about that."

Kate frowned.

"This was an initiative that had the best of intentions. If it gets picked up that our diversity program excluded female students, we can get a lot of bad press and bad feelings."

"Rightfully so," Kate ventured.

"Agreed. Just so we're clear, I had nothing to do with the selection. That was delegated to—"

"I'm not blaming you at all. I'm just wondering what's going to happen to make this more equitable."

"They're expanding the program to thirty-two. They'll be finding the sixteen females to invite, and we'll integrate them in."

"Twice the students?" She put her hand on her forehead. "I ordered supplies for sixteen. It's more money. More work getting the resources together. More work getting these students caught up unless they'll be added to the class straight away."

"Straight away isn't going to happen. It'll take a couple of weeks. We have to go through a process. The principal's no happier than we are. It's a mess, for sure."

"Especially because I'll be out."

"We knew that going in. You were by far the most qualified CSI teacher who applied."

"That seems odd to me. I only have the one semester teaching CSI."

"Ah, but you worked the most crime scenes. That background working with police and doing the work hands on, with a decade in the classroom? You were gold. We just hope you don't live up to your reputation around here."

"I have a reputation? I just got here Sunday."

"Sure." Dave rocked his head back with a sarcastic smile on his face. "Your job in Scarborough, you get there and within the first week, you're involved in murders."

Kate pressed her lips together. "I was the CSI intern. Crimes would be an expectation."

"Murder in Scarborough, Virginia? That was not the expectation. The last time there was a murder there was never. Then you get a job in Boonestown. Teaching. The first week you find a clue and start pursuing a murder."

"I didn't pursue a murder. I was simply trying to return someone's watch. That was happenstance both times."

"Two murders? A coincidence. Three? That's just bad juju as Lexi would say."

"I have no intention of being involved with a third murder." Kate swung her feet down and wiggled toward the edge of the chair so she could stand. "I do believe I've filled my quota."

"Good to know." He rubbed the back of his neck. "What are you doing now? Home and resting, I hope."

"I'm going to see Ryan first. There's an imaging study that's in FDA trial that Ryan's doctor found. She was talking to him last night about it when I went home. I wanted to hear what he has to say about the possibility of participating."

"What will that do for him?"

"Dr. Carlon hopes to get images that show her why he's in such constant pain. If she can figure it out, she hopes to fix it. Out of the box thinking, because the straight road isn't getting us to where he needs to be." She stood, remarking how this was getting more awkward by the day.

"Man, I hope that works." Dave grunted to his feet. "Come on, I'll walk you to your car."

"You're not afraid to be walking with me? I mean it is the first week of my new job. With my track record, that you so kindly pointed out, being near me could be dangerous for your health."

5

"THE CLASS SEEMS to be warming up," Dave said, holding the front door for her.

She looked up, startled by the clang of ropes against the aluminum pole as the wind whipped at the school's American flag.

"Just because I linked science to playing basketball, well, exercise. They interpret that as they like." It was a surprisingly warm day for January, and Kate didn't bother to do up her coat.

"Whatever works."

"Amen to that." They moved down the front stairs and toward the teacher's parking lot.

"This imaging thing with Ryan, where is this happening?"

"I didn't ask. I hope to figure all that out tonight." She adjusted her purse on her shoulder. "I don't know how to get him there if it's far. He has to be flat on his back to get any kind of relief from the pain."

Kate's phone buzzed. Since she was thinking of Ryan, Kate

pulled it from the thigh pocket of her tactical maternity pants to make sure it wasn't someone from the care facility. "Romeo," she said as she swiped to unlock and read his text: **My mama out here AND she not happy I'm playing ball. She don't believe this is my science homework. Immabout to get my a** whoop.**

Kate showed it to Dave, and he chuckled.

Kate texted back: **I'm happy to talk to your mother if you'd like to call.**

Romeo: **She think I have someone staging like you. She won't believe you.**

"Smart woman. I wouldn't believe you either if I were Romeo's mama," Dave said. "I bet she's had just about as much of Romeo as one woman can handle."

"Do you think they're far from here?" Kate looked up at Dave.

"They play over on Spring Hill. It's about five minutes down the road."

Kate: **I can be there in about five minutes if your mother would like to talk to me. Are you at the Spring Hill court?**

They had to wait a moment for the answer: **"My mama say that be just fine. She'd like a chance to talk to you."**

"I do believe you got on Romeo's mama's bad list."

"Yeah, maybe." Kate dug the car keys out of her jacket pocket. "Will I see you tomorrow?"

"How about we take my car over to the court?" He took her by the elbow and spun her toward a different row of cars.

"You worried I can't hold my own with Romeo's mom?"

"Nope. I just want to have a front seat and a bag of popcorn when you do."

Kate was secretly glad that Dave was going with her. She could maybe close her eyes and take a five-minute power nap on the way over.

She climbed into the front passenger seat of Dave's car, pulled on her belt, and leaned her head back with a sigh.

Little Guy had waited until Kate laid down last night, and that's when he woke up to play what Kate could only describe as a soccer match in her belly. She had never been so tired in her life.

Thank goodness Kate's Aunt Emma was going to come and stay after the baby was born, Kate might get some stretches of sleep. In theory anyway.

Dave nudged her. "We're here. I can go talk to her if you need to sleep."

"Sorry," she said meekly.

"Don't be. I've got the twins. Luckily, they came early, and my wife would be delivering about the point you are in your pregnancy. But up until then, Cathy was *miserable* and exhausted. I remember. Whatever I can do to make things easier, I'm fine with that, okay?"

"You are one really nice guy, Dave. Thank you." She popped open the door, focusing on the woman jiggling a baby carriage and watching what looked like most of Kate's students playing ball.

"Mrs. Gander?" Kate called as she shut the door.

"You Mrs. Hamilton, the science teacher?"

"Yes, ma'am, and Detective Murphy who co-teaches the criminal justice class." She made her way over to stand near Mrs. Gander.

"You want to tell me what criminal justice has to do with playing basketball? Romeo out there tell me he's doing his homework."

"Yes, ma'am." Kate peeked into the carriage. A sweet baby girl with a pink flower headband was eating Cheerios off the front tray. "Hello sweetheart," Kate said then stood. "Basketball and criminal science. One of the things that Detective Murphy and I want to do this semester is to prepare our students for their potential careers. One thing we know is that after a work day, dealing with the criminals and the horror show that criminals create, it's important to let go of stress and have a transition between the dark world of crime and their homelife. Stopping and playing some ball with friends is one of the habits that might serve these guys, and their spouses and children, well. Better to blow off aggression and stress out on the court, than to walk through the front door with it in their system."

Mrs. Gander pressed her lips together. Romeo had warned her in one of his stories that meant Mrs. Gander was about done with his foolishness.

"Beyond that, studies tell us that exercising between school and homework helps the student to absorb information better. It makes their study more effective. So tacking onto the other pieces of homework I give them—"

"Like playing chess?"

"Another skill building exercise with long term good outcomes, yes. Beyond asking them to exercise I ask them to eat a healthy snack or dinner. Food as brain fuel." Kate suddenly felt uncomfortable thoughts about inner city food deserts and the idea of lack filled her thoughts. She hoped she wasn't being disrespectful of the family's circumstances to have brought that up.

"Speaking of snacks," Dave said. "I'm going to run over to that corner store and get a coffee. Can I bring you something Mrs. Gander? Something for the baby?"

"Yeah, I'll have some orange juice if you don't mind." She dug in her pocket and brought out a couple dollars.

"No worries," Dave touched her hand, so she'd put the money away. "Kate?"

"A bottle of water, please."

Mrs. Gander looked down at Kate. "Tell you the truth, I thought Romeo was pulling one of his stunts."

"He has a big personality."

"When your baby coming?"

"End of February is what they tell me. Detective Murphy will be handling the class, and we have some interesting speakers—"

A scream went up, loud and high.

Mrs. Gander reached out and gripped at Kate's arm as Mrs. Gander tucked down over her baby.

Kate couldn't duck. Her belly was too big. Her eyes scanned, and she saw Oliver standing in the dumpster with the ball in his hand, holding it shoulder height. Just standing there screaming.

Half the guys playing took off running in the opposite direction.

Kate's students ran toward him.

Kate was running too.

"Oliver. Oliver look at me," she called, pressing her hands against the rusted dumpster, tipping her head back. "Look. At. Me. Oliver. What's happening?"

Slowly his chin dropped down, his gaze found hers. Tears dripped down his cheeks. "The ball went into the dumpster," he stuttered out, and his gaze drifted toward his feet.

Kate looked around. She pointed at Romeo. "Romeo stay with your mother and protect the baby." She turned and pointed at another student. "Jamal, run to the corner store and get Detective Murphy. Run!" She pressed onto her toes, trying to get a look at what was happening inside the dumpster. "Oliver, are you hurt?"

He shook his head, his whole body trembled, the basketball squeezed between his hands.

"Tell me. Just one thing. One small thing. What's happening?"

"There's a dead guy in here with me. He holding my ankle."

6

———

KATE REACHED to grip the rim of the dumpster, looking for a foothold to hoist herself up. "Royce," she called when she saw him in the street guarding the area like a sentinel. "Royce, come here and give me a leg up."

"You're not going in the dumpster with a dead guy, Mrs. Hamilton," he said as he came up beside her and put his hands on the top ready to vault himself over. "I'll go in."

Kate put her hand on his back to stop him. "He can't be dead if he's holding onto Oliver's leg. I need to do first aid. And you need to help Oliver get out of there." She locked her fingers together. "Just lace your fingers together, yeah, just…" She leaned her head back. "Oliver, stop screaming and get out of there." Royce bent and let her step into his hands. Steadily, he hefted her (God bless him) and her fat pregnant belly up the side of the dumpster.

The next couple of minutes wasn't pretty as Kate writhed to

get her bottom onto the lip of the dumpster to see in. She held out her hand to Oliver. "Come on, get out."

Oliver tossed the ball down then rounded a leg over the side of the dumpster sitting away from the form crumpled amongst the rubbish.

The smell of old garbage was thick as it wrapped her in its nauseating pong.

Kate pulled off Ryan's jacket and dropped it to the blacktop beside Royce.

"What she doin' in the dumpster pregnant like that?" Mrs. Gander sounded pissed. "Why you lift her up like that?"

"She's my teacher, Mrs. Gander. She told me to."

Kate dialed 9-1-1 and had her phone pressed between her shoulder and her chin. She reached into one of her tactical pockets and pulled out the CPR key chain she always carried. It had a mask, two children's chewable aspirin, and a pair of Nytril gloves. She wriggled her fingers into the gloves.

"9-1-1 where is your emergency?"

Kate huffed out. She couldn't remember where they were. She needed to hand this off. "Royce, here you help me communicate. This is the 9-1-1 operator. Tell her where we are." She held the phone down to Royce. She aimed her feet and dropped as gingerly as possible into the dumpster, gripping the top for stability as she sank knee deep into the bags of waste. "Royce, can you hear me?"

"Yes, ma'am."

"Tell them. Male. Late twenties, early thirties." She flattened her hand across the man's back. He was dressed in a pair of washed out fatigues and a blood-soaked t-shirt. "Labored respiration. Blood. These look like stab wounds to the torso. We need police and a rescue squad. Tell 9-1-1 the victim is in a dumpster, they'll need equipment to get him out. I'd guess he weighs about a-hundred-and-sixty—a-hundred-and-seventy pounds at least."

"Kate!" It was Dave. He didn't sound happy. "Get out of there and let me take care of this."

Yeah, now that she was in here, Kate didn't have a strategy for how to get back out. "Dave, get your first aid kit out of your car." She assumed he'd carry one.

"Sir, can you hear me?" Kate tapped the man's shoulder. "Are you okay? Can you open your eyes?" When she got no response, Kate wrestled the guy around to lay him out the best she could so she could find his wounds. Her feet kept slipping down in the bags and debris, throwing her off balance.

The smell squeezed her chest and roiled her stomach.

Little Guy was kind enough to lie very still. Her bottom found a kind of seat on one of the bags. "My name is Kate." She used her teacher's voice, calm and authoritative. "I've been trained in first aid, and I'm going to help you until the ambulance gets here. I won't leave you. Help is here." She ripped the t-shirt open from one of the stab wounds. Those holes were evidence, but when it came to applying first aid and preserving evidence, life always came first.

One of the thin slits in his skin went into the man's lungs.

His labored breathing sounded wet.

Kate pushed up from her squat to peek over the lip of the dumpster. She saw Dave running full out in her direction.

"Did you have the first aid kit in your car?" she yelled to him.

He held a white box aloft as he ran toward her.

"I need some tape and something plastic I can use for a seal. He's got a sucking chest wound."

Normally, she'd ask for the whole box, but the environment was just too filled with germs. It would contaminate everything.

She looked down at Royce who held the phone to his ear. "Royce, tell them I'm applying a three-sided seal to a sucking chest wound."

Royce dipped his head, finger in his ear as he updated the dispatcher.

Dave planted a knee on the cold blacktop as he opened the kit and rummaged around.

Kate waved her hand at him, impatient for the tools she needed to help this man.

Dave pulled on a pair of protective gloves, then grabbed tape and a handful of gauze pads and stretched them up to her.

With the corner of one gauze pad between her lips, Kate stuck the others in her back pocket for easy access.

Dave pointed his finger at Oliver. "Hey, all of you with your phones out, no posting to social media. None. If you already started to post get it down *now*."

"The police can't tell them not to post," Kate heard Mrs. Gander say as Kate moved gingerly into a better position.

"I'm not here as the police, ma'am, I'm here as their teacher." Dave's voice had gone to patient reassurance, the kind he'd use with emotional witnesses. "I'm asking them to be good criminal justice students."

Kate got the seal in place using the plastic-coated bandage wrapping and taping three of the sides. That seemed to help. Kate readily saw three other wounds. She picked the two biggest bleeders and topped them with gauze bandaging, placed the flat of her hands, applying pressure.

"No room for me in there?"

Kate glanced up to find Dave sitting on the corner of the dumpster. "None. Please stay up there."

"You're in there, eight months pregnant. You should have let me do this."

He sounded like Tim's scolding, the voices of reason when it came to her and Little Guy's safety.

"You weren't here. Police and their doughnut runs." She

looked down and saw a tear in her gloves. "I have a rip. Do you have more gloves?"

"You get blood on you? Here lift your hand up. I'll help you."

Kate extended her hand toward him. Dave removed her glove following protocol and helped her wiggle her fingers back into another one. And then put a second one on to give her a double layer of protection. He tore open more gauze and handed that down to her.

"I'll be right back." Dave swung his legs out of the dumpster, and Kate heard a smack as his feet hit the ground.

Kate didn't see a rise and fall of the man's chest.

Last summer, Tim and she had been closest available when there was a medical emergency in Scarborough. They ran into the house to find the man collapsed on the ground in his dining room and had applied CPR and artificial breath. They labored to save him until the rescue squad arrived. The paramedic pronounced the man's death. She'd been trying to blow life into a dead man. That sensation still woke her up in a cold sweat.

Kate's body trembled as she lowered her cheek to the man's nose to see if she could feel him exhale.

"Thank you," whispered against her cheek.

"I'm with you. I won't leave you. Help is here," Kate repeated.

His fingers moved toward the waist of his pants. She watched to make sure he wasn't pulling out a weapon. But it was a colored piece of paper. "I won't need this anymore. I give it to you. My gift. To you. Thanks." His voice was a mere wheeze. His eyes were slit open. He was tapping the paper onto the back of her hand.

That she didn't take it from him seemed to agitate him.

So she released the pressure on his wound long enough to move the paper to her back pocket. And went back to the compression.

"Thank you," she said. "I'll just hold it for you. We're going to get you fixed right up. Tell me your name. What should I call you?"

He whispered.

"Alf? Is that right? Stay with me. Stay awake."

"Short. Annoying little f..."

She focused on the military tattoo over his heart. "Call sign. Okay. Marine. Here's the deal. You *will* stay awake. You *will* stay with me. You *will* fight. That's an order."

"Yes, Ma'am." But his eyes drooped closed and his mouth went slack.

She checked again for breath. Air not words whispered over her cheek.

Kate pressed her elbow at a plastic bag that was caving in on her. "Help is coming. I won't leave you. The ambulance is almost here."

Oliver reached down, grabbed the bag that was trying to tumble on top of her and tossed it out of the dumpster.

Kate found herself chanting, "Come on. Come on. Come on."

$$7$$

THE RESCUE CREW set up a ladder system and came in at the victim's feet.

Kate continued to hold pressure while the paramedic did a quick vitals check. He added another layer to Kate's gauze and took over for her.

Another responder bent over the lip and caught Kate under the arms, helping to heft her out of the heaping garbage.

His *oof* at taking her weight was understandable. He kept his hands on her, even after her feet found the rungs, and she climbed up and over.

She removed her gloves, and they gave her a once over to make sure she hadn't hurt herself and the tightness of her belly was just a Braxton Hicks contraction. She hadn't thrown herself in to labor by jumping into the dumpster.

Royce held up Kate's jacket for her and helped her into it. Kate couldn't have imagined this kind of behavior from him on their first day of school. Goes to show you, people were multifaceted.

"Your phone." He handed it to her, and Kate slid it into her coat pocket as they moved away from the rescue activity.

Kate scanned to check on her students. They were in a huddle by the fence, where a police woman looked like she was noting names and statements.

Dave was talking to an officer.

Oliver was down from his perch on the dumpster. His phone was still up. He was slowly pivoting as he recorded the scene.

"You're not live streaming this or putting it on social media, are you?" Kate asked, moving toward him.

"No ma'am," he said a bit of shock in his voice. "I…I…I… I thought that it might be evidence. I mean the guy was obviously…it seems to me there's been a crime."

"Excellent thinking."

Dave moved toward them. "You get all that?"

"I think so," Oliver said. "I tried."

"Can you forward your images to me?" Dave pulled his phone from his pocket.

KATE WAS BELTED into the passenger seat of Dave's car as they motored back to the school parking lot. Her elbow rested on the side window; her forehead was cupped in her hand. Kate's brain kept popping up the images of Alf. "Annoying Little F—" He'd stopped from saying the f-word. That meant he was with it enough to not want to use that word in front of a lady, right? That boded well for him, right? He could survive. He was heading toward help.

"You don't disappoint," Dave said, pulling up next to Kate's car.

Kate dropped her hand and focused on him. "How's that?"

"First week in Scarborough you're on a murder scene. First week in Boonestown, you land on the watch that led to the murder scene. Welcome to Washington D.C." He threw the car into park next to Kate's car.

"That's not fair." She released her safety belt. "This isn't a murder. A crime, yes. The responders got there. He should survive this. They will treat him, won't they? Even if he's seemingly homeless. He could be a disabled vet and have insurance. There are laws."

Dave's face was neutral, nothing to read there. "They have an obligation to treat him in a life-threatening circumstance."

"I hope he has ID on him. And an insurance card."

"Chances of that are slim to none." He glanced toward her car. "You okay to drive? I can take you home and bring you back in the morning."

"Thank you. That's nice of you to offer. But I'm not heading home. I need to go check in on Ryan."

"I can take you. Honest, I don't mind. It'll give you a chance to decompress between stressors."

"Thank you for being so nice to me." She reached for her purse strap. "I won't put you out. Last night I had to wait for an hour while Ryan was in PT. I never know. I'm fine. I promise. But thank you."

"No buts, remember? *And.*"

She sent him a thin-lipped smile.

Kate climbed from his car and looked down at her clothes, she'd need to change before she went to the care facility. She couldn't be traipsing in covered in germs.

KATE, now showered and dressed in yoga pants and one of Ryan's sweat shirts, tapped on his door at the care center and walked in.

His eyes moved her way briefly, before he refocused on his video game.

This was part of his therapy. It was experimental, but Ryan said he was so messed up at least he was useful in trying to figure out what might help others. What more harm could it do him?

She moved into the room and pulled the throw blanket from under his feet at the end of the bed and wrapped it around her shoulders as she sat on the cold vinyl chair and waited.

Oh, Ryan was very much aware that she was there and would stay there until they had spoken. Back in the day, he'd stop whatever he was doing and focus his eyes, full of love and mirth, on her, and she'd feel emotion move between them like liquid silk, binding them and holding them together. It was *the* best feeling knowing that they belonged to each other.

Ryan was consciously depriving her of their connection, trying to sever it. He was still on his campaign to get her to leave him for some fantasy other guy who would make a perfect husband for her and father for Little Guy. Then, Ryan would slide into the shadows to get out of the way. It was insulting. Hurtful. And everything she would expect of Ryan, putting her happiness before his own.

He slipped up though. Every once in a while, the mask would shift, and she caught a glimpse of his truth. That silken ribbon of belonging still tied him to her. She had to believe that, or she'd just be a terrible person for not allowing him out of their marriage.

His argument had always been though, she, Kate, was safer without him. He had never said, "I stopped loving you."

Kate focused on the first-person shoot 'em up game. She wasn't sure what to think about it. She'd read the peer reviewed articles. From a scientific point of view, Kate didn't like that the findings were mostly anecdotal measurements instead of hard numbers. She got the theory that having those who developed PTSD on a battlefield could use the games as desensitization and reintegration tools— "exposure-based PTSD therapies." She got that these video games, with their virtual reality and photoreal characters and scenes in the first-person shooter games, helped survivors feel that they had some level of control, and that even bad outcomes in the videos, taught the soldiers' brains that they could walk away.

Kate was still not convinced, though.

If nothing else, the FPS gaming gave Ryan something to do in the day. A box to check off that said he was working toward recovery and not just staring at the ceiling in pain.

Granted, Ryan played the game silently so as not to exacerbate the headaches. Kate hadn't found anything in the literature about the efficacy of this type of therapy without the sound component—the explosions and the screams.

Ryan wouldn't talk to her about his experiences on the battlefield. She didn't know if he heard anything at all when he was caught up in that last blast, or if he could even remember the explosion that damaged his brain.

"I was watching my students play basketball today," she said to the wall. "We discovered a man who had been stabbed. He was in the dumpster with a sucking chest wound. I hope he lives."

Ryan rolled her way. "You're kidding."

"Nope."

"And you did what in the scenario of stabbed man in the dumpster? You don't have to tell me because I know. You didn't want your students to be in harm's way, so you somehow got yourself into the garbage to give him first aid."

Kate rubbed the edge of the blanket between her fingers.

"You put yourself in danger. And more, you put your son in jeopardy. That was a risky decision."

"Ours," she murmured. "I put our son in danger."

Ryan closed his eyes.

"The victim was passed out, and I was wearing Nytril gloves. I guess there was some small amount of danger to it. It's true that I wasn't processing as much as just acting. But in the end, if I knew he was alive, and I chose to do nothing other than dial 9-1-1?" She stopped to press her lips together. "I told Zack about it last summer, I don't know if he shared my story. But in Scarborough, I gave mouth to mouth to a guy who was dead. Did he tell you about that?"

"Yeah, I know about it."

"Sometimes, about once a week or so, I wake up, and I hear him." She waggled her fingers beside her head. "Just there. He says, 'breathe harder. Why aren't you helping me? Breathe harder.' It always makes me cry." She stopped to swallow. "And there's that woman, the teacher who was killed in Boonestown, the one Lexi's dogs found. She wakes me up, too. She laughs at me and says, 'tick tock, tick tock, time's almost up.' I get an adrenaline dump like I did when the guy came to the house looking for the watch that ended up getting him convicted." She pulled the blanket tighter. "I hope that guy from the dumpster lives." She swallowed. "I don't need any more ghosts haunting me."

She looked up to see horror and compassion in Ryan's eyes. But when their gazes caught, it was like a curtain falling over his emotions.

Kate cleared her throat. "So, Dr. Carlon was talking to you last night about the FDA study. Do you think you'll do it?"

"I'm going up tomorrow."

"Where's up? How are you getting there?"

"Boston. Dr. Carlon wrote a prescription to put me out while I travel up in an ambulance. I'll stay with Zack and his family Wednesday and Thursday nights. The ambulance will bring me back here to the care center on Friday," There was a trace of bitterness at his being brought back.

Understandable.

Kate was actually glad that he'd get out of here for a few days, though she was surprised that he'd allow Dr. Carlon to medicate him for the trip. Ryan could be hard headed with some things. After seeing the effects of pain meds on his brothers, opposition to taking opiates was one of them.

"Zack and his family. That's nice." Kate bit down on her own bitterness that Ryan thought that it was fine to stay around Zack's wife and kids but not her and Little Guy. She got that Zack would be monitoring Ryan and could physically intervene. Still… "And Houston? Is she going with you?"

"She'll stay with me tonight when Ridge brings her back from training. In the morning, Striker's going to take her to Iniquus to stay with Tripwire."

"It must be odd to live on Iniquus campus, just up the road, when you have your own house nearby. Lexi isn't staying in her side of the duplex right now." Kate decided to move away from emotional topics to something more banal. "Deep is there. His fiancée Grace is down visiting from New York. She lives with Deep's mom. Grace Del Toro. An unusual last name and really unusual that she and Deep have the exact same last name. Don't you think?"

Ryan shifted his eyes back to the screen, crossing his arms over his chest.

"You remember Molly Edwards, though. My colleague from my Boston school. I just heard that Molly married Clay Edwards. When they got married, Clay got upset that she wouldn't be giving up her maiden name for him, so she did. Per the tradition, she replaced her middle name with her maiden name and now she is officially Molly Edwards Edwards." Kate offered up a tired smile when he glanced her way. Her whole body drooped with exhaustion.

She knew Ryan registered it. There was a flash of concern, a twitch of his body as if he arrested himself from reaching out to her.

"How much is the ambulance going to cost?" She'd need to work that into her budget.

He turned his focus toward the ceiling. "The study is providing it."

"They must really want you up there."

"SEAL brains are the golden ticket to research participation."

"Okay, gone until Friday night. I guess I'll see you again on Saturday." She wriggled to the edge of her seat and pressed into the arms of the chair to get herself up. "Houston is cared for. That's good." She folded the blanket and stepped toward Ryan's bed. "I really hope this produces something that will help." Kate knew better than to try to give him a kiss. She gently laid the blanket back across the end of his bed. "Good night. Have a safe trip." She left, shutting the door softly behind her.

As Kate walked down the hall, her phone rang. "Hey Dave."

"I thought you'd like to know. I'm up at the hospital and our John Doe made it through surgery."

"It's looking good for him?"

"At this point, all I can say is he's alive."

8

"I KNOW the first thing you'll want to know is, how the victim is doing," Kate said as her CSI class dumped their book bags onto the floor and took their seats. "The answer is that we can't be told much because of HIPAA. That's a law that protects the privacy of your health. I do know that he was taken to the hospital, he had surgery, and remains in the hospital." She paused to take in the stoic faces of her students. "He would not have made it this far had the ball not gone in the dumpster." Kate held off on saying that the guy had a chance. She needed to keep her words neutral. If she gave them hope that the man would survive the attack, and then he didn't make it… Yeah, better to be neutral until she could gather a better feel for how he was doing.

Little Guy started his dance moves, and Kate put her hand over the place he was elbow gouging her, trying to give him a target and protect that spot from getting too sore.

"Let's talk about yesterday from a scientific point of view." She perched on the corner of her desk.

"Oliver screamed like a girl." Jamal guffawed.

Oliver slunk down in his seat with his long fingers draped over his face.

"Interesting," Kate said. "Why not say Oliver screamed? Why did he scream like a girl?"

"Girls scream. Men suck it up," Antonio said.

Oliver sunk lower.

"Oh? I would say that depends on the circumstances. We are all—males and females, every single one of us here—we are all the product of our amazing ancestor's determination to stay alive and produce a next generation. In order for you to be here," she scrolled her finger from the right side of the room to the left to encompass all of her students, "your ancestors had to survive to an age of procreation and beyond. They needed to live long enough for their offspring to produce the next generation."

"And they had to find someone to procreate with. Which, to be honest, for some of us," Romeo touched his hand to his chest, "is a might easier than for others." He tipped his head toward Malik and rolled his eyes for emphasis.

"To survive to the age of procreation in our cave-dwelling past, was not easy to do. We have to understand, our being here is pretty amazing."

"What's that got to do with Oliver screaming?" Xavier asked.

"Let's figure that out." Kate slid further onto the desk top and planted her hands on either side of her, wrapping her fingers around the wooden edge. "First, can we all agree on the premise that what happened yesterday is not a normal part of your day?"

The heads nodded.

"Can we agree that Oliver took in information through his senses, and it was processed by his brain as not only unusual but also cause for concern about his survival?"

"Only if he's afraid that a little blood was going to hurt him."

"Contact with someone's blood can kill." Kate raised her

brows to emphasize the point. "In CSI we always use precautions. It's why we got him out of the dumpster the way we did. Picture this: A man in peril. Possible peril around us. Should Oliver have been quiet about the situation?"

"No."

"But he shouldn't ah screamed like that, neither," Antonio said.

"I disagree. And so would Oliver's brain. Remember, his brain holds the limbic system, his lizard self-preservation tool. If Oliver had shouted in a normal voice, how many times would he have to call out to get you to pay attention? You were all shouting and calling to each other as you played basketball. If Oliver had used a happy tone, what kind of reaction would he have?"

Silence met the question.

"He screamed. It was the perfect survival thing to do." Kate pointed around the class. "For those of you who were there, that scream lit up your limbic systems and made you dump adrenaline into your body. Your eyes could see better. Your hearing was better. You had power pumping through your muscles so you could run from danger or fight. That tone of voice—that scream is a gift from Oliver's ancestors to not only keep him alive but to protect his clan."

More silence. This argument was taking root.

"Remember our ancient ancestors depended on everyone else to survive. That's true today, *and* it was particularly true for our forefathers. If you were cast out of the cave or tribe, you had little chance at survival and no chance at procreation—making a next generation. So while Oliver, given the opportunity, would probably have chosen to react differently to avoid your teasing, his brain *forced* his body to do the right things. So everyone thank Oliver's survival brain."

"Thank you, Oliver's survival brain," a good seventy-five percent of the room intoned.

"Okay. With Oliver's call, an alarm was raised. We've already talked about what effects the alarm had on your bodies. Very quickly, you were able to process that there was a fellow member of your tribe who was signaling trouble. Here's an interesting thing that happened. The young men playing basketball, whom I didn't recognize as being part of our class, ran away from the scene. While those who are in this class, and who were there for that game, ran toward Oliver. Some to the dumpster some to the perimeter to guard the location. There was no coordination; it just happened. We'll circle back to that in a moment. But once everyone ran to their spots, what happened next?"

"You went into the bin." Antonio said.

"I didn't get into that bin by myself."

"Royce hefted you in," Xavier said.

"I'm a pregnant woman. What would my condition mean to the cave?"

"The future. The next generation," Jamal said. "So we gots to protect you. That way, when we be old, you made another generation to get in there and feed us and what not."

"Exactly. While hesitating to help me into the dumpster, and offering to go himself, Royce ended up helping me. I am a team authority figure, and I demanded it. Royce's behavior—trying to put himself in the danger instead of a pregnant team member, then complying with my demand that it be me as a team leader—is perfect team survival behavior. Thank you to Royce's ancestors." She stopped and smiled.

The class was focused. She loved when this happened, when she could see the cogs whirring in her students' brains.

"I get into the dumpster and the group of basketball players are used to working as a team. Romeo was guarding his mother and the next generation baby. We have Royce on the phone doing comms. Oliver sat out of the way videoing the event to preserve information. Someone went after Dave. Dave ran in with supplies.

Right? Is that team behavior new to you? Or do you think that practicing team sports are an important training tool for survival?"

Royce tipped his chin up. "Yeah, I can see how playing sports all along the timeline would be a fun way to get the body strong and to, you know, teach a team how to work together—who was good at what role. Who were the leaders."

"Excellent. Let's conclude that Oliver's alarm brought the team together with the right hormones in our bodies to contend with a life or death situation. Team sports are something that our brains enjoy because they prepare us for times when we need to rely on each other for survival. Preparing us physically, mentally, and strategically to function." Kate stopped to scan her students. "I couldn't have been prouder."

She let that statement sit in silence so it could be absorbed.

"Now, I want to turn our lesson to the videotaping. The victim's identity should be protected. He was vulnerable and the tapes were made of him without his consent."

Oliver shifted around uncomfortably.

"I'm not saying it was wrong to take the video as a tool for understanding the situation. I'm saying it would be wrong to expose the victim for sensationalism. I know you guys told me that this wasn't going to be seen around. That you wouldn't post this on the Internet. I hold you to your word. That time was sacred to him, but also—how do you think it might impede a criminal case to have a video out there being consumed and shared by the community?"

Nothing.

"Did any of you get to your reading last night? I know it was an emotional time. I'm not grading you down. Just show of hands, did anyone read?"

The hands that went up were the students who hadn't been on

the scene. They looked unhappy that they weren't in on the event and weren't part of the first-hand experience.

Royce's hand went up. Kate took note of that. She was wrong about their butting heads. He might just be the one who was going to shine in this class.

"Fine. Let's go over that information and see how you applied your knowledge to a real-life scene." She slid off the desk and rounded over to the board where she started writing as she lectured.

- *Only someone with a good reason to be at the crime scene is allowed in the area*

She turned to the class and tapped the board with her pen. "This precludes the media, the family, even detectives from contaminating the scene. This pertains to Lokard's principal. Those of you who need to catch up with your reading will discover this tonight as you hunker down with your books. Basically, Lokard said that people come with debris and leave it at the crime scene, and they can pick up debris from the crime scene and take it with them. That's why everyone on scene is covered up—gloves and booties and so forth. That's why each person on scene is logged into the area and logged back out again. What kinds of contaminates could be left?" She listed as the students called out.

- *Contaminants:*
- *Fingerprints*
- *Footprints*
- *Hair*
- *DNA*
- *Fibers…*
- *Candy wrappers* (that one got a laugh.)

"When extra information is introduced, it slows the process and creates extra work for the investigators because they have to sort through all of the data. Okay." She put the top on her marker and set it on the lip of the white board. "Another reason to keep others at a distance?" Kate cocked her head to the side. "Think about those videos. Why would the police want to keep the public away from a crime scene?"

"One of my cousin got shot up in Chicago." Mason laced his fingers and rested his hands on his desk, rubbing his thumbs together in a self-soothing gesture. "Before the police could go tell the family, they already knew." He had to pause. "It was all over the Internet and everyone seen it. That really upset the family. Seeing a loved one messed up on the ground like that. And people who didn't know him or care about him, makin' jokes. Talkin' smack about him."

Kate nodded. She couldn't imagine the pain of that, seeing someone she knew dead on the street in a video she scrolled past on Instagram, and that was how she found out? She rubbed a hand under her belly and left it there. "I'm so sorry for you and your family. My condolences. And a very good point, so thank you for sharing. If you posted the pictures of the victim that might be how the family finds out."

"But we don't know who he is. So that could be a good thing," Royce said.

"There is a process for trying to identify the man. I'm sure that the police have his fingerprints and are searching their data bases, trying to get a name. He did have a Marine tattoo. I'm sure the DCPD will reach out to the military with the fingerprints to try to get the victim IDed. He might even have had identification on him. We don't know."

"And he could just wake up and tell folks who he is," Romeo said.

Dave tapped on the door and came in. Kate lifted her chin his way.

He took a seat while Kate focused back on Romeo.

"That would be the best. None of you have seen that man before?" Kate looked at the shaking heads. "All right, more. Besides potentially traumatizing friends and loved ones, what are some good reasons not to show tapes of a crime scene?"

"Well what if this isn't personal, you know?" Romeo asked. "If this is a serial criminal, he could have an MO."

"Right," Anthony added. "Or if there was someone who wanted to copy cat to throw the scent off them. They might want to make it seem like an MO, he could match it to the scene."

"Could be," Xavier said, "that they left some piece of evidence. He see it on the film, and he go back and clean it up later."

"What about false admissions?" Royce asked.

"Good, tell me about that," Kate asked.

"Folks sometimes don't understand their rights. They might not have the education. They might not have the mental health. They just tell the detective, yeah, I did it. A shady detective and prosecutor could accept that. Throw the guy in jail. Get another notch on they belts. But a good detective who kept key pieces of information secret about the scene could tell if the guy was making up a story or not."

"Very nice. Wow. You all impress me." Kate pulled her chair around toward the side of her desk

"So what happens if Alf dies?" Oliver asked.

She sat down with her knees wide, glad to be wearing tactical pants and a pregnancy-length shirt. "In what sense?"

"How does he get a proper burial if we don't know his religion or his family? Will the military do that? Bury him with military honors and all. Respectful."

"I believe they'd have to know who he is and prove that he

was in the military. It would be odd, but it's possible that he got the tattoo without having served. Not for reasons of being fraudulent but for example he might have gotten the tattoo to honor a fallen friend or family member."

"We should at least know the man's name," Romeo pushed. "What if he had a wife? She should know her husband's been bad hurt and could die. She'd want to be there, so he won't die alone."

"I don't disagree." Kate's mind conjured up the scene of walking into Ryan's empty room and thinking he could die at any time, and she might not be there to support him as he walked on to Valhalla to join his fellow warriors. There was always the chance that she wouldn't get the chance to say good-bye. She swallowed down those overwhelming feelings. "The police will be working on that."

"No they won't."

Kate and Royce were eye to eye. "Why do you say that?"

"He's a homeless dude. Looked like one anyways. He doesn't have money. He doesn't have community standing and people who can call and put pressure. He don't have no friends that go to cocktail parties and golf. He's a nobody and a *nothing* to the system. He was thrown in the trash—that's what folks think of him. Homeless. Useless. Not worth the time or energy. Probably just think that it was a drug deal gone bad."

"I think he was killed for the lottery ticket," Romeo said.

Kate tipped to the side to see Romeo. "What lottery ticket?"

"The one he gave you as a thank you present."

Kate stilled and looked at the floor between her feet. Nope, she didn't remember any of that, she shook her head.

"I got it on the video." He pulled out his phone and cued it up.

Kate watched it. She watched it, again. She waved Dave over, and they watched it together.

She'd not clocked it. She hadn't even looked at what he'd pressed into her hand. She'd slid it in her back pocket. Kate had taken off her pants in her bathroom to get cleaned up to go see Ryan and put the pants in the clothes hamper. Sure enough, Alf said she could keep it. And it sounded like he was saying lottery ticket.

"Huh. Okay, add to our list of lectures. We need to talk about tunnel vision. I don't remember this happening at all. But it must still be in that pocket. Detective Murphy, can you come to my house and collect it as evidence? Or should I call the officer assigned to the case? It might give them some clues."

"Or we can split the money," Markus said.

"If there is any money," Kate said, "it belongs to the victim. Any money that might be associated with that ticket is *not* ours."

"You seen though, it's on the tape," Romeo protested. "The dude give it to you. It's yours."

Kate held up a finger and waved it across the classroom. "No. It's not." She turned back to Dave. "Can you call the officer assigned to this case, Detective?"

"On it."

9

———————

KATE SHUT the door on the officer and pulled her phone from her back pocket to see who had kept buzzing her.

Tim had called her three times and left a text—**Give me a call when you get free**.

Okay, that didn't sound like it was an Aunt Emma emergency.

Tim picked up on the first ring. "Hey there. My Kate meter is pinging. Are you settling in okay?"

Kate threw the deadbolt then walked toward the kitchen. "It was an easy move since Zack's wife packed up our personal stuff in Boston, and they brought it down last fall. It was just a matter of unpacking my suitcases from Scarborough." She opened the fridge. "I need to find the grocery store, though. I've been grabbing fast food for the most part."

"Okay. So… Why am I picking up danger vibes?"

Tim listened patiently as Kate told him the dumpster story. "Right before I called you, I shut the door behind the officer who came to pick up the lottery ticket."

"Was it worth anything?"

"Yeah." She opened the cabinet to get a mug.

"A lot?"

"It was their Gold ticket, five hundred grand." She raised her voice to speak past the running water.

"Kate."

She put the mug in the microwave and tapped the minute button twice. "I'm glad to get the ticket out of this house, out of my hands, and on its way. I want nothing to do with it. I learned my lesson about curiosity when I found the watch in Boonestown."

"Don't go looking for the criminal, Kate."

She pulled out a kitchen chair and maneuvered her way down. When Kate could bend in half to do a sit up again, she wouldn't complain about how much she didn't like them. She never thought that she'd miss that part of her workout routine. "No way I'd do that."

"Don't go trying to identify this guy."

"No, I won't, there's a police officer assigned to the case."

"Promise?"

"Tim, I'm freaking 31 weeks, now 32 weeks pregnant, making it through my day and over with Ryan is all I can manage. Ryan's gone for the next few days. He's up in Boston having some scans done."

"Where's Houston?"

"He thought it would be too much for me. The Iniquus Cerberus Tactical K-9 guys took him back with them. Tripwire will bring Houston back when Ryan gets home." She looked at the microwave when it dinged. That meant she had to get up again. Was tea worth the effort?

"When is that?"

"Friday, he comes home, well, back to the care center. He's staying with Zack and his family while he's up in Boston." Kate wiggled back upright and moved to the cupboard to get a tea bag and some raisins.

"There was a hitch in your voice." And concern in Tim's.

"Zack has a wife and children. Ryan can go there and stay in their house, and it's all okey dokey. But Ryan's *own* wife and his *own* son?"

"Zack probably has rules like his family isn't around Ryan if he isn't right there with him."

"In case he turns into the Incredible Hulk? He hasn't had any dissociative episodes since he started the hormone therapy."

"What about his other symptoms?"

"Hard to tell. He lays flat on the bed to manage his pain."

"Houston alerts doesn't she?"

"She did before the accident." Kate made it back to her place at the table. "But not since Zack brought her down. Why? Is it because those symptoms are gone, and it wasn't PTSD but the hypopituitarism caused by a blast concussion? Is it because she isn't doing her job? Is it because she is doing her job, but it looks different now that Ryan is further incapacitated? No one knows. Houston is a comfort to him. That I can tell. And Houston is devoted to Ryan, that I can tell too. Watching over him is her job."

"And you by extension."

She blew across the tea water. "It seems that way, which is why I have a glimmer of hope."

"Tell me about that."

"It seems to me that if Ryan didn't love me, didn't care, that Houston would protect Ryan from me. But Houston isn't that way in the least."

"Did you ever think Ryan didn't love and care for you? My impression through all this is that he's doing everything he can think of to keep you safe, and he thinks he's your biggest threat. He's sacrificing his feelings for your safety out of love."

"That's the story I tell myself to stay sane. Okay, look. I'm really tired. Sorry if I distracted you from anything with danger vibes."

"Katydid, I vowed to always be there for you. I meant it. I am here for you. You're family to me."

"Yeah. Just don't let Pam hear you say that. No reason to go borrowing trouble. And same here. You're family of the heart. I only want good for you."

"Before you hang up, Kate, I just want to offer one observation, and I don't want you to comment. Just listen. You love me. Not in a *let's have an intimate relationship* way. But you love me. You saw that your being here, living at your Aunt Emma's house was causing me some grief. You felt terrible that was happening. And you left as soon as you could. You wanted to leave before anyone knew about your pregnancy so no one would know, and no one would gossip about your baby being my son. And even now, you're watchful that I don't say anything that might rile Pam up. This is a small, tiny, minuscule example of just what Ryan is doing for you. He thinks he's the cause of pain and doesn't want you to feel that. Right or wrong, it's what he can give you right now. And I'm sure it frustrates the heck out of him that you won't just let him do this for you. Not suggesting you should, just offering perspective. Night, Katydid."

There was a knock at her door.

"Night, Tim."

Kate wiggled herself up and went to find Dave standing on her porch.

"Hey there." He held a plate in his hands with a cloth over the top. "Cathy wants to make sure you're eating."

"She is so nice to me." Kate stepped back to let Dave in, accepting the plate. "Everyone is *so* nice to me." And Kate couldn't help it, she burst into tears. "Hormones," she choked out as she turned toward the back of the house.

"I went through this with Cathy. You do what you have to do." He followed her to the kitchen where she set her plate on the table and pulled a fork from the drawer. "Can I get you anything? A glass of water? I haven't been shopping yet so I have cupboard food. Raisins?"

Dave sat in the chair across from her. "I'm squared away." He lifted his chin toward the plate. "Eat while it's hot."

Kate put her napkin on her lap. Cathy had sent lasagna, tossed salad and a gloriously huge slice of garlic bread. She waved the fork over the plate. "Cathy spoils me. Tell her how much I appreciate this. I was about to make yet another PB and J." After taking a bite, Kate asked, "Any update to give the kids tomorrow?"

"On the dumpster victim? No identification. Alf was stepped down from ICU to telemetry."

"That's good isn't it?"

"Might be. Could be a budgetary decision. I have no way of telling. I'm sure the nurses will do their best keeping an eye on him."

Kate covered her mouth so she could speak before she swallowed. "Officer Parker came by and got the lottery ticket."

"Did you see what kind it was?"

"I took a picture of it." She pulled out her phone, scrolled through to find it, and texted it over to Dave, then picked up her fork to get another bite of lasagna.

"A Roaring Cash Gold ticket? Are you kidding me? That's a half-million-dollar prize."

"It's a lot of money." She stabbed her fork in his direction. "People have killed for less. It would certainly be a motive for an attack. But why didn't the attacker take it?"

10

———————

Thursday

"Class before we get started, I want to remind you that you have your first quiz tomorrow, as you will every Friday on that week's topics." There was a general shuffling around in the seats and the display of stink faces that Kate would expect. "The quizzes are *not* easy. This isn't a fluff class. People's lives might just depend on your abilities. And I take this subject very seriously. Your hard work is expected. I want everyone paying attention."

She pulled a chair around to the front of the room. She was going to try to avoid writing on the board today or standing for that matter. Her feet and ankles were swollen and uncomfortable. "Today, I want to expand upon the idea of creativity and science. This past week, we've been talking about creativity and how success has been scientifically correlated with hard work, practice, and experience. Think about scientists like Edison who have created things that help us in our everyday lives. Thomas Edison was asked by a reporter, 'How did it feel to fail a thousand times?'

Edison replied, 'I didn't fail a thousand times. The light bulb was an invention with a thousand steps.' This to me sounds an awful lot like Mozart and the number of compositions he made in his short life."

Meh, this wasn't interesting them.

"Another step in developing expertise is having a mentor. In our class our mentor is Detective Dave Murphy."

"And you too," Jamal said.

"And me. You're right. Thank you. I hope you see me in that light. A good mentor not only encourages us, but points us in the direction of discovery, and will constructively criticize us. When we know where we're making our mistakes—because someone cares enough to help us see them—how can we respond? We could mope. Feel down. Feel attacked and misunderstood. Or we can pick another emotion like gratitude. A good mentor pointing out mistakes on the front end saves years of trial and effort like Thomas Edison worked through in his thousand experiments. Our mentors have walked the path we're travelling and can share their experiences."

Still no sparks. Well, if they didn't like this warm up, they were going to be bored to tears with the chemistry behind predictive blood tests. Kate took one more shot at pumping them up and trying to find a little intrinsic motivation. "An interesting study by Guilford looked at spies who stayed alive. Guess what skills predicted success?"

"Mad gun skills."

"Martini and lady skills," Romeo suggested.

"Smarts."

Kate pointed at Nicholas. "Interesting. Smarts was my guess too. But, no. The most successful spies were the ones who demonstrated the most *creativity*—Guilford was a scientist who studied spies and their traits to try to figure out the question. He discovered what kept them alive and successful in their spying roles was, as he put it, quote, 'divergent thinking, the ability to see many options, to be able to create alternatives. Problem solving skills.' End quote. And thus survival. You all have the capacity to develop your creativity and not just survive but thrive. But science says you have to *want* it, you have to *go after* it by studying, practicing, learning from your failures, trying again." She paused as she scanned the room. "You are important. Your potential is *important*. We need you. We need what only your amazing minds can imagine and create. So I challenge you, find the thing that makes you curious, the thing that feeds your drive and pursue excellence there. It's in you." She nodded. "Today we're going to be looking at the science behind—"

"Mrs. Hamilton, how is Alf?" Royce asked.

Kate focused on him with a tug pulling her lips down. "I have very little news, and it's from last night. Alf was moved from ICU to telemetry. Telemetry is a step-down unit. Alf still gets close attention. It should mean there's been some improvement. But I don't know that as fact. It could just be procedure."

"Or, it could just be that he's poor," Royce said.

Kate scratched at her brow. "I simply don't have factual information about any of that. And I can't get it because of HIPAA. I know about his move from Detective Murphy. And I spoke with Officer Parker when he came by my house to pick up the lottery ticket."

"Was it a lot of money?" Jamal asked.

"Yes," Kate said, not sure how much she should say here.

Oliver leaned forward. "Enough to get killed for?"

Kate felt tension radiating down her back. A sciatic burning poker striking into her thigh. She shifted around in her seat to relieve the pain. "I've read cases where someone was killed over too few chicken nuggets in their box. The amount isn't predictive."

"Is there a reason you won't tell us?"

"Yes. There is. If you know, you might tell others. We have no idea what happened, so we don't want to muddy the case. When it's all over, I'm sure they'll make the findings public."

"Will you use your prize money to take us to dinner or something?"

"New York," Xavier said. "I've always wanted to go there."

"It's not my money. I want nothing to do with it. Hopefully we can find his family."

"Yeah, we working on that. We got pretty far too."

Kate stilled. "What does that mean Antonio?"

"I'll tell you what it means." Royce sent her a scornful look. "I ain't buyin' that the police are going to do the right thing here. Alf in the dumpster is just that, some nameless man thrown away by society. The police don't care none about him. Like I told you yesterday, Alf ain't got no family with clout pestering their high-tone friends to find the guy who stabbed their family. This is just a file on some guys desk that'll get moved to the file cabinet with nothin' done. And you know how I know that true? 'Cause we all sat down and played chess." He swiveled around and swept his hand to encompass the class. "Only it wasn't on those boards you handed out. We played crime chess."

Kate got a sick feeling in the pit of her stomach.

"We thought it through and tried to run that crime in rewind. We found the store where the ticket was bought. The police didn't track it down. When you handed it over, they could have called the lottery and got that information and jumped on it. It was important, and it was time sensitive. The police know that, and still, they didn't look."

"You know that to be a fact?" Kate wished Dave was here.

"Yeah, we hunted down the store that sold the ticket to Alf." Romeo grinned. "And Royce is right. We asked. Nobody came by. And if we hadn't, what then? Those tapes are on a seventy-two-hour loop. They get taped over. Lost. We got there just in time."

"Antonio's friend's girlfriend was working at the Shop and Go," Jamal said. "And she let us download the tape about the time we figured Alf had to have been there. And sure enough. There he was buying the ticket."

Kate rolled her lips in and rubbed them together while she listened.

"Then we figured out what path he had to have followed to get close to the dumpster. We asked the businesses along the way for the tape of that time so we could follow Alf walking and see if we couldn't see someone else there. Unless he waving his lottery ticket in the air. Had to be someone who saw him at the Shop and Go."

"You told them why you were doing that?" Kate asked, staring straight at Royce.

"Yeah," he said. "They all knew. Guy gets stabbed in the neighborhood, it's not like it was a secret or nothin'."

"We saw this other guy in almost all of the videos with Alf from the Shop and Go and then on down the street," Romeo said. "He was tracking Alf the whole time."

"The assault is on video?"

"No, ma'am," Romeo said. "We moved past the shops to people's houses, and we run out of cameras to ask about. We had Alf up until two blocks from where Oliver found him in the dumpster."

"Tossed away like so much debris." Royce's moral indignation seethed from his skin. "Tossed away like a piece of trash. But you know who's the real trash? It's not Alf. It's the do-nothing police officer assigned to this case."

Kate swallowed. She couldn't defend Parker, as far as she knew, besides picking up the lottery ticket, he hadn't done anything. Or maybe he did a lot of things. "Do you guys have that footage?"

Jamal grinned. "Yeah, we have both the original and the ones that got fixed."

Kate tipped her head. "How was it fixed?"

"Xavier has a cousin who's at college. He's dating a girl who has a brother who's studying film technology."

"Okay."

"So we sent Barry the file of all the clips, so we have that one, unchanged. Then he put the clips together taking out the extra footage, so it be easy to see Alfie walking down the road."

Kate was focused on Xavier. "Why did you call him Alfie?"

"That's what my friend's girlfriend called him," Antonio said. "The one that work at Shop and Go. She say he go in there all the time. She told us that he was a nice guy, friendly, and that he stopped by to play the cheap lotteries once a day and the big one once a week."

"Did she know the other man on the tape?"

"She don't remember him," Antonio said.

"All right." Kate wished that the police had done this and not these kids. This was bringing up memories of Boonestown. The ghost of Carolyn Lambert whispered, "Tick tock. Tick tock." Kate scraped her teeth over her lips. "You have the original file you downloaded and the edited file. Okay."

"And the augmented file," Xavier said.

Kate's brows pulled together. "I don't know what that means."

"Here." He reached in his back pack then walked toward her, handing Kate a thumb drive. "Can you put it up on your computer and up on the screen?" He pointed at the screen that was available for Power Point presentations.

Kate set the system up and pressed the icon that said, "edited footage." She took the time to watch Alf's ten-minute walk away from the store. Kate clicked that off and tapped the icon for "augmented footage."

She watched the same ten minutes, only it was much clearer.

The men's facial features much easier to distinguish. And, yeah, Alf must have felt someone behind him, he kept turning around to look. He sped up his pace. The other guy seemed to blend into the doorways as Alf turned.

"Okay." She released the thumb drive. "Can I have a copy of this to give Detective Murphy and have him take it to Officer Parker?"

"Yeah, I made that one for you," Xavier said.

"Thank you. I'll replace the thumb drive with a new one." Kate slid the thumb drive into the thigh pocket on her tactical pants and patted the flap to make sure the Velcro sealed shut. "You worked hard on this," Kate acknowledged. "You were persistent. You were creative. And you used your resources."

"Intrinsic motivation." Royce cocked his head to the side. He obviously was picking up her ambivalence. "Right, Mrs. Hamilton? It makes a difference if you're personally involved. When you've got skin in the game."

"Yes. It makes a huge difference." Kate reached up and wrapped her hand around her throat.

11

———————

KATE'S PHONE wasn't supposed to be on in the waiting room. Somehow, they must think that might violate someone's privacy. Or maybe they had too many loud conversations that disrupted the Zen-spa feel that the designer was trying to engender. Kate wasn't willing to put her phone on airplane mode. She was too worried about what effect the trip up to Boston was having on Ryan's symptoms.

When she felt the vibration against her thigh, Kate glanced toward the reception desk and found it empty.

Dr. Carlon's name showed on the screen.

Kate quickly swiped and brought the phone to her ear. "Is Ryan okay? Is the test helpful?" she asked without preamble or salutation.

The nurse pushed the door wide. "Hamilton?"

Kate stuck a finger in the air. "I'm at the OBGYN and the nurse is calling my name. Just quick. Ryan?"

"Everything is the same with Ryan. I do want to talk to you today though."

Kate sent an apologetic smile to the nurse as she got to her feet. "I have my appointment here, and then my CSI intensive, and then I can talk. Is that all right?" Kate pointed to her phone and mouthed, "Doctor," for the nurse's benefit.

"Sounds good. I'll call you when I take my dinner break, then."

"Thank you."

"Mrs. Hamilton?" the nurse asked.

"Yes, that's me. Sorry about that." Kate gathered Ryan's coat around her and made her way down the hall to get weighed.

Now, lying on the exam table with her pants pushed down her hips, Kate's OBGYN, Dr. Bendrick, stretched the measuring tape over her belly. "Your blood pressure is elevated today. You're having more swelling in your feet and ankles."

Kate tightened her fingers into the fabric of her shirt she was holding high on her chest.

"I know you can feel that being on your feet while you teach. I need you to sit as much as possible while you're instructing." When Kate wrinkled her nose, she said, "It's just until you give birth. The students can put up with it for Little Guy's sake." She took a step back from the table, so she had better eye contact with Kate. "Have your stress levels come down now that you've moved here permanently instead of coming in on the weekends? I'm used to your having last appointment of the day on Fridays and that's after a long drive."

"Stress levels down? I think it's too soon to tell. I'm relieved not to have to make that four-hour trip each week now. I get to swing by the care facility and see Ryan every day."

"Does that increase the concern or alleviate it?"

Kate pressed her lips together. She wasn't big on personal sharing. But this had to do with Little Guy's well-being. "Ryan speaks to me like I'm an administrator of affairs and not his wife. He won't touch my belly or feel the baby kick. He's in terrible pain day in and day out. It's taking a toll on him. It's in the lines on his face. I don't know how long he'll hang on. I'm not sure if he'll want to."

Dr. Bendrick nodded. "Who's going to be there with you when you give birth?"

"My friend Lexi, and another friend Sarah who lives across the street. She's the one who will be caretaking for Little Guy once I'm back on the job. The neighborhood is great. Supportive. Like an extended family. I couldn't have a better living situation. Well—unless Ryan was well enough to come home. I guess what I should say is I'm fortunate that in the practical world—with only my Aunt Emma as family—it's nice to have landed in my situation on Silver Lake Road." She rubbed a hand over her exposed belly. "Little Guy and I are luckier than some." Playing in Kate's mind was Tony's funeral last September. Tony had been one of Ryan's SEAL team members. He died from PTSD, suiciding. His wife Marybeth sat in the pew squeezing her children so tight that they cried and struggled to get free of her grip.

Dr. Bendrick squeezed Kate's hand. "This isn't easy. I need you to do what you can to relax, put your feet up, and take care of you. For Little Guy's sake."

Kate rolled her lips in tightly and offered a slow nod.

"It's time to move your appointments up to every two weeks. Everything's looking good for you carrying to term. You're right where you should be for this stage of your pregnancy. We're still looking at an end of February, beginning of March arrival date for Little Guy." She gave Kate a smile. "Have you worked out his name yet?"

"Not yet. No."

WHILE HER CSI students worked on their quizzes, Kate drew four circles on the board, each was a different size. She labeled them A, B, C, and D.

B was clearly the smallest. This experiment had been impactful at Boonestown High. Now to see if it had the same force here.

Kate had texted with her students who normally sat in the first row this morning. She hoped she could trust them to be good accomplices.

Kate started on the right side of the room, working across student to student. "Which of these circles is the smallest?"

"D," J.J. said.

"D," Kendrick said

"D," Antonio said.

"D," Royce said.

As each of her accomplices said that "D" the medium sized circle was the smallest, the other students squirmed uncomfortably in their desks, squinted their eyes. Leaned left and right. Assessing.

Kate continued her trek through the students. As they offered their answers, Kate tallied their replies under the appropriate letter. She paused to count the "B" votes and the "D" votes. She subtracted the votes given by her accomplices from the "D" votes on the board.

"Seventy-five percent of you were influenced to answer 'D' by my coconspirators in the first row. 'B' is clearly the correct answer."

Romeo balled up some paper and sent it flying to hit Antonio in the back of the head.

"Now—I don't want you to self-judge. This is a natural inclination. Obviously, it is, or the majority would not have added to the number of people who said 'D'. There are important reasons for this. I want you to harken back to our conversation about our ancestors and how those at the crime scene behaved the way you did in an urgent situation. We all have behaviors that are imbedded in our DNA. Out of natural selection, it was our ancestors who survived. This data point," she tapped the seventy-five percent number on the board, "is evidence that our brains developed in a way that makes a group of people conform."

Kate moved to a clean space on the board and wrote: *Benefits of conformity.*

She turned back to her class. "Let's list some. As you think about this, remember, it's all about survival."

"Conforming is easier than putting in the effort to think for yourselves. I don't care which circle is bigger. Sure, I'll go along with the rest," Xavier said.

It's easier than putting out the effort, Kate wrote.

"Right, yes. There are a couple ways that this relieves someone of their effort. For example, there's the energy of coming up with your own answer, and the energy of defending it. Sometimes it's just easier to go along to get along. What is that old worn out saying? 'If mama ain't happy, ain't nobody happy.'"

"Truth!" Romeo said.

"So you might go along with what mama—insert here any authority figure—and you just let it go. Another phrase—Don't rock the boat. Right?"

"Sometimes we're working together and say I don't want to go lift weights," Jamal said. "I'd rather eat a cheeseburger and catch a game on TV. But I go on with them anyway."

"Right!" *Conformity to a group helps with collaboration,* Kate added to the list.

"We learn from each other," Kendrick said. "We see something that's working for others and then we do it."

"This is incredibly important to understand as a CSI. This week we're going to see how conformity to blood spatter and fire forensics put people in prison and even got them executed, and it was all based on fake science."

"What now?" Royce asked, leaning forward.

"We'll be talking about that for the next week," Kate said as she wrote:

Norms

Practices

Rituals

She tapped the words to get the students to focus. "When we conform, we fit in. In the caveman days, not fitting in and being ostracized from the group meant certain death. Conformity meant survival."

"Don't question just get along."

"Not questioning is something that can be important for survival and is part of our caveman brains. Let's have a scenario —who can paint a picture of someone doing something that might lead you to do it, too."

No one answered.

"Have you seen on YouTube videos parties where folks start jumping into the swimming pool fully dressed in their formal clothes? All it takes is one person to jump in and get a positive reaction. Wanting that positive reaction for themselves, others quickly follow."

"Fights at a ball game," Oliver said.

"Right. Exactly. You all know that it's against the law to fight. But if your friends are jumping into the fight. Most likely," she tapped the seventy-five percent number on the board, "a goodly portion will follow. Why do you need to know this and be thinking about it in your criminal justice work?"

Nothing.

"Yesterday, we talked about the importance of creativity in developing CSI protocol. Unfortunately, while scientists need to be creative about their approach to advancing scientific knowledge, they also have to fit the hard science pieces. First, the experiments are conducted. Then, their methodologies need to be scrutinized in peer review. Peer review is when fellow scientists look at your work and point out the holes."

"Like mentorship."

"Quite a bit like mentorship, yes. One of the things that peer scientists will do to make sure the scientific data is good is to replicate the findings of the experiment. The experiments need to be replicated over and over to show that under the same conditions, the outcomes are also the same. This is an example of creativity followed by conformity."

Little guy was thundering around her pelvis, and Kate moved to sit down. She had to take a minute to breathe. "Sorry." She licked her lips. "We have to be assiduous—assiduous means tireless—we have to be assiduous with our methods. In our work with CSI, our methods—what we do—and just as importantly what we *don't* do—has the potential for lifechanging impact. Take notes please. This will be on next Friday's quiz."

She waited for her students to get situated.

"The National Academy of Sciences in 2009 produced a study entitled, 'Strengthening Forensic Science in the United States: A Path Forward.' This report looked at the scientific basis for virtually every forensic discipline that has been used to send people to prison. With the exception of DNA analysis, it found that, and I quote, 'No forensic method has been rigorously shown to have the capacity to consistently, and with a high degree of certainty, demonstrate a connection between evidence and a specific individual or source.' End quote.

"Wait what?" Royce's outrage was painted across his face. "They put people in prison based on the say so of expert scientific testimony that wasn't science at all?"

Dave opened the classroom door and stuck his head in. When he caught Kate's gaze, he signaled her out.

She waddled to the door.

"The SRO is going to take over for a minute. We need to go talk to the principal."

Kate stared hard at Dave.

He nodded his head.

"Class, I need to step out. Officer Clemmons is going to sit with you. I suggest you use this time productively. Work on your homework, read ahead in your textbooks. Don't conform to bad actors, make good-for-you choices. Once you're aware, then the choices you make rest on your own shoulders."

12

THEY WALKED SILENTLY DOWN the corridor until they passed all the classrooms. There, Kate stopped and turned to Dave.

"Alf died, Kate. I'm sorry."

She deflated. Right there in the hall. Sank to the ground. It was the tattoo. He was part of the military family, and she hadn't been able to help save him. She knew this was tied into her sense of helplessness with Ryan but... Man. It was like a blow to the diaphragm.

Dave crouched down next to her with his hand on her shoulder. "Breathe."

"I'm fine. I'm fine. Just. That's disappointing and sad." She put her hands on the floor, coming onto all fours. "Close your eyes. Don't watch this."

Dave stood up with a chuckle as he turned his back to her.

Kate did a modified down dog to get herself, ungainly and ungraceful, up to her feet.

When Dave turned her way, Kate could tell by the twitch at the corner of his lips that he'd watched the whole thing. Probably so he could intervene if she were to do a face plant. He steadied her by holding her elbows. "You good?"

"Absolutely not. I'm sad. And disappointed. The class is going to be devastated. Which reminds me. You need to have this." Kate reached into her pocket and pulled out the flash drive Xavier had given her, recounting the tale.

"Okay. It's a murder case now. They'll assign a detective. I'll make sure they get this stat."

They moved into the principal's office. He stood beside the window and turned his face toward them. Lips pursed. "During school hours, I don't want you to tell the students about that man's death."

"But why? They need to know," Kate said.

"Most of your class wasn't there."

"While that's true—"

"The incident didn't occur on school property."

"I thought you might be bringing us in here to talk about getting a grief counselor involved."

"It wasn't school time."

"Their teacher was involved at the scene," Dave said.

"I don't want this brought up in your class."

"It's a criminal justice and forensics class." Dave stepped forward and put his hands on the back of the guest chair in front of the principal's desk. "They were witnesses to a crime. Do you think they won't want to talk about it? They're invested. They're teens."

"Detective Murphy and I should be allowed to use our discretion when it comes to interacting with the students on the subject."

He shook his head. "There's a murderer out there. Say it's an ongoing investigation, you can't talk about it."

"Have you ever met a teen?" Kate was almost cross-eyed with frustration. "The moment you try to make something out of bounds, they push back. Hard."

"Regardless."

"You know that I have a unique role here," Dave tried. "I'm not paid by the school system. I'm employed by the police."

"You're operating on my turf. My sandbox, my rules."

Kate took another step closer to the principal. "Can I at least go tell the students that the victim died and that any further discussion of the case will have to be suspended while the crime is under investigation? I'm in my first week here. I'm building rapport. I believe I'm building trust. If I take a couple of students to the side after school and ask them to pass the news around, I will lose the classes respect forever. Give me this much."

SHE SAT THERE, a little numb. A lot tired. She had promised Little Guy that she'd go by the store on the way home to get some wholesome food. Then, she'd put on her pajamas and stay in bed the whole weekend, binge watching funny things, and working on getting her blood pressure down. *I'm going to take care of you, Little Guy.*

On the drive home, though, it started to rain. Kate couldn't bring herself to get out in that mess. She decided she'd order a couple of pizzas instead. A habit that she and her Aunt Emma had taken to after berry season was over and cobblers were no longer their go-to dinner. They decided that if they got the veggie laden ones, it was healthy enough.

Kate threw the car into park in front of her house, deciding to wait until this particular deluge let up a bit.

Dave and she had gone back to the class.

She'd stood there looking at the curious faces and searched for the right words.

"Aww man! The dude died," Royce said.

When push came to shove, Kate had turned to Royce for leadership, and he stepped up. She could see briefly the look that moved over his face. It affected him. He wanted the miraculous outcome. That was good. The humanity. Kate hoped Royce could hold on to that despite the jaded front that he showed people.

"I'm so sorry."

A long silence followed, and Kate allowed it. They needed time to assimilate the news.

"And the funeral?" Romeo asked.

"Alfie's body will be autopsied. Detective Murphy will invite the medical examiner to come and talk to you and answer your general questions. She won't be able to answer specific questions about Alfie while this case is under investigation. We won't be able to update you either as we are now witnesses in a murder case. We need to stop discussing the case in the classroom. If either Dave or I have information about the man's funeral arrangements, I will email all of you."

The bell rang. The students gathered their bags and moved silently out the door.

Dave fell into step beside her as they made their way out to the parking lot. "Do you want to come down to the precinct with me? We can find out who got assigned to the case, bring them up to date."

"I can't do this today, sorry. I'm going to bail on you. Dr. Carlon needs to talk to me about Ryan." Kate put her hand on her forehead and started swinging back and forth like she was looking for a direction to run to get away from everything.

"Hey." Dave reached out to still her. "No worries. But should you be driving right now? How about you take a Lyft?"

"I'm okay. Thanks though, Dave."

As she looked through the curtain of rain at her house, Kate knew she shouldn't have driven. One minute she was in the parking lot, talking to Dave, and the next, she was driving into her neighborhood, deciding that she'd forego the grocery shop. She didn't remember the drive at all.

Autopilot was never safe.

13

———————

HER PHONE BUZZED as Kate pushed her car door open. She'd been anticipating a call from Zack to tell her how Ryan was doing. That call hadn't come in. Not knowing what was going on there, she didn't want to make any situation worse by calling him.

She had decided to wait.

Kate stepped down into a puddle she hadn't seen past her belly. Water slid into the sides of her shoe as she quickly stepped back and looked down at her screen. Dr. Carlon.

Kate checked her watch; it was only four o'clock. They were supposed to talk over Dr. Carlon's dinner break.

A cold chill raced down her body, catching up with the icy freeze that shot up from her shoe.

Kate slammed the car door and hustled toward the stairs and under the porch roof before she swiped the screen and brought the phone to her ear. Breathless from the quick jog and a swift kick of displeasure from Little Guy, she panted, "Hello?" into the phone.

"Kate? It's Dr. Carlon." Cheery.

Kate wasn't sure how to interpret that. Some people got overly bright when they delivered bad news and then tried to paint a silver lining into the picture. Kate wasn't in the mood. "Hi there. Hang on just a minute, I'm…" Nope, she couldn't get her lungs functioning enough to get words out.

She kicked off her muddy shoes outside and felt the frigid air brighten the cold water on her socks as she made her way into the house.

The screen banged shut.

Kate turned to shove the door closed behind her, blocking out the wind and rain.

"I'm sorry." Her words were a whisper of air. She wasn't ready for this. They must have found something awful, or this would be Zack. "I need to sit down first." She shucked Ryan's coat and let it drop to the floor then got herself down onto the sofa, her eyes closed, her lips reflexively pursed like she'd learned in Lamaze, a means to deal with pain.

"Are you okay?" Dr. Carlon asked.

"Ready." Kate fixed her eyes on the empty black void of the fireplace.

"I had a few minutes. I thought I'd see if you could talk."

"Yes. Yes. I'm just walking through my front door now."

"Have you spoken with Ryan or Zack?"

Kate spread her knees wide and dropped her stomach between her legs, getting an elbow onto one thigh as she held the phone in shaking fingers. "No. I can look back at my call history. But, no, I haven't spoken to either."

"Okay, I'm not surprised. They were trying to catch a flight."

"A flight? Not the ambulance home? I wasn't expecting them until later tonight."

"They flew to California. Another trial."

"Wait. Ryan was just doing a trial. Well, helping research.

What did the imaging turn up? Let's start there. Did we find out anything helpful?"

"If we learn anything as a byproduct, it might help us address his issues. But that study wasn't geared to making Ryan better. It was data for their work on what happened to Ryan's brain over so many concussive events, and then the final two major blows—the explosion and then the accident."

"Yes, yes. That was Ryan giving back. I get that." Kate rubbed a hand over her face then reached down to rub her stomach, hoping to stop Little Guy from his distracting kicks. "I had my fingers crossed that they might see what it was—by using this new kind of imaging—that was putting Ryan in so much pain. I mean, well, we've said this before, Ryan was having a rough time of it already when he was medically discharged from his military duties. But he could do things, workout, tinker, have some kind of life. Since the accident, he just lies there, trying to survive." She rubbed a hand over her mouth. "He's involved in a new study?"

"Right, a study I hadn't found in my research. In this case, it might be a little bit of who you know as well as what you know. The researchers up in Boston who are doing the imaging were telling me about it, and they reached out on Ryan's behalf. Let me start there. I've got you on speaker phone right now. I'm driving. If you hear traffic or me cussing, I'm going to offer you a blanket apology now. But I have a patient who was just admitted, and I need to get over to the hospital."

"It's good. It's fine. Please. Do whatever you need to do. I'm appreciative. You said Ryan and Zack were headed to a plane."

"Right. So we've learned a lot over the decades of war about TBIs and psychological impacts. From the work done to help soldiers, we have him on the hormone regiment, and we know that we've got that balanced out. You and I have talked about how it's hard to tell how he's doing. The headaches are causing him so much pain that we can't tell if they are masking the symptoms of

TBI/PTSD he was exhibiting before the accident, or if we were able to effectively treat some of the pieces to his medical puzzle. If we could get the pain out of the way without medication, then we'd know."

"Yes."

"The military is interested in knowing what we're doing and how it's helping or not helping. And again, Ryan's finding that his being involved in experiments both gives him hope and makes him feel purposeful. So when offered this opportunity in California, he jumped at it."

Kate didn't want to interrupt Dr. Carlon's stream of thought, so all she said was, "Okay."

"I had sent Ryan's medical charts ahead of him to the folks in Boston. His MRIs from Boston from before the accident, the ones from here after. The more data the better."

"Right. We signed the papers. Did they see something new?"

"You might say that. They saw that Ryan was a SEAL."

"Oh."

"There's an experiment going on that focuses on SEALs. Double blind experiment. Forty percent of those who get the procedure see a change immediately. Sixty percent see a change over a month."

"This is for TBI? How would we know if there's a change or not with the pain possibly masking Ryan's symptoms?" Kate pulled off her wet socks and flung them toward the brick hearth away from the wooden floor. "You said double blind. He might be in the placebo group, flying all the way out there and deal with the air pressure changes and the pain to do something that has zero chance of helping him."

"I always forget that I'm talking to a biologist instead of one of my clients without a scientific background, until you start asking questions. It's a risk, yes. That's part of the problem with being a human guinea pig."

"Tell me about the trial. Is it a pill?" She put her hand to her forehead, asking, "What has he gotten himself involved with now?" more to herself than to Dr. Carlon.

"Maybe you should sit down for this."

"I am sitting."

"Okay, maybe you should lie down for this."

"Oh dear Lord. Give me a second, please." Kate swiped at her phone to check the call history and sure enough there were about twenty calls coming in repeatedly from Zack's number. She felt sick to her stomach. This was what happens when you put your phone on airplane mode at work and don't check the call history.

Kate swung her legs around and eased down on the couch with a throw blanket under her head, pulling a pillow between her legs. "All right, I'm safe from passing out and hitting my head on the floor—I guess you don't want another patient."

"Certainly not one that's due in a few weeks. Okay, starting at the beginning and working through what I know. You can stop me to ask questions or hold them. I have two kids, so I know first-hand about pregnancy brain." She chuckled. "Why don't you go ahead and ask as we go."

"That's nice of you, thank you." *Come on already!* What was Ryan doing? Maybe she still had time to throw her two cents out there and stop this from happening—if it was too crazy. Would she?

"…this is a good thing," Dr. Carlon said.

"Wait. What? I'm so sorry. I spiraled into a panic, and I didn't catch anything since I said thank you."

"Okay. Let me try that again. There is an ongoing study at Newton Brain Research Laboratory. NBRL focuses their research on brain-based medicine. They're in the last phase of an FDA clinical trial to judge the effect and the risk associated with a new therapy on a whole constellation of brain disorders from depression to aggression without drugs."

"No drugs," Kate repeated.

"Here's where the Boston guys got excited about hooking Ryan up with the California guys. The study at NBRL is focused on SEALs. The process they're using is called Magnetic EEG/ECG guided Resonance Therapy, or MEERT."

"Wow that sounds scary. Like something out of a sci-fi movie. Can you put it into layman's terms for me?"

"The way it was described to me, it's a pretty cool idea. Ryan will have an electroencephalography cap on his head to measure his brain's baseline electrical activity."

"You have that don't you?"

"They'll want to do their own for the study. The therapy is to take a device by his skull, oh about the size of an ultrasound wand and introduce small bursts of current into Ryan's brain. Each spot will be focused on for about twenty minutes and the whole inter-vention lasts about an hour."

"Electroshock therapy? For someone with a TBI? That sounds like madness. He's already in pain."

"I'm told that at its most painful, it feels like someone tapping on your head."

"They've seen significant changes in symptoms?"

"To those actually receiving the therapy, yes. It can be profound."

"You said they're focusing this study on SEALs. Not military in general, though? I don't know that I get that."

"I asked the same question. They want the research subjects to have approximately the same physical and mental qualities. They're trying to take out variables. In that regard, the SEALs are a good fit for the study. When they are selected for the BUDs they're in great shape. From what I've been reading over the kitchen table at night to understand Ryan's medical issues better, the SEALs go through specialized training geared to enhance their mental and physical strengths and alertness. Their job, both on a mission and in training, includes a lot of breaching by explosives."

"Yeah, they're called 'door kickers' but they usually kick a door open with det cord and C4."

"By choosing to populate their experiment with SEALs, the NBRL get both a high functioning baseline and those with persistent post-concussive symptoms."

"Did you tell them about hormones?"

"They actually asked me if I had tested him. Had I not, that's the first thing they do. They want me to watch his levels, because this process might recalibrate his brain to the point where he doesn't need hormone therapy. I've added that information to his chart."

"How long will Ryan be there?"

"The whole protocol is five days a week for four weeks."

"Zack can't stay away from his family that long."

"To be part of the study they have to have at least three interventions. After that, it's determined by the researchers and the SEAL how they'll proceed. It has to be done in California, and not everyone can get away from work to stay there that long."

"So various levels of disability."

"Yes."

"Randomized—so Ryan could be going out to California to watch a light bulb flash?

"If he did, it would add to the body of the work. The idea would be that once approved by the FDA it would become available to him."

"Yes, I know that's how it works. I just…to go all that way and to have hope."

"I understand."

"So what does that hope look like?" Kate draped her arm over her eyes. "Not a cure."

"'Cure' isn't a word they're associating with the therapy. But they've seen dramatic results in over sixty percent of those who go through the process."

"Could this make things worse though? I keep picturing shock therapy."

"Okay, let me paint a different picture for you. The first thing they're going to do is measure Ryan's EEG/ECG biometrics to find out what his baseline is. Everyone is different. No two people experience brain health and brain disorders in the same way. PTSD has a long list of symptoms on the menu, and they can have any combination of those symptoms."

"Okay." Kate patted her belly hoping to sooth Little Guy's gymnastics. He was a distraction. "The pain is Ryan's biggest issue right now."

"They're finding success relieving pain in some of the participants that show headaches as one of the symptoms. I'm sitting at the red light outside of the hospital parking lot. I'm kind of proud of myself. I haven't cussed yet."

"No worries."

"The theory states that these problems share a common origin. The TBI and PTSD are disruptions of a person's brain rhythm. That the beat of the brain's natural information-processing rhythm is off. The natural rate is called a 'dominant frequency'. They run somewhere between eight and thirteen hertz. That rate is the speed at which we encode information."

"The SEALs must all register on the high end of that spectrum, then."

"Exactly right. Eleven to thirteen."

"I wonder if it's as high before they go to BUDs or if it gets faster through training."

"Good question. My understanding is we're born with a rate. But it would be interesting if it could be influenced. I'm pulling into a parking spot, now."

"I appreciate you're taking the time."

"Look, you're eight plus months pregnant. You need to let others focus on Ryan while you focus on the baby. And by focusing on the baby, I mean that if something happens to you it happens to both of you. So you take care of you."

"I'll do my best."

14

———————

KATE HAD FOLLOWED HER PLAN. She had spent the entire day in her pajamas curled up on the couch watching Netflix.

A pizza box sat on her coffee table. Whenever she felt hungry, she'd lean over and grab another slice of veggie pizza.

This had been needed. She could feel some of the stress easing from her shoulders. When this show was over, she decided, she'd take another long soak in the tub, maybe do some yoga stretches, maybe go to bed with her Kindle.

Those thoughts were interrupted by a knock at her door.

She peeked through the peep hole to see Deep standing there with a pot in his hands. He was looking over his shoulder at something.

Kate threw the door wide. "Hey there."

"Grace thought you might like a break from cooking, so she sent over some stew."

"That's awfully kind. If you wouldn't mind setting it in the kitchen."

As Deep moved through the door, she saw Dave making a beeline her way. She pressed the screen wider. "That's not a happy look."

"Have you seen the news?" He took the steps two at a time.

"No, I'm binge watching a comedy." Any peace that Kate had been able to coax into her system flew out the door before she could slam it shut against the cold and rain.

Dave held out his phone, and she saw a newscaster on the screen. He tapped the arrow and there were renderings of Alf and the possible criminal front view and side view in pencil. Under Alf they had another rendering, this one was in color, of Alf's tattoo. The scene changed to the weekend reporter, standing in front of the dumpster, telling the story of what happened to Alf. There was police cam footage of the paramedics getting her out of the trash. Luckily, they didn't show Alf. They mentioned Kate's name, and Dave's. The students' names were being withheld since they were minors.

"I am so uncomfortable having my name out there," Kate said.

"It would be hard to find you. This house belongs to Lexi. You haven't had time to get a D.C. driver's license. You don't work for the school. Anyone who wanted to contact you would have a heck of a time doing that."

Kate nodded. "How did they get the renderings? They're really good. Did the detective—who's on this case?"

"Detective Mallory."

"Did Mallory put this together? Why would he use our names?"

"He called me to see why we were interfering in the case. He's pissed."

Kate stood there and blinked. "This isn't our students. They *understood*. We *told* them."

"Mallory got a heads up that it was all over social media when a local reporter tracked him down and was getting footage from the responding officer's vehicle and a copy of the police report. I'd say the likelihood of it being them is high. They didn't do anything we asked them not to do. There's no footage of the crime scene that they took. No photo of Alf. No mention of the lottery ticket or the footage they put together from security cameras."

"But the renderings are first class. They look almost photoreal." Kate looked up from the screen when Deep approached. "Deep is there any way to figure out how a story originated on social media?"

"I have software that can trace it. Why what's going on?"

Kate's phone was ringing, and she turned to dig it out of the crack in the sofa. She checked her text.

Zack – **Call me.**

She looked up to see Dave and Deep walking toward the door. "We'll be back," Dave said, as he went out.

"I'll leave it unlocked. Just let yourselves in."

She tapped quick dial number one. "Hey. It's Kate."

"What are you doing?"

"Worrying, to be honest."

"You talked to Dr. Carlon? You know we're in California?"

"Zack. I can't thank you enough. This is impacting your life."

"I can work from anywhere. And my mother-in-law is in town. So I'm extremely grateful for an opportunity to be gone."

"You love MeMaw."

"I do. But my family's happy. No need for a guilt trip. I bet you were surprised I didn't call and talk this over with you. I tried."

"I saw. I had my phone switched off. It feels like a big deal letting someone zap you like that."

"It's a huge opportunity if it works. And he's a SEAL. He's lucky."

"I guess."

"He can't live a whole life lying on his back, Kate."

"No. I agree." She put her hand on her forehead and stared out the window. "I'm just scared."

"If people were dying or going insane, the FDA would shut this down." Reasonable. Steady.

There were times that Kate relied on that in Zack. She was wrung out and hormonal. "It's been a big week and things haven't gone smoothly here."

"The baby?"

"No. I saw the doctor yesterday. My blood pressure is a little elevated. I'm planning on being a slug all weekend."

"Ryan's worried about you. He said you tried to help a crime victim. You don't have a good track record."

"True. But if Ryan's worried, Ryan can tell me that himself. He's a big boy and doesn't need an intermediary."

"He's in the lab right now undergoing the procedure. He's doing his best."

Kate sat silently. What could she say? She reached down and grabbed up a blanket from the sofa.

"Kate, you're very pregnant. I think it's dangerous for you to be involved with a crime under normal circumstances. Certainly now."

Kate hugged her blanket to her like a teddy bear. "Oh you don't need to preach to me about how vulnerable I am. I am well aware. But this is in the hands of the officers. I was just a good Samaritan. Why would anyone come after me? I applied pressure to the guy's wounds. And he died anyway."

"He died?"

"Yes, yesterday."

"They didn't say that on the news. I'll tell Ryan. Don't be surprised though if one of the Iniquus guys shows up with a duffel bag and is moving in with you. You know what? I'm going to call over to Striker and have him bring Houston to you. You keep her with you."

"Ryan said Houston would endanger me because—"

"Houston's not going to endanger you. Ryan just didn't want you burdened. He wanted to hand off her care to his military brothers. Houston adores you."

"I don't like these new games he's playing with me. I liked it better when we could just talk things through. Look, Deep Del Toro, who's on Striker's team, is living next door. So I'm covered. And he's here now so I need to go. I love you Zack, even when you push my buttons."

"I love you, too, even when you're hard headed."

Kate tapped her screen and looked up as the men came in.

Dave handed her a list of their students' names. "These are the accounts that started it. And it started Friday afternoon."

Kate scratched under her nose, thinking. She swiped her code design and texted Romeo: **I know you don't normally talk on the phone. AND I need to talk to you. Please, call me now.**

She answered the phone on the first ring. "Thank you, Romeo."

"Yes, ma'am."

"You guys started a thing on social media, huh?"

"We wanted to find a way to identify Alf. Sooner rather than later, you know? Royce thinks no one's ever gonna look."

"Who did the drawings?" Kate worked to lighten her voice. "They're pretty impressive."

"Yeah, yeah, my girl she got an aunt that got a cousin who dating a guy who do sketches in the park on the weekend for some side hustle. We sent him the piece of tape from the Shop and Go that was clearest. And he done them up for us."

"And the tattoo."

"Yes, ma'am. We did. My uncle's friend's brother was a Marine and he say that those tattoos sometimes are specific to a unit. You know all the war buddies getting the same one. And he had the bullet scars and all. I'm pretty sure he's been to war. Or hey, maybe he grow up in the wrong neighborhood. But this guy we was talking to, he didn't recognize the tattoo when we showed him. He did recognize the scars, though. He say Alf is most likely a war hero."

"You've put a lot of effort into this. I hope you get the results you need one way or another."

"Thank you."

"Thank you for calling me, Romeo."

She hung up. "I'm scared Dave. I told you what happened with the watch that my students found. I keep hearing that woman —sorry, I'm going to sound crazy, I hear her in my ear, 'Tick Tock. Tick Tock. Times almost up.' When I survived the attack by her murderer, I was fighting the guy off. I thought I could kill him with my bare hands I was so enraged he would put Little Guy in danger. But that was the second time I narrowly escaped. I feel like I hid from the grim reaper. And he's been looking for me."

Dave was perched on the coffee table. The pizza box pushed to the side. He reached out and squeezed Kate's arm. "You said that's your husband's call name. Reaper. You think there's anything in that?"

"That Ryan would hurt me?"

"I'm not suggesting that. I'm not a therapist. But you've been through an awful lot in the last year, and I don't think it's a bad idea."

She frowned.

"We talked about the students and how important it is to get habits into their lives that would help them handle criminal justice jobs. If you saw someone in your position, you'd want them to get help, so they didn't burn out."

Kate stared at her belly, her lips pulling into a deep frown.

"This already shows they're listening to you. They did the leg work, but you planted the seeds in their head."

Her gaze came up, hot with anger. "To try to track down a killer when they don't have the skills to handle the repercussions? I most *certainly* did not."

"They're teens. They're invincible."

"Yeah, I forgot about their bullet proof egos."

"You asked them to be strategic and creative and to act on intrinsic motivation. They implemented your lessons. As much as we're upset with the class being all males, I will say that the guidance counselor and school resource officer did a good job. Those kids were *excited* by this. I'm excited to see what they've done. They didn't do anything we asked them not to do. And the most important thing was that they weren't driven by their bullet proof egos. They were driven by righteous indignation and compassion."

"I am equal parts deeply profoundly proud of them and scared. If it gets out that there was a lottery ticket, it's the watch all over again."

15

___

Monday

"I'm HANDING out your quizzes. Some of you will find your grades disappointing." She laid the stack of papers on her lap and scanned the room. "I don't want a single one of you to let this grade define you or define your time here in this class. Now is the time when you decide for yourself what you want for you. This could be the best failing grade that you've ever received if you let it teach you that if you want something, like a career in criminal justice, then you need to fight for it. You need to love your textbooks. You have to go after it. I know you can. I've seen it with my own eyes last week."

The class sat completely still.

"The quiz was asking a lot of you. I *expected* you all to do well. I don't know if people haven't asked much of you, because they don't think you are capable or if you thought this was the kind of class you could blow off. Either way, *know* this: I see how smart and capable you are. I'm holding you to my *highest* standard, because you have the capacity to reach that level of professionalism *and* because as we've discussed before, if you go into this line of work, people's lives will depend on your seriousness. This is serious stuff."

She was met with silence. But the energy rose.

"Failure is not a bad word in this classroom. Well, that's not entirely true. Here's the deal, there are two kinds of failures, there's the good kind and the bad kind. Let's start with the bad kind. It's the 'I don't give a flip' kind. It's the, 'I'm not doing my assignments, I'm not studying for my test, and I'll sleep through class' kind." She waggled the test papers in the air. "It's the 'No effort equals no outcome' kind." She laid the quizzes back down. "Then there's the good kind. There's the 'I tried hard to do it, and it didn't go well' kind. It's the bravery to live in that space of failure to *feel* the discomfort as you try again, and again, and again, and again. This applies to anything. Before I was pregnant, I wanted to get upper body strength. I wanted to do pushups and I face planted instead. Since I couldn't do a regular push up, I did them from my knees, then I did one properly. Just one. Every day, I did it until that was easy, so I added another. It took time. Dedication. I struggled to reach my goal of fifty pushups in a row." She rubbed her belly. "Of course, if I get into push up position right now, I barely dip until I tap my belly on the floor. But the fact remains that I tried and failed and tried and failed until I edged forward, made progress, and hit my goal. It's a silly example. There are other more important examples. Remember Mozart, striving from the age of three, and his music impacts us hundreds of years later, influencing our modern artists like Kelis. Remember Thomas Edison and the lightbulb—a *thousand* fails. If he'd given up, how long would we have been in the dark?"

The kids shifted around now, a bit of shame for not holding themselves to a higher standard.

"Your effort will lead you to amazing places. Maybe this class isn't your future. Maybe this isn't the kind of science that triggers your curiosity and motivates your effort. Remember though, one thing we know about creativity and success is everything you know and everything you experience goes into your toolbox. You never know when you'll need to pull something out and use it, when you'll be working on something that truly excites you, and the thing that makes you successful is some little tidbit of knowledge that you picked up in your CSI class, or your English class, or your underwater basket weaving class. If you are given the opportunity to learn, use it. When life gives you things you find hard, *embrace* it. Learn from it. Put it in your tool box. Let that tool box help build the kind of life that you want for yourself."

That looked like it took. Good.

"Okay, climbing off my soap box now. The grades are disappointing. For everyone who learns from this experience and raises their grades twenty points or greater on the next test, I will average the two grades and replace this grade with that average. But you have to earn it. You have to *want* it. You have to *motivate* yourself toward it."

Dave came over and took the quizzes from Kate. He whispered in her ear, "Go home. Get off your feet. I've got this." When he started passing out the papers he said, "Mrs. Hamilton is going to let me take over the rest of the class today. I wanted to talk to you about my job and some of the real-life dangers that are part and parcel with trying to find murderers."

KATE STOOD outside her door with her keychain in her hand, picking out the front door key. She was so glad for this extra little respite. She checked her watch. Zack had said yesterday that Ryan was on his third protocol. And Sunday night they'd be making some decisions about how to proceed forward. With the time differences, she hadn't been able to check in and see what the plan was this morning. She'd called from the school parking lot, but she'd been sent straight to voicemail.

Kate slipped the key into the knob, turned and pushed. The screen resting on her shoulder.

She decided to try Zack again, now. Kate kicked off her shoes and turned to shut the door.

"Hey, Teach."

She looked up to see a man dressed in a suit with a pad and pen.

It could very well be the guy from the videos and the artist's renderings. It could be. She wasn't sure. This was so familiar. *Run,* her limbic system screamed. But that was absurd. Kate reached her arm around her stomach.

"I'm a reporter. I have a few questions for you about your heroic efforts saving the homeless man with your high school students."

"Thank you, I have nothing to say about the incident." She pushed the door, trying to close it. But the man had slipped his foot in the way.

"I think you're probably right. But I have a few things to say. Let's talk about this in your house."

He slid the hand with the pen into his pants. Kate thought about screaming, but as she scanned over the neighborhood, she knew everyone was gone. It was time for the moms to pick up their kids at the elementary school. And the dads were at work. Grace was at work. Kate was alone on the block.

When the guy pulled his hand from his pocket, he was palming the handle of a tactical knife. The blade laid along his forearm.

Yes, this was the man. And he'd come because he must think she knew where the lottery ticket was. And just exactly like in Boonestown, she didn't have it. It was with the police. That had done nothing to protect her before. And she was in a position to save herself back then.

Kate backed into her house and over to a chair by the window. She dropped down, holding her belly like a basketball between her knees, and she tried to do some Lamaze breathing. She thought about the biologics of survival. Humans were hardwired to help a woman who was pregnant. If she had to, she'd go all in on his caveman-survival brain.

It's all she had by way of weapon.

Kate knew this was the man who had sliced into Alf. And if Alf couldn't protect himself, a military vet, she had no chance. Any slices to her torso would be aimed at Little Guy.

"Whatever you need," she panted. "Please, help yourself." Then she groaned and feigned closing her eyes, panting and unfocused while she counted to sixty in her head. If he had any kind of training in babies, she needed this to be as realistic as possible. "Wow, that was unexpectedly intense." She looked at the wall clock and said, "Two forty-three."

"What's that? What are you doing?"

"I think…I might be ready to have this baby. They sent me home early from school because I was having contractions. They're getting closer." Kate wiped a wrist over her head and grabbed at her belly again. "My neighbor's supposed to go with me to the hospital. I need my suitcase."

The guy stood there his eyelids stretched wide. "Okay. Okay yeah, you should do that. Go to the hospital. But first I need Alf's lottery ticket. He said to pick it up for him."

The guy didn't know Alf had died. Kate thought back to the news and the Internet posts, no one had mentioned Alf's death. They also didn't mention the high school where she taught. But the school was right up the road from the basketball courts. He must have gone there and waited to follow her home. How many teachers were this pregnant, after all. It wasn't like she was hard to miss.

"Oh, okay. Great. Hang on." Kate pretended not to have seen the knife. She might have missed it if she wasn't a SEAL wife and seen how the guy's used their tools. "I have it here."

The guy licked his lips.

Kate pulled out the card Dave had given her for Detective Mallory. And at the same time, she tapped her emergency button that when she dropped the phone would automatically send a message to 9-1-1 with her location. She handed the card out and dropped the phone to the side hard enough that it would bounce. She looked down at it and reached, then grabbed her belly with an "Oh!"

The guy grabbed at the card in her hand. "This ain't no lottery ticket! This is the detective's card."

Kate held up a finger for him to wait as she huffed and puffed and made faces. After she counted to sixty in her head, she wound things down. "I'm not ready for this pain. Who the hell would have more than one kid with this much pain? It feels like my insides are ripping apart. I don't want to do this. I'm done. Nope. Not going to do this." Her gaze roamed the room, and she tried to make herself look wild-eyed. Little by little she calmed the act down.

She waved her hand at the card in the guy's hand. "I gave him the lottery ticket. He has it in the evidence locker. Tell Alf that the detective said he just needs to sign for it, and he can have it back."

"You're lying. You wouldn't do that. It was worth too much. You would have hidden it away."

"That would be a crime. And it was only two hundred and fifty dollars."

"Five hundred thousand dollars."

"No. No, I promise you. It was a couple hundred bucks." She

got a good look at the guy now and, yeah, he wasn't looking good. "You're pretty shaky. Here I am yelling about epidurals, and I bet you need a fix. My husband is a disabled vet. The detective said Alf is too. Are you? I don't mind helping you. I know how the VA is. There's money in my wallet." She pointed at her purse. "I can't get up to get it right now. How much will it cost you to feel better? Let me help you."

"It was *not a couple hundred bucks*. That was the golden ticket that's Five hundred *thousand*. Are you trying to cheat a war hero?"

"Take the money from my wallet. Get yourself what you need now. Then we can figure out how to get you more money. I don't have the lottery ticket—like I said it's with the police. I—" She stopped to make terrible noises as if she's having a contraction. "So close together, aren't they? Really close," she gasped.

If Deep or Grace came up onto the porch, they'd hear her. Surely, they'd look in and see the scene. What time did they get home? Hopefully, Grace wouldn't knock or come through the door. Just call for help. Someone with a skill set to launch themselves on this guy. Deep—or one of his buddies from Iniquus. Someone with bad guy pouncing skills. She blew out and put her head back. "Wow that was strong. I mean, you hear stories about the pain of childbirth, but you can't really imagine them. It's like my insides became a volcano and it took over my brain." She panted, playing this for all it was worth.

"You got something to drink around here? Alcohol?"

Kate was eight months pregnant; she had no use for alcohol. *Oh wait!* Tim had put a bottle of champagne in her car with her bags to pop open when the baby was born. It was in the dining room. Should she tell him? Would drunk help? Well it would take time and maybe Dave would come by and check on her after school. "Champagne. On the table in there." Kate pointed.

The guy kept his eye on her as he went in and found it.

Kate wasn't going to run. It was absurd to think she could get away from him. No. Chess was the only way to win here. She'd call it a win if she was able to get to a place where this guy wasn't. Whole and healthy.

He found the bottle of champagne. He popped the cork and poured it into the water glass Kate had left on the coffee table last night. "A toast to my lottery windfall. All that money. How much money? Five hundred grand." He pointed his finger at her. "You can't fool me. You think you're a smart teacher, and you can lie to me."

Kate swiped her hand through the air to shut him up as she went into her next fake contraction. "Hospital," she grunted and counted to ninety this time. "Longer and more frequent. I can't drive there. I need an ambulance. Look," she said as she came back to sitting. "Take my wallet. Take my car. I'll give you my pin number. Go get what you need. I need an ambulance." She grimaced.

He was belting back the champagne like it was ginger ale. He drank the bottle down then belched long and hard. Surely with the carbonation, that alcohol would go straight to his head.

He wiggled the bottle at her. "You got more?"

She faked another contraction. Louder and longer this time hoping to god to attract attention. She thought she heard footsteps on the porch. Her imagination? Wishful thinking? The last time she was confronted by a killer, she had fought him off tooth and nail. That was last September when she wasn't a freaking whale — "The baby! The baby! I think it's time!"

"That was fast wasn't it?" He was waving the knife around. It was slicing close to her face. "That was too fast wasn't it?"

He looked at her horrified as the two oldest parts of his brain fought—save the mothers and babies and survival. Looking at the guy's teeth and skin, he was a meth addict. And Kate knew that addictions rubbed the survival part of the brain raw.

Kate thought she heard something again on the porch.

"The baby! I feel the head."

He stood there, knife in hand, his head wagging from side to side.

"I have a baby coming out of me!" Kate let out a terrible scream of pain. Her whole goal was to keep this man's brain from settling on a plan of his own. She needed to give him a direction to get him away from her.

Once that fake contraction was over, she said, "Okay, I don't have time to get to the hospital. This is what we'll do. Go fill the tub upstairs with hot water."

"Hot water?" he slurred.

"We need hot water for the baby. Upstairs. Fill the tub. Quick hurry!"

He walked to the stairs and put his hand on the post.

As soon as she heard the tap go on, she'd run to her car and lock the doors.

He wasn't moving so she called out in anguish. The guy wove his fingers into his hair and pulled. The knife resting on his head.

"Water!" She was afraid to stand with him looming there.

"Okay. Okay. But you'll run away."

"I have a baby's head pushing its way out of my body, and you think I can run? Are you for real?"

"Okay. Okay. Water in the bathtub."

"Hot as you can get it!"

He spun toward the stairs and just as he put his foot on the tread, a flash of brown sailed into the room.

A sharp scream and a tangle.

Kate pushed back into her chair as her brain tried to make sense of this new information.

Houston! Houston was tearing into this guy.

Sirens were sounding. People pooled into the room.

Ryan was beside her. "The baby is coming? I've got you, Katie. I'll help you. Can you feel the head?"

She wrapped her arms around his neck. How did he get here? "I'm fine. Everything's fine. I was just acting to get out of the situation. The baby's fine. See?" She pulled Ryan's hand onto her belly to feel the baby kicking against his hand. The first time he had allowed this.

He stilled with a look of awe on his face.

She smoothed her hand over his cheek, looking at him. He looked so different from the last time she'd seen Ryan lying in his care facility bed. This man actually looked like her husband. The man she married. Her Ryan.

He pulled her hand over his mouth and kissed her palm.

"The pain?" she asked, aware out of the corner of her eye that others were in the room and dealing with the situation. She didn't want to pull her attention from Ryan, afraid if she did this would all vanish. A mirage.

"Pain, still. But a great deal better. They think I'll continue to make improvements."

Kate collapsed against Ryan, shaking as the adrenaline left her system.

Looking over Ryan's shoulder, Deep had his knee in the guy's back.

Zack was holding Houston by the collar.

"Good, girl, Houston. Good, girl," she called, and Houston dragged Zack toward Kate.

"Are you going to tell us what was happening in here? The guy with a knife?"

"He followed me from the school, I'm guessing. I'll explain later."

"Cops are pulling up," Deep said. "Do you need an ambulance?"

"I'm not hurt," she managed. Too much going on, she needed

a point of clarity. "Okay quick, why are you here, Ryan? Dr. Carlon told me you were doing a month-long study."

"I go back for that next Saturday. I had to get home and see you. Hold you."

Kate nodded her head. Her lips in a tight frown, trying to hold back the sobs.

"I'm not cured. Don't get that into your head, Kate."

She shook her head.

"They want me to come in five days a week for four weeks to finish the protocol." He pulled her hand to his lips and kissed her again. "I think this is the golden ticket. I think this is going to be the thing that makes the difference. I'll go and do the study, and I'll be home by beginning of February, in plenty of time to be with you for our Little Guy's birthday. Right son?" he whispered against her belly.

EPILOGUE

Kate turned her head as Ryan opened their front door for Tim. "Hey there, sorry for the quick turnaround. Aunt Emma says she can't sleep with all the car noises."

Tim stretched out his hand to shake Ryan's. "Congratulation's, man." He rounded to the couch where Kate was snuggled up with her newborn sleeping on her chest.

She leaned her head over and breathed in the honey-sweetness of him.

"Zachariah Timothy Hamilton is a mighty fine name." Tim reached out and wiggled Little Guy's foot.

"Yes, we decided that naming Little Guy after the two men who stepped in and helped my wife protect him would be fitting." Ryan came around to perch on the sofa arm behind Kate, gently massaging her shoulders.

Kate leaned her head back. "Aunt Emma," she called toward the kitchen. "Your knight in shining armor is here to whisk you back to Scarborough."

Aunt Emma moved through the dining room drying her hands. "Thank goodness. I tell you, I love Little Guy so much. I hate to have to leave him. But cities make my skin crawl, always have."

"No worries, Mrs. Jenkins. It gives me a chance to say hi to this little guy. When I brought you, I had to turn right back around, and I felt like I missed out."

"Can I get you something to eat or drink, Tim?" Aunt Emma asked. "I've got a nice pound cake fresh out of the oven."

"No, ma'am, but thank you." Tim took a seat at the other end of the sofa and looked at Ryan. "Kate says that you just signed a contract with Iniquus. What will you be doing over there?"

"I'm going to start out on Strike Force for a few months while I get the lay of the land. I'll be shadowing Deep Del Toro while he brings me up to speed on the capabilities of the various strike teams."

"You're not going to be operating again, are you?"

"Kate has put the kibosh on anything that might aggravate my brain. No, after I'm up to speed, I'll be working with their Cerberus Tactical K-9 Team. Training. I won't be taking the dogs into the field."

"That's what you did with the SEALs, I think Kate told me."

"K-9 handler? Yeah, that's right."

Kate looked up at Ryan and smiled, and he dropped a kiss onto her lips.

"With Ryan working, will you get to take more time off?" Tim watched Aunt Emma move through the room.

"Tim, I'm going to put the last of my things in my suitcase, then I'll be ready to go. I know you've got duty tonight. I don't want to hold you up."

"Yes, ma'am."

"My kids in the CSI class are important to me. I'm not going to abandon them. I was able to work it out with the DCPD that Dave Murphy and I can finish teaching this semester, then I'll end my contract."

"Was DCPD upset?"

"I think, under the circumstances, being held at knife point and all, they understand that I'm no longer gung-ho about this position. That guy, by the way, Bob Starr, pled guilty in exchange for life in prison instead of the death penalty. Get this, one of the things I didn't understand was why he didn't just take the lottery ticket from Alfred. After they fought, Starr threw Alfred in the dumpster to go back in the middle of the night when he could search through Alfred's pockets and not attract attention. Cold. At least, he's off the streets."

"Three notches in your belt, Kate. Not bad at all. Matter of fact, I just have the one. And I'm a detective."

"I'd prefer none. The good piece of news is that Oliver did capture Alfred giving me his lottery ticket. I was able to sign it over to the scholarship fund. Every one of my students who helped solve Alfred's murder will have a good chunk of money to pay their living expenses while they're in college. They were already earning scholarships for criminal justice."

"You're going to keep teaching? Maybe something safer, biology?"

"I'll finish up this semester, then the plan is for me to spend some time home with Little Guy and Ryan. We've had a rough couple of years. We're ready for this new start."

Kate and Ryans story continues in the World of Iniquus with FEAR the REAPER, part of the Strike Force series.

Readers, I hope you enjoyed getting to know Kate, Ryan and the little guy. If you had fun reading The Kate Hamilton Mysteries, I'd appreciate it if you'd help others enjoy it too.

Recommend it: Just a few words to your friends, your book groups, and your social networks would be wonderful.

Review it: Please tell your fellow readers what you liked about my book by reviewing, The Kate Hamilton Mysteries. If you do write a review, please send me a note at hello@fionaquinnbook s.com so I can thank you with a personal e-mail. Or stop by my website www.FionaQuinnBooks.com to keep up with my news and chat through my contact form.

Join the fight for greater good with the first book from the World of Iniquus:
Weakest Lynx

Turn the page for a sneak peek:

WEAKEST LYNX

SHE WANTED A SIMPLE LIFE. WHAT SHE GOT
WAS ANYTHING BUT…

1

LYNX

THE BLACK BMW POWERED STRAIGHT TOWARD ME. HEART pounding, I stomped my brake pedal flush to the floorboard. My chest slammed into the seat belt, snapping my head forward. There wasn't time to blast the horn, but the scream from my tires was deafening. I gasped in a breath as the BMW idiot threw me a nonchalant wave—his right hand off the wheel—with his left hand pressed to his ear still chatting on his cell phone. Diplomatic license plates. *Figures.*

Yeah, I didn't really need an extra shot of adrenaline—like a caffeine IV running straight to my artery—I was already amped.

"Focus, Lexi," I whispered under my breath, pressing down on the gas. "Follow the plan. Give the letter to Dave. Let him figure this out." I sent a quick glance down to my purse where a corner of the cream-colored envelope jutted out, then veered my Camry back into the noonday DC gridlock, weaving past the graffitied storefronts. I recognized that the near miss with the BMW guy probably wasn't his fault. I couldn't remember the last ten minutes of drive time.

I watched my review mirror as a bike messenger laced between the moving cars on his mission to get the parcel in his bag to the right guy at the right time. Once he handed over his package, he'd be done. Lucky him. Even though I was handing my letter off to Dave, the truth was that wouldn't be my end point. I wasn't clear about what an end point would even look like. Safe. It might look like I was safe, that I had my feet back under me. But that thought seemed like it was far out on the horizon; and right now, I was just looking for something to grab on to to keep me afloat.

When I finally parked in front of Dave Murphy's mid-century brick row house, I sat for a minute, trying to regain my composure. I'd pushed this whole mess to the back burner for as long as I could, but after last night's nightmare… Well, better to get a detective's opinion. Dave had handled enough crackpots over his time with the DCPD that he'd have a better grasp of the threat level. Right now, even with all my training, I was scared out of my mind.

I glanced down at my hands. The tremor in them sent the afternoon sunlight dancing off my brand-new engagement and wedding rings. I felt like an imposter wearing them—like a little girl dressed up in her mother's clothes. *I'm too young to be dealing with all this crap,* I thought as I shoved my keys into my purse. I pulled my hair into a quick ponytail and stepped out into the February cold. Casting anxious glances up and down the street, I jogged up the stairs to bang on Dave's front door.

The screen squeaked open almost immediately, as if he'd been standing there waiting for my knock. "Hey, Baby Girl," he said, stepping out of the way to let me in. Dave had been calling me Baby Girl since I was born, because my parents couldn't decide on my name, and that was how I was listed on my hospital ankle tag.

"Glad I found you at home." I walked in and plopped down on the blue gingham couch. It had been here since I could remember. The fabric was threadbare and juice stained by his five-year-old twins. On a cop's salary, fine furnishings ranked low in priority. Right now—edgy and confused—I appreciated the comfort of familiarity.

Dave shifted into detective mode—hands on hips, eyes scanning me. "Long time, no see."

"Where are Cathy and the kids?" I asked.

"They've got dentist appointments. Did you come to tell us your news?" He lifted his chin to indicate my left hand and settled at the other end of the couch, swiveling until we were face to face.

"Uhm, no." I twisted my rings, suddenly feeling drained and bereft. What wouldn't I give to have my husband Angel here? The corners of my mouth tugged down. I willed myself to stay focused on the reason for the visit. My immediate safety had to take priority over my grief.

Dave raised a questioning brow, waiting for me to continue.

"Angel and I got married Wednesday. I'm Lexi Sobado, now." My voice hitched and tears pressed against my lids. I lowered my lashes, so Dave wouldn't see. But his eyes had locked onto mine, and he never missed much.

"Married? At your age? No introduction? No wedding invitation? Why isn't he here with you now?" Dave angled his head to the side and crossed his arms over his middle-aged paunch. "I'd like to meet the guy," he all but snarled.

Dave probably thought I'd come here because my husband screwed things up already. I pulled the pillow from behind my back and hugged it to me like a shield. "I'm sorry. I should have let you and Cathy know what was going on—I was caught up, and I just..." I stopped to clear my throat. "Angel and I got married at the courthouse and no one came with us. Not even Abuela Rosa."

"Angel Sobado. He's kin to Rosa, then?"

I gave the slightest tip of a nod. "Angel is her great-nephew. I couldn't bring him with me today because he deployed with the Rangers to the Middle East Thursday. That's why everything happened so fast. He was leaving." The last word stuck in my throat and choked me.

Dave leaned forward to rest his elbows on his knees. Lacing his fingers, he tapped his thumbs together. "Huh. That's a helluva short honeymoon. Married Wednesday. Gone Thursday." Dave's tone had dropped an octave and gained a fringe of fatherly concern.

His compassion gave me permission to break down. But those Angel-emotions were mine. Private. Right now, I needed to hold myself in check long enough to get through my mission of handing off the letter. I shifted my feet back and forth over the rug as I glared at my purse.

"Might even explain the expression on your face," Dave said, narrowing his eyes. He slouched against the arm of the over-stuffed couch.

Stalling wasn't going to make this any easier. I reached a hesitant hand into my bag, pulled out a plastic Zip-loc holding the envelop, and held it up for Dave. "The expression is because of this," I said.

Dave took the bag. After a brief glance, he hefted himself to his feet. Over at his desk, he pulled on a pair of Nitrile gloves, then carefully removed the letter.

Dearest India Alexis,
O my Luve's like the melodie
That's sweetly play'd in tune!
As fair thou art, my bonnie lass,
So deep in love am I:
And I will love thee still, my dear,
Till a' your bones are white and dry:
Till a' your veins gang dry, my dear,

And your skin melt with the sun;
I will luve thee until your heart is still my dear
When the sands of your life shall no more run.
And fare thee weel, my only Luve,
And fare thee weel a while!
And I will come again, my Luve, so I can watch you die.

Dave read the words aloud then stared at me hard; his brows pulled in tight enough that the skin on his forehead accordioned. "What the—"

"Someone shoved the poem under the door to my room, and it's scaring the bejeezus out of me." I gripped the pillow tighter.

Dave peered over the top of his reading glasses. "Last night? This morning?"

"Wednesday morning." I braced when I said it, knowing it would tick Dave off that I didn't bring this to him immediately. Ever since my dad died, his buddies had stepped in and tried to take over the fathering job, even though I'd be turning twenty in a few days.

True to my expectations, Dave was red-faced and bellowing. "*Wednesday?* You waited two whole days to tell me you've gotten a friggin death threat?"

Yup, this was exactly the response Dad would have given me.

Dave jumped up, pacing across the room. Obviously, he didn't think this was someone's idea of a joke. Fear tightened my chest at his confirmation. I had hoped he'd say, "No worries—someone is having fun pranking you," and then I could go on about my life without the major case of heebie-jeebies that tingled my skin and made me want to run and hide.

"It was our wedding day." I worked to modulate my voice to sound soft and reasonable. "I only had a few short hours before Angel had to take off. So yeah, I decided to focus on us instead of this." I motioned toward the paper in his hand.

Dave took in a deep breath, making his nostrils flare. "Okay." I could almost see his brain shifting gears. "When you first picked up the letter, did you get any vibes?"

"You mean, ESP-wise?"

He nodded stiffly; his eyes hard on me.

Vibes. That wasn't the word I would have chosen to explain my sensations. "I didn't hear anything. It was more like an oily substance oozing over me." I tucked my nose into the soft cloth of the pillow and breathed in the scent of cinnamon fabric freshener. "I vomited." My voice dropped to a whisper. "It felt like evil and craziness, and I can still smell that stench." A shiver raced down my spine.

Dave's lips sealed tightly; he was probably trying to hold back a litany of expletives. Finally, he asked, "That's all?"

"Yes."

"Did any of your neighbors notice anyone unusual lurking around? Did you check with management and run through the security tapes?"

"Dave, didn't you hear? My apartment building burned to the ground three weeks ago. I assumed you knew. It was on the news."

Dave's eyebrows shot straight up.

"I've been living in a motel the Red Cross rented out for all the families displaced by the fire. But to answer your question, no, nobody saw anything, and there were no cameras trained on my motel corridor." I curled my lips in to keep them from trembling. I was used to holding my emotions in check. I trained myself to present a sweet exterior, a costume of sorts, but right now I was filled to over-flowing, and my mask kept slipping out of place.

"Shit." Dave ran a hand over his face. "I had no idea. I'm letting your parents down. Apartment burned, married, husband gone, and now a death threat." His eyes narrowed on me. "Do you think that about covers all of your surprises for me today?"

I paused for a beat. "Yeah, Dave, I think that's it for today." Okay, even if he was like family, the way Dave was talking pissed me off. I was frightened. I wanted a hug and his reassurance. What I was getting was… Dave's brand of love. He wouldn't be this red-faced and agitated if he wasn't worried about me. Tears prickled behind my eyelids, blurring my vision.

"Hey, now. Stop. We'll get to the bottom of this. Did you already let Spyder McGraw know what's going on?"

I wiped my nose with the back of my wrist. "Spyder's still off-grid. I have no idea when he'll get home."

"Were you assigned a different partner while he's gone?"

"No, sir. I only ever worked for Spyder—he sort of wanted to keep me a secret." I still couldn't believe Mom had sat Dave down and told him all about my apprenticeship with Spyder McGraw. Under Spyder's tutelage, I was following my dream of becoming an Intelligence Officer, learning to out-think and out-maneuver the bad guys trying to hurt American interests. And like anyone heading toward a life in the intelligence community, my skills needed to go under the radar. Now that my mom had died, only four people—Spyder, the Millers, and Dave—knew that side of my life. I would prefer Dave didn't know.

"Still, did you consider bringing this to Spyder's commander? Iniquus would probably give him a heads up. Get a message to him."

"Iniquus is my last resort. Sure, Spyder told me to talk to them if I ever found myself in trouble." I sucked in a deep breath of air. "Bottom line? He never wanted them to know I worked for him, well, for them. Safety in anonymity and all that." My fingers kneaded the stuffing in the pillow. "Besides, I guess I was hoping this would all just go away."

Dave's eyes were hard on me. "You know better. Once some

psycho's caught you on his radar, you're stuck there until someone wins."

"Okay, so I make sure it's me who wins."

"Exactly right." He considered me for a minute before he asked, "You've kept up with your martial arts training?"

"I have a sparring partner who's pretty good. We rent time at a Do Jang twice a week."

Dave lowered his head to read over the poem again. He put the letter and envelope back in the Zip-loc and placed it on his mantle. Pulling off his gloves with a snap, he looked down at them. "I hate these things. They give me a rash. Look, I'm going to take this down to the station and open a file. If you get anything else, I want you to bring it to me right away. Understood?"

"Yes, sir."

"This is the only poem, letter, communication of any kind you've gotten?"

I nodded. For the first time since I walked into Dave's house, I became aware of sounds other than our conversation and the thrumming blood behind my eardrums. A football game played on TV. I glanced over as the announcer yelled some gibberish about a first down, then moved my gaze back to Dave. "You must have taken graveyard shift last night," I said.

He picked up a remote, zapped off the TV, and sent me a raised eyebrow.

"It doesn't take a psychic. You look like an unmade bed."

Dave ran a hand over his dark hair, thick on the sides, sparse on top. He hadn't used a comb today or bothered to shave. He was hanging-out-at-home comfy in jeans and beat-to-hell tennis shoes. It looked like the only thing I was interrupting was the game re-run.

"Double homicide. Turned into a long night up to my ankles in sewage."

"Yum." I tried on a smile, but it was plastic and contrived.

Dave narrowed his eyes. "We need to move you. Pronto. It's priority one. You need to be someplace secure where I can keep better tabs on you."

"I've been looking since the fire, but I haven't found anything."

"Would you consider buying?" he asked.

"Yes, actually—I'm looking for a low-cost fixer-upper I can work on to help me get through this year without Angel." I followed Dave into the hallway. "Diversion, and all that."

"How about here, in my neighborhood? I could keep a better eye on you—and you won't be showing up at my door with a suitcase full of surprises." He grabbed his coat from the

closet and shrugged it on. "I'm taking you over to meet my neighbor. She has the other half of her duplex on the market." He looked over his shoulder at me. "You shouldn't be running around without a jacket." He handed me an oversized wool parka that smelled like raking leaves. He kicked a Tonka truck out of the way, and we moved out the front door.

On the front porch, I slid into the shadows and took in the length of the road. No cars, no barking dogs, everything quiet.

Dave glanced back. "Coast is clear."

I tucked the coat hood up over my ponytail. Screened by Dave's broad back, I started across the street. Down the road, a car motor revved. I reached under my shirt and pulled out my gun.

Continue reading *Weakest Lynx(Book One of The Lynx Series)*

Turn the page for The World of Iniquus in chronological order.

THE WORLD of INIQUUS

Chronological Order

Ubicumque, Quoties. Quidquid

Weakest Lynx (Lynx Series)

Missing Lynx (Lynx Series)

Chain Lynx (Lynx Series)

Cuff Lynx (Lynx Series)

WASP (Uncommon Enemies)

In Too DEEP (Strike Force)

Relic (Uncommon Enemies)

Mine (Kate Hamilton Mystery)

Jack Be Quick (Strike Force)

Deadlock (Uncommon Enemies)

Instigator (Strike Force)

Yours (Kate Hamilton Mystery)

Gulf Lynx (Lynx Series)

Open Secret (FBI Joint Task Force)

Thorn (Uncommon Enemies)

Ours (Kate Hamilton Mysteries)

Cold Red (FBI Joint Task Force)

Even Odds (FBI Joint Task Force)

Survival Instinct - (Cerberus Tactical K9 Team Alpha)

Protective Instinct - (Cerberus Tactical K9 Team Alpha)

Defender's Instinct - (Cerberus Tactical K9 Team Alpha)

Danger Signs - (Delta Force Echo)

Hyper Lynx - (Lynx Series)

Danger Zone - (Delta Force Echo)

Danger Close - (Delta Force Echo)

Fear the REAPER – (Strike Force)

Warrior's Instinct - (Cerberus Tactical K9 Team Bravo)

Rescue Instinct - (Cerberus Tactical K9 Team Bravo)

Heroes Instinct - (Cerberus Tactical K9 Team Bravo)

Striker (Striker Force)

Marriage Lynx (Lynx Series)

A Family of the Heart Cookbook

Guardian's Instinct - (Cerberus Tactical K9 Team Charlie)

Beowulf - (Certified Cerberus Tactical K9)

Red Line (CIA Color Code)

Sheltering Instinct (Cerberus Tactical K9 Team Charlie)

With more Iniquus novels to follow!

For the most up to date list go to FionaQuinnBooks.com

This list was created in 2025.

ACKNOWLEDGMENTS

My great appreciation ~

To my editor, **Kathleen Payne**

To my cover artist, **Melody Simmons**

To my publicist, **Margaret Daly**

To my Beta Force, who are always honest and kind at the same time.

To my Street Force, who support me and my writing with such enthusiasm. If you're interested in joining this group, please send me an email. **FionaQuinnBooks@outlook.com**

Thank you to the real-world military and FBI who serve to protect us.

To all of the wonderful professionals whom I called on to get the details right. Especially, D. Hall, for her plotting input; Bart Drummond for his rescue input; M. Carlon for her expertise. Please note: this is a work of fiction, and while I always try my best to get all of the details correct, there are times when it serves the story to go slightly to the left or right of perfection. Please understand that any mistakes or discrepancies are my authorial decision making alone and sit squarely on my shoulders.

Thank you to my family.

I send my love to my husband, and my great appreciation. T, thank you.

And of course, thank YOU for reading my stories. I'm smiling joyfully as I type this. I so appreciate you!

ABOUT THE AUTHOR

Fiona Quinn is a USA Today bestselling author, a Kindle Scout winner, and an Amazon Top 40 author.

Quinn writes smart suspense with a psychic twist in her Iniquus World of action-adventure stories, including Lynx, Strike Force, Uncommon Enemies, Kate Hamilton Mysteries, FBI Joint Taskforce, Cerberus Tactical K9, and Delta Force Echo Series.

She writes urban fantasy as Fiona Angelica Quinn for her Elemental Witches Series.

And, just for fun, she writes the Badge Bunny Booze Mystery Collection with her dear friend, Tina Glasneck, under the name Quinn Glasneck.

Quinn is rooted in the Old Dominion, where she lives with her husband. There, she pops chocolates, devours books, and taps continuously on her laptop.

Visit www.FionaQuinnBooks.com

X   x.com/fionaquinnbooks

⊙   instagram.com/fionaquinnbooks

BB   bookbub.com/authors/fiona-quinn

g   goodreads.com/fionaquinnbooks

COPYRIGHT

The Kate Hamilton Mysteries is a work of fiction. Names, characters, places, and incidents either are the product of the author's imagination or are used fictitiously, and any resemblance to actual persons, living or dead, business establishments, events, or locales is entirely coincidental.